66711

W9-BNP-880

A Place Called Wiregrass

Center Point Large Print

**This Large Print Book carries the
Seal of Approval of N.A.V.H.**

A Place Called Wiregrass

MICHAEL MORRIS

CENTER POINT PUBLISHING
THORNDIKE, MAINE

For Melanie—
whose faith, love, and encouragement
never wavered

This Center Point Large Print edition
is published in the year 2005 by arrangement with
HarperSanFrancisco, a division of HarperCollins Publishers.

Unless otherwise indicated, all Scripture quotations
are taken from *The Holy Bible, New International Version.*
Copyright © 1973, 1978, 1984 by International Bible Society.
Used by permission of Zondervan Publishing House.
All rights reserved.

The text of this Large Print edition is unabridged. In other
aspects, this book may vary from the original edition. Printed in
Thailand. Set in 16-point Times New Roman type.

ISBN 1-58547-569-6

Library of Congress Cataloging-in-Publication Data

Morris, Michael, 1966-
  A place called Wiregrass / Michael Morris.--Center Point large print ed.
    p. cm.
  ISBN 1-58547-569-6 (lib. bdg. : alk. paper)
    1. Large type books. 2. Abused wives--Fiction. 3. Runaway wives--Fiction.
  4. Grandparent and child--Fiction. 5. Alabama--Fiction. I. Title.

PS3613.O775P57 2005
813'.6--dc22

                                                            2004021197

Acknowledgments

To my editor, Renée Sedliar, thank you for your wisdom and humor. I also value the tremendous support that I have received from the sales and marketing teams at HarperCollins and HarperSanFrancisco. To my friend and agent, Laurie Liss, thank you for your persistence and dedication.

I am grateful for the wisdom, guidance, and enthusiasm of Chris Ferebee, Jeff Dunn, Debbie Justus Collins, and Susan Downs. My gratitude also goes to Mary Ellen Wells and Hospice of Wake County and to Dr. Bert Losken for keeping the writing within the lines. And to Tim McLaurin, thank you for motivating me to move forward with four simple words—"You're a good writer."

One

———•———

"What you wearing them sunglasses for?"
      I'd felt Roxi's shifty glances for the past thirty minutes. I knew the square black frames with gold specks made me look like a June bug, but I still hoped Roxi would drop the subject. As I figured things that morning, I had two choices: either wear the insect spectacles or miss a day of work. And I never missed work.

The thunderous drill of sewing machines provided an easy out. I proceeded to sew another zipper and added the completed product to the bushel of blue rayon slacks piled in a plastic carton at my tennis shoes. *I'm gonna get wrote up if I don't hustle,* I thought and tried to dismiss Roxi's coal-eyed glances.

"Erma Lee, you fixin' to be a movie star or something?" Roxi asked with her rugged laugh. I didn't know anybody else who could laugh and talk at the same time. Glancing at the big white clock on the factory wall, I knew I couldn't ignore her any longer. It was another twenty minutes until Roxi's smoke break. The comments mixed with her cigarette-induced laugh would only get stronger.

"Yeah. I'm on the first bus to Hollywood this evening." I avoided her stare and concentrated on my machine. The hammering needle put a perfect stitch in the crotch of a pair of navy pants.

Her gravel laugh let loose again. "I know that's right. Take me too." Roxi tossed a pair of khakis into the carton.

The zigzag of sixty industrial needles was the only sound I heard. *Good, she'll be on to something else directly.*

"You got home trouble?"

I shot a quick look across at Roxi's station. She wasn't laughing anymore. Her silver-framed glasses perched on the edge of her nose. The way her black eyes rolled upward made me feel like a schoolteacher was getting onto me.

"No." To make it look like I was really telling the truth, I shook my head. *I didn't need her getting all in my business.*

"Girl, you forget I been here as long as you. I hope them sunglasses ain't a return to when you . . ."

"I'm gonna miss my quota if we keep flapping our jaws like this." I was scared to death to look at Roxi. Terrified she'd know the truth.

Who are you fooling? She already knows, I told myself. *And so does everybody else in this metal building. Why didn't I just call in sick?*

Roxi sighed and for a couple of minutes focused again on the khaki slacks. "I ain't seen no woman who's tough as you put up with crap like that. You know what I'm saying?"

I shifted my eyes behind the dark bug frames. Roxi was hunched over the white sewing machine, smacking a piece of gum. "My cousin Darlene—you know the one I'm talking about. She put up with that

8

same mess. And then one day she just hauled off and knifed that no-count husband of hers." The rugged chuckle erupted again. "Yes, ma'am. He punched her one too many times is all. You know what I'm saying?" Roxi suddenly stopped sewing and put both hands on her seated hips. "And she not half the woman you are."

Roxi's unexpected glare made me flinch. Just when I turned to look back at the strip of metal zipper, it happened. Like a mosquito gone mad, the steel needle pounded my right index finger. Numbing pain shot up my fingernail to the top of my shoulder. Snatching my foot off the control pedal, I flew backwards and screamed, "God bless America!"

Roxi jumped to the rescue and pried the needle from loose, bloody skin, tearing more in the process. I moaned, trying not to call more attention than was already coming my way. When I looked up and saw the crowd of women gathering, my right hand began to throb. It was almost worse than the throbbing I'd felt the night before, when Bozo slammed his fist into my eye.

The passenger's seat in Mama's silver Escort pressed hard against my back. I stroked my hair, which draped over my shoulder in a ponytail. Mama said long hair was a luxury we didn't have time for. Mama always used the pronoun *we* when setting ground rules for herself.

I adjusted the sunglasses, hoping she would notice the big square frames and ask why I was wearing them. I mapped out my response. I'd say, "I got a bandage to

9

cover twenty stitches, just like I got a disguise to cover my banged-up eye."

But Mama never was one for questions about cosmetic matters.

"That hospital ain't nothing but a first-aid clinic," Mama yelled. "We coulda got the same treatment at the factory clinic and saved me hauling you into town. As it is, I'll get docked for the past three hours."

"Well, I'm so sorry, Mama. Let me just see if I could've planned it a little better for you." I edged closer to the passenger window. A haze blanketed the cold glass.

After a few miles, the hum from the engine filled the car. She could care less if Bozo had hit me or not. Mama made her opinion known the day after Bozo and me adopted our granddaughter, Cher.

"You cause him to leave you, and you're up the creek. And now you with that grandbaby to raise."

I still remember Mama shaking her silver head like she had hornets flying around the boyish mane. "And don't think I can take care of you and that young 'un. No siree, not me."

Not that Mama would realize it, but whenever there's been any caring to do, it's been me. Ever since Daddy walked out, I was expected to step up to the plate. Mama took a job at the new Haggar factory, and at fourteen I took a job raising my six brothers and sisters. "If we plan to eat, you gonna have to sacrifice," Mama reminded me on her way out the door each morning.

I married Bozo two years later to escape the toll of

10

being a full-time mother. Of course, Bozo wasn't his real name. His birth certificate read Bozell Jacobs. He only put up with a nickname best known for a clown because he thought his given name sounded too much like a sissy.

A year after we said our "I dos," I resumed the duties of mothering all over again with my own daughter. But this go-round, I had to work for a paycheck too. Bozo told me flat-out that babies were expensive, and if I planned on having them, then I had to help pay the bills.

After we married, Mama was decent enough to recommend me at the factory, and ever since that's where we've spent eight hours a day together.

The little green clock on the dashboard informed me it had been ten minutes of silence. "I guess you know why I'm wearing these sunglasses."

"Didn't reckon it was none of my business," Mama said. I saw her hand move upward on the steering wheel, gripping the leather tighter.

"He's back to drinking again." I sighed and sent dust on the car dash flying in a million directions. "Hanging out at the Brown Jug. Nothing but trash."

Mama adjusted her black cat-eye glasses and continued to stare at the asphalt ahead of us. "A man will get into a mess once in a while, Erma Lee. At least he won't lay up. He will hold a job."

"I decided on that hospital table, there's gonna be some changes around here. I'm not having Cher raised up in this mess. I made that mistake once already."

"Now Bozo's drinking ain't got a thing to do with

11

Suzette's trouble. The girl was always into something or other."

Mama never did believe the letter that prison psychologist sent me. "A head shrinker," she called him. The psychologist wrote me on thick beige prison stationary stamped with the seal of Louisiana. His typed words explained that the abuse I endured while Suzette was at home made her also seek abuse. Put in those terms, my daughter was a major success. And I guess so was I.

"Look, Mama . . ." I shut my mouth when I looked out the windshield and spotted the Haggar factory. Being so close to our destination, I wasn't in the mood to fight and hear the same lines over and over. Instead, I chose to notice for the first time that the bright green building didn't have any windows.

"All I'm saying is you can't go blaming everything on somebody else. Look at me, Erma Lee. I got dumped with seven young 'uns. You do what you got to do."

I did look at Mama then. Her cropped silver hair with yellow streaks was cut above her ears and close to the back of the lined neck. The deep-seated wrinkles on her face looked like scars from some horrific car wreck. I looked at her battle wounds and thought how sad this woman of sixty-four had turned out. She looked more like one of the oil riggers Daddy used to work with instead of the feminine creature I once thought she could be.

There were only sixteen years between Mama and me. A chill snaked down my spine. I pulled the zipper of the gray flannel jacket up to my neck.

"And what you gonna do now? Quit him? You ain't got no education. No training. The next time Bozo comes at you, just do what you did last time."

In Mama's mind there was only one last time. Bozo hadn't come home from work for two days. When I finally found him in a shack behind the Brown Jug, he was laying on a floor pallet with two hussies. He wore nothing but a once white T-shirt, now stained with a cocktail of mud, liquor, and body fluids. He was so drunk I pulled a muscle dragging him, buck-naked, out of the house. A group of black men stood outside, passing a wrapped brown sack as they stood around their makeshift bonfire. When I think back hard enough, I can still hear their howls of laughter—entertained by watching me load my better half onto the tailgate of his pickup as though I had just purchased a sack of feed. The men weren't the only ones entertained. Cross City, Louisiana, was a small town where gossip spread overnight.

The next day, Bozo managed to show up for work, where he spent the entire day being made fun of by members of his logging crew. That evening he entered the house with an all too familiar stagger. I quickly tried to shoo the kids outside, but he blocked the door with his left hand and used the right one to strip off his belt. "I'll learn you to make a bunch of pulp-wood no-counts laugh at me." The sweet lilac smell of whiskey moved closer. He yanked my hair and ordered Suzette and Russ to watch. "I catch any y'all not looking, I'll give it to you next. This here's what you get when you go behind Pop's back." After four stinging licks to my back, I dug my nails in his arm and managed to reach for the stove. The iron skillet seemed weightless when I landed it against the side of his head. My only regret was that it wasn't loaded with hot grease.

While Bozo recovered from his hairline fracture in the hospital, I packed up our meager belongings and set off for Mama's. "All I need is a couple of days till I can get an advance in my pay." I always hated to beg. Especially standing there on the front porch I used to oversee.

"I ain't getting in the middle of this," Mama said. Her thick arm stretched across the width of the front-door frame. "He might tie one on and burn my place down. Then we'd all be in a fix."

We returned home with a fracture of our own. Russ ran right back inside the house, but Suzette lingered. During late nights when sleep won't come soon enough, I close my eyes and try to erase the picture of Suzette sitting in that backseat staring right through me.

Bozo got better, sort of. He was never going to be one of *Family Circle*'s "Top Ten Husbands." Still, he did promise to stop drinking. I even noticed a new-found respect from him. But Suzette never got better. Her troubles had just begun.

When we turned into the factory entrance, the rough-ness of the gravel made Mama's steering wheel vibrate. She kept control by squeezing harder and jerked her head towards me. "And what you and the girl gonna do for groceries? Now, you with this bum finger. If this just ain't one big mess."

My eyes landed on the dusty back window of my 1984 Monte Carlo. My one piece of property, bought five years ago with cash. I ignored Mama's shaking head and sat in silence until her car had reached the employee parking lot.

"Don't come crying to me. 'Cause I ain't got it. You got a man who makes a good living. But no, that ain't good enough for you."

I snatched the car door open and slammed it so hard I thought I heard the window shatter. Roxi and the usual group were gathered under the metal awning taking a cigarette break.

Roxi held a cigarette in two fingers and cupped her mouth. "How many stitches?"

Mama jumped out, screaming, "Your problem is, you're never satisfied. One of them kind ain't nobody can please."

A hush fell over Roxi and the others. Their necks craned towards the once candy-red Monte Carlo, now a faded orange.

I looked at the group and then at Mama. She stood behind the open car door, and her hands rested on her hip-hugging navy pants. "How do you know? You sure never tried," I screamed and jumped into the one thing with my name on the title.

When my foot slammed the gas pedal, the car skidded to the left and then to the right. Tightening my grip on the steering wheel, I screamed right out loud. It felt good to be out of control.

In the rearview mirror, I saw gravel and dust form a

cloud that floated over the smokers. I imagined Roxi tilting her head back like African royalty and blowing smoke from her lips, *"You go, girl."*

Two

Fourteen weeks and two days had passed since I last saw Mama standing outside the factory, hands on her hips, glaring at my car. She never did like me. If she'd been pressed, she'd probably say she loved me, but only because she'd fear eternal hell for not loving her firstborn.

I went back to work later that day to pick up my last check from the Haggar factory. The front-office ladies looked nervous when they saw me. I started to stick my tongue out, just to see them flinch. Mr. Warren, the shift manager, lifted his arm like he was going to offer some grasp of affection or sympathy. I folded my arms and moved to the side. "Now, darlin', you sure you want to do this?" he asked.

They all acted like I was gonna kill somebody— Mama, I reckon. But I wasn't about to waste time with any good-byes, permanent or otherwise. I picked Cher up from school, then packed up. I even left Bozo a note, though he deserved nothing and knew it. Cher whined a little bit, but seemed to come around when I told her the truth about my black eye. *She's thirteen,* I kept reminding myself. *I have to stop babying her so much.* Like Roxi and the other women in the green

16

metal building, she most likely already knew the truth anyway. We left Cross City, Louisiana, that January day and almost never have looked back.

My next big decision was where to go. Cher pressed the point, sitting in the passenger seat and holding a worn-out atlas, its cover half ripped off. Ever since she was a little thing, she'd gnaw something to the bone until she got her answer. To buy time, I told her it was a surprise. When my Monte Carlo came to the last stoplight in Cross City, I remembered my cousin Lucille.

Last summer at the Thomley family reunion, Lucille drew a crowd when she pulled up to the community center in a brand-new white El Dorado Cadillac. The men tucked their hands in their pockets and walked alongside the car, while little kids dared to touch the shiny chrome hubcaps. Her new husband, J.W., was a welder, she reported over potato salad and fried okra. To hear her tell it, Wiregrass was the place to be. "Jobs galore," she said, holding a drumstick with her pinkie acrylic nail stuck out. Lucille, with her bright red hair, orange-colored nails, and thick gold-coin necklace, certainly seemed the image of prosperity. So, on a rare impulse, I decided we would join my rich cousin in Wiregrass, Alabama.

Only thing was, Lucille lost her newfound prosperity soon after the reunion. And that El Dorado everybody had such a fit over was really an Alamo rent-a-car. The man, J.W., wasn't even her husband. I would've still been mad at her for lying to me, but the poor old thing had gained a pile of weight, and those nails were back to the half-chewed-up mess I remembered. Before those shiny fake things, it always hurt me to look at Lucille's nails, bitten off near the quick. Standing at the door of her ice-cold apartment, I scored her as being worse off than me and decided not to ask if we could stay. My Aunt Stella used to say everything happens for a reason. So I guess I have to give Lucille credit for directing me to the Westgate Trailer Park.

Miss Trellis, the trailer-park owner, was a seventy-five-year-old widow who said she ran a clean place with forty-two trailers and wouldn't take a single one more. She moved around the one-room office under the sway of a polyester housedress. "No loud music, no speeding, and no gossiping about neighbors. What they do in their castles is their business," Miss Trellis told me before handing over the leasing agreement. She tacked on an extra hundred dollars for letting me use her hand-me-down furniture.

Cher settled in for the last semester of school and seemed to be doing good. She was always a whiz with numbers. The friends would come soon enough, I assured myself, and tried to concentrate on finding us some grocery money. Along with the job demand in Wiregrass, one of the only truthful things Lucille reported, also came stiff competition. My odds weren't increased on account of me quitting high school just shy of my senior year. Having secretly wanted to be a nurse when I was a kid, I even tried to get on at the big hospital in town. After dead ends, I finally found a job in the food industry.

The cafeteria at Barton Elementary seemed perfect

for the time being. I was able to be home soon after Cher's middle school let out, a luxury I never had with my own two children, and the manager, Sammy, seemed to like me. Not that he felt sorry for me or anything. I think he had a natural affection for me since he was raised by his grandmother and respected the way I was bringing up Cher. "Foxy Grandma," he'd call me. "You sure don't look like any grandma I know."

The upcoming spring break was the only thing that made me real nervous. Up to that point, we were managing just fine. But since I asked for all my pay up front and didn't slot any out for holidays and summertime, I knew financial trouble was around the bend again. Two weeks before school let out for Easter break, Sammy told me Mrs. Murray wanted to see me.

This is it for sure, I thought as I walked down the brick walkway towards the principal's office. *If she lays me off, so be it. Under no circumstances will I go back to Cross City with my tail between my legs begging for my old job back.*

"Sammy says the best things about you, Erma Lee," Mrs. Murray said. She was a full-figured woman and had a singsong voice that made me think she was either stupid or stuck up. Judging by the string of degrees on her wall, I put my money on the latter. Her light brown hair was teased as big as a basketball, with tuffs of bangs over her right eye. She wore so much makeup, I couldn't help but think she must've gotten in the way of somebody painting a fence red.

"I appreciate it." I pulled at the bottom my white polyester top. As much as I hated that uniform, I hated the black hairnet I had to wear even more. All I could think the first time I caught a glance of my reflection in the gigantic mixing bowl was the skit Ruth Buzzi used to do on *Laugh In.* The one about a bent-over old woman. *I'm forty-eight,* I wanted to scream each time the frumpy, twisted shape stared back at me.

"You crop that hair like I told you to, you wouldn't be wearing that thing," I imagined Mama saying. I quickly tucked a loose strand of hair behind my ear.

"I'm real happy here, Mrs. Murray."

She waved a hand at me. "Now, you call me Patricia. And we appreciate you, just so much." Patricia's wide smile revealed a red dot of lipstick on her front tooth. She seemed like she could claw somebody to pieces and never lose that fakey smile.

Patricia leaned forward and propped her elbows on the glassed desktop. "The reason for our little visit is personal. My mama, bless her heart, took a bad fall a few weeks back. She's just not getting along like she should. And with it being Easter break and all. Well, I was just wondering if you'd be interested in helping her out. Little things like picking up the house, some washing maybe."

Years ago, I promised myself I'd never be a maid. The idea of cleaning someone's toilet was just too humiliating. "Sure. When you need me to start?" The groceries, the rent, and the electric bill made me put pride on the shelf.

I still wasn't real familiar with certain parts of Wiregrass yet. Certainly not familiar with the type of neighborhood Mrs. Claudia Tyler lived in. I thought Patricia Murray would come from a rich family. In Cross City, anybody who went to college was either rich or a good enough football player that LSU snatched them up.

As I held my city map in one hand and steered my Monte Carlo with the other, I couldn't help but gawk at the big brick homes. Looking at manicured yards, water sprinklers running, and gigantic oak trees guarding the two-story homes, I could only guess how stuck up the Queen Mother would be.

Mrs. Tyler's home was a two-story brick building with two white columns and black shutters. It reminded me of a courthouse. Two oaks as big around as four elephant legs towered over the row of pink azaleas leading up to the front door. The covered porch was as big as my trailer and ran sideways towards the garage. Her shrubs were cut neatly, and when I got out of my car, I noticed a rose garden. *Needs a full-time staff to keep this place up,* I thought.

"How you doing? Richard Tyler. I'm the other child," said the man who greeted me at the door. He squinted his beady eyes and chuckled for no apparent reason. I thought of Roxi. He was a little older than his sister, Patricia, and a little fatter. His white hair hung in strands, and his round face reminded me of a moon pie.

After pleasantries and questions about my background—thank God he had never heard of Cross City—he led me to the downstairs bedroom that Mrs. Tyler was occupying. I had never seen so many clocks in all my life. The oak-paneled hallway leading to her bedroom not only had two different clocks on the wall,

21

but also a dark grandfather clock standing guard at the end. Ticking rang through my ears, and the hardwood floors creaked under the weight of my work shoes.

The room was dark in muted colors, and the mahogany canopy bed didn't help lighten it any. A tall bronze lamp formed a backlight against her wavy black hair. She was holding some sort of red book and looked every bit like the Queen Mum I'd imagined.

"Mama, she's here," Richard announced and promptly chuckled. The room smelled of Pine-Sol cleaner and expensive flowered perfume.

Mrs. Tyler adjusted herself on the bed and pulled at the pink chiffon nightgown. When she looked up, I saw her hair was all fixed and a touch of pink lipstick covered her thin lips. Not as much makeup as the daughter, but enough to strike me as strange that this woman who was bedridden would even bother. Another extravagance Mama never allowed. To this day I don't wear any makeup except for special occasions. And I couldn't tell you the last time that was.

"Well, it's just so good to know you." Her hazel eyes danced underneath wire-rimmed glasses. "Come sit where I can get a good look at you." She pointed to a wingback chair next to the bed. "I guess you know I had to go and fall. Right after I pulled the clothes from the dryer. I just thank the Lord nothing was broken."

I nodded my head and tried to look pleasant, thinking that if she didn't like me the job was off.

"Well sir, they want me to lay up here on this bed for a few weeks, and Patricia insists on getting me some help."

Richard was just beginning to take a seat on the padded chest at the end of the bed. "Richard, you go now. You've got that appointment with the dentist, remember." He tucked his head and babbled something undetectable when he bumped into the hallway wall. The Queen Mother, just as I guessed.

I tried to cross my legs and look ladylike. Then I saw the black lace-up shoes on my feet. The pair Cher called Grandma Walton shoes. I quickly hid them under the chair and settled on looking ladylike with my hands folded in my lap.

"Richard's a nerve patient," she said in a stage whisper. "Once a big-deal lawyer in Birmingham and now . . ." She raised her arms and opened empty palms. "That's why I need help. Got his own apartment. Lives by himself, just over yonder above my garage. But as far as lifting or anything like that, well he's just as worthless as teats on a boar hog."

My eyes widened. I tried not to look surprised, but I always was the world's worst at hiding my expressions.

"I'm just talking plain now. And as for Patricia, well she's so busy tending to that schoolhouse and all her parties, I never can get her to do a thing."

"Who helps you with the cooking and cleaning?" I refused to let her think I was some mousy something or another she could lecture.

"Sugar, you're looking at her. Bertha worked for me thirty-two years. When the Lord took her, I decided I would do it myself. And then I had to go fall. Oh, gracious, enough about my mess. You got any children?"

"Yes, ma'am. A boy and a girl. They're all grown now. But I'm raising my granddaughter."

"Does your husband help out with raising the grand-daughter?"

I looked down at the Oriental rug and then, thinking I might seem pitiful, I looked back into her forgiving eyes. "We been separated for the past few months now. He's back in Cross City, you know in Louisiana, where I come from."

"I don't guess I know that place. Near Monroe? I got a third cousin who lives in Monroe."

"No, ma'am. Near New Orleans." *Maybe this was getting better after all.*

"Well, tell me about your granddaughter."

If a thermometer had been set up to measure my confidence level, it would have overheated. "She's thirteen. Well, soon to be fourteen. She's a good girl. Good with her school work. Likes to read. I told her she must've read every horse book this library has." I tried to chuckle.

Mrs. Tyler propped the blue-veined hand on her chin. "She sounds precious. What's her name?"

I was hoping to skip that part for the time being. Older folks like Mama never understood why anybody would name a child after Sonny's partner. The words rang in my mind as clear as they had the day Cher was born. *"Why couldn't Suzette give that baby a decent name?"* Mama had asked. *"Cher, like that singer? Don't you remember how that trashy thing showed her belly button on TV? And had to drag that young 'un of hers on TV too. You sure don't see somebody with a decent name like Carol Burnett dragging her kids on stage.*"

"Her name's Cher," I said with eyes closed.

"What a pretty name. And how about her mama and daddy?"

She adjusted a pillow, and I hoped had not seen my cheek flinch. The question struck me as too personal and something she had no business asking this early on. "Well, her mama, my daughter, is . . . uh . . . a nerve patient like your son. She's in the state hospital up in New Orleans."

A lie was the first thing I jumped for. I couldn't very well say Suzette was in the Louisiana Correctional Institute doing time for drug trafficking and child abandonment. She'd throw me out on my ear for sure. And before I made it out the driveway she would've called that principal daughter of hers too, probably interrupt one of the woman's parties and really make her mad. Then I'd lose the cafeteria job on top of everything. And it's not all a lie. If Suzette would've had a decent lawyer, she probably could've gotten off on insanity.

"Well, I declare," Miss Claudia said and wrinkled her brow. "Richard was forty-three when he had his nerve attack."

After she offered me more money than I expected, we discussed my hours and general responsibilities. Maybe I'd been wrong about Claudia Tyler—"Miss Claudia" she said everybody called her. As I approached the bedroom door, she held up her hand. I leaned forward, still uncertain whether I could take

25

her and her mansion on.

"I really only had Bertha around because the poor old thing needed the money that bad. Her with that little retarded boy and all." Miss Claudia gazed at the comforter covering her legs. "But I never called her my housekeeper. And at eighty, I'm not starting now. Just tell folks you're my companion."

Three

The key was almost in my assigned mailbox when the swish-swash of polyester made its way out of the cinder-block office. Miss Trellis carefully stepped, to avoid a puddle deposited by her window air-conditioning unit. The way she worried so, you would've thought the black cloth shoes she wore had been bought in New York City. She leaned to the left and then to the right like her swollen midsection was the balance between her two feet. *Poor old thing,* I thought and pulled a postcard advertising a tire store and a missing Hispanic boy from my mailbox. My heartbeat resumed a normal pace. No bills.

"Oh, me," Miss Trellis groaned and put her elbow on top of the metal mailboxes jumbled together in birdhouse fashion. A mound of flesh plopped where a tricep might have once been. "Your grandbaby told me you was working two jobs now," she said, barely managing to catch her breath.

"Yes, ma'am." I made a mental note to remind Cher

to be careful what she told Miss Trellis. All I need is for us to break her rule about gossiping and get thrown out. My cousin Lucille was my only fallback, and she hadn't returned my last phone call.

"Poor old Claudia Tyler," the worn-out woman said. "Me and her used to sew together down at the Emporium. Oh, I forget you ain't from here. It was the big department store uptown. Anyway, we was the tailors, me and her. She was a Ranker back in them days."

I turned my eyes from the postcard and studied Miss Trellis. I wanted to call her a liar because I knew the woman who lived in the courthouse-shaped home could've never been a seamstress. "You did?"

"Oh, yeah. Back in them days she didn't have it so good. No siree." She paused to slap a gnat. "Not until the old man Tyler's son up and quit his wife. Then things got a whole lot better for Claudia. Next thing you know, Tyler's son and Claudia up and married— real fast like." Miss Trellis stuck her neck out long and bugged her gray eyes. I could see the crooked red lines in her sockets.

Lord, she's crazy as a coot. "Well, that's real nice."

"I ain't even gonna say what all us girls knowed about it. So don't even ask me." She drew her neck back into its double-chinned shell and closed her eyes.

"Well, let me get going," I said, taking a step towards the Monte Carlo. She made me nervous, and I couldn't help but think she was trying to set me up to break her gossip rule. Besides, I could hear the air conditioner running in my car and knew I didn't have the gas to waste listening to some pathetic hag like her.

27

But Miss Trellis was on a one-way journey. "And then the Benson's Department Store come to town and bought out the Emporium. Just gave Claudia's husband a plumb pile of money. That's how they come up with all they got. Old Man Tyler was long gone by that time. Wade, Claudia's husband, he just got ever dime of it."

When I saw a white pickup pull in behind Miss Trellis and park, I jumped at the opportunity. Just when I was fixing to get in my car, I heard the last comment that confirmed my impression. "If you was to give me all her money, I wouldn't take it. No, ma'am," she said. "She's got so many problems, bless her heart. Money ain't gonna buy you happiness."

She didn't move from her position when the man with a ruddy complexion and an orange cap with the word *Caterpillar* opened a mailbox. What I didn't hear her tell the man as I drove off was how sorry she was for me and my poor little granddaughter. But I didn't have to hear her words. I knew her type and could've written the lines for her. Old or young, black or white, bitter spirits speak the same language.

The blaring sound of screaming turned my attention away from tales about Miss Claudia to the inside of the metal frame box I called home. I jogged to the silver handle and tried to picture the tragedy unfolding. *Bozo,* I first thought. But he would never lay a hand on Cher. Not unless he's wasted out of his mind and decided to beat information about me out of her.

"Cher!" I bolted inside the trailer. The TV blasted, and I surveyed the room to make sure nothing was out of order. I saw the white phone cord spring behind the kitchen wall. Cher leaned against the pantry door.

Just as two women began to fight over their lesbian cousins, I turned the talk show off. "I could hear that mess screaming all the way out to the car. You like to give me heart failure with that thing."

Cher tucked a strand of brown hair back behind her ear. She created a breeze when she swept passed me and picked her book off the red-and-white-checkered couch. If it had been my furniture back in Cross City, I would've gotten after her for plopping down so hard. She sat Indian style, pulled her bare feet under the couch cushion, and tried to retreat into a world of fiction. I never did know why she liked reading so much. Halfway through any romance book I ever tried to read, I'd jump on to the end. Just say what needs to be said, too much rattling for my tastes.

The end of the phone cord was lightly swinging against the kitchen wall. "Who was on the phone?" I asked and put the lid back on the jar of peanut butter.

"I wasn't on the phone." Without opening her eyes, she turned back to her book. Its cover was bright and cheery, with a young blonde-headed girl holding the rope to a horse. The white cord on the kitchen phone was still bouncing.

With my own kids, I'da blistered their tails for sassing me. But I tried to be more patient with Cher. Counting to ten in my mind always helped. She deserved special measures. Especially with me and Bozo splitting up.

"Did you get that math test back yet?" I asked, laying

29

the car keys on the kitchen countertop.

"Ninety-three. And it's algebra, not math." She chewed on the ends of her brown hair, never looking up.

Opening the refrigerator door, I chose again to ignore her pissy attitude. "Miss Claudia said she wants to meet you. I was thinking maybe this Saturday we could . . ." I turned to the sink, which looked out over the living-room area, and she was gone. The slamming of her bedroom door reminded me that she was stuck between a child's world and a teenager's.

Hormones, I decided. I stood at the closed pine door, but decided not to knock. She'd started her period when we first got to Wiregrass. She's got a lot going on inside that little ninety-eight-pound body of hers, I reminded myself. Trisha Yearwood's voice oozed out of the space between the pine door and the gold linoleum floor. I figured she was daydreaming of a boyfriend or dreaming about riding a big horse like the one on the cover of her book. It was only while she was taking a shower that I discovered her dreams were more ridiculous than any schoolgirl fantasy. A fantasy that Cher needed to dismiss from her mind.

The picture was torn at the edge and a little faded. She had hidden it from me inside her pillow. I would've never found it unless some of the pillow stuffing had not been hanging out the corners of the half-closed zipper.

They didn't look like convicts, her mama and daddy. But then again, in the picture Cher didn't look like the smart girl she was. In fact, she didn't look like a girl at

30

all, just a bald six-month-old leaning on her daddy's tattooed arm. Her little ears displayed two tiny gold balls. I told Suzette piercing a baby's ears was trashy, and now I was holding the celluloid proof. Suzette had her brown hair parted on the side and, looking into her wide brown eyes, there was no denying she was Cher's mama. The blue plastic background with smoke drifting from the chimney and snow on the ground looked weird with them in the foreground. Why were they all dressed in short sleeves? And it probably was the dead of winter when they had the picture made. Most likely at the grocery store or some other unplanned place. No wonder when I found that picture in a kitchen drawer back in Cross City, I promptly threw it in the trash.

The first week with Miss Claudia was a settling-in time. By Friday, I knew my way around the place, and it didn't seem quite as huge as it had before. Her regular friends came and went from two to four o'clock. My pick was a real sweet black lady. The tiny woman with round glasses stopped by mostly on Tuesdays. I decided she must be one of the late housekeeper's relatives still keeping check on Miss Claudia. Rich people always seemed to have hired help who were just like family. But I refused to be put in that category. *This was just a way to keep up with the bills,* I reminded myself every day when I pulled up the long concrete driveway.

Richard got on my last nerve, as I predicted he would. I call it the "Short Man Syndrome." All he'd do

31

is talk big about how much money he made in stocks and how he used to own racehorses. So much for Mr. Big Shot—he couldn't even keep an appointment without his eighty-year-old mama reminding him.

Only once did he start to get out of hand. I was washing the dinner dishes and had half tuned out his lecture on the mysteries of the Bermuda Triangle when I felt the digging glare. My back was to him, but I could picture him leering at me from the kitchen table. Still in uniform, I knew he was looking through my cheap polyester slacks at my panties.

"It's a pure shame my mama don't live closer by. She just loves interesting stuff like you talk about," I said, turning to him with the crystal tea pitcher in my hands. "I bet she'd be after you, seeing how y'all about the same age." When he scrunched his face and retreated to his garage apartment, I couldn't help but get tickled. The idea of Mama, whose hair was shorter than his, ever going on a date with a nerve patient was hilarious. She'd stomp on his nerves like a bull in a china store. Before I knew it, the chuckle erupted, and I slapped my soapy hand over my mouth. For a second I felt lighter. It was the first time I had laughed since leaving Cross City.

Ladies from First Methodist paraded through the afternoons at Miss Claudia's. I let each enter through the big white door with the brass door knocker. Big or skinny, with gray or dyed-blue hair, they all had the same little turned-down smile that I decided must be required with the Methodists. A woman by the name of Elizabeth was the worst. I'd say some pleasantry like,

"How you doing today?" She'd just turn her ash-blonde head ever so slightly and give me a tired smirk. And I know the worn smile was not because she'd been cleaning house all day, but instead was her way of saying, "Who do you think you are talking to me, White Trash?" without exercising her voice.

The good thing about Prune Face—the pet name I secretly gave her—was she never stayed long. Soon she'd appear in the living room again, with her brown Bible in tow. After I closed the door, I'd watch from the living-room window as she got into her big Chrysler. I imagined her sitting in a metal chair the following Sunday reporting to her Sunday school class that she had visited the ailing Claudia Tyler. Check one more visitation off the sick list for Prune Face.

Not that I ever understood why Prune Face brought her Bible. They were in plentiful supply at Miss Claudia's house. She kept one in every bedroom and even a small black Bible in her downstairs guest bathroom. During the end of my first week, I found her propped up on four pillows with unusually flat hair. She had her big book spread across her lap. I was dusting the antique armoire and had almost made it to the legs when I heard the voice.

"See, I am doing a new thing! Now it springs up; do you not perceive it? I am making a way in the desert and streams in the wasteland." For a second, I wondered if Miss Claudia had taken one too many pain pills as she sat there, eyes closed and red lips grinning. Within a twinkle of my eye, she was back onboard.

"Isaiah 43:19," she said and opened her eyes real

big. I smiled and kept dusting.

"Do you own a Bible, Erma Lee?"

With my back to her, I bit my lip. I had told all I wanted to about personal business. "Yes, ma'am." I thought of the little white Bible Aunt Stella's church gave me decades ago when I joined Antioch Missionary.

"I just love this verse. It lets me know that, even at my age, God's not done with me yet."

I turned to face her, and she was swinging her glasses as easy as she'd swing a jump rope. "He's got a plan for all of us. For Patricia, for Richard, and you too, Erma Lee."

Now don't even start this religious mess with me, I thought. *It makes you weak and pious, like that old Prune Face, who visits you just so she can go brag to the preacher what a good Christian woman she is.* "Yes, ma'am."

Religious fanatics were all over Cross City. I was used to them. And I decided to say what she wanted for the sake of a paycheck. As I watched her painted fingernail move across the thin, white sheets, I felt sorry for her. *How on earth could this woman even know what the wilderness and desert her Bible spoke of were really like? Had she gone hungry? Had she gone to the emergency room to get stitches above her eye after her old man broke a plate over her head and then worried the next day because she was missing work and couldn't pay the electric bill? No, I know better. And no matter what Miss Trellis claims about Miss Claudia sewing at some store, this woman had it good now. I*

34

had the scars from the wilderness and the blisters from the desert, and I survived it by myself. I was the only one I could count on.

By the beginning of April, Bozo's calls dwindled down to one or two a week, most often after he'd tied one on. I could predict them. He'd call at twelve-thirty or one in the morning and either cry like a baby, begging forgiveness, or rant and rave so loud I would hold the phone ten inches from my ear and could still make out the cuss words. After the first week, I learned to hang up and unplug the phone.

The day before the week-long Easter break, I had one of the worst days imaginable. The morning started with me running late, then the solenoid switch on my car giving me a fit. I borrowed the old man's pliers from next door and rigged it enough so it'd crank. A trick I have Bozo to thank for teaching me. At school, a little girl threw up her corn dog right by the conveyer belt that ships the trays for us to wash. Then Miss Claudia's leg was acting up, and I had to haul her to the doctor's office. After waiting two and a half hours for the doctor, I took Miss Claudia home, then cooked Richard supper, and washed his last pair of underwear.

When I walked through the door at eight-thirty that evening, I found the trailer pleasantly still. The only sound was the popping of the metal as it adjusted to the cool night air. Cher was spending the night at a new friend's house, Laurel Krandle, who lived in a trailer across the Westgate driveway. After checking in with Cher, who actually seemed in good spirits, I unplugged the phone and slept the best I had in months.

My newfound rest was short-lived. I arrived at Miss Claudia's the next day to find her actually sitting up at her kitchen table. That was good news. The bad news was she said my better half had been calling for the past hour. I licked my lips and ran my hand over the top of my pulled back hair. "Lord, I'm so sorry."

"He's an impatient thing," she said and then sipped her coffee.

I wanted to ask if he was drunk, but then I doubted if she'd ever been around such behavior. Miss Claudia looked angelic sitting at her pine table in a cream robe with embroidered roses on the collar.

"You might as well call him. Richard's still sleeping, and if there's any straightening out to be done, I'd just as soon him not hear it." She pulled at one of the little satin roses. "His nerves, don't you know."

I knew her own nerves were probably running on high, thinking my old flame was gonna come gun me down on her manicured lawn. Most likely, I'd fall over on top of one of her pink azalea bushes and shed blood on her concrete walkway. Then there'd be CNN and all the little ladies from First Methodist congregating after the unfortunate incident. Prune Face would probably stand over me clutching her purse and shaking her head. "Pure D trash," she would say and squinch her mouth up.

The living-room phone was the most private place for the butt-chewing I wanted to give Bozo. I sighed and entered the red-walled room. I almost couldn't remember the phone number. But instead of worrying that it was the sign of some brain tumor or Alzheimer's, I was relieved. One more thing I was forgetting about that place I once called home. He cleared his throat into the receiver and welcomed the caller.

"How'd you get this number?" I imagined icicles snaking through my voice to Cross City. I wanted to scream, but I knew Miss Claudia sat in the kitchen, glued to the edge of her chair.

"My grandbaby give it to me. Right after you left the house without fixing her no breakfast."

Adjusted to Wiregrass or not, I'm gonna blister that girl when I get home. "She spent the night . . . Look, that's none of your business. And don't be calling here again. I mean it."

"Don't you tell me where and who . . ." He sighed. "Fine. I just got one thing to say to you. Either you get your tail back here by the end of the month, or I'm getting me a lawyer."

I wondered if Bozo would get that quack who represented Suzette the first time she got arrested for dealing drugs. That man with long nose hair and a bright yellow tie that ended at the crest of his big belly. "Well, hallelujah!"

"Listen, I mean this thing. Me and your mama done talked it over, and she knows I'm—"

In the background at my former home, a female voice mumbled something about eggs. The clanking of a spoon hitting the frying pan rankled in my ear. I could hear Bozo trying to conceal the evidence by muffling the phone receiver.

Funny, I thought. *He never tried to hide it before.*

"Which juke joint did you find her in?"

"Don't you never mind. Hey, I got rights, you know. Don't you forget them adoption papers list my name as Cher's daddy. I can get you for custody, gal."

The one bullet I didn't think he'd fire. I giggled, the type of giggle that said, "Kiss my butt" and "You're an idiot" all in the same octave.

"And just what judge would put some thirteen-year-old girl in the same house with a wife-beating, whore-hopping drunk like you?" I was too loud with that one and was sure Miss Claudia heard every word.

But it worked. Bozo went off like a cherry bomb. "Hey . . . hey, she ain't no . . . Hey . . . Hey . . . anyhow a man got needs. Any judge knows that. And how's about you . . ."

"Send my best to your whore there. Tell her she better learn how to handle that frying pan, 'cause sooner or later she'll need it." I slammed the phone down as hard as I could.

He wouldn't even think of fighting me over Cher. Not even Mama could go along with him on that one. The slightest chance made my heart race. *I'm stronger than this,* I reminded myself. *But what if he does fight and finds some crooked judge?* Lord knows Louisiana was full of them. I sat on the edge of the shiny black piano bench and tried to let my nerves settle. My breath grew deeper, and soon my heartbeat withdrew from the base of my neck. As I sat there looking at a painting of two brown rabbits, which hung over the phone table, I couldn't help but wonder if this was how Richard felt during one of his nerve attacks.

With my head held high, I walked briskly back into the kitchen. Miss Claudia, standing with the help of her silver cane, was taping something on the refrigerator door. She did her best to act like nothing out of the ordinary had taken place. My attention was diverted by her upright position. She was much taller than I expected, and she shook her head as she smoothed out the edges of a piece of notebook paper.

I began pulling out the usual equipment for breakfast, and she sat back down at the kitchen table. When I turned to the refrigerator, I paused to notice the white paper with block letters: CLOSE!

"That's not for you, sugar. That's for Richard. He's gonna run my electric bill sky-high. Can't remember to leave that door shut for the life of him."

I tried to smile and moved quickly to retrieve the frying pan. The clanking spoon against the frying pan in my old house drummed in my mind. Before I could close the cabinet, the black cast-iron tumbled to the floor. I scooped it up and mumbled an apology. Turning around three times, trying to remember where the eggs were, I suddenly felt lost.

"Eggs are right behind you, sugar." Her smile was warm and comforting, like someone who wanted to keep a secret.

No, don't fall into that trap. I've told her too much as it is. Lord only knows how much she heard.

"You're just all to pieces. Come over here and sit down." She patted the wooden chair like she was enticing a disobedient child to behave.

I was sure she was gonna tell me if I don't leave my

personal problems at the house, she'd have to let me go. My heart moved up to my throat again. I thought for sure she could see the pulsating rhythm in my neck. Flipping my ponytail over the base of my neck, I rested my hands on the table as if everything was hunky-dory.

Her eyes closed, and she sighed. "Some men just ain't worth spit." My palm flinched when she put her blue-veined hands on top of mine. She gazed out the kitchen window and shook her teased hair.

"I'm real sorry you had to hear all that." I sighed, trying to find words to explain and at the same time censor the details of life in Cross City. "He just . . . I mean, it was just too much and finally . . ."

"You felt like you were just about to suffocate."

I wanted to stand up and yell "Yeah" and go off on a testimony about Bozo and what a waste he had been in my life. But I just sat there, mesmerized by this woman who suddenly seemed foreign compared to her circle of friends who participated in the First Methodist sick-list parade. She stared at the blots of yellow and pink in the rose garden just beyond her window.

"Not many people know I was married before. Down in Apalachicola, Florida, where I was raised. Richard and Patricia hardly know a thing about all that. It comes to me now and then. Like just now when you were talking to that man." She rubbed my hand, but never looked down. I knew the reprimand was just a few breaths away.

"My first one, Luther Ranker, was not good to me a'tall. If Daddy would've lived, things would've been different. I can still remember the salty sea smell on

Daddy's shirtsleeve. He'd come in from fishing after a long day and still find time to tussle around on the floor with me and my little brother, Jack Henry. He was only thirty when he came down with typhoid fever. I remember noticing that the dirt was still fresh on his grave when we buried Jack Henry next to him three weeks later. Mama and me cried and begged the Lord to give the fever to us. Mercifully, we were spared.

"I declare, Mama looked like a scarecrow when Old Man Maxwell came calling a month later. I never had any use for that man the minute I laid eyes on him. Well, for one thing, he was old enough to be Mama's daddy. Old Man Maxwell thought he was something because he owned the mercantile with a bait and tackle shop on the side. I tried to convince Mama we could make it on our own. I was getting pretty good at shucking oysters, and Mama took in wash from some of the fishermen. But she said I was too young to be burdened with such. I never could get her to understand she wasn't a piece of property. And with his store and his land, Old Man Maxwell had the highest price.

"For a while me and my newfound daddy tolerated one another. I even liked working in his store. I learned all about fabrics and studied the latest styles in the Sears and Roebuck catalog. By the time I turned fourteen, I was making dresses for me and Mama. And if I say so myself, they looked just as good as mail order."

I nervously chuckled and nodded my head in agreement, but Miss Claudia never drifted her attention away from the rosebuds outside her kitchen window.

"Directly, Mama had another baby. Little Madeline. Oh, she was just the sweetest thing you ever did see. After the store closed, I'd hurry and get my lessons done so I could rock her before fixing supper. I liked to pretend I was Madeline's mama. Problem was, Old Man Maxwell pretended I was her mama too. One evening when Mama was still in bed recovering from the birthing, he made his intentions known.

"I was used to closing the store by myself, so I was surprised to look up and see Old Man Maxwell's long, bearded face in the glass front door. The image disappeared as soon as I pulled the green shade down. But he had that musky scent, just like a water moccasin lets off before it strikes.

"When I began cleaning out the cash register, he moved in on me. I edged away from the cash register, still clutching pennies in my hand. His old, prickly beard rubbed against my neck. I yelled for him to behave, but he just kept on with it. I can still feel his dry tongue on my neck. I reckon it was reflex that made me throw those pennies as hard as I could at his baggy eyes. It was the first time anybody ever slapped me on my face.

"Poor Mama was so weak with anemia from having the baby that I thought it best not to talk about such things with her. I could fight him off, I decided that night with the covers pulled tight over my sweaty head. The next morning over his runny eggs, I looked him dead in the eye and told him if he ever tried to touch me again, he'd be sorry. The dishes in the kitchen cabinet plumb vibrated from his laughing."

Miss Claudia's hand trembled when she adjusted her glasses. I was on alert, waiting for her to stop talking and go to crying—my cue to jump in and rescue her by changing the subject.

"Mama got better, but my situation sure didn't. Whenever I'd try to mention his behavior, she'd just start chirping about how Old Man Maxwell saved us from the poorhouse. To keep away from him, I started working in the bait and tackle shop. I'd dig for earthworms, slice minnows, and put weights on fishing line, anything to keep away from that creature. In the process I ran right into another one.

"Luther Ranker was a regular in the bait shop. He owned two fishing boats and hired out three colored men to help him. Mama always said he tried to get by on his looks. He seemed sweet at first. Every day he'd come in the shop and tease me about us running off and getting married. I called him silly, handed him his minnows and new hooks, and sent him into the bay. Two months later I stood at the courthouse and promised to honor and obey him.

"I still remember the day I made up my mind to marry Luther. It was a hot morning. July, I believe. I was getting everything ready to open the shop, when the Old Man caught me by myself and pushed me to a corner where some nets were stacked. 'I put a lot of money into you, girlie, and it's time to pay up,' he said. The bacon my mama had made him was still fresh on his breath. When I heard his zipper go down, my vocal cords dried up. I just . . . never thought it'd go that far. And my poor mama . . . just inside the store putting

43

money in his cash register. If only I could've done . . ."

She squeezed my hand until the knuckles ached, her gaze set far above the pink and yellow roses beyond the window. We both jumped at the slap of the screened kitchen door.

"We're not having breakfast this morning?" Richard stared at the empty frying pan.

Miss Claudia quickly released my hands and dabbed the sweat beads on her forehead with a nearby napkin. A ghostly white imprint remained on my fingers.

"Umm . . . yeah, I'm getting a late start this morning." I returned to my proper place at the frying pan and began melting the butter. Imagining the black coils as Old Man Maxwell's beard, I slammed the pan on the eye of the stove. The loud bang made Richard turn towards me.

Miss Claudia casually patted her hair like she had walked through a gust of wind and smiled. "Sleep good?"

"Yes, ma'am. I did." Richard joined her at the table and went over all the drama that had taken place in Wiregrass the night before—knowledge thanks to the police scanner that ran constantly in his garage apartment. "You never know when a good lawyer might be needed," he reminded us this morning, like he did every time he reported a car wreck or burglary scoop learned from his faithful mechanical friend.

I eyed Miss Claudia real close, trying to think of some question to ask Richard in case she needed more time to gather herself. She gracefully propped her left hand on her chin. While Richard told of a fire downtown, she nodded her head in agreement, and the white rock on her left hand sparkled. He never realized she was sitting at the table for the first time since her fall. He just continued his 911 report, spoke of his need of prescription refills, and asked about his doctor's appointment for the day. "Remember they changed the appointment to three o'clock," Miss Claudia said with a point of her finger. The lady of the house was back where she belonged.

Four

After repeated attempts to get me to see a lawyer, Miss Claudia finally set up a meeting with the one she used. I knew I had to go meet with him as soon as Richard offered to represent me. Miss Claudia winked when Richard made the offer over a plate of chicken and dumplings. A wink similar to Patricia's when one of the third-graders reports a tall tale in the cafeteria. Albeit, my lawyer couldn't have been more than twenty-nine, my own daughter's age. Miss Claudia insisted he was top-flight. Like Patricia, he had a line of framed degrees decorating his fancy downtown office. The baby-faced man with slicked-back blonde hair addressed me as Mrs. Jacobs and made me feel confident that quick action would be taken. While he rattled on about no-fault, unfit parenting, and quick proceedings, all I could think of was my ailing car out in the parking lot. The pair of pliers had become a trusty companion, but sooner or later that switch would need replacing. He took a breath, and I jumped at the chance to ask the cost. He simply waved his hand and continued talking pending divorce.

Every evening when I stepped inside the trailer, the first thing I'd see was the white phone cord spring from behind the kitchen wall. Cher told me she was talking with Laurel, her first friend in Wiregrass. The girl was a year older than Cher. Her bright blonde hair and a hint of too much eye shadow made me question what kind of girl Laurel might be. I thought it curious that Cher would spend so much time talking with Laurel since she lived in a double-wide across from us. Why didn't the two girls just meet in the middle of the crumbled asphalt street to do their talking? But after raising two kids, I knew all sorts of odd things the early teen years did to kids. Besides, I trusted Cher. I always told her I'd trust her until she gave me reason not to.

Then the phone bill came in.

Our bill jumped to seventy-five dollars, decorated with phone calls for various area codes in Louisiana. She passed it off as trying to locate her missing friends. I refused to let this one go by. Although I didn't want to involve Miss Claudia in this, Cher had to learn a lesson. I brought her with me to work the last two days of her spring break, and she washed all of Miss Claudia's downstairs windows.

"Morning. Time to get on up," I said on the second day.

She lay in bed, mumbling and grumbling, until I took an ice cube and tossed it in her bed. She screamed and told me I was a child abuser for making her go through such torment. Maybe Mama was right about her being spoiled.

Stopped at a red light just a mile from Miss Claudia's, the car died. With blaring horns and the roar of automobiles, I jumped out of the car, and with the aid of my handy pliers we were back in business. An old man in a long blue car pointed his finger at me and shook his head. "Yeah, Buddy," I screamed with raised hands. *What did he think, I had planned all this to slow him down?*

Cher slumped down to the floorboard and refused to lift her head above the door for fear she might be recognized. I laughed at her and threatened to put a sign on the car the next day saying I was her chauffeur and that she hired me to drive her around. "Nuh-uh," she said while shaking her long brown hair. Even she laughed at that one.

Miss Claudia made a fuss over Cher the minute she laid eyes on her. "Erma Lee, this child has the prettiest skin I ever did see." By that time, Miss Claudia was doing much better and dressing herself. Even sitting around the house, she wore the nicest clothes. Cher picked up on her fashion sense and asked her all about the store her husband once owned. They hungered for each other, Miss Claudia never having had any grandchildren, and Cher looking to someone who could be a grandmother image. I was too busy trying to be Mama and Daddy for her. After an hour, I had to remind the two of them why Cher was there. As Cher washed and rinsed the windows, Miss Claudia sat outside on her porch, praising her work. Miss Claudia could always give a compliment that made you feel like she really meant it.

On Friday afternoon, Miss Claudia hobbled on her cane and tried to make lemonade. When she scared me to the point of picturing her falling on the knife she was carrying, I took over. She said she wanted to go outside and have a lemonade party. My warnings that she was spoiling Cher fell on deaf ears. "You hush. A little spoiling never hurt nobody." So we sat on iron chairs surrounded by latticework, carpeted grass, and award-winning roses and listened to Miss Claudia's lecture on the finer points of nature. I loved to watch Miss Claudia's hazel eyes dance as she carried on about this rose or that one.

"Do y'all know the story about the dogwood tree?" She pointed with her cane to the tree decorated with white blossoms.

We shook our heads. With a lift, Miss Claudia sprang up from the chair and put her arm in Cher's as she escorted her towards the tree.

Miss Claudia carefully opened the bloom and informed us that the tree had a message for us. As if reading a tea leaf, she told us about Jesus dying for us and how He rose up. I stiffened to think she was going to start preaching. Cher pulled her chin down, intently listening to Miss Claudia, and then she examined the white petals shaped like a cross. "See here. The red stains on the tips of the bloom reminds us that He loves us so much He died for us. You know today is Good

48

Friday, the day Jesus went to that cross."

"Today?" Cher cupped the bloom in her hand.

Miss Claudia smiled and nodded her head. She made it all seem just that simple.

"And Sunday we'll celebrate the resurrection. The new life He gives us, don't you know. I just love Easter. Patricia and her husband will take me to church. Maybe even Richard will go this year." Miss Claudia leaned on her cane and raised her head to soak in the full beauty of the big tree. Without looking away from the branches, Miss Claudia said, "I declare, I'm just falling in love with the two of you."

Cher looked at me for guidance. I didn't know what to say. The woman surprised mc at every turn. I wondered what she wanted from me and racked my brain to recall if there was a doctor's appointment next week. Did she want me to bring her?

Holding her cane, she reached out her arms. Afraid she'd get drunk-headed, I quickly grabbed her arm, and she pulled me into her bony chest. Cher leaned into her other side, and she roped her arms around us. Her silver cane pointed forward with all the authority of a compass. I tensed, not knowing why this woman I had met only a couple of weeks before was acting so suspicious. Maybe she had the beginnings of Alzheimer's? Maybe shc thought Cher needed the attention? Cher didn't liked to be babied, I could've told her that. I felt Cher's arm snake under my chest to hug Miss Claudia. A young child taken in so easily.

"Why keep love in your heart, when you can give it away for free?" Miss Claudia said. For a minute I was terrified Cher would go to crying. Then what would I do? But nobody said or did anything. We just stood together on that thick-carpeted grass, feeling the rising and falling of each other's chest. Three females entwined together by a past of hurts.

Saturday night was a welcome relief. After Cher paid off her portion of the phone bill, I let her use what was left over to go skating with Laurel. Laurel's mama offered to take them and everything. After the week I had, I needed the time alone to unwind. I had finished washing my hair when the phone rang. I knew it wasn't Bozo, because on Saturday night he and his frying-pan girlfriend would be at a honky-tonk.

"I hope I'm not calling at a bad time," Patricia said, not giving me time to respond before she continued. "Well, I'm in the doghouse with Mama." She offered a long, dramatic sigh. "Mama is just all to pieces. Doctor Tom and I promised her we'd take her to church tomorrow and then have lunch at the club. Well, naturally I assumed Mama would want to go to First Methodist like we always do. Then this evening she springs on us that she wants to go to Missoura's church."

I stood holding the receiver with one hand and combing the conditioner through my hair with the other. "Uh-huh."

"Now Erma Lee, you know I don't have a prejudiced bone in my body. You see me at school. I hug on the little black children just like I do the white ones. But with Doctor Tom being a dentist . . . Well, some people around here are just small-minded. It won't look good."

"Missoura?"

Patricia paused. "You know her. She comes to visit Mama all the time."

I had forgotten the tiny woman's name. She never lolled during a visit. She went straight back to Miss Claudia. "Now is she kin to that woman, Bertha, that used to clean the house?"

Another pause. "What?" Her voice was shrill, and I sensed she didn't want to answer any questions. Patricia probably was off to some party, I imagined.

"No, no. She and Mama are both from Apalachicola. Old-time friends. But anyway, I had no idea Mama promised Missoura she would go to Easter services at her church. It's not my fault, you know."

I sensed she wanted an agreement. I sat silent this time.

"Now, if you have plans just tell me," she said, not really meaning it, knowing full well I had no plans of my own. Cher had asked soon after the dogwood story if we were going to church for Easter. I was aggravated with Miss Claudia for pumping her up. Cher knew how I felt about religious holidays. If you didn't go throughout the year, then why be two-faced and show up for Easter and Christmas?

"But it would be so nice if you'd call Mama and offer to take her. Don't say I called or anything. You know, just call to check on her."

I hated being on call like this. "And will Richard go?" *He could at least drive a car,* I thought, wondering why on earth he couldn't take her.

"Honey, you should know the answer to that by now. Every single little thing he sees fit not to do becomes a bad case of nerves. I tell you, it's just left all up to me. That's why I'm so grateful you're here. Mama just thinks the world of you. Oh, and Cher too."

Don't do this to me, I wanted to shout. *Don't try to reel me in with some decorated compliment.* I visualized Patricia at home on the phone either showcasing that toothy grin of hers or shooing her husband to wait for her out in the car. As she rambled about my sainthood, I remembered how excited Miss Claudia was about Easter. She said it was her favorite holiday. The woman had been through the wringer.

"I'll take her," my words sliced through the phone line of bull.

Cher paraded in and out of my cramped bedroom, modeling a little black sundress with yellow flowers. Saturday night when I told her we were going to church, she jumped on the phone to Laurel and ran across the street to borrow the dress. I couldn't believe Cher didn't have a decent church outfit. But then again, there was no need for such fancy things as dresses. I only had one myself. The white one with big black flowers. And had it not been for Aunt Stella's funeral ten years ago, I wouldn't have had it on hand.

I looked for unsightly bulges as Cher zipped me up. *Good thing I've kept my frame in line.*

Instead of the usual rubber band to hold my hair in a ponytail, I dusted off the black cloth barrette and clamped it to the long braid Cher had created. I gave a final inspection in the wooden mirror nailed to the back of my bedroom door. "You think this looks okay?"

Cher smiled and nodded her head in approval.

Miss Claudia had us walk around the living room one at a time while she sat in a wingback chair and bragged on us. Cher ate it up and twirled around with her hand on her hip. I felt silly and waved away Miss Claudia's compliments about my braided hair and slim figure. I have to admit, her words made me feel like a tall woman.

Richard used Miss Claudia's Polaroid camera to make a picture of all of us in front of her rose garden. He made an extra copy for me and Cher to keep. I studied the picture and marveled at the way Miss Claudia's wide white hat with its navy band made her look so glamorous. She smiled and directed what setting and which person was to be photographed. If she was upset with Patricia and Doctor Tom for standing her up, she didn't show it. "I'd rather go with y'all anyway," she had said when I called her the night before.

I was nervous driving Miss Claudia's long Lincoln. Cher leaned over the front seat to watch the computerized dashboard. As Miss Claudia directed me to Bethel AME Church, I asked about Missoura.

"Oh, goodness. I guess I've known her almost my whole life. Well, soon after I married the first time."

"You were married before Mr. Tyler?" Cher asked leaning over the front seat.

"That's right. He was a fisherman. Lost at sea." Her scripted answers let me know she didn't want to talk about him. "Anyway, Missoura's husband, Aaron, worked for my first husband. She's just as sweet as she can be. I'd walk through fire for that gal."

Cher persisted. "Did she move to Wiregrass the same time you did?"

"Soon thereafter." Miss Claudia clamped the handle of her white purse.

"Did her husband come with her?"

"Oh, sure. There was more work here, don't you know. He passed away five years ago. Now Erma Lee, you're gonna turn left at the next red light. Cher, tell me about that little dress. I just imagine all the girls are wearing that kind." She managed to direct Cher away from any more questions for the time being.

I couldn't help but wonder what the little ladies from First Methodist would think if they saw what they believed to be one of their own entering the clapboard church. A marquee that would have been fitting for any movie house sat in front of the church with the words: *Bethel AME, Dr. Carlton Granger, "He Is Not Here."* The marquee was appropriate. A movie premier could be no more glamorous. Everywhere I turned there were hats in various styles and colors. Suddenly I felt naked with my hair slicked back over my scalp and braided like a show horse's tail.

Missoura was waiting for us in the foyer. The tiny woman was engulfed in Miss Claudia's arms. A gold stick with a stone-colored bumblebee stuck out of the top of Missoura's big black hat. I thought any minute she might fall over from the weight of the thing. She offered hugs to Cher and me too. "I'm just tickled y'all got to come. We gonna have a blessing today."

A tall man in a navy suit escorted us to the tenth pew. Missoura's appointed spot, I decided. I was surprised he didn't sit us in the front row. Roxi always told me whenever white people went to her church for weddings or funerals, they were seated directly in the front. At first I thought it was a sign of honor, but then she told me it was because everybody wanted to keep an eye on them. Seeing how underdressed I was, I sighed, relieved we didn't get placed up in the very front.

When the organ music swept over us and the singing started, I had to tap Cher's arm to stop her from turning around and staring. People were swaying all around us and lifting up their hands. A few shouted "Amen" and "I know that's right." Whatever we may have thought, we couldn't knock the peace and confidence they had that Sunday morning.

While a big bald man in a black robe wiped sweat off his brow, we heard a booming voice deliver the same story told to us by Miss Claudia. One of divine appointment, crucifixion, and resurrection. Even Miss Claudia let loose with a few amens of her own. At one point, when the pastor asked everyone to turn to their neighbor and declare they'd been blessed, Miss Claudia quickly turned to Cher and me. She put both of her cold hands on our cheeks and said, "Oh, I've been blessed."

A warmth cut through me. I started to reach up and put my hand on hers. But I sat silent, searching her hazel eyes. Her eyes were the softest I had ever seen—eyes that made you feel like you were the only one in the room who meant a thing in the world to her.

It was one-thirty before we ever made it to the circular driveway of Miss Claudia's country club. The church service had to go on record as the longest in history. "As long as the Spirit is moving, who's gonna argue?" Miss Claudia whispered after Cher voiced her shock at the length of the sermon. I had to agree with Cher.

After the service, I was afraid Cher had put her foot in her mouth when she asked Missoura if she was going to join us for lunch. "No, y'all go on. I got other plans." I knew she hadn't been invited. Couldn't have gone even if Miss Claudia wanted her to. I thought it crazy how this petite elderly woman, who was dressed much better than me, couldn't enter the doors of the very place Miss Claudia was taking a cafeteria worker. Believe me, I'd rather be eating dinner with Missoura than the crowd I had to face at that club.

I swallowed hard and carefully maneuvered the car up the hill to the covered portico. The big white brick building had white columns everywhere you turned. Cher had her head pressed against the backseat window as we made our way up the azalea-lined driveway. The grounds were manicured as perfectly as Miss Claudia's, but five hundred times bigger. I couldn't even imagine how many people it must take to keep the place in shape.

The good thing about the long church service was that most of the Methodist, Baptist, Presbyterian, and

Episcopalian crowd had already eaten and gone. But one of the old guard remained. As soon as we stepped foot into the red-carpeted foyer, I laid eyes on that prune-faced Elizabeth. Cher and me stood next to the planted palm and watched as she offered air kisses to Miss Claudia.

"That hat is just precious," Prune Face said, actually showing teeth. "We missed you in church today," she said with that pointy chin tilted towards the carpet.

"My friend Missoura wanted us to go to her church." Miss Claudia turned to point in our general direction. Prune Face shot us a quick look and then blinked her eyes, seeming to want to take us out of focus.

"Well, now. Do I know this lady? She attend the Baptist church?" Elizabeth folded her arms and leaned sideways, as if concerned she'd have to stop Miss Claudia from joining a cult.

"We go way back to Apalachicola. You know her. Her husband, Aaron, worked for us down at the store."

"Aaron?" Elizabeth straightened up and slightly tucked her head. "You mean the colored man who ran the elevator?" By the way she whispered the word *colored,* you would've thought she was using the most vile four-letter word known to man.

Miss Claudia was unaffected. "Bless his soul, you know, he died five years back. Anyway, I just think the world of his wife, Missoura. We all went to services with her. And brother did that preacher lay it on us." Miss Claudia turned to look out the double-glassed doors. "In fact, I'm expecting her any minute. She's going to join us for lunch."

57

Elizabeth's big blue eyes bugged even wider. "Here?" She leaned over and pointed down to the carpet.

"Well, where else? Oh me, where are my manners. You know my companion, Erma Lee Jacobs. This here's her granddaughter, Cher." Miss Claudia waved her hands for us to stand by her.

Prune Face stood frozen, finger pointing down to the floor. Cher looked up at me all nervous-like. I hated that she had to see this, but I was just doing handstands on the inside. If I'd had control over the Wiregrass newspaper that day, I would've run with the headline: "Prune Face Gets Hers."

"Now, Claudia. You do realize there are rules the club abides to and . . ."

Prune Face was saved by her skinny, bent-over husband, who had strips of thin gray hair covering his balding head.

"Well, lookie here." He wiped his mouth with his handkerchief and had a more pleasant grin than his wife. "Claudia, you look like you're doing good. Hip getting back to normal?"

While Miss Claudia updated the husband on her nasty fall and the bruise that still lingered, I saw Elizabeth pinch him on the sleeve of his jacket. As if pulled by a string, he quickly said, "Well, y'all have a nice lunch," and they departed. I turned around to look through the glass doors and saw her bony hands chopping air as I'm sure she recounted the shocking news that a colored would be having lunch at her exclusive club.

I tried to contain myself by biting my tongue. The soft piano music coming from the center of the room seemed too dignified for a fit of laughter. When the man in the white dinner jacket sat us outside on the balcony, I was relieved. The clapping of rotating sprinklers on the fairway would help to weaken any misbehavior that might burst forth. Finally the picture of Prune Face bent over, pointing with her skinny finger, was too much.

Cher looked at me like I'd lost my senses when I erupted. Unfortunately, Miss Claudia had just taken a sip of iced tea and spat the liquid across the table. All the sudden I forgot that she lived on Elm Drive. She was still all refined in her white-and-navy hat, but the way she bent over sideways, clutching her shaking bosom, made me believe she could pass for one of my neighbors at Westgate Trailer Park. A couple behind us peered to see what the commotion was all about.

I have got to straighten up, I kept telling myself. But every time I tried to stop laughing, Miss Claudia would mimic Prune Face by dropping her chin, bugging her eyes out, and pointing to the floor with her index finger. Then it would all start right back up again.

"Y'all are embarrassing me." Cher held the menu up to her face.

Through a blur of tears, I finally staggered to the ladies' room, leaned against the magnolia-printed wallpaper, and howled. The deep stomach holler felt good. Miss Claudia really didn't like that Prune Face after all.

Five

I had never been late before in my life. Not even when Bozo would get on a drunk and keep me up until two in the morning. That play only had two scenes. Either I'd try to find him and drag him away from one of his watering holes, or he'd find me with his raging fist.

But when I faced the morning late for work because my car wouldn't crank, I knew I had to take action. Not even the pliers trick could make the engine come to life.

Kasi, Laurel's mama, appeared out of nowhere. I barely knew the woman who lived in the double-wide across from me. Her bleached white hair was shorter than Mama's and stuck up all over the top of her head. To look at Kasi, you'd think she never ran a brush through that spiky mess. She approached me as I tinkered under the hood of the car, mumbling every cuss word I knew.

"Sounds like you got you a mess."

When I leaned from under the car hood displaying my evil eye, as Cher calls it, she took a step backward.

"I just . . . well, thought maybe you needed me to call somebody or something." She took a drag on her cigarette and pulled down her already too tight black T-shirt with a face resembling Vince Gill spray-painted across her bosom.

"This piece of crap just got on my last nerve is all."
I slammed the hood down. "As it is, I'm already going
to be late for work." I didn't want to tell her I had no
one to call for help. Richard first entered my mind, but
fearing he might have an attack of his nerves under the
pressure, I decided against it.

"Well, my shift ain't for another hour. I'll run you to
work." The ride to Barton Elementary in her sapphire
blue Toyota pickup was risky on my part. I still didn't
know who to trust.

"That old bat Miss Trellis give you her rules yet?"
Kasi squashed out a cigarette in the ashtray while
trying to steer the truck at the same time. "Don't tell
her nothing you don't want the whole entire trailer
park to know." She squinted her eyes and held the fire-
orange bulb of the truck lighter to a second cigarette.
"Oh, and about that car. Take it to Gerald Peterson,
down at Peterson and Son. He'll give you a real good
deal. Tell him I sent you. Just down past the trailer park
on Naples Road."

When her blue truck made its way up the circular
school driveway, I wanted out of there. I was hoping
Patricia wouldn't look out her corner office window
and see me, late for work and talking to a spiky-
haired creature in a pickup truck. "I sure do appreciate it. Let me know if there's any way I can help
you sometime," I said. If the closing truck door had
squeaked any louder, I would have missed Kasi's
parting words.

Kasi leaned towards the open passenger window and
nodded her head. "Awright. Sounds good. Maybe we

61

can go out partying. When Cher's daddy comes to visit, you'll have a full-time baby-sitter then."

Before I could get the questions I wanted to ask out of my opened mouth, the blue truck lurched forward and gained speed. I was so shocked at Kasi's announcement of unexpected company that I forgot to be nervous about being late for work.

By the time I had mixed up the potato-burger loaf, I went from being worried to angry. What did Kasi mean that Cher's daddy was coming to visit? How dare Bozo plan to come down here and pay a visit to Cher? He had only talked to her three times since we had moved here. And only then to find out what I'd been up to. But then again, was Cher really telling the truth? Maybe she just told Laurel and her mama that he was coming to make them think Bozo gave a flip about her. *Poor little thing*.

As we put the trays of food out on the cafeteria line, Sammy continued to prod my quiet mood. He kept asking me if I was in trouble. "Nothing's the matter," I lied. I wanted to scream and tell him to watch for a murder on CNN, because I knew if Bozo showed up something bad would happen. After the attack I dreamed up, I pictured Sammy being interviewed and saying what a good worker I was. From down the line of third-graders ready to graze, I spotted Patricia with her arms draped over the shoulders of two little boys. She would be interviewed too. She'd wax her face up but good and act all sad over the horrible misfortune. I just hoped the killing wouldn't happen right in front of

Miss Claudia's house. After all, Bozo did have her phone number.

"Mama said y'all had the best time Sunday," Patricia drawled with one hand on a lunch tray and the other straightening the shirt collar attached to a little black boy. He rolled his eyes up towards her shiny red mouth. When she grinned and pursed her glossed lips, I cautiously guarded the potato-burger loaf. I knew that just any minute the honey-looking stuff on her lips would drip off into the food.

"It was real nice," I said, handing her a plate. With my car dead and me soon to be next, I was not in the mood for her fakey ways. *Keep moving down the line away from me.* The image of my green paycheck gave me the strength to smile real nice at Patricia.

"I just hate that I missed it." She released the little black boy, and he quickly stepped two paces ahead of her. Patricia's hand dangled at her lips as if she was telling me the secret recipe to Kentucky Fried Chicken. "It just didn't look good for Doctor Tom and me to go, you know." She pursed her lips, closed her eyes, and shook her head real fast to emphasize the inappropriateness of it all.

Why Patricia called her own husband by the title of doctor, I never did know. When I first started working for Miss Claudia, I thought the word *doctor* was part of his first name. Just like I got two first names. Then I realized that this man, whose first name Patricia always threw the *doctor* to, was really a dentist. I guess if he spent all that time in school, he wanted to make sure he was appreciated for his hard work.

63

During lunch cleanup, I watched Sammy out of the corner of my eye. He twisted and turned to help this one and that one remove empty trays from the steaming bed. And with a prance, he was in the main kitchen, where he appointed Miss Dot, who was still ailing from hip surgery, the easy job of wiping down tables.

When he approached me, my stomach churned. I imagined the little kids who had earlier that day bravely stood on the cafeteria stage and spelled words longer than my arm. Swallowing hard and trying to imitate the spelling-bee bravery, I wondered whether I should go on offense or defense in justifying my squirrelly behavior.

"You know when you asked me what was the matter earlier," I said, creasing the lines of the dishrag. "Well, my car is tore up. I had to catch a lift here this morning. You know, that's how come me to be late, and I just hate to ask . . ."

His mustache spread wide, and he gently placed his hand on my white polyester shoulder. "You need a ride to Mrs. Tyler's?"

While he drove me to my second job, Sammy talked about taking his cat to the vet. I leaned against the window, offering a few "uh-huhs" in the right places. *Why couldn't I get my new life in order? Why was Bozo showing up now of all times? If he would've come at all, I'da thought it would've been when we first moved down here.* Dread brewed in my chest. Some things aren't fitting to talk to others about, and most the time nobody really cares anyway. So I sat there in the passenger seat of Sammy's black El Camino, letting the Wiregrass sun pour on me as I listened to the ailments of Spooksie.

The clanging of the piano drifted onto the street. Richard was sitting on the side-porch steps reading a book. Learning more about the Bermuda Triangle, I figured. As I drew closer, the noise of the piano increased. It sounded like the old-timey piano playing at Aunt Stella's church. The rhythm had a one-two-three, one-two-three tempo. The song even seemed familiar.

"Mama's getting ready for Carnegie Hall," Richard said, squinting his eyes together and laughing.

I didn't even bother with one of my usual fake grins. His silliness was not finding me in good humor today. The old fool didn't even realize somebody had dropped me off. I decided when it got time for me to go, I was going to have to come out and directly ask Richard for a ride home.

When I began to walk past him, Richard blocked me by stretching his left arm across the concrete step. Stroking his thin black book, he said, "I'm reading about the domestication of modern-day cats in the Egyptian world. It's just fascinating. Erma Lee, did you know that Cleopatra . . ."

"Oh, goodness. I think I hear Miss Claudia needing some help." I stepped over his arm and continued up the porch. *Too bad Sammy and Richard couldn't get together,* I thought. *With all Richard's so-called knowledge, maybe he could save Sammy a vet bill by diagnosing what ailed Spooksie.*

The one-two-three rhythm engulfed me when I walked into the living room. With her eyes closed and swaying like Ray Charles, Miss Claudia hummed some song, and I fished for the name in the deepest corner of my mind. Her cane was propped up against the big black piano. I wondered how she ever learned to play with such an awful childhood. I knew that trashy step-daddy of hers didn't pay for any lessons.

With the last touch of the ivory, I forced my mind to dump the image of Bozo, drunk, with a loaded shotgun. Instead, I clapped my hands. As bad as my day had been and with my life now ending, I hoped her home with its warm colors and fancy paintings would offer a refuge.

"Good gracious alive." She clamped her hand to the periwinkle blouse. Her hair was done, and her makeup dewy fresh. "I didn't know I had an audience."

I began picking up pieces of Richard's trademarks: sections of the newspaper scattered on the floor near the sofa. "I mean to tell you, you're good now." I continued to work and talk. With a talker like Miss Claudia it's the only way I could get my work done and be able to visit at the same time. After Easter, I'd come to realize part of my duties was to keep her entertained. Patricia never came right out and said it, but even Miss Claudia claimed me as her companion. "How long you been playing the piano?"

She flipped through the faded green hymnal and shook her head ever so gently. "I declare. Let's see. Missoura taught me back when I was seventeen, somers in there. Here we go. How about 'How Great Thou Art'?"

Some of my favorite things in the home on Elm Drive were the cobalt blue glasses stored in the white living-room shelves. Miss Claudia had told me her late husband, Wade, had given her the antique glasses as a wedding gift. After a good dusting, I always loved standing back and watching the sun seep inside the swirls of blue and teal.

As I inched the dust rag inside each glass, I found myself humming along with Miss Claudia to the steady rhythm. Then, as clear as the pictures Miss Claudia made with her instant Polaroid, I remembered where I had heard the song. I remembered the flowers, the preacher, and the sweet one-two-three rhythm of that old-timey piano just like it was yesterday. But Aunt Stella had been gone ten years now.

When I looked inside that frilly gray casket and saw my aunt's face all sticky-looking, I started to cry. From the time I was just a little thing, I knew she was the one person who really loved me. Mama quickly reached across the flowers on top of the casket and squeezed my elbow. Her eyes pierced me as if to say, "If I can stand my own sister's death, then I expect the same out of you."

Mama didn't like for me to cry. Said it made me look weak, and people would feel sorry for me. I just hope that after Bozo shows up with his shotgun and blows me away in front of this safe haven, Mama won't expect Cher not to cry.

What about Cher? If I go, who'll end up with her? Mama?

I felt the blood drain from my face and neck. The very idea of that cold woman taking thirteen years of my training and turning Cher into an empty shell made me want to throw up. I tipped to the right and caught myself on the edge of the grand piano top. Before I realized it, the blue cobalt glass blasted into pieces on the hardwood floor.

Bozo's shotgun blast won't sound much louder, I thought. Paralyzed, I stood looking at the scattered pieces. The chips of glass looked like hundreds of expensive blue stones ready to be mined.

With the shrill crack of glass, Miss Claudia stopped playing and turned towards me. I had my hands up in the air like something gone wild. My mouth flew open, but nothing came out. Tears puddled in my eyes.

"Don't you cry, girl. You want this woman to think you're weak?" I heard Mama yell in my mind.

Miss Claudia picked up her cane and approached the rubble. She put her hand on my shoulder. I still couldn't look at her. My hand shielded the side of my face as though I expected a strike from her blue-veined hand. Mouth still open, all I could manage was some sort of half-human moan.

This is it for sure. I'll never be able to work off how much this thing cost.

"It was an accident is all. No reason to let your nerves get keyed up." Her bony fingers squeezed my shoulder tighter.

I could only turn my head away from her. "I'm so . . . so . . . sorry. And these the glasses your husband . . ." Some sort of matter seemed to gather in my throat.

Looking down, I saw an escaped tear mark a spot on her hardwood floor.

"People make mistakes every day. You know what my husband Wade used to tell folks down at the store? He'd tell 'em, if you're not making one mistake a day, then I question if you're really working."

If I'd had a tail, it would've been tucked between my legs. Instead, I tucked my head. When I turned to face her, I let myself fall into those hazel eyes. I dropped the invisible shield and bit my lip to keep from squalling. Soon I felt her bony fingers again, pulling me into her bosom.

"All this fuss over some blue glass. Oh, I can get Patricia to get me another one. It's just a thing, sugar, not a human being."

Her hand patted my back while I clung to her soft, silky shoulder. I would not cry. I couldn't cry now and stain her pretty silk blouse with my weak tears. Without the release of a single tear, I erupted. "I'm gonna get killed. Cher won't even be able to cry, and they'll all be telling you what trash I was."

She pulled me back to examine my face. Her raised eyebrows and gaped mouth seemed to question if I had been struck by one of Richard's nerve attacks. Instead of calling for a straitjacket like she probably should have, she and her cane led me to the kitchen table.

"Now, you need a Coca-Cola to help settle your stomach?"

"No, ma'am," I said, knowing full well I had to tell it all now. But instead of dread, I felt protected. For a moment she didn't say anything. She just sat there with her hands folded, looking down at her lace tablecloth. I was relieved when the air conditioner kicked on and provided background noise. The humming sounded soothing.

"Now what in the world was all that about? And just drop that old pride, Erma Lee. It's me you're talking to."

Her soft hazel eyes did me in again. Before I knew it, I was telling all the ugly, tattered holes that were missing from the puzzle. The holes I'm sure she had figured out, but gave me the dignity of acting like she didn't know.

When I began to describe the drunken attacks, the last night before I left Cross City, and what I knew about Bozo coming to town, I somehow felt silly. Nobody said anything about him wanting to kill me. Like always, I assumed the worst. Maybe because if I prepared myself for the worst, the truth never seemed so awful. I expected her to tell me I was making a mountain out of some little molehill, or some other silly expression that older people like to use.

She wiped her hand across the tablecloth as if she was scattering invisible after-dinner crumbs. "You can't play around with men like him. You think he'd be so crazy to come here?" Before I could say anything, she verbalized my deepest fear. "Well, if he got liquored up, no telling."

"I don't know what to think anymore." I pulled my ponytail over my neck and twirled the ends of my hair with my finger. "And just when things were going good . . ."

"We'll call the lawyer directly. I just imagine he can get papers drawn up to stop that Bozo person from coming within any distance of you. You got a tag number for his vehicle?"

As I searched my pocketbook, fishing through tissue paper, female needs, and pieces of Juicy Fruit, I thought how wrong I'd been about Claudia Tyler the first time I met her. I assumed I could put her in a neat little box because she lived in that nice big house on Elm Drive. Miss Claudia would tear out of any box anybody ever tried to put her in. And I suspected she had done so before.

While she sat at the kitchen table and used her portable phone to ensure my safeguard, I could make out bits and pieces of the conversation.

"So the divorce papers were already served. I see." Shaking her head, her hazel eyes locked on me. I knew my eyes were all big and scared-looking. In my mind, when those papers got handed to Bozo, he probably went slam nuts.

I could just see him driving to the Brown Jug and telling everybody how I kidnapped his grandbaby and how he would rot in jail before seeing me keep her. "Them papers say I'm her daddy by law," he'd shout at no one in particular. Knowing full well he couldn't raise Cher and she was better off with me. It was that pride thing he had. The same thing kept me from telling Miss Claudia about my black-and-blue past.

Once I confessed my fear and she made the phone calls, I felt stronger. I'd never leaned on anybody before and wondered if I was venturing on shaky terri-

71

tory by letting Miss Claudia get so wrapped up in my business. To be honest, at the time I felt like if she didn't get involved, I very well might have one of Richard's nerve attacks. I decided telling her about things that shouldn't be discussed in public was better for her in the long run. The other option was her seeing me run down Elm Drive in broad daylight screaming and pulling my hair out.

"Sheriff Thomas will handle things from his end too. He's a good man," Miss Claudia said and fingered her pearls. "You know, sometimes the law likes to look the other way at messes like we've been through."

I stopped twisting the ends of my ponytail and looked up at her. "Well, you got to trust somebody, don't you?"

She just offered a soft smile, and I hoped she was not about to tell me that the man who set her up with all these nice things had violated her in any way. Right then, I needed the image of a good and decent man. Wade Tyler's picture hung in her bedroom and offered a glimpse of a soft man with a receding hairline and a shy smile. I imagined him running his department store and letting Miss Claudia take the limelight by fellowshiping with all the customers, complimenting a woman on this dress or flirting with a man over the new suit he was having tailored. I wanted to plug my ears and not listen. I needed that image of Wade Tyler.

She looked down and drew circles with her index finger on the white tablecloth. "I never will forget the time I called the law on my first husband. That Luther Ranker. We'd only been married two months before I knew I'd gone from one hell on earth directly to another. Funny, I don't even recollect what the problem was. Me just a girl, don't you know. But anyway, he set in to pounding on me for something I should've done or shouldn't have done."

Miss Claudia stopped drawing imaginary circles on the tablecloth. Instead, she squeezed the lace into a ball.

"The next morning after my beating, Luther went off in his boat, and I went straight to the sheriff's office to file a complaint. I still remember how the sheriff's fat chin glistened with sweat. He leaned back in his chair and put his big hands behind his round head. The sheriff said he didn't like to get in family matters. He asked me if I had talked to my folks about this yet. I wanted to yell at him and tell him my real daddy was dead. If he counted that no good Maxwell as my papa, I did not share his opinion. I thought at the time if he knew what Old Man Maxwell had done to me, he would've locked him up too. I was such a silly thing back then. Sitting in that hot office with the black iron fan rotating in the open window and thinking that if the sheriff locked Luther and Old Man Maxwell up, Mama, my baby sister, and me could all live in the big store on Main Street. But instead, I was a good girl and followed the sheriff's order.

"Only problem was, Old Man Maxwell stood in the door to his store and told me in no uncertain terms that I made my bed and would have to sleep in it. I knew he was lying when he told me Mama didn't want to see me. I tried to push my way inside the door. He grabbed at my breast and squeezed hard, pushing me out the door like some old drunk being tossed out of a saloon. 'Get from here, before your mama sees you looking like some beat-up whore,' he yelled and closed the store door. While I laid there on that nasty wooden sidewalk, I just didn't know what was worse, getting that beating from Luther or being kept away from my own mama by the devil incarnate.

"I even wrote Mama about how I made a mistake marrying Luther. I never did go into details about the day before I ran off and the liberties Old Man Maxwell took with me. Some things are just better left alone, I decided. I just wrote about the current hell and begged Mama to contact the sheriff and get me some help. I worked on that letter every day for a week and planned on dropping it off at the store when Luther took me to town on Saturday. When I hid it in the closet, I had no idea Luther would be smart enough to find the letter tucked inside my shoe.

"Luther waited until we were riding in the truck on the way to town before telling me to give him my pocketbook. He claimed he had a piece of money for me and wanted to personally put it in my pocketbook. I don't think I could've gripped that little black pocketbook that carried the letter I wrote Mama any tighter. After a few minutes of teasing, Luther yanked it out of my grasp and pulled over on the edge of the dirt road. It was right near Yorkshire Pond. I can still hear the locusts sounding off out in the pines.

"When he saw that letter, I never heard so much yelling and swearing in my life. Luther went plumb crazy. Telling me how I thought I was going to pull something over on him and how he was watching my ever move. Then, he just leaned against the driver's door and started kicking with his boots. He only caught me with one good jab to my arm before my hand found the door handle and I jumped out. He screamed that I'd be six feet under before he'd let my mama get in our business. I didn't see what he pulled from under the truck seat until the tree limb above my right shoulder dropped to the ground. Before the pistol smoke cleared, I took off running.

"I ran all the way around the pond and through the briars and underbrush. The briar bushes tore my legs to pieces, but I never felt a thing. It was only after I made it to Aaron and Missoura's place that I noticed the blood on my legs.

"Aaron was hoeing in the garden when I came running up to him, crying and carrying on. Missoura later told me that I jumped right at his big chest like a little young 'un excited to see her daddy. He saved me that day and time and time again. A more gentle soul you never did know."

Miss Claudia drew zigzag lines all across the tablecloth. Her face met mine, and she flinched as though she just remembered something she had to accomplish. "Oh, my goodness. Listen to me just rattle on. Not a bit of use in talking about things that are best left buried."

She held the edge of the pine table and lifted herself up. I didn't move to try and assist her. I remained at the table feeling embarrassed over how my own problems had somehow peeled away years of hurt that were draped with cobwebs in her mind. I could not for the life of me imagine this woman I was looking at putting up with the life she described. But then again, maybe she thought the same of me.

"But what I was getting at is our sheriff." She leaned on her cane and lectured with her pointed index finger. "He's not like that sorry excuse for a lawman in Apalachicola. Wiregrass's sheriff respects a woman and will take her word. You got nothing to worry about, Erma Lee."

I never was any good at taking care of myself. I was too busy caring for Cher or Mama or, until a few months ago, Bozo. And now I saw another purpose with Miss Claudia. I wanted to protect her from further heartache. Those early weeks with her had been spent worrying she'd feel sorry for me. Now that had all changed, and the feeling that came over me was strange, an aching for a person I barely knew that good. An aching for what she had lost at such a young age.

At such a young age . . . sixteen. Only a year younger than me when I married Bozo. Sixteen. The same age Suzette was when she got pregnant with Cher.

"We're just all thimbles on the big Monopoly board of life," my Aunt Stella used to say. That afternoon sitting at Miss Claudia's kitchen table, I couldn't help but wonder if the God Aunt Stella worshiped had sent me to Wiregrass for a reason after all.

Six

As soon as Miss Claudia confirmed that Gerald Peterson was the best mechanic she knew, it made me feel a little more confident about advice from my spiky-haired neighbor. Kasi claimed Gerald Peterson was good, but she didn't say how good-looking he was.

He pulled up to my trailer in a shiny black tow truck, and with a nod of his Auburn University baseball cap, he lifted the truck bed conveyer to rescue my ailing car. I caught myself pulling at that white polyester cafeteria uniform while he leaned over, hooked, and prodded all kind of equipment under the hood of my car.

Gerald was probably in his early fifties. He had a square build and a thick neck. I imagined him rushing down the Wiregrass football field decades earlier, scoring for the home team. A combination of curly blonde and gray hair stuck out underneath his cap. His mustache was still blonde with a few gray patches. He moved like a man determined to complete the mission before supper time.

Most likely he had a wife and kids to get to, I decided. Maybe he was even a grandfather. I caught myself embarrassed by studying his build for so long. Quickly, I glanced to see if Cher had noticed.

She stood by me with her hands on her hips, drawing rings in the sand with the tip of her big toe. She seemed to consciously ignore the other trailer-park kids who had gathered on bikes and skateboards to witness the faded Monte Carlo's elevation to the car ambulance. The humming of the tow truck's diesel engine drew kids from every corner.

Looking at Miss Claudia's big Lincoln parked in my driveway, I couldn't help but think how out of place such luxury looked at Westgate Trailer Park. Half of my home was the same size as that car.

When I had shaken my head *no* to Miss Claudia's first offer, she stood firm. "Mercy, Erma Lee. If I can't do this, what can I do? Me with this bum hip, how much driving you think I'll be doing?" With a toss of the keys she sealed the deal. "You're taking the car, and that's all there is to it."

"Well, hey, Gerald," Kasi said as she slipped through the growing throng of kids.

He nodded and, without looking back up, asked, "Where's your old man hiding these days?"

She took a deep drag off her cigarette and bent down to the side mirror on the door of my Monte Carlo. "He's working a job up in Huntsville. Getting paid time and a half. I told him just keep them checks coming, baby," she said, stretching the ends of her platinum hair.

Gerald ignored Kasi, and she eventually slid over towards Cher and me. "Cher, baby, why don't you run over and help Laurel get ready for skating?"

Cher looked at her and then glanced at me. I knew she didn't want Kasi to know I had to give my permission first.

When she walked in front of the kids gathered on the street, Cher flung her hair over her shoulder and never said a word. I worried she was getting a big head because we had that shiny Lincoln parked in our lot.

Kasi stood next to me dragging on a cigarette and pulling at her denim miniskirt. The diesel engine of the tow truck hummed along with the crickets of early evening. The noisy mixture made me nervous, and I tried to think of something to say to Kasi. I never did know how to act around women like her, the flirty kind that hid behind a pile of makeup and had big breasts that hung out every which a way.

"He'll fix it up for you now." She laid hard on the word *now* and took another drag. "Me and Ricky met him down at the Moose Lodge one night," Kasi said while smoke escaped her black-lined lips. "He sure can dance. Gerald I mean, not Ricky."

"I hope it won't cost me a pile of money," I whispered.

"He'll do you right. He's fast with his hands."

I shot my eyes towards Kasi, wondering if she was talking from personal experience.

"Works on them cars day and night," she added.

"I expect his wife gets tired of all that working." I shocked myself by bringing up the mechanic's home life. It was at times like this when I wished I was equipped with a built-in tape recorder and could recapture dumb words by pressing a rewind button.

Another long drag on the cigarette, and then her head flung backwards as though she was looking for the first evening star. *Oh great,* I thought. *Now she's going to make it worse by asking me if I'm interested.* I hated games women like her played.

"You're not going to believe this. He's a widow," Kasi said. Rings of smoke escaped with each word.

"Widower?"

"You know, his wife died. He won't talk about it. And all Miss Trellis would say is that it was tragic." Another long dramatic drag of nicotine. "You know how the old bat is, making you beg for answers. Well, she can kiss my tail before I beg anything out of her grubby little mouth. You heard what she done when Laurel rode her bike up by the office the other day? She went and . . ."

"I believe that's got it."

I didn't even hear him walk up. He was wiping his hands together, I guess hoping the grease would somehow disappear. Fearing he heard my earlier comments about his marital status, I felt a streak of heat roll up my neck.

"You got my work numbers to call when it's ready?" I was busy pulling my ponytail across the base of my neck. Not allowing myself to look at his walnut-shaped eyes, I looked down at the circle of dirt he was standing in.

When he casually walked away, he stuck his hand up in the air and cocked it forward. Skateboards and bicycles scattered to the shoulder of the pavement, and the shiny black truck departed with my worn-out car.

Cher was in the height of her glory riding with Laurel in the backseat of Miss Claudia's big Lincoln.

"Where to, Miss Cher and Miss Laurel?" I knew I shouldn't have encouraged them to act like big shots, but I tried to remind myself that you're only a young 'un once.

"To the penthouse apartment, darling," Laurel said a little too convincingly. *All those trashy soap operas she watched,* I thought.

"Onward to the club," Cher said in a throaty whisper. She leaned sideways onto Laurel and giggled. Cher's silliness comforted me. Her developing body had not evaporated my little girl yet.

Just because I wasn't allowed to act silly doesn't mean it will hurt anybody else, I decided early on with Cher. Maybe if Suzette could have escaped her problems in silly giggles and make-believe, she wouldn't have had to escape her heartache with dope.

After the girls were dropped off at the skating rink, I found myself not wanting to go back home. Emptiness seemed to be sucked into my pores from the very air that spewed from the air-conditioning vents. Would Kasi want to talk if I stopped by her place? But then the mental image of her getting all fixed up and spiking that hair out to go juking flashed across the windshield.

I was sure Gerald Peterson was out on some date too. I pictured him cleaned up and capless, sitting at a restaurant cutting his T-bone with those big powerful hands. After a big meal, he would go out to a club and dance. Maybe one or two beers, but he wouldn't overindulge. He'd keep one elbow on the bar and turn his head to grin at all his friends.

As I turned up the soft echoes of the steel guitar on

the radio, I tried to capture Gerald's voice and guess what he would say to the girlfriend he may be with tonight. All I could think of was his hair and how wavy it was. For a second I caught myself wanting to put my hands in it. But who was I fooling? Speaking of hair, I remembered mine when he first laid eyes on me. Pulled back like some bald-headed fool with a ratty ponytail dangling down my spine. Gerald Peterson was the type of man who could only be with a brassy woman, probably some beautician who spent hours pulling out all her eyebrows and drawing perfect new ones on with a black pencil. I took my knocks, but nobody could ever call me stupid. I knew where I could be accepted.

"Now, I hope I'm not bothering you or nothing," I said under the dim yellow light of Miss Claudia's porch.

"Oh, don't be silly," she said, dressed in a long white silk robe with big butterflies and pink flowers. "I'm just in here looking at TV." She held the front door open, and I entered with the McDonald's bag.

"I went on a hunch here. You like chocolate milkshakes?" I held the bag up trying to entice her.

Whether she did or not, I would never know. She clamped her hand on her chest and closed her eyes. "It's just what I needed right now."

We decided to take our milkshakes in the family room. It was warm and inviting, with fashionable furniture. Old photographs of Patricia and Richard were scattered on the mantel and the coffee tables. A big built-in bookshelf took up one wall of the room, and I wondered if she'd really read all those books or just had them there for show.

"They tell me Gerald Peterson is just the salt of the earth," Miss Claudia said when I updated her on my car. She paused to suck up the last remaining drops of milk chocolate from her straw.

"My neighbor Kasi, she said he works all the time." I sat with my bare feet insulated under the sofa cushion, and rolled my eyes to see if my bait had been accepted.

"I expect he has to."

"Does he have a bunch of kids to feed or something?"

"Erma Lee Jacobs. You ask more questions about him than I ever heard you ask about me." She slapped the arm of her chair. "And here you are all propped up on my love seat. Are you wishing Gerald was here to share that love seat with you?"

I bolted my feet from under the cushion. "That's a lie," I yelled, trying to drown out her laughter. All I could think of was how I sounded like Cher teasing Laurel over some boy she had couple-skated with. "I mean, I was just wondering why he had to . . ."

"Oh, me." She wiped a tear away from her eye. "You're still a good-looking woman. You're expected to notice men, don't you know."

I wondered if she knew her compliments got me every time. Whenever she made such a comment, and she did often, I always wanted to run and look in the hallway mirror to see if I could see the same qualities she claimed I had. But I usually just looked down or waved my hand, believing I could shoo away her silliness.

"To my knowledge, Gerald Peterson is still a single man. Or he was the last time I had my car tuned up." Miss Claudia jiggled the straw in her cup. "He's sure had some bumps along the way."

Oh, Lord, here it comes, I thought. *Prison, crackhead, most likely a womanizer.*

"It's probably been three years. His wife was killed in a most terrible car wreck out on Highway 431. They tell me she was coming back from prayer meeting when a drunk ran right into her head-on. Naturally the drunk survived."

I thought of Bozo and all the nights he went on drunks and how I stayed worried not for his safety, but for the safety of everybody else on the road.

"After I heard about it at the beauty shop, I took a pot of chicken and rice over. That big giant man just sitting there with his hands on his head. Lord, it liked to tore my heart out."

"He got any kids?"

"There's a girl. I say girl, I think she's married now. And a son. Gerald Peterson is a good man, Erma Lee. You like his looks, I suppose?"

"No, ma'am. I mean, he's attractive and all." I felt guilty for talking like this over a poor dead woman's husband.

"I don't want you thinking every man is like that Bozo person. It took me some time after Luther was lost at sea . . . well, before I could think of another man. Not because I mourned him, don't you know," she said and pointed the tip of her straw. "But because I was scared to death I was a magnet for meanness."

"How did you get over all that?" I suspected there were more stories of beatings and ugliness. She was like me in that way. We pulled from our memory file and shared the first that came to mind, not necessarily the worst, but the most convenient.

She shook the empty cup and sat it by the edge of her recliner. "I have to credit the good Lord for healing those mental scars. I leaned on Him mighty heavy and Missoura for healing the physical scars. She was so sweet to me. She'd ever so lightly put the lard on my broken skin. I often think now what a terrible predicament I put Aaron and Missoura in by running to their house after I thought I'd be killed. After all, Aaron worked for Luther, and him being colored was just inviting trouble. But where was I to go? My mama was under a spell of doubting where her next meal would come from, and the sheriff left it all up to Mama. Well, there you go." She tossed up her arms to emphasize the desperation, then looked down at her painted toenails.

I always hated times like these, not knowing whether to speak up or let the person catch their thoughts. The grandfather clock in the hallway chimed eight times. If she didn't speak on the tenth, I would say something.

"To keep it from looking like he was involved, Aaron paid off Nettie, the lower quarter's concubine. She let me stay at her place. Naturally Aaron paid an even higher price. Every day searching for oysters, Aaron had to listen to Luther tell him how disgraceful I was to live like the worst kind of trash. Like Luther was supposed to be better, mind you.

"But Aaron knew how to keep his nose clean by playing stupid. And him a hundred times smarter than that sorry Luther. So Aaron got by with offering a 'Yez zir, boss man' to Luther's tirades about how horrible it was that I was living with a colored harlot. I reckon if Luther would've figured out Aaron was involved, he would have killed him right there on the boat and used him for bait."

Miss Claudia dropped her chin and stared over the tops of her glasses. "So you see why I'm so crazy about Missoura? I was the same way by Aaron, don't you know.

"Gracious, I saw and heard things in Crazy Nettie's shack along Howard's Creek that a girl had no business knowing. But I just chose to look the other way. You might as well say I had to. Missoura would take me to her house in the daytime, and then, before Aaron got home and Luther would have a chance to check up on me, I'd go to Nettie's for bedtime. Luther said he'd kill every colored in the quarters if I didn't go back to him. But the day he showed up to take me home, Crazy Nettie was standing on the gapped wooden porch holding two live water moccasins. She jabbered some mumbo-jumbo and claimed she put a spell on Luther. He yelled at her, 'Get out of my way, you crazy whore.' He hadn't made it up the first step when Nettie threw those moccasins at him." Miss Claudia slapped the arm of her chair and howled with laughter. "Luther fell over his feet trying to get away from there. He was so eat up with meanness the snakes wouldn't even touch him."

"And that's when you moved to Wiregrass?"

She pulled at the folds of her robe like she might be exposing herself to a room full of men.

"That's when I wanted to move. I was hoping to earn enough money by helping Nettie sew clothes that I could buy a bus ticket and have a nest egg. She made me a better seamstress and complimented me on being a quick learner. Whenever she went into Old Man Maxwell's store to buy material, I'd sit outside hoping Mama would look out the window so I could mouth her an SOS. She never did." Miss Claudia straightened the wrinkled armrest.

"Many a time I've wondered if Nettie told Mama I was outside. I felt like a trapped beaver. Maybe worse than that. Believe you me, if I could've chewed my leg up for freedom, I would have. Instead, I chose to earn it by making dresses and hemming seams for the folks in the quarters.

"The day after I bought my bus ticket to Montgomery, I realized it wasn't just nerves making my cycle late. I really was pregnant. Nettie told me she couldn't entertain menfolk with a screaming baby in the background. They had already cut back their visits on account of a white girl on the place. Aaron and Missoura begged me to go on with my plans to leave, but that paralyzing fear set in. The kind that whispers to you in the middle of the night. Me with a baby and no means of income, in a strange town and nobody to help care for it while I worked. I let the demons convince me that the hell I knew was better than a potential unknown hell. And when Luther showed up to try and once more talk some sense into me, I gave in. Before sunset, I was back in that house on the bay, washing his dishes, shucking his oysters, and agreeing with him how stupid I was to ever leave. He waited until the second night to whip me for leaving to start with."

I was leaning forward with my knuckles resting on my chin. I racked my brain trying to think of a positive direction for the conversation. "What about your baby?"

Miss Claudia sighed. I was scared to death she was growing tired of me. Then she looked up and smiled. "Little Beth. She was the one piece of joy in those days. She lived two years on this earth." She looked down and put her hand on the edge of her eyeglasses. "Typhoid fever took her away. Just like it did my daddy and brother."

I just sat there looking at the upturned cushion with my bare feet curled under it, wanting to bury all of me inside the padding. My nosy landlady, Miss Trellis, had been right after all. The woman who sat before me on a throne of padded khaki had suffered in a way I think most people only relate to in a movie.

"That's why I respect you, Erma Lee. And don't you ever for one minute think you should've stayed." Miss Claudia pointed her finger at me and almost screamed the words like the preacher at Missoura's church. "If the car, the trailer, the whole ground caves around you, don't you think differently."

It was only when I saw her finger shake and her lip quiver that I moved to the edge of her recliner. My turn had come. I draped my arm over her soft shoulder. Instinct told me to put my head against hers, but I did not. I knew what it felt like to want to keep an inch of pride.

She sniffled and patted my hand. I quickly moved back to the sofa.

"We all have our cross to bear, don't we? But I won't have anybody feeling sorry for me, don't you know," she said and pulled a tissue from a gold box next to her chair. She asked me to help her up, and we walked into the formal living room with her holding my arm.

"They say music is food for the soul. How about it?"

I just smiled and tried to nod, but all that came out was a halfhearted movement of my head. Too much honesty always embarrassed me. *How could you sing right now?* I wanted to scream. *You just tore your heart wide open and now—sing?*

But sing we did and repeated the chorus five times: "Count your blessings, name them one by one."

Seven

*D*ays passed, and still no sign of a shotgun-toting Bozo. Maybe that court order mandating that he keep five hundred feet from me paid off. My sleep grew sounder, and every day my nerves settled a bit more. I decided to take Miss Claudia's advice and not

89

question Cher about her declaration of Bozo's return. Miss Claudia reminded me of the adjustments Cher had made and that she was most likely making it all up. I reasoned with Miss Claudia. Cher was just living in a dream world. It was her age. And I know it had to hurt Cher that Bozo stopped calling to check on her. Anytime he called it was only to cuss me out and order us back to Cross City.

So when the phone snatched me out of a deep sleep one night, I decided there had to be something wrong with Miss Claudia. *An emergency call needing my help,* I thought and flung the hair from my eyes. I fumbled down the darkened hallway, stubbing my toe on a doorstop en route to the phone. *Has Miss Claudia fallen out of bed? Did Richard go into one of those fits she was always talking about?*

"Hello."

"Where you get the idea I want to come after you?"

I dropped my head on the kitchen counter, and my hair created a curtain over my face. The screaming on the other end of the phone seemed foreign in the otherwise still, dark trailer.

"I warned you you had till the end of the month to get back here. And it's been two months. You think you're so popular I can't get shut of you, gal?"

Every time I opened my mouth against the cool counter, he blasted through my incoherent mumbles. After what seemed to be thirty minutes of Bozo's tirade about how he wouldn't waste his gas to come after me, I flipped my hair back and stood erect, forcing the slits of my eyes to open. The red light of the microwave clock read three thirty-seven.

"Is there any rhyme or reason to all this, or do you just like tying one on so you can harass me?"

"Me harass? Me? What about the harassment you give me by having that deputy come to the shop and give me them papers?"

The court order protecting me from this lunatic. *Funny,* I thought. *Over the phone he seems more pathetic than scary.* "Maybe if you hadn't been telling Cher you were coming down here, they wouldn't have to serve no papers."

"I ain't told nobody nothing. Hey . . . hey, I don't give a flying rip. Stay down there on welfare for all I care."

That did it. Me busting my tail to live paycheck to paycheck, and him accusing me of welfare. "Bozo, let me tell you one thing. I got connections here. And if you ever so much as call me drunk again, I'll tape-record you raising sand and turn it over to the law. By the time I'm done with you, you won't be able to step foot outside Cross City."

"Don't you threaten me, woman. I can always come see my grandbaby if I want to. You can't stop me. Hey . . . hey, I signed them papers as her legal . . ."

"Legal daddy, maybe. But you don't care a thing about Cher." When I turned around, I caught a glimpse of Cher's bare feet and the slip of her white cotton nightgown. While Bozo rambled about how sorry I'd be when he signed the divorce papers, I could only hope that Cher hadn't heard me. I ended the call the usual way, hanging up the receiver fast and furious.

The second step was taking the phone off the hook.

Cher's foot dangled off the side of my bed. Her soft brown hair swept up on the pillow. Her eyes were closed tight, and I tried to convince myself that my voice had not been heard. Maybe she had just had a bad dream and slipped into my bed.

I scooped my body against her and draped my arm around her tiny waist. I could feel the steady rhythm of her pulse in the base of her stomach. We laid there together in the quiet of the night hearing only the faint chirp of the misplaced phone receiver.

Regardless of the unpleasantness of my premature wake-up call, the touch of her skin made me feel all was well. In times like these she was my baby girl. My special project. The one I would clear a different path for. I wanted to squeeze her and keep her body from changing. I wanted to hang on to the little girl inside her.

Twilight was just settling back in my mind when I heard her mumble, "Pop didn't do right by us."

It hurt my gut that she knew she was deserted by the man who was both the only father and grandfather she had known. I wanted to say nothing. I wanted to squeeze her against my chest, to stroke her hair.

"Did he?" She leaned up ever so slightly and then fell back down on the mattress. We were alike in that way. The easy way was never our way.

"No, I guess not. He loves you in his way. I think at one time he even loved me. But then he just . . ."

"Good night," she said and squeezed my hand tighter.

Cher never did like excuses. At least now she won't go around telling folks her daddy would be coming for visits. I suspected now she'd tell Laurel and Kasi that he'd been killed in some bad accident where she'd sketch him out to be a hero or maybe announce he moved away to drill for oil in Argentina. Either way, I'd back up whatever lie she settled on. My baby had enough hurt to last for a while.

As she clasped her hand in mine, I wished her sweet dreams. Dreams of riding a black horse down a country dirt road. Dreams a thirteen-year-old girl should have, not fantasies of a make-believe family that only lived in her mind.

I would not allow myself to park Miss Claudia's big Lincoln in my regular spot at school. I couldn't have Sammy and the ladies in the lunchroom looking at me and making jokes about my fancy transportation. I settled for a remote parking spot, across the street in a field used by the kids for soccer games after school.

"You got a phone call, foxy grandma. And it's a man. You been holding out on us?" Sammy raised an eyebrow at me.

I dried my hands on a dish towel, hoping that it would not be a rerun of Bozo. A sober Bozo crying and asking for another chance. A depressed Bozo telling me how much he loved me and that he wanted his grandbaby back home.

"It's ready to go anytime."

Between the shrill drill I heard on the other end of the line and the clanging of metal pots in the deep sink near the phone, I had to put my finger in the free ear to make out a word he said.

"What? My car?"

"Yes, ma'am. It's Gerald Peterson. We got it ready for you."

Ma'am. I repeated his words in my mind and cleared my throat. Cher must've been right about my black rubber-soled shoes looking like something from the Depression. "Well, how much you think it'll be?"

I heard another voice in the background and some papers ruffling. Then the shrill drill again. *He's bracing me for the worst.* My pulse throbbed against the base of my neck. The light bill was due next week, and Cher's birthday was right around the corner.

"Somers around fifty dollars. You need a ride out to get it?"

I cleared my throat again and tried to make my voice sound higher, younger. "That'd be real nice of you, Mr. Peterson."

"Now you sit still," Miss Claudia said, hobbling to the door with her cane. I knew most she wanted to throw that cane across the room and welcome the gentleman caller in a way Scarlet would be proud of. She had been looking through the sheer living-room curtains for the past twenty minutes waiting for Gerald to appear.

"Well, Gerald Peterson. I haven't seen you in a month of Sundays. You getting along okay?" She swept her arm, welcoming him into the home.

He took off his cap and planted both thumbs on the

waist of his jeans. With smooshed-down hat hair, he stood there in the foyer shifting his weight from one foot to the other. He must've felt as uncomfortable as I had the first time I entered Elm Drive. "Yes, ma'am, doing good."

That was it. He called Miss Claudia *ma'am* too. He put me in the category with an eighty-year-old. I scooped up my purse and cussed my white polyester cafeteria uniform.

The long fingers were busy creasing the insides of his cap. He stuttered as if regaining his train of thought. "And you? That leg acting up on you?"

"Oh, me," she drawled, thicker than usual. "Gerald, I might need you to take me in and rework me but good. You got any new hips you can tack on?" She giggled, and soon he laughed too. I made the first move towards the door.

Sitting in the cab of his truck, I watched while Miss Claudia stood behind the half-closed door, waving good-bye. Suddenly, I felt like we were two high-schoolers going on a date. I cussed myself for telling Miss Claudia too much of my business.

The forgotten knots in my stomach prevented me from saying much on the drive to his shop. We just sat in the pickup in a sea of air-conditioned air and soft country music.

"Solenoid switch give out on you."

I flipped my ponytail around my neck and leaned forward, afraid the butterflies in my stomach were affecting my hearing.

"I had to replace the switch in your car," he said,

looking at me. He was probably trying to determine if I was some kind of idiot who couldn't talk.

"Oh, okay. Well, I'm glad it wasn't much worse," I said, not knowing if this was something damaging or not. For fifty bucks I figured it could be worse.

His hands were large and tan. The grime of honest work gathered around his cuticles. His sideburns were short and doused with gray. What really made my insides tingle were his eyes. They were blue, heavy, and deep-set. The small scar right above his eyebrow kept him from being a pretty boy. I couldn't help but wonder if I went to his mama's house and found a picture from high school, if his eyes would've been that heavy and set back in his head. Or were the hollows caused by the loss he lived with?

"Where you from?" He turned to look at me.

I quickly turned my head and looked out at the field of watermelons we were passing. I knew I had held my stare on him too long. "Cross City. It's in Louisiana."

"There's an old boy I know works up there during a plant shutdown. Don't they got a plant?"

I could only nod my head. I knew my luck would run out and there would be someone who had a connection to my past. *Of all people, it had to be him,* I thought.

"You like it here?"

"It's growing on me. You're from here, right?" *I shouldn't have asked it like that. Like I already had the answer. Now he would know I'd been asking questions about him.*

"Born and raised. Live in the same house my great-granddaddy built." He seemed to talk more when he looked straight ahead and didn't look at me. "You got any kids?"

"A boy and a girl." *Please don't ask me to give their locations,* I begged.

Russ I could handle. The boy was making good by himself. After a string of DUIs and constant pestering from the principal's office, Russ had finally given in and joined the Marines. For the past year or so, he'd been doing a hardship tour in Korea. I have to give credit to the Marines for undoing a good portion of the damage his daddy'd done.

But Suzette. I would have to lie about Suzette, and I didn't want to lie to him.

"That your girl I seen the other night?"

"Actually she's my granddaughter. I got custody of her." *Shut your mouth before you tell it all,* I scolded myself.

He just nodded his head, and we stared at faded black asphalt for another mile.

"You got any kids?" I finally produced the words after debating whether it seemed too forward.

"Marcie's my daughter. She's twenty-five. Got a boy, Donnie. He's seventeen."

We pulled into his sand driveway, and I tried not to look big-eyed with wonder. My first thought was how odd it looked with that garage shop and its rusting tin roof placed next to the white two-story house with black shutters. With a paint job and new porch steps, his house could be something off *Gone with the Wind.*

On the other side of the house a horse and a dozen cattle grazed in a bright green field.

A massive oak tree and a row of automobiles separated the yard of the home from his mechanic garage. A separation of the old way of life from the new. In my mind I sketched a black-and-white of a gentleman farmer raising peanuts and tobacco. His great-grandson, for the sake of paying bills, tossing that life to work on horseless carriages.

I pointed at the horse, which was biting a fence post with its front teeth. "Cher, uhh . . . that's my granddaughter I told you about. She'd love that horse. She's the craziest thing over horses."

He carefully got out of the truck and squinted his eyes towards the field. "That's my son's doings."

I used the hood of his truck to prop my checkbook and write out the fifty-dollar check. Every time I wrote a check, I always tossed figures in my mind, verifying it wouldn't bounce. Before I signed my name, I estimated the check to Peterson and Son was safe. *That's nice,* I thought. *He must have named the business so his boy would have a permanent job.* The idea made him that much more appealing to the ounce of dreamer still left in me.

A shrill drill like the one I heard on the phone echoed from the garage. A young man, either chewing tobacco or a wad of bubble gum, glanced our way, then returned to his assignment.

"Thanks," I said and turned towards my car parked under the oak tree.

"We appreciate the business. Let us know if we can

help any way." He cocked his head sideways and smiled.

"Okay, then." I looked down at the crushed acorns on the dirt. Right before I turned to walk away, I saw him look at the length of my body and wipe the side of his chin with his thumb. For a minute I forgot the polyester uniform and the no-nonsense shoes. I forgot the bruises, cut eye, and broken arm that were long healed, but still glowed in my mind against a black light of revelation. During the bumpy ride down the sand driveway away from the shop and the old-timey home, I forgot the past and tried hard to let that ounce of dreamer in me grow.

Eight

While Cher washed Miss Claudia's car for its proper return to Elm Drive, I walked to the mailbox. I wanted to spin around when I saw Miss Trellis. One hand held the edge of her glasses while the other was propped on the side of her red polka-dotted tent dress. Her stance and complaints to an older man with gray whiskers on his chin made her seem every bit the authoritative figure I knew she wanted to be.

Just as I walked up, the old man looked mercifully at me and smiled. "Have a good one," he said and hobbled off towards his cream-colored trailer.

"Hey. I seen a new car yonder in your lot." She

99

hadn't even waited long enough for me to get my key in my mailbox.

"Mine was tore up." I snatched the mail and tried to think of an excuse to skip away.

"You and Claudia must be regular Mutt and Jeff. I sure wouldn't let any of my help ride off with my vehicle."

"She's a fine woman." This time I shot Miss Trellis one of my looks and hammered down on the word *fine*.

"Oh, yeah. Bless her heart. And I seen that Peterson boy haul your car off last Tuesday evening."

I actually felt a little sorry for the poor old thing. I saw Miss Trellis every evening when I drove into the trailer park. You couldn't help but see her, sitting in the small block apartment tacked on next to her office. Her blinds were always wide open, and the knobs behind her TV stuck out under the blinds. She probably kept a journal next to her easy chair and, in between orders on QVC, noted each entrance and exit of her kingdom.

Miss Trellis rested both hands at the base of her back and stuck her round stomach out. "You talk of another poor old soul. That Peterson boy had it something awful. His wife getting killed on the road like that. They tell me after that drunk hit her, the Peterson boy laid in bed three weeks, not eating, not speaking. Nothing."

When a black truck jacked up with big tires and a loud muffler idled past us, I moved closer to Miss Trellis. For once, I did not want to miss a single word.

"A great big man like him, I had an idear he'd go beat the tar out of the trashy thing that killed her. And,

100

honey, he was trash. He was a Driggers, the whole outfit just public nothings. Anyway, the Peterson boy just stayed there in bed, staring at the ceiling. They tell me the doctor had him so high on nerve pills he looked plumb scary at the funeral."

"Did you know his wife?" I regretted asking her, but the nosy side of me won out.

"I just can't talk about her or I'll go to crying." She looked down at the ground and shook her head.

Why was I so stupid to take the bait? I thought of Kasi's warning about Miss Trellis.

"Poor, poor thing." She looked sideways and then glanced at me. "You might near say we was kin. Her mama was my husband's brother-in-law's cousin."

Before Miss Trellis could suck in enough air to renew momentum, I fled back towards the sound of spraying water hitting car metal.

"You gonna let me go skating if I clean the inside out too?" Cher asked as I flipped through bills and money-saver coupons.

"I thought riding you around in that fancy Lincoln would be payment enough."

"Yeah, and now I'm back in that piece of junk," Cher said and propped her cut-off jeans hip out. "When we gonna get a new car like . . ."

I never looked up from the mail and walked past her. "When you go to college and get a good job. Then you'll buy us whatever you want."

Once inside, the kitchen counter served as my makeshift desk. I sorted the mail and ripped check after check out of my wallet to meet the collectors' due dates. Giggles and squeals vibrated against the door. Laurel had come over under the pretense of helping wash Miss Claudia's car. The only help she offered was luring Cher into a water fight.

I looked out the kitchen window and shook my head in amusement at the sight of them running around Miss Claudia's Lincoln with Laurel holding the water hose. When I opened the phone bill I lost my grin.

That girl, I cussed. Another bill over seventy dollars. On top of the unexpected car repair and the monthly payment to the divorce lawyer, I didn't know how I was going to pay it. I tried to teach her a lesson last month by having her work off the charges. "I have had it," I yelled.

And who in the world did she even know in Shreveport anyway? I quickly ran my finger down all the charges to the 8774 number. All the calls were made after three o'clock in the afternoon and before I got home of an evening. Those evenings I had opened the door and saw the phone cord bouncing, she told me she had been talking to Laurel. All I could think was that she had gotten connected with some pervert off that Internet she worked on at school. I had seen all sorts of horrible stories on TV about how weirdos seduce kids.

I hammered my finger on the phone numbers and waited. It took six rings for him to pick up. By the time he said hello the second time, I knew it was him. The worst monster I could imagine. Much more corrupt than any pervert off the Internet. *This couldn't be LaRue. He is supposed to be locked away,* I reminded myself. I slammed the phone down. *You only thought it was his voice.*

The second time I called, he answered the phone all smart-alecky, like he was part of the prank phone call. No doubt it was him. The worst piece of trash that I could ever imagine. My heart began to pound, and my breath grew shorter. I wanted to scream obscenities at this unwelcome intruder; to tell him he had no claim on Cher. The words bubbled at the base of my throat.

I slammed the receiver down and leaned against the wall, wishing this day had never happened. I always thought she would be older when I would face this. *Let this be a bad dream,* I wished, but her laughter rolled in tides from outside the door to remind me what I had to face. I had successfully hid her from LaRue and his seedy life for twelve years. Now Cher had found him. Pages from the phone bill shook in my hand, and my first instinct was to whip Cher and then flee again. Atlanta. That was a city big enough to hide from LaRue. Cher had disrupted our new life. She had turned over a rock and discovered the very slime that shared his seed to create her.

Nine

*"W*hat's the matter with you?" Cher seldom saw me idle, and for a second I was touched that she thought I might be sick. Sick all right, but not from any ailment of a physical nature.

I looked up from the couch and saw drops of water falling on the plastic green welcome mat. Normally, I would have chased her with towels and told her she would catch cold coming into the air-conditioned trailer all wet. Her sopping gray T-shirt clung tightly to her flesh, reminding me once again of her development into womanhood.

I could only manage to hold up the telephone bill.

"What's that?" She stepped closer, drops of water landing at her feet.

"I want to talk to you." I patted the couch, knowing full well her cut-off jeans were too wet for her to sit on furniture.

She sat on the edge of the checkered couch like she was at a tea party instead of the courtroom I hoped to create. "Is something the matter with Pop?"

I shook my head. Part of me wanted to knock her beside the head and scream words like *disgusting* and *stupid* to her. Instead, I silently counted to ten like some head doctor had recommended on a radio talk show.

"Whose number is this?" I tossed the pages of the phone bill at her, and two pages floated to the floor.

She examined the pages and sniffed a couple of times. I wasn't sure if she was crying or if it was the cold I'd failed to warn her about now settling into her system. "Oh, that's Becky Pitts."

"No, not the Cross City number. The numbers for Shreveport."

She closely studied the page and wrinkled her brow. She shrugged her shoulders and got up. My mouth dropped as she prissed down the hallway.

Right when she reached to open the towel cabinet in the bathroom, I blocked her. Standing in the doorway with my hand against the cabinet, I decided she would not turn me off like her clock radio. She looked at my reflection in the bathroom mirror, but I just continued to look at the side of her wet head.

"Gah, all I need is a towel," she moaned.

"All you need is to tell me the truth." I decided to count to twenty this time. I watched specks of water drop from her ear lobe.

"I know who it is. Did you think I was so stupid I wouldn't check the number?"

She folded her arms and looked down at the floor.

The words I should have said earlier to LaRue erupted onto his offspring. "I'm surprised he even has a phone. Probably just for his drug deals. I wish I could've had five minutes with that parole board. Oh boy, they'd be sorry."

"He's not like that anymore. He's got his own business now," she said in an unsteady tone.

I wondered how many times she'd practiced that line, hoping to convince herself of his truthfulness. If I wasn't so mad, I wonder if I would have laughed. The idea of this three-time drug offender owning anything other than a pharmacy was too ridiculous to even waste breath on. And so much for that white-haired judge telling him twelve years ago LaRue would never see the wickedness of a crack house again.

"How did you even get his number?" The very mention of his name seemed to harass something vile in my soul. I tried hard not to say his name, choosing instead to use only pronouns and filthy words not fitting for polite conversation.

"The library, okay?" She looked up and then withdrew once again. And there I was thinking she was spending those days after school seeking out books about horses, not searching phone books for a jackass.

We stood our ground, still and silent. She broke first by reaching up to open the towel cabinet. I moved outside to the door frame and allowed her access.

I decided to take the sympathetic route. "Baby, I love you and just want the best for you. You know that. There're just some things you don't know . . ."

"You just try to control me. Why can't I call him? Why? He is my daddy, you know."

Controlling accusations. The questions. This was all too familiar. LaRue's influence once again. He put Suzette up to that kind of talk too. "I don't care if you talk to him," I lied, not wanting a rerun of another life pushed towards disaster because of my objections. "It's just the calls cost so much. And well, I just don't want you to get all confused."

"It's too late," she screamed and slammed the door.

I stood outside the pine door and heard the lock click. I didn't even try to knock. I'd let her count to whatever number she needed to to cool off. As if we were playing a game of hide and seek, I dashed into Cher's bedroom.

The picture was still zipped inside her pillow. I glared at LaRue holding my baby on his lap. Had it not been for my fear of completely losing Cher, I would have ripped the cheap celluloid into a zillion pieces. No amount of counting could harness my anger towards that thing, that LaRue LaRouche.

Even though I thought the world of Missoura, I was not pleased to see her sitting in Miss Claudia's living room. I had waited all weekend to tell Miss Claudia about Cher's calls to her biological father. My nerves were just about shot, and now I had to wait that much longer for some guidance.

"Erma Lee, I want you to look. Dedrick Aaron Jackson, Missoura's grandson." Miss Claudia held up a photo. I had just hung my pocketbook on the coat rack.

I sighed, remembering the fine line I walked between employee and friend. I held the photo of the Army captain and remarked he was nice-looking or something to that effect.

Missoura talked about how good he was doing and how he liked Fort Benning. "So lucky to be stationed close to home," Miss Claudia added and sipped her iced tea.

I guess I was not the only one who found Miss Claudia to be a good listener. I swear, I had washed three loads of clothes, mopped the kitchen, and cut three roses and put them in a vase by Miss Claudia's bed before Missoura left. Right when I opened my mouth to ask for my own guidance, the phone rang.

"Why yes, she is. Who may I say is calling? . . . Oh, I liked to not have recognized your voice." She nuzzled the phone against her blouse. "Come on over here. It's Gerald."

I wiped my hands on my pants and grabbed the receiver. "Hello." I was conscious of Miss Claudia standing next to the kitchen sink.

"This's Gerald." The clanging in the background would have given him away. "You want to uh . . ." Louder clanging. This time I heard a muffling sound and Gerald's voice yelling something undetectable. The clanging stopped. "Yeah . . . uh, like I was saying. They having a fish fry this Saturday at the Moose Lodge. Well, I mean, with you not knowing a whole bunch of people yet, I thought . . . Do you want to go?"

Not now, I thought. *This is not a good time.* "Well, I might need to help Miss Claudia that day. You know, do some stuff for her and everything." Dead silence. I always had a tendency to talk more whenever the other person dropped the conversation. "Her with her hip and all." Miss Claudia turned to look at me. I was sinking with each second. "Just let me call you back."

"What in the world was all that about?"

I knew she had every right to ask since I brought her name into it. "Nothing."

"Sure didn't sound like nothing to me."

I went back to the sink and finished washing casserole dishes. She kept her perch next to me.

"Erma Lee, what did you mean, doing things for me?"

"Saturday. I told you I'd go get you some fabric on Saturday, remember?" I didn't look at her, concentrating instead on the scorched corners of grime on the dish.

"I declare. We can pick up that old fabric anytime. I hope you weren't using that as an excuse for whatever it was Gerald wanted?"

I looked at her. Both her hands were propped on the cane, and her head was slightly turned. Sometimes she was so dramatic that I thought she could've acted on one of those afternoon stories.

"Just some fish fry at some lodge or something."

"You don't mean the annual fish fry down at the Moose Lodge?"

Right then I hated the fact she knew every nook and cranny of Wiregrass. I decided she must rank right up there with the courthouse as a Houston County institution.

"Well, if he asked, you have to go. Richard went a little while last year. Stayed as long as he could. His nerves, don't you know. But anyway, he said they had the biggest crowd he ever did see."

I blew up at the loose strands of hair that were hanging over my eye and continued washing the casserole dish. "Yeah? Well, I don't think it's good right now."

"Now, Erma Lee, I sat right in that living room a week ago and heard you talking about that man."

I sighed, realizing how a horse had to feel after being ridden on a long journey.

"I certainly hope it's not because you're afraid of still being a married woman. You're for all intended purposes divorced. Just a matter of . . ."

I scrubbed the brush on the last remaining bits of scorched food. "It's not that. I just . . ."

"Well, I hope you certainly don't think you have to baby-sit me. And speaking of that, Cher can stay with me. We'll cook us some popcorn and . . ."

The thud of the dish crashing to the sink made her jump. "Look, I got too much on my mind to decide right now."

She blinked hard and looked over my right shoulder. "I see," she said and then patted the silver top of her cane.

"I'm sorry," I said, brushing suds of dishwashing soap on my forehead.

Her expression never changed. She just reached over and put her blue-veined hand on my arm.

"I just found out this weekend that when Cher said her daddy was coming, she didn't mean Bozo. She meant her biological father." I never used the phrase *real daddy,* because LaRue could never reach this standard no matter how hard he tried. "Me and her had it out, and now she won't even talk to me."

Miss Claudia wiped the suds from my forehead. "When did all this happen?"

I laid out the naked details and was even sort of honest about his time in prison. I told her he was in for drugs and left off the charges of child abandonment.

"When I was a girl going through all that mess with Old Man Maxwell, I used to daydream what my daddy would've looked like if he'd still been alive. How many wrinkles would he have around his eyes? How many streaks of gray would he have around the temples? I even made up an image."

"This is different. You had a good daddy. Hers ain't worth squat."

"Makes no difference. Sometimes a fantasy is easier to face than the truth. Especially about the person you're supposed to love."

Miss Claudia didn't ease my worrying, but she did help me understand what Cher might be thinking. That night when Cher got in the shower, I called Gerald back. It was such a brief conversation I wondered why I had picked up the receiver three times before finally dialing his number.

"I hope that fish fry ain't dressy," I said with a chuckle, knowing I was scared to death I would be out of place.

"Ain't nothing but a bunch of boys frying fish and having a little fun. I'll pick you up at seven," Gerald said.

After he hung up, I held the receiver against my chest and wished life could be as easy as Gerald made everything out to be.

Ten

"I have stared at four walls until I'm about half crazy," Miss Claudia said, standing in the doorway of her side porch. She was on a mission, dressed all pink: hot pink skirt, light pink blouse, and a white scarf with little pink roses on it. A khaki wicker basket draped her arm, and at first glance I thought she had packed for a picnic. When I helped her down the porch steps, I realized the basket served as her pocketbook.

"Bum hip or not, we're going to town," she declared and handed me her car keys.

Fabric World was our first stop that afternoon. She lingered with the sales clerk, asking all about the young woman's origins and telling about her years as a seamstress. I noticed by the way Miss Claudia looked down and nodded her head that she was disappointed the young woman did not know of the Emporium. "This is my companion, Erma Lee Jacobs. She's not from Wiregrass either," she said, allowing the auburn-haired girl with a fair complexion to join my outsider sorority. "Tell me, what are the young girls, oh, say high-school age, wearing now days?"

The young woman escorted us to a big counter with jumbo-sized books filled with patterns. "Oh, Lord have mercy. I wouldn't let my dog wear that thing in public," Miss Claudia said when the young woman pointed to the first selection. Her comments were met with laughter from the sales clerk.

Charmed another one, I thought.

"I'm going to need Cher's measurements."

"Now, Miss Claudia," I said with one hand on my hip. "I can't have you doing this."

She continued to flip through the pages of the plastic binder and pretended to ignore my presence. "And just who will stop me from making an outfit on my own sewing machine in my own house?"

I leaned over the catalog filled with patterns. "Your hip. You can't be sitting up sewing. What about the pedal?"

Over the top of her wire-rimmed glasses she looked up at me. "I already thought of that. I'll use the good leg to pedal and prop the bum one on a chair."

"I just can't have you . . ."

She raised one eyebrow and dropped her chin even lower. The same soft hazel eyes could slice through concrete when she found something blocking her way. "This is my business. Not another word out of you."

I could only mumble and roll my eyes.

"What? If you have something to say, Erma Lee . . ."

"I said you didn't take us to raise, you know."

She resumed looking at the catalog. "You hush. Here, how about this periwinkle one for you?" When she tried to shove the bulky book in my direction, two pages flipped over the spot her thumb marked.

I glanced at the soft sleeveless top with big blue buttons and the short skirt cut somewhere at the model's knee. On the rare occasion Bozo practiced romance, and on the more frequent occasion of kissing up after a drunken rage, he would tell me how crazy he was about my legs. "Oh no. You're not going to . . ."

"All right. You win. You can set a pillow under my leg and run in and out fetching me tea while I sew. Happy now?"

The pace of my heart slowed a little. I actually pictured a wave of my nerves settling to a lake ripple. She was spoiling me rotten, and I never let myself forget it.

Miss Claudia made the bad times seem distant and

strangely unimportant. I felt safe with the tall woman who used a cane. The truth was, I did not see her much older than myself. All I saw was a confident, determined woman who could overcome any obstacle set in her path.

Days leading up to the big to-do at the Moose Lodge, Miss Claudia worked steady on her sewing machine. Her bedroom was set up like a makeshift tailor shop, with a step for me to stand on while she pinned the skirt hem and held a tomato-shaped cloth ball full of pins. The concentration of her wrinkled brow and the couple of pins sticking out of her mouth showed me a hint of the top-rate seamstress she once was. During the creation, I stuck my head in the room every so often to make sure her left leg was inclined on the wooden desk chair and that the pillow cushioning her leg had not flattened.

The final product was as good as anything from the mall. I stood in the mirror of her bedroom and fidgeted with the skirt, wondering if I was too old to wear such a short length.

"You just look so pretty," she said, cupping her hands up to her chest. The way she looked at me made me think how she might have reviewed Patricia in her coming-out dress. The painted picture of her in that very dress hung in the formal living room. When I asked Miss Claudia what exactly the event was, she dismissed the Cotillion as "a bunch of high rollers thinking their you-know-what don't stink."

"I mean to tell ya, you're good now," I said, turning

my head to get the full-mirrored view in every possible direction. "No wonder Mr. Wade went and married you."

"Oh, my word," she said, playing like she was embarrassed.

"I'm serious. This is the best sewing I ever saw. And that's coming from a trained seamstress herself." Another moment I longed for a built-in eraser in my mouth. I was afraid that last part sounded big-headed. To counterbalance, I quickly added, "You just don't know how much I appreciate this."

"I'm just tickled to do it. You know, Wade did fancy my skills. I remember the day after his daddy hired me. I fixed up a suit with a New York City label, not knowing who on earth it was for. When I placed the thread in the needle, I pure shook, racking my brain to remember all the lessons Nettie taught me.

"The next day, Wade walked in the back to where we girls were and had on that very suit I worked on. He wanted to know who did the job. Thinking something might be the matter with the suit, everybody turned and pointed at me. That woman who runs your mobile-home park was the worst—Trellis stood up and pointed." Miss Claudia leaned over the machine and stuck her tongue out. "Might as well had put a spotlight on me. Anyway, he just came right over and shook my hand. I was such a timid thing back then. I just looked down at the scraps of material on the floor. And even though he wasn't a loud talker, he made sure everybody in the room heard him say it was the best-fitting suit he owned.

"Later he told me he liked my looks and told them to give the suit to me just so he'd have a reason to get better acquainted with me." She shook her head the same way I did whenever Cher acted silly.

"Did he ask you out on a date then?" I asked, knowing full well Miss Trellis had already told me the man was married at the time. I don't know why I asked it. I guess part of me still had some doubts and wondered if I could catch Miss Claudia in a lie.

"No, not then. Wade was married, don't you know." She tapped the sewing machine with her polished nails and rolled her big hazel eyes up towards me.

I shrugged my shoulders and felt ashamed that I had doubted this woman.

"Oh, yeah. He was married to poor Colleen. Her problem was beyond nerves. She had certifiable craziness." Miss Claudia licked her lips and sighed. "One day she'd hear voices and come running in the store screaming somebody was trying to kill her. The next day she'd walk the streets not knowing where in the world she was. I don't care what anyone says, Wade was good to her."

I nodded my head in agreement, recalling the adulterous scandal Miss Trellis had alluded to.

"Wade would come in the back and talk to me about all the problems he was having with her. That's how it started out with us, strictly friends. After all I'd been through, don't you know. But Wade was different in his ways. He had the softest voice. Nothing sissy, mind you, just caring and honest." Miss Claudia chuckled and gently patted her hair.

116

"Then the next thing I knew he missed an entire month of work. The girls in the store said he had Colleen put away in the crazy house. They talked about how cruel he was to lock her away like that. I just never let on that I knew one way or the other.

"He didn't court me for a few months after all that. And even then, it was only a meal or two in the room I rented over the bakery. But one evening when he was leaving, Trellis and that husband of hers were driving by real slow like, snooping for a robbery. They got the scoop all right, just in time to see Wade walk down the side stairs of my room. The next day at work, you'd think I was at a home for the mute. When I sat at my sewing machine and said good morning, they just all looked at me. Only later, I learned those girls were going around telling the whole town what a home wrecker I was and how I had taken advantage of the boss.

"Those women at the store thought they knew it all. Before Wade locked Colleen up, she ran around the house with his pistol shooting holes in the wall big enough to put your arm through. A few weeks later he came home and found her in the bathtub with her wrists slit. She was half dead when he rang for the doctor. Old Dr. Miller never breathed a word. He just shipped her away by ambulance the next morning. Wade protected that woman as long as she lived. After his divorce and during all our married life he paid for her hospitalization. I kept the payments up until three years ago, when they sent me a letter saying Colleen died of a stroke."

Miss Claudia patted the tomato pincushion. "That's the real story those biddies don't know. And never will as far as I'm alive." She shooed away the past with a quick bat of the eye and a shake of the head. "Well, there's a Trellis in every crowd. I expect you've known a few."

I sure had. The only problem was I had to deal with the real one.

It was not her fault she caught me on the same day that the story of the good and decent Wade Tyler had been recounted. But when I got out of the car that day, the last person I wanted to see was Miss Trellis. Before I closed the car door, she appeared behind the big pine tree next to my trailer.

"Oh, me," she moaned.

At first I thought a cat was in distress. Then I turned to see the swagger of her knit black shoes.

"Doctor told me to take exercise and lose some of this lard. I expect I'll be walking up and down this street morning and evening," Miss Trellis said, holding her back and pouching her stomach out like she was expecting any day.

"Good luck," I said, pulling a bag of groceries out of my backseat.

"You working all the time, I don't see how you have time for grocery shopping."

"I manage." I was still fuming with her for being so hateful to Miss Claudia. Thirty years ago or thirty minutes, I was always bad to hold a grudge.

"Claudia still having all them health problems?"

I juggled the paper bag and slammed the car door with the side of my leg. *Don't start,* I wanted to scream. *Don't act as if you care about Miss Claudia when you really like the fact she's suffering, even in the slightest.* "She's getting along fine."

"I heard she wasn't taking that chemotherapy. I got an idear it's because she don't want to lose none of that pretty black hair."

"Uh, no. I think you're confused. Her hip is acting up, but other than that . . ." I leaned forward and shrugged my shoulders.

She flattened her matted gray hair and used her flabby forearm to wipe sweat off her brow. "They tell me she's eat up with cancer."

She squared off with me, both hands on her hips.

"Well, *they* must've misunderstood, because . . ."

"Don't tell me." Miss Trellis stuck her pointy chin out and bugged her eyes to the point of retina damage. "I reckon my daughter-in-law knows. She works for Claudia's doctor. Does filing three days a week. They said she won't take no therapy neither."

I wanted to run and slam into her with my grocery bag, hoping the bottle of spaghetti sauce would knock the wind out of her so she couldn't speak such non-sense. After two steps, the threat of eviction talked me out of it. "Well, how come she don't have any symp-toms?" I carelessly asked. Then the big ugly bruise on her hip flashed through my mind.

"Look, I ain't arguing about it. Ask her if you don't believe me. Or maybe she don't want you to know. I reckon, best leave some things alone." Then, as if I had been pestering her, "Let me get on with my exercise, hear?"

The bags became heavier while I watched her swagger along the cracked asphalt. I did not believe her. I refused to consider it. Who did this old gossip think she was—a doctor? I remembered the telephone game where information whispered to the first person was all messed up by the time the information reached the last person in the group. Obviously, Miss Trellis was the last person in the circle concerning the health of Miss Claudia. I was the lead in this game.

Eleven

The day of the fish fry with Gerald, Cher was actually happy for a change. She was busy running around helping me get dressed. After I scrubbed the pine door down with a towel to remove any dirt that could gather on my new outfit, we hung the blue top and skirt on top of the closet door. I wondered if Cher thought I was silly to treat the new skirt and top like it was laced with gold, but since it had been over a year since I had a new shirt, it might as well been laced with rubies too.

The new outfit was one of those experiences you read about in a magazine, one of those binding moments for Cher and me. She held her hand up to her heart and stumbled backwards when I agreed to let her fix my face a little. "Nothing heavy," I said while pulling her up off the floor by her arm. "Quit acting silly," I said in a whisper. I didn't know whether to laugh like her friend or to act stern like her guardian.

She used her curling iron to design the back of my hair. Since I counted my first date with Gerald as a special occasion, I had her finish me off with the black cloth bow. She loosely gathered hair and centered it at the crown of my head. Long flowing curls fell below.

Once completely dressed, I felt Cher was finally pleased with me. "Go on with it," Cher yelled. She had never seen me show my legs before. I sensed a new chapter for us. Her fast becoming a young woman who could show me the trends, and me being able to caution her against life's heartache. We both were cautious not to mention LaRue, and since he hadn't called, I was satisfied in knowing my words had sunk in Cher's brain.

I was scared to death the wind would mess up my hair and ran out of the trailer with my hands held up on both sides of my head. Like in an eight-millimeter home movie, Mama's skeptical face flashed through my mind. But I forced myself to empty my mind of fertilizer for one night. I sat in the car watching Cher awkwardly juggle the three videos that she had previously censored for Miss Claudia's viewing.

Miss Claudia greeted us at her door and patted her hands like a little child expecting candy. Her rosy cheeks, wide smile, and bright hazel eyes solidified my wrath on Miss Trellis for spreading lies about ill health.

"You're quite the Cinderella tonight, sugar," she

121

drawled. I didn't try to shoo her comments away.

Richard stood in the hallway, smoking a cigarette. "Erma Lee, you look absolutely breathtaking," he said and bowed. Even though he was silly, Richard could make words dance to the tune of his baritone voice.

"Now stand over by the piano and let me make a picture," Miss Claudia said, holding the instant Polaroid camera.

Standing behind Miss Claudia, Richard leaned against the hall entranceway and declared he might see me at the fish fry. "I always have been a good dancer. You remember my senior ball at Vanderbilt, Mother—how I had those two dates to juggle."

Miss Claudia gave me an animated wink, like someone might offer when a child said a naughty word without knowing the full meaning. "Oh, yeah, I remember."

As the flash fired and the square white prints discharged from the camera, I wondered if this was how a prom feels, all giddy and braggy. Picture after picture—she produced at least a dozen—I posed by every piece of strapped-down furniture in the living room. My favorite was the picture made of Cher and me by the mahogany staircase. I felt nervous, self-conscious, and hesitant that night. But above all, I felt like a woman who learned to, as Miss Claudia said, "accent the positives."

She'd sat at her sewing machine that day and announced that she was altering the pattern by dropping the neckline. "Nothing trashy," I came running into her bedroom yelling.

"Use it before you soon lose it," she said above the hammer of the machine.

I felt like I was going to throw up on the way to the fish fry and almost had Gerald pull over. *You're out of your league,* I told myself. The boot-shaking music on the radio didn't help my nerves any, and I finally asked if we could turn it to another station.

Gerald looked better than ever, capless, with his wavy blonde and gray hair combed back. The back of his hair was still wet, and I liked the tight curls it created. I was intoxicated by his evergreen aftershave and hoped that it was not the cause of my nausea. His black pullover shirt and khaki pants made his tanned arms and neck seem even darker. I especially liked his brown cowboy boots. As with my pair of low-heeled shoes, the boots were probably the only dress pair he owned. Whether it was true or not, I kept telling myself so, trying to convince myself that we were alike in some way.

My only other big fear of the night was that I would have to dance. I don't know what I was thinking. Maybe that the band would be only a small portion of the evening, and I could plead a headache and go on back to the house. The minute I walked into the dark banquet room with black lights on the ceiling and a crystal ball, I knew I was in trouble. White circles bounced off the crystal ball and onto the paneled walls. A mammoth stage was decorated with a steel guitar and drums. The place looked how I imagined a fine dance club in Nashville would look.

Miss Claudia was right. This fish fry was the social event of the year. People jammed into the concrete building and spewed across the front lawn, where two large boilers were set up under the direction of four serious men armored in white aprons. After surveying the crowd, I breathed satisfaction knowing my new outfit looked as good as any other lady's wardrobe. And, thanks to Miss Claudia, my clothes looked better than what many wore.

At first I thought the squealing was due to a pig running loose, but then I saw the bright blonde hair as she landed squarely in Gerald's arms. The first thing I noticed about her was her teeth. They were big and shiny, and her hair stood straight up on the top of her head. Between Patricia, Miss Claudia, and now her, I decided big hair must be the thing in Wiregrass. The blonde bangs fell low to her blue eyes, and when she turned I noticed her hair was as long as mine, only a kinky texture.

"This here's who I been telling you about. This is Marcie," Gerald yelled over the roar of the crowd.

Before I could smile or even speak, she was in my arms too. She loosely grabbed me, and I felt a rib when I clasped my arms around her. "So good to meet you," she said in a high-pitched voice. "I'm just so glad you could come with my daddy," she reached over and placed her head on Gerald's chest. He put his arm on her shoulder and grinned wider and longer than I knew he could.

Whenever I answered Marcie's questions, she would lean back and swing that blonde mane over her shoulders. Marcie's moves reminded me of when Suzette was little and how she would put a towel on her head to imitate Cher's hair swings from the *Sonny and Cher* show.

Marcie was just as excited when I met her husband, Chase. He was short and stumpy with a crew cut. I remember thinking that the cut must be back in style, because I could not imagine Marcie paired with someone out of trend's favor.

She wore a gold choker necklace and a ring on every finger, even her thumb. I thought that was a little trashy. As we lined up for fried catfish, I held a paper plate and heard all the details of her attempts to have a baby. Marcie was brutally honest, to the point of embarrassment.

"I just feel like I've known you my whole life," she said, smiling and massaging her thick necklace. When I spoke of Cher and Miss Claudia, her eyes would scan over my shoulders. While I talked, I saw her mouth "Hey" to the people passing behind me.

After the food, the lights dimmed, and the whine of the steel guitar filled the building. Every time I saw Gerald approach the table, I would start moving my hands to whoever I was talking to, to making Gerald think I was deep in conversation. But really, there was only one deep conversation that night.

Kasi joined us at our table. After my third beer, I explained everything to Kasi concerning Cher lying about her daddy visiting. Even though my head was feeling lighter, I didn't tell too much, but just skimmed the surface to prove Cher had some denial about the situation.

"Poor little thing," Kasi said and took a drag of her cigarette.

"No, it's nothing like that." I refused to have her feel sorry for Cher. "She's just confused." I leaned closer to Kasi, wanting to make sure she understood how stable and happy Cher was.

She looked across the table, her eyes sparkling with amusement. "Well, hey," she said, flicking the long ash into the ashtray.

Richard's squinty eyes and wisps of white hair seemed magnified in the black light of the banquet room. "Erma Lee, are you surprised?" he asked and laughed. I worked hard not to let my face be a billboard for the shock I felt. I could only wonder how on earth he slipped away without Miss Claudia realizing it.

"Hey there," I managed.

After a brief introduction, Kasi offered him a cigarette, and within the length of two songs they were dancing. I couldn't help but wonder how this loud music might play on Richard's protected nerves. But his twirls and side steps indicated he knew more than me. Kasi screamed and threw her head backwards when he spun her around by the tips of his fingers.

After watching Richard glide across the dance floor with woman after woman, I decided how convenient his nerve disability was. Between him and Marcie, I think the bartender could have liquored up the entire town. I was really impressed when I saw Richard slow dance with the big-butted woman wearing a denim miniskirt and sip from his plastic cup all at the same time.

When the band played "Boot Scootin' Boogie," Marcie let out another squeal that reminded me of a hog-calling contest I had heard about on the news. She rounded up her followers, and soon the entire dance floor was filled with women and a few men scooting across the concrete floor, shaking their behinds to the faithful drum beat.

"She's flat sure crazy about that dance," I heard Gerald yell across the table. I watched while Gerald shook his head and grinned at her. His intense stare made me wonder if she had some invisible string pulling his eyes towards her.

As the crowd twisted and turned through the maze of shuffles that Marcie directed, I worried that she would take an eye out with that blonde hair. The ends of her hair flew like a bullwhip as she flipped it over one shoulder and then the other. My concern soon turned to laughter when I saw Richard in the back of the group turning in every opposite direction. Waves of cocktail spewed over the edge of his glass and onto the boots of a lady dancing next to him. The big-haired woman with embroidered roses on her denim shirt shouted something at him. By the way she curled her upper lip, I decided it must have been something harsh. He took it in stride, waving at her and twisting his butt in a half-cocked manner. If only Patricia were here to see this. But I knew the band's guitar amplifier would not yet cool before one of these fish-eaters would call her with an update on his foolishness.

The music died, and the boot-scooters scattered in various directions. I heard Gerald behind me. "This here is the old boy I was telling you about." I turned and saw Gerald standing next to a fat man with the speckled face of a twelve-year-old boy. "He's the one worked up at that plant in Cross City."

I heard the steel guitar whine, and my lungs went on suspension. "Oh, yeah." I gagged a little and tried not to act scared.

"Jarvis Pettry," he said. His wide smile revealed a missing tooth in the corner of his mouth. When he pulled a metal chair next to me, I thought for sure my luck had run out. I casually looked across the table at Gerald, hoping at least he would not be able to hear anything said by this connector to my past.

"I don't know no Jacobs. Worked with some Petroes, though. They Cajuns."

I smiled, and before he could ask me what part of town I once lived, I did it. "Gerald, you 'bout ready to dance?"

I barely knew how to walk in high heels, let alone get out there in front of everybody and show my ignorance. What if they started up with that boot-scootin' song again? I pictured my tight skirt splitting right down the middle. *"If you'd kept your tail at the house, none of this mess would be happening,"* Mama echoed in my brain, louder than any amplifier the band could ever hope to own.

My heartbeat climbed up to my throat, and the twenty paces it took to reach the dance floor from our paper-clothed table might as well have been twenty miles.

"I'm not real good at all this," I mumbled. Gerald ignored my revelation and put my hand in the base of his callused palm. I felt the thickness of his fingers on the small of my back.

"You're doing just fine," he whispered. I felt the directions within his hand. Left and right to the music, all with that magical hand. The horses in his field couldn't have been guided any better than I was that evening. I swallowed hard, hoping not to ruin it by stomping on his cowboy boots.

This big man, with his roughness and power, seemed so smooth and gentle under the black light. I thought I heard Gerald hum against my ear, but knew enough not to get too close. I would not allow myself to rub any inch of my material against his black shirt or his big silver belt buckle and its gold-crested scene of a cow roping.

The few minutes in Gerald's arms made me lift my head a little higher. I was in the middle of that paneled room with a man. A man who drank Coke instead of Jim Beam. A man who could beat the fire out of anybody in the room, but would never be brutal to me. His hands felt smooth against my back, and had I not known better, I would've thought he might be wearing velvet gloves. I wanted to place my head on his shoulder like I had seen on the late-night movies when worry kept me hostage and sleep was far away. I realized I was experiencing that too often used word, *romance*. But I didn't care. I just gave in and let the music flow me into comfortable dreams.

"Now, I ain't telling you again. You want some of

me?" The yell spun me back to the black lights and paper-covered tables. Gerald craned his neck a few inches, and I leaned sideways.

When I edged to the side of the crowd, I saw a man in a cream-colored western shirt shove Richard. Two ladies with matching yellow sundresses jumped from their seats just before Richard landed like a decoration on the top of the table. The screeching of metal chairs vibrated like fingernails inching down a chalkboard. Richard managed to hold his empty glass and catch the side of the table with his free hand, ripping the paper tablecloth in the process.

Gerald grabbed the would-be offender's arm. "That pinhead got excited dancing with Kasi. She felt him. He was feeling her up," the man yelled.

Kasi stood in the corner calmly smoking a cigarette. I was unsure if she was embarrassed or pleased at the attention being dished her. *What was she thinking? Him with his case of nerves.* I couldn't help but wonder if this was a rerun of other scenes played out with pitiful men under her strict direction.

Gerald pulled Richard upright by one arm. Richard slurred something undetectable and pulled at the untucked portion of his dress shirt. Another slow song was starting back up. I wanted to push him out the door, tell him to sleep it off in the safety of his car, and get back to dancing. But then I pictured Miss Claudia, dressed in her housecoat and rollers, frantically looking for him the next morning.

"We can't let him drive," I mumbled to Gerald, half hoping he wouldn't hear the words. He pulled Richard to the door and put him in between us in the pickup seat. I rolled down the window hoping Richard would get enough air and not throw up on my new outfit. By the time the truck snaked down the crooked driveway to the main road, the steady whine of the steel guitar had been permanently drowned out by the heavy snore of the nerve patient. *Life as Cinderella,* I thought and wiped Richard's drool off my bare arm.

Only the next day would I learn from Kasi what the real scene had been that evening. The dramatic exit Marcie made, running out the front door with her hands over her face with a bunch of female followers trailing. Her show was timed to the minute I made my journey with Gerald to the dance floor. Upon hearing the news on the steps of the trailer, I rolled my eyes and mumbled, "Whatever."

I didn't need a man anyway, and besides I was still really a married woman. But he did call. Gerald was even good-natured enough to laugh about Richard, and he brushed aside my apologies. While leaning against the paneled door where I kept canned goods and laughing, a peace floated by me. I knew deep within my gut, the same spot that had told me it was time to leave Cross City, that Gerald Peterson was different from the rest.

Twelve

*D*uring the first of May the sticky air of summer rolled into Wiregrass just as my own problems began to evaporate. Bozo had stopped his regular late-night phone tirades, and my young lawyer reminded me that in another three months I would legally be a freed woman. Typical of my luck, I would have to end up in a state where the law made me wait six months for a divorce.

I stood at the kitchen window and watched as my lawyer got out of his black convertible sports car. He was walking around the trailer, snapping pictures as though the apple green trailer would be the featured layout in *Southern Living*. "If he gives us one ounce of trouble with the agreement, I'll threaten alimony," the young man said, loosening his red-and-white-striped tie.

"Now hold on. We said just child support. Nothing about no alimony." The least amount of contact my new life would have with Bozo, the better I'd be.

"Relax, it's just a threat," he said, never looking up from the shutter of his fancy camera. I had no doubts that I was his charity case. I could tell it by his sassy comments and the clipped answers he provided. The shiny silver-and-black camera he carried stood as another reminder that I would never have this repre-sentation had it not been for Miss Claudia. I'm sure I was the only client he had on a monthly payment plan. And the few times I ventured into his two-story brick office, with its Oriental rug and hardwood floors, I felt a spotlight of either pity or disgust by the manicured ladies guarding the front desk.

When Miss Claudia's loaned lawyer stood on the upside-down car-wash bucket to get a shot of the rusted roof, I vowed never to accept Bozo's handouts. The only reason I agreed to child support was so that I could fill in some of the blanks in Cher's college savings account. Alimony was crossing the line. It would be too much like a payoff for the mess he dished out to me during our thirty-one years of marital bliss. Besides, he would hold it over my head forever. And if I put him into too much of a financial bind, I worried he'd literally hold it over my head with a red-tipped ax.

My days in Wiregrass working at the cafeteria and caring for Miss Claudia were so pleasant that I vowed never to return to Cross City. On a borrowed piece of notebook paper from Cher's school supplies, I carefully noted that upon my death I did not want to be returned to Cross City. They could just plant me at a cemetery here in Wiregrass. Now I think it's silly, but at that time it felt good to drag that ballpoint pen across the straight blue lines.

In those early days of May, Gerald and me settled into a routine of spending every Saturday evening at the local steakhouse, and never once did he mention Marcie being upset with me over our dance at the Moose Lodge. As much as possible I avoided Marcie's name altogether. The evening Marcie called I tried not to stutter from the shock of hearing her voice on my phone line. I took a deep breath and hunkered in for a real knock-down drag-out.

"I've been so busy with work and church I just haven't been able to think straight," she said. As she railed on about her stressful job, as a dispatcher for the Houston County Sheriff's Office, I was trying to arrange the right words. I would tell her that she had misunderstood the dance at the fish fry. *We're just friends,* I planned to say.

"Anyway, it's about time we all get together," Marcie said. "I want us all to have a big cookout at Daddy's this Saturday. You and Claire can come over, say at around three? And we can just talk and ignore fat grams for one night." She giggled a high-pitched sound that caused me to pull the phone receiver away from my ear.

I tried to correct her on Cher's name, but every time I inhaled, she let loose on details of the menu and how I shouldn't bring anything before I could even offer.

After ten minutes, I forgot she ever called Cher by the wrong name. I was just glad she was not paying long distance for this call.

"Gotta go. Chase just got in from softball practice. Oh, y'all doing okay? Hadn't seen you since the fish fry."

I was ready. "Yeah, and I just want you to know . . ."

"No, Chase. Get out of that refrigerator. I got a plate for you in the microwave."

I chuckled like an idiot, not knowing what else to do.

"Well, I'll see you around three and don't worry

about bringing anything. Looking forward to meeting Claire."

Saturday's clear blue sky was perfect for a cookout. Not that I could claim to be an expert on such events. The one time I hosted a family cookout with the stainless-steel charcoal grill I splurged on at Wal-Mart, Bozo paid more attention to sipping his paper cup filled with Jim Beam than he did to grilling the hot dogs. And Mama offered swats with her hands in the air, predicting every ten minutes that a mosquito would carry one of us off into the thicket of woods behind my former home. After a throw-down with Cher before leaving the trailer, I wasn't so sure this second cookout in my lifetime wouldn't be a rerun.

Cher sat in the passenger seat with her arms tightly folded over her orange-and-white-striped T-shirt. The scowl look dared me to say anything to her. She had first refused to go and only gave in when I told her we would leave whenever she wanted to. Up until that morning she was acting nice.

I even tried my hardest to look the other way about Cher's phone calls to LaRue. His number still appeared on my phone bill. But instead of raising Cain, I would simply circle the Shreveport numbers in red ink and provide the figure owed at the bottom. We developed a telephone-bill ritual. While she showered in the morning, I left my calculations on the kitchen counter for her review and payment. Before I left for work, she would snatch the bill off the counter and stuff it into her book bag. I saw her one morning, standing at the stop sign, surrounded by a misty, early morning haze, running her finger down the page to verify my calculations. A week or so later, the money would appear—wrapped in the original phone bill and placed on the counter. On account of Cher's fund-raising drives, the windows and automobiles at Miss Claudia's home remained spotless. Miss Claudia never would tell me how much she paid her. "She's just needing some independence," Miss Claudia would say, waving her hand for me to hush.

No matter how many times I pulled into Gerald's driveway, I would always look at that two-columned wood house, built in the 1800s, and hear violins. Gerald seemed like a foreigner around his home place. He was an everyday kind of man with grease under his fingernails, his elbows stationed on the dinner table with a fork in his left hand and a biscuit in his right. He was too down-to-earth for this prissy house. Cher even came alive when we almost bottomed out in the washed-out place in the driveway and rebounded to get a wide view of the structure. "This place looks like something off TV."

Then we saw the home's version of Scarlet standing on the front porch, waving her arm like we were part of a rescue squad coming up the sand driveway to save a life. Marcie wore a short navy skirt decorated with sunflowers and a yellow top. A top so yellow, it almost matched her hair. Her face paint and hair were done up perfectly. When we got out of the car, I forced myself not to pull at the ends of my top. I was wearing that blue top Miss Claudia made for me. Try as I might to convince myself otherwise, I knew Marcie would remember it was part of the outfit I had worn at the fish fry.

"Chase, go check the grill. And put the chicken on first. We'll do the steaks next. Daddy, they're here." She said her hostess lines in one breath. Then she bounded down the wooden steps and pranced towards Cher. I wanted to run over and intercept. To guard my baby from the Marcies of this world. But I stood frozen, saying a silent prayer that Marcie would at least call her by the right name.

"Hello," she said in a tone similar to what I imagined her using when singing "Yankee Doodle Dandy."

"Marcie, this is Cher. Cher is my granddaughter. Cher is the one I told you about," I said with the rhythm of a twenty-one-gun salute. Each time I said the word *Cher* I went up an octave.

"Oh, I know all about Cher," Marcie said, touching Cher's shoulder.

Cher half smiled and continued to stare over the lowest oak limb at the horse feeding in the grass pasture next to the house.

Beneath all the hype and comments of "cute" and "precious" when describing us and every item of clothing we had on, Marcie was civil. While Marcie gave me orders on where to place the paper plates and plastic cups, I watched from the back porch as Gerald pointed Cher towards the open pasture. The chestnut-colored horse grazed in the meadow against a steady hum of locusts. Cher slightly flinched when Gerald put two fingers in his mouth and whistled.

Marcie's sigh was deep and heavy behind me. She began knocking plastic cups off the wooden table and sighing louder.

"What you throwing cups for?" I turned to see Chase behind me, puzzled, with crumbs of potato chips falling from his mouth.

"Maybe if I had some help," she said in a clipped voice. "All you're doing is sitting in there watching that stupid car race, and me working myself to death."

I knew the comments were branded for me. But I let Chase jump down the old creaky porch steps and pick up the cups she had tossed in her fit. *She had one more trained,* I thought.

The smell of steaks and chicken searing on the grill had long drifted miles away when Donnie finally arrived. I first noted his arrival by the pounding bass vibrating from inside his little silver truck. The vehicle was so low to the ground, I wondered how on earth he ever made it through the washed-out place in the driveway. He pulled the toylike truck right up behind the house next to the picnic table. Like a veil being uncovered off a dedicated statue, he slowly opened the door. The windows were so black, all I could make out was the dashboard of the truck through the front windshield.

He was tall and skinny. If he hadn't been wearing such tight Wrangler jeans, he might have looked like he had more meat on his bones. The silver-and-gold cowboy belt buckle looked heavier than he did. He was tan like all the members of this clan, and his hair was blonde, just not as bright as Marcie's.

As he used his thumb and index finger to thump the edge of his little round Skoal can, we were introduced. "And this is ol' Donnie," Gerald said with his large hand engulfing Donnie's bony shoulder blade. We all looked at him, even Gerald. Donnie murmured something that I thought might be "Yeah," while he poked the particles of tobacco he'd pinched between his thumb and index finger inside his bottom lip.

If I had been in any position to say anything, Marcie beat me to it. "Dipping? And us about to eat supper?"

Donnie didn't look up at her. He just brushed the left-over grains of his supply on his jeans and then took his appointed place at the table. Marcie groaned like she was in labor, and Gerald laughed in a way I couldn't quite read. Either he was embarrassed, or he was making an excuse for this rudeness.

Cher had a tomato with a spot of dressing up to her lips when Marcie bowed her head and clutched her hands, "Dear Father." While I listened to her return thanks for the portion of food we almost put into our mouths, I could only picture her drunk on the dance floor slinging the ends of her blonde hair.

The talk of the table drifted back and forth between the horses and Marcie's job. Marcie did all the talking. Cher and Donnie would simply nod their heads in agreement.

As the sun lowered over the field, we all helped clear the red-and-white-checked tablecloth. Gerald helped until he was pulled away for a conference by Donnie. I held the white salad bowl and heard mumbling. All I could make out was "money" and saw

Gerald retrieve his wallet and land two bills into the open palm of his male heir. Donnie had not yet made it three steps to his little truck, when Gerald spoke. "You gonna say bye?"

"Oh, yeah," he said, sheepishly rolling his green eyes towards us. "Good to meet you." His attempt at a smile only resulted in a smirk, and I gave him the benefit of at least trying.

Gerald and me stood still, watching as his lowered truck with black windows departed in a trail of dust. "You know how these boys are. You got one," Gerald said and nervously chuckled.

I kept my stand at the kitchen sink, washing every item lips had touched during our feast. Marcie chuckled when she saw me washing the plastic cups. *Not everyone makes good money like you and Chase,* I wanted to snap. But I continued with what I did best, cleaning up a mess. She dried the items and continued with stories of her coworkers and the inmates. I filled her up with more fuel by asking all sorts of questions, anything to keep the conversation off me. I just knew she would question my personal business with Bozo and why I came to Wiregrass.

When I saw Marcie standing next to my side with what I first thought was a piece of cardboard clutched to her chest, I was afraid she would cry. She batted her eyes and smiled, much like I imagined her doing when the announcer called out her name as first runner-up in the Peanut Festival beauty pageant. An accomplishment shared twice during dinner. "Wiregrass has a big peanut festival each year. Did I tell y'all I almost won it," she said and rolled her eyes up to the plucked eyebrows.

Standing in the living room with Marcie, I felt every muscle in my neck tighten. She handed me the photograph of Leslie, the one that sat on the TV. I needed no introductions. The dishwater blonde and soft green eyes gave her away as the mother of the two children who favored her. This could be a turning point, I decided, and no matter how much discomfort my brain told me I should feel, I acted sweet. "Oh, lookie here. She's so pretty." I gazed into the gold frame and imagined myself speaking of a little baby.

"Whoever comes in here has mighty big shoes to fill," Marcie added. I did not look up at her, because I knew all that mascara she had on was smeared from tears.

I decided to prevent her from causing a scene and pretended that I did not hear her remarks. "And she looks so much like you and Donnie," I said.

The screen door screeched and then slammed against the wooden door frame. I looked up and saw Gerald standing in the doorway. He glanced down into my hands and then back up at Marcie. By this time Marcie was using her index finger to blot the tears that pooled around her eyes. Her mother's eyes. The eyes of the woman he first loved. I watched his neck strain when he forced saliva down with a hard swallow. I opened my mouth, but could only shake my head, producing nothing but air. What could I say? We just all three stood there for what seemed to be an hour when Cher came running up behind him, peering through the heavy screen of the door, her hands and face pressed against the mesh screen.

"Grandma, Paintbrush ate an apple right out of my hand."

"Is that right?" I said, lowering the photo slowly down towards my leg.

"Yeah," Gerald added. "He . . . uhh . . . he took a liking to Cher, all right." He turned, opened the door, and ruffled Cher's hair.

Marcie went into the bathroom to apply more cover-up. Try as I might to let go, my hands were frozen on Leslie's photo. I simply stared into the tan face with lines on the edges of the green eyes. I was in this woman's kitchen with her husband, tolerating her daughter. I felt odd and hated being the other woman. There's an old saying that the dead and the living can't live together. In this house, Leslie Peterson was held prisoner. She never could drift away.

Thirteen

Standing in the hallway with the toilet brush and yellow plastic gloves on, I knew Miss Claudia was really my guardian angel.

"How about it? School term is almost up. You want to stay on with me full-time for the summer?" My laughter was one of joy and humor at her typical no-nonsense approach. We were a lot alike, me and her.

I almost flung the blue toilet brush towards the high

142

ceiling in victory. I knew I had been foolish to arrange to have all my pay from the Houston County school system paid out over the course of the school days and not have it spread out over the summer, but at the time I had extra costs tacked on from renting Miss Trellis's ratty furniture. And truth be known, at the time I was not certain how long I would stay in Wiregrass.

But since the day I first started with Miss Claudia, I realized she needed me more than she probably admitted. Her need wasn't merely because of the many orange prescription bottles I moved from her marble bathroom counter in order to clean up. Those pills and her trusty cane, which she claimed was temporary, were the only two reminders she was not my age.

Her sign of dependence on me was detected more in her inability to get out. She kept her faith by attending church, even the Wednesday evening services, and kept her aging in chains by making the two-mile trek across town to her beauty shop, Cut Ups. But other than that, she sat a lot with her leg propped up on one of her cloth ottomans. I even took the weekly grocery list and made the run to Winn-Dixie. So when I found her that Friday dressed in a yellow dress and wearing a straw hat with a plastic sunflower on the side, I was stunned.

"We're adding some beauty to this place. I got a mind for flowers."

I helped her in the car like I imagined a polite Wade Tyler doing on his first date with her, and we made the rounds of all her favorite nurseries in Wiregrass. The garden-center owners knew her by name and seemed excited that she was at their door. *Most likely because they know she could run up a big bill and pay cash,* I decided. I knew I wouldn't get that treatment all by myself. I liked the way she would include me in her decisions as we created a rainbow of petunias, impatiens, and crepe myrtle out of the plastic containers. She even had me pick out a flat of petunias for my own place.

I got so carried away, I just slipped up without thinking. "Petunias are my daughter's favorite. When she first moved into her own place, I bought a big tray and helped her plant them around the front door." By my light tone, you would've thought Suzette and me traded Hallmark cards with each other on a weekly basis. What I didn't tell her was that the only reason I bought the flowers was an attempt to put some sort of beauty into Suzette's dark existence.

Miss Claudia, sipping from her Wendy's cup, revisited the subject I had raised earlier at the nursery. "You and your daughter close? I mean, I didn't know if she was able to have visitors with her nerve condition?"

I looked down and removed the plastic lid from my cup. *This was my own fault. I should have never agreed to even stop at Wendy's. Who ever heard of stopping at a restaurant just for a cup of sweet tea anyway?* "No, they got her in solitary confinement." At least that was half true. In prison, Suzette was confined.

Miss Claudia just smiled with her usual childlike innocence and held the cup away from the table like she was afraid of damaging the pepper-strewn tabletop. "It's hard, isn't it? Having a child with an affliction like that." She sighed and shook her head. "I lost one child, and I swear I refuse to lose another one. If it takes my last breath to see after Richard, I'll do it."

All I could think of was Richard's liquored-up state at the fish fry and hoped Patricia had not passed on the gossip.

"Patricia doesn't see Richard's problems the way I do. She's so impatient. I stay on my knees many a night, praying for the Lord to protect him."

"They say it's hard, losing a child like you did." I wondered who I thought I was—acting like I had mine. Suzette was locked up in a prison behind steel bars, and I could count on my left hand the number of times my son had written me since hooking up with the Marines.

"It just tears your guts out. I hate to be so vulgar, but it's the gospel truth." She propped her chin in her hand and looked far off as if searching for meaning. "Then, I sometimes wonder if the Lord didn't take Beth to spare her the hell on earth I had born her into. In her two years of life, she saw enough meanness from her daddy. He never beat on her. I'd kill him first, and he knew it. When she'd cry too loud, I'd run with her out the door before he'd yell. It was a house with Luther's needles all over the floor. I had to be careful where I stepped."

I tried to laugh and ease the tension. "I think you and me had the same builder."

She took my hand and squeezed it. "Kindred spirits,

me and you. I just thank the Lord you came here."

Those needles Miss Claudia spoke of felt like they were in the seat of my chair. As my legs and arms twitched, I looked down and wiped the leftover pepper off the tabletop. "You 'bout ready? I need to get on home to Cher."

While I watched her sip the last remaining drops of tea, I wished I was good with words. In the past four months, she told me she loved me more than my own blood mother had in the past twenty years. But all I could do was jingle her car keys and feel stupid by getting so embarrassed over her affection.

"You ready for this?" He asked like we were about to take a journey to Mars.

"I reckon I'm as ready as I'll ever be." I laughed at Gerald's nervousness.

I bounced and tried to hold on to the passenger door without him seeing. I didn't want Gerald to think I was scared each time his truck dipped and leaned down the sand embankment behind his house. I watched him hold the black steering wheel with both hands. The veins in his forearms bulged, and the muscles strained to keep the steering wheel under control.

Just as fast as the bouncing began, I looked out of his dusty windshield and saw a creek with currents of water cutting over large rocks. Tire tracks, which after hundreds of treks had cut out a road that ran parallel to the creek.

Gerald leaned over the steering wheel, grinning at the ripple of water running over two rocks and down the little stream. It was only knee deep at best, but the way he studied it you would've thought it was the mouth of the Mississippi.

"It sure is pretty," I said, hoping that was what he expected me to say.

As he drove up the path that ran alongside the creek, the branches of oaks screeched across the metal of his truck. I couldn't really enjoy the beauty of the land without worrying he'd have a thousand scratches on his truck when we got back to the house.

"This is my piece of paradise," he said, still looking straight ahead.

"It's beautiful all right."

"Not many people even been back here." He glanced at me.

I wondered if he thought I wasn't acting excited enough. "This piece of land is just about the prettiest thing I've seen."

Soon we passed the clearing of trees and drove up onto a clear parcel of land. Nothing but bright grass and the creek that ran down the middle of the land. It looked so bizarre, so set apart from his home, which rested just beyond the thick treetops.

"My goodness," I said and moved towards the edge of the truck seat.

"Told you," he said, grinning broadly. "This place is my sanity. When I get too much going on inside my brain, I come out here and drive it away." He suddenly turned the steering wheel to the right, and we were off the path and onto the bumpy, untamed part of the field. Oak trees stood at a distance on either side. He pressed down on the gas pedal, and soon it felt like we were soaring over the rough terrain.

We rolled the windows down and opened the back window of the cab. The ends of my ponytail fluttered from the teasing of the wind. I considered giving into the wind and letting all my hair free to the whips of current, but decided against it after picturing myself looking ridiculous.

Gerald drove the length of the meadow, and when he pulled up so close to the creek that I thought he would drive through it, he hit the brakes. We sat there still and silent with swirls of grass particles and dust floating over the vehicle. The water trickling over rocks was the only sound for a long time. Not the awkward type of silence I first felt with him. A silence that let us know we didn't have to think of words. The words spoke for us within the ripple of the stream.

"How'd you find this place?" I finally asked.

"Since I was a boy, I used to come down here and mess around. But then I got busy with life, you know." He continued to stare through the windshield and into the steady stream of water.

I pictured him as a boy with a head full of blond curls, flying a kite out in the field, climbing up an oak tree, target-practicing with his first rifle. I was proud he was sharing this with me. "Well, when did you start coming out here again?"

He looked down at the floorboard of the truck and pushed a half-crushed 7–11 cup with the toe of his boot. "Last year," he said, drumming his thumb on the steering wheel. He quickly looked up. "Look yonder, two quails across the creek," he said with the first hint of animation.

The silence told me not to say any more. This was his place. I was meant to be a spectator.

The trickle of the water called me out of the truck, and without saying a word I got out and walked to the edge of the bank. I leaned down, pushing the edge of grass back enough to see the steady stream. The clean currents looked like running glass. I reached out my hand to break the smooth slickness.

"Careful for moccasins," he said behind me.

I jumped up so fast he had to catch me by one arm to keep me from falling on my tail. When I saw the smirk on his face, I gave him a quick jab in his side. My hand touched the soft portion of his belly against the denim shirt. A flush of blood rushed through my chest, and for a second I had half a mind to touch him again.

Gerald threw his head back towards the cloudless sky and showed me just how hard he could laugh. It was more high-pitched than I imagined a man his size capable of. I got tickled just watching this six-foot-something man squealing like one of the eight-year-old boys in the cafeteria line.

For the next two hours, we sat close to each other on the edge of the bank and just listened. The chirps of birds and streaming water created reverence. For most people, it was probably a place more ideal for being alone than together.

"I came out here after the funeral." He slapped the toe of his boot with the end of a long green weed.

His words struck me while I was staring at the gray-

and-black-streaked rocks in the stream. Thank goodness I didn't jump and say, "Excuse me." He just assumed I knew the details leading up to his life as a widower. Even though my feet were beginning to fall asleep, I didn't move. I wouldn't even have breathed if I didn't just have to. Part of me wanted to hear about this part of his life, and another part wanted to find the pair of quail to point out.

"Everybody kept worrying me. All I wanted to do was run off someplace. I'd lie in bed and picture my truck heading down I–10. Texas, maybe. Heck, I didn't know where. And me a grown man with two kids." He half chuckled like he thought I'd think he was a fool.

"I want to run off lots of times."

He looked up at me with his mouth slightly open and continued slapping the tip of his boot with the weed.

All I could think of was Miss Trellis and the picture she painted of Gerald, a man half crazy with grief. I wanted to get right up, brush the leftover grass off the seat of my jeans, and get on with our time together. All this talk of depression would ruin our day. But the seat of my jeans was a magnet to the patch of dirt I sat on. His patch of dirt.

"Somers around the third week, I dreamed about this place. I done forgot what this meadow looked like back then. In the dream it sort of reminded me of what heaven might be like."

The slowed beat of my heart echoed inside my ears. I worried about him crying. Would I hold him and stroke his hair and run my hands over the base of his neck? Or would I ignore it and hope that pair of quail would reappear?

Gerald broke the weed and put the broken end in the corner of his mouth. "I ain't told nobody none of this. But I wanted to kill that piece of crap who . . ."

He didn't have to finish the sentence. I even wanted that trash Miss Trellis called "a public nothing" dead. He deserved it for putting this man through torment. That drunk probably had a suspended license when he drove to the bar that Wednesday night. Suddenly I wondered what Leslie must have thought the minute before that slime hit her on the highway. *What would she think now with me sitting so close to her husband?*

"But I don't know, when I come out here I just forgot all that. It was like the good Lord gave me an understanding about that thing. I found this creek when I was full of hate. And when I left, I don't know . . . I was all still inside. You know, sort of like a lake right at sunset?"

He turned to look at me. I smiled and slightly nodded a lie. Gerald was talking in an unknown tongue. I certainly never felt settled like any lake. But I did feel a tingle of peace when he reached over and stroked my cheek with the back of his hand. The roughness of his fingers slid over my skin. The touch made me want to reach over and kiss him. I wanted to kiss this man before he realized he had a lack in judgment concerning me. How could I compare with this man? All I had was a mixed-up world of tidal waves.

"You're easy to talk to, you know that?" His green eyes ran the length of my naked face. I turned my head slightly away, squinting towards the overpowering rays of sun.

The roughness of his palm was again on my cheek. Gerald softly pulled my face towards him. And before I could ask him if he was about ready to go, he leaned over and kissed me. Not the kind of hard kissing Bozo taught me. His lips were light as a feather's brush, and before it was over I reached out and ran my hand through his coarse blonde hair.

Fourteen

*T*he phone rang just as Patricia pulled out the brochure of the fancy resort she and Doctor Tom would stay at during the Dental Association Convention. When I told her I had never heard of Marco Island, she fluttered her hand like a little bird flying beside her head. "Down in Florida, somewhere. It's just nice is all I know. Now Mama, look at this place we'll be staying," she said, unfolding the brochure on Miss Claudia's kitchen table.

I was put out to have to answer the phone. I wanted to see this fancy resort that Patricia had been going on about for the past twenty minutes.

"Mrs. Jacobs?" The voice on the other end of the line was unfamiliar and nasal.

I quickly inhaled, knowing that if the call was for me at Miss Claudia's house, it could only be bad news. I closed my eyes, hoping Bozo had not reared his

152

liquored head again. "This's her."

"I'm Rachel Baxter, guidance counselor at Houston County Junior High. It appears Cher had a little altercation this afternoon. Unfortunately, she's suspended for two days."

Patricia's words of hot tubs, tennis lessons, and massages drifted through the phone receiver while I stood frozen. *This is a lie,* I thought. *Not my honor-roll Cher. This part of my life was over. This was the life of raising a bobcat son and a delinquent daughter. Not Cher.*

"Mrs. Jacobs?"

I wanted to scream *liar* and slam the phone down, but the background noise of described luxury kept me calm. I had two bosses in the room and had to keep my wits, however loosely strung together they may be. "I'm on my way."

"Now, Mama, I want you to look at this. Doctor Tom got us one of these bungalows right on the beach." Patricia towered over Miss Claudia such that when I told them I had to go pick up a sick Cher, I only saw Miss Claudia peep over Patricia's arm.

Walking down the concrete sidewalk towards the red brick principal's office of Houston County Junior High, I could only think that there was some explanation. Some mistake. Or was it another tidal wave to remind me that, no matter how enjoyable my Saturday afternoon with Gerald was, my life was not a lake of stillness?

I listened as Ms. Baxter, the guidance counselor, sat behind her gray metal desk and read from a manila folder. Normally I would have been struck by how young this Ms. Rachel Baxter was, but I had to concentrate on every detail to find the slipup. The missing piece this young lady could not figure out. The responsibility must fall elsewhere.

"It happened in the lunchroom line when Cher evidently began clawing Lacretia Hightower. Of course Lacretia said she did nothing wrong."

"Umm-humm," I mumbled in a sassy tone.

Ms. Baxter glanced up from her file. I'm sure she was calculating just how much trouble this redneck grandmother would cause. Raising a grandchild was a special type of discrimination. I learned long ago whenever teachers found out I was the grandmother, not the real mother, they immediately expected problems from Cher. They had tested Cher from the first grade on to make sure there were no emotional problems. Until now, all they got back were the highest marks.

"Cher proceeded to then hit Lacretia in the head with her shoe until a teacher's assistant pulled her off."

"Give me a break," I said, slapping my pocketbook. "And just what started all this?"

"Kids in their class said Lacretia had been making fun of Cher's name for a few weeks now." The young counselor put down the file and took a sip out of her apple-shaped coffee mug.

"There's more to it than that," I said a touch too loudly. "With a name like hers, I taught Cher from first grade to laugh off any teasing about her name." I settled back against my wooden seat and racked my brain to think of other incidents when having the name of an entertainer proved embarrassing. All I could come up with was Mama's protest at the hospital when Suzette announced the name, which had been permanently placed on her birth certificate. I considered changing it when me and Bozo got legal guardianship, but decided changing the first and last name both would be too much of a jolt, even for a two-year-old.

"You know, at this age kids can be so cruel." She smiled and batted her long eyelashes.

"Huh. She's seen cruel," I yelled and then quickly changed emotional gears, fearing Cher would be forced to take more mental testing. "Look, Miss Baxter, all I'm saying is that the girl has never give me one ounce of trouble."

"New names are an adjustment. Especially at this age."

"Well, like I told you, I always . . . What?" I was getting irritated at this young educator's poor listening skills. "I told you Cher was her name the first day she started school."

The young lady tucked strands of hair behind her ear and leaned forward. "I'm sorry?"

"Her name's not new—she was born with it." I sat tall with the wooden chair, spine pressed into my back, pleased I had outsmarted someone with two diplomas hanging on her office wall.

Miss Baxter opened the manila file and quickly ran her fingernail down the white page. I just imagined mistakes were far and few between for the likes of her.

The most pressing issue in her life was most likely whether she had the time to get those fingernails manicured weekly.

"Okay, here we are. Four weeks ago, Cher told her teachers that her last name had changed. She said that she was taking her father's name of LaRouche. Lacretia began calling her 'La Roach' and pretending to spray insecticide at her." Miss Baxter crinkled her perky noise.

I jumped up from the wooden chair and threw my bag over my shoulder. "Where is she?"

Miss Baxter looked up, her mouth opened. "Mrs. Jacobs, Lacretia was suspended as well. Now there is no . . ."

"Get Cher out here right this minute."

During the ride home I said nothing, and Cher sat in the passenger seat with her arms folded. Fingernails had left crimson marks down her right cheek. A sign of valor over the name of the man who stopped contributing to her well-being the second his seed helped form her. The very idea made me hit the steering wheel with the palm of my hand. It was still vibrating when we pulled up to the trailer.

Cher bolted from the car and stomped through sand and crabgrass. I studied this stubborn human who weeks earlier snuggled with me in my bed. I could only wonder what air castle LaRue LaRouche had seduced her with over the phone.

She tried to open the door, and when she realized I had the key, she put her hands on her hips. Her toe tapped the concrete steps like she was too important to wait.

This had gone on long enough. The phone calls, the daydreams, it would all burn up today. Slowly walking towards the door, I plotted my next move.

When I unlocked the door, she bolted to her room. The pine bedroom door had almost slammed when I blocked it with the base of my arm.

"Oh, no you don't," I said, still feeling the tingle of the door on my arm.

She jumped on her bed and reached to turn the radio on. I leaned over and grabbed the radio. Brushing up against her, I could almost see rays of anger bouncing off us. I slammed the off button so hard, the radio tumbled to the floor.

"What's gotten into you?" I stood with my hand propped on the closed door. I had her trapped, and she would listen to me if I had to hold her down and pour the words into her ear.

She rolled over on to the bed, her face buried in the pillow. The same pillow that entombed the photo of the family that was never meant to be. "Leave me alone!"

"How can I? I'm the only person on the face of this earth who cares a thing about you. And what do I get for it? Your hateful words, your bad attitude, and now this."

"You hate me," she said, swinging her face up to glance at me and then retreating into the pillowcase.

"No, uh-uh. You're not pulling this crap on me. I love you, and I'm the only one."

"My daddy loves me." I could make out the muffled

words as they fought to be heard from under the pillow.

"That does it. Look at me!" I fell to the bed on my knees and pulled her shoulders upright. She tried to let out a scream, and the terror in her eyes reminded me of how I must've looked the times Bozo came after me. My grip loosened. "Please don't do this," was all I could say.

So much for my big plans of truth and honesty. I wanted to cry, to beg her to stop calling LaRue. To make her push him out of her life. This was all my fault. I had let it go too far, and now didn't know if I could tell her the truth that would stop it.

"I am, you know. I am a LaRouche. Why can't I be called by his last name? It's mine. It's mi-i-i-ne," she screamed. Her tortured screams brought to mind a toddler falling to the floor and tightening her legs in a fit of rage.

I looked inside her blank brown eyes, clouded with tears. "Trust me, he doesn't want you," I calmly said.

"He does so," she screamed and threw her head back in torment. The tears and moans tore the fibers of my being, and when I tried to hold her, she pushed me away with her fists.

The thuds on my chest reminded me of when I tried to tell Suzette she should never marry LaRue, pregnant or not. She fought me, tried to slap me, and refused to let me break her dreams. I gave up and she won. She said she refused to allow me to rule her life. Instead, she let him break her and throw her into prison when he was done with her.

Sitting on the bed listening to Cher's tormented

screams, I decided I would die before seeing family history repeat itself. "He doesn't care a thing about you," I continued in the most civil tone I knew. "I love you. I love you."

"Shut up," she said, sticking her fingers in her ears. I yanked her arms down and forced her to hear me. "He didn't care anything about your mama, and he won't care anything about you." Her arms twisted in my grip.

She gagged and carried on so that I thought for a second she might be having some sort of spell. Like a mental patient. Like Richard.

"I love you. Me—not him. I'm the one who loves and sacrifices for you. It's me. *Me.*"

"I hate your guts." A stream of clear liquid ran from her nose. "I hate you!"

Tough love ended right then. I was not prepared for this. She said it as forcefully as I had told her I loved her. Cher would drop me and the sacrifices I made for her over a make-believe daddy. An air castle that had a big crack down the side of the wall. A crack invisible from where she sat on her puffy cloud.

"Fine." I dropped her arms and let her cough and gasp for air. "You want to live in a dream world, go right ahead. But I'm telling you, he ain't like you think."

I had my hand on the knob of her bedroom door when she screamed for the last time that afternoon. "You'll see when I'm living with my daddy in his brick house. And you're here in this dumpy place!"

Like daggers landing in the flank of a bull, the anger overwhelmed my hurt. I turned and stormed the eight

159

steps to the end of her bed, and she jumped with a scream. I snatched the zipper of her pillow and pulled out the little photo of her dream world, the biological parents she was too young to clearly remember.

"This is what you think life with him is?"

"How . . . How did you?" She stood at the end of the bed, hair matted on her face by the tears.

"Well, honey, you got another think coming. This is your dream, and this is reality." I tore the wallet-size photo faster than any store-bought shredder. I kept the pieces tightly in my grip, knowing if she could she would glue the memory back together. As soon as I cleared the way, she slammed the door as hard as she could. Walking past the door to the garbage can, I could hear her muffled cries over the baritone-voiced radio announcer. *"Mostly sunny skies today with a high reaching eighty-six. Just a gorgeous May day here in the Wiregrass area."*

The smell of butter melting in a frying pan filled the trailer the next morning. After a sleepless night, I decided to offer an olive branch. But I knew it would take more than French toast to cover up the lashes we gave each other with our tongues. At three I got up and eased into her bedroom door to make sure she was still there. Cher was curled in a fetal position, fully clothed; her red blanket was tossed to the end of the floor. *If only she could stay so peaceful,* I thought and laid the red blanket across her bare feet.

I had already called and told Sammy I would not be at work. "Under the weather" is how I explained it, but in reality I was sick with fright. She barely mumbled when I greeted her with "Good morning."

"I made you some French toast."

She stumbled in her wrinkled blue jeans to the kitchen table and drowned the brown bread with maple syrup. I sat down with my cup of coffee and tried to offer another branch.

"Listen, last night . . ."

"Am I going with you to Miss Claudia's today?" She looked me dead in the eye like we were negotiating a contract. Then when she licked a stream of syrup off the side of the plastic bottle, I was reminded that she was not the adult in this situation.

Cher's punishment for impersonating someone she was not amounted to cleaning all of Miss Claudia's windows and painting the wicker swing on the side porch and the flower boxes. She would also wash Miss Claudia's and Richard's cars, her usual job. But this time I refused to let them pay her, even for the car washes.

"Erma Lee, don't be too hard on the girl." Richard stood at the kitchen door, sipping his coffee.

With Miss Claudia I would take advice. From him I dismissed it the moment he parted his lips. "Need more coffee, Richard, before I throw this pot out?"

Cher even had her lunch outside under the oak tree, the same seat where Sam, the yard man, ate his lunch the two days a week he worked at Elm Drive. "Bless her heart," Miss Claudia mumbled while poking a fork at a breast of fried chicken. She took a bite of the crispy meat and turned to look at Cher from her

161

kitchen window. But I was unmoved. Mama was right about some things, I decided. I had spoiled Cher and was now reaping the consequences. I said little to Miss Claudia and Richard that day. I wanted to be the hired help. I wanted to come and go as I pleased without them interfering in my life.

"You and Gerald go out for your usual steak supper last Saturday?" Miss Claudia asked while I dusted the mahogany stair rail.

"Yes, ma'am."

She stood a minute longer and opened her mouth to speak, but then walked away. The tap of her cane faded, and she closed her bedroom door.

I was in no mood for such foolish thoughts of romance; I had a crisis in my midst. Miss Claudia was sitting in her bed, reading the newspaper, when I entered with an armload of folded underwear to place in her chest of drawers.

"Cher was just here washing my window, tapping the glass, and making all sorts of monkey faces." Miss Claudia pouted her lips and scrunched her nose. She giggled, and I only offered a smile.

"I declare," she said, and her laughter died. "Erma Lee, you said this all started over the kids teasing her about her name?"

With my back to her, Miss Claudia could not see me roll my eyes. "Yes, ma'am."

"Has this happened before?"

"No, not really. Where do you want your scarves to go?" I slightly turned to see her hazel eyes burning a hole through the inside of me.

"Top drawer is fine, thank you. Listen, turn around where I can look at you."

Just what I did not want to do. I sighed a little too loudly.

"Now what in the world is going on? It's me now. I'm your friend."

"She just got in trouble at school is all. Some girl picked a fight with her." I hand-dusted the top of the drawer. Anything to prevent looking at her.

"All this over her name. Why, Cher is a lovely name. I don't see anything a'tall wrong with . . ."

"It's her last name. Her last name," I said out of utter frustration to make her comprehend my problems. "She changed it. Told all the teachers she was going by LaRue's last name . . . her da . . . her biological father."

Miss Claudia picked up the magazines off her bed and tossed them on her nightstand. "The poor girl's just confused."

I sighed, not expecting Miss Claudia to understand. Whatever we had in common concerning taking licks from a man, she didn't have all the problems I faced. She had an imperfect child, but he lived next door, not in a prison. She didn't face the loss of love and hope from the one person you believed would change a mess of destruction. "It's more than all that. You just don't understand."

"Well, try me."

"No, just forget it. I just never should have . . ."

"Erma Lee, you're just all to pieces. Now I'm concerned about you. You don't want me to worry about you now, do you?"

I stepped towards the chair by her bed and ran my fingers over the brocaded fabric on the armrest.

"What's the matter with the child pretending? She's having an identity crisis. She needs to know who her people are."

"I'm her people," I said, pointing into my chest. "She needs nobody else but me. He won't have her, I keep trying to tell her." My voice echoed down the hall and greeted me once again. I reeled my emotions back and got onto myself for getting out of control. She sat there and looked at me. She was expecting more, signaling me with her eyes that she was tough and could take it.

"Is this man dangerous for her?"

All I could do was look down and nod my head in shame. Shame that my own daughter had brought evil into our lives. Shame that I couldn't stop it. Finally, after what seemed two hours of silence, I sat down in the chair by her bedside.

"He's real dangerous. That's why this is not just some schoolyard fight. I should've seen it with Suzette too. My daughter was raised with fighting and screaming all the time. You can just imagine how bad. And I don't blame her for running off and marrying the first thing who looked over his shoulder at her. Not much different than me, I reckon. I tried to tell her what a mistake I made marrying so young, but Suzette knew more than me.

"Bozo or me, neither one liked LaRue. Can you blame us? She met him when the carnival came to town. He called himself a ride engineer. I saw through that bull. The carnival was always littering the airport field after they left town, and in my book LaRue was just one more piece of trash they left in Cross City. LaRue got a job working construction, and after his third paycheck Suzette got pregnant. Lord knows, I begged her not to marry him. I told her I would raise the baby while she finished school. She cussed me for everything under the sun and told me I wanted to keep her chained. That was LaRue talking, I know that now. They snuck away the next morning. I didn't hear from her until a week later when she told me they found a rental house in Shreveport."

"Well, I declare," Miss Claudia said with her chin propped on her knuckles.

"Yeah, LaRue always had a big scheme. He was going to paint houses, or he was going to own a gas station, always something. Except any money he made went straight up his nose. But I will say at first Suzette tried. She was even a good little mama for a few months. I don't know how long it took her to get doped up, but soon we knew something wasn't right. Cher was just a year old when they were flying high. New vehicles, lots of jewelry. Then next thing you know, we weren't hearing from them. I'd send a letter. No response. Call on the phone and get no answer. I called for a solid week before one morning I called and got a message saying the phone had been disconnected. I called in sick at the factory and drove straight over to Shreveport. Calling it sixth sense or whatever, I knew something wasn't right.

"I went up the small steps of the blue rental house

expecting nobody home. The yard was scattered with plastic bags and beer cans. I pried the front door open with a rusty jackknife I found by the side of the house. As soon as the door popped open, the smell of old beer and urine nearly knocked me back out. Clothes and shoes were piled all in the middle of the floor, and the sofa Bozo and me gave them as a wedding gift had been torched. I first thought some type of Charles Manson gang had come in and killed them all. I pulled my shirt over my nose and stepped over beer cans and bottles of Wild Turkey. Half-eaten McDonald's hamburgers with white mold on the buns still sat in yellow containers on the kitchen counter.

"The kitchen table and chairs had been tossed in all directions. You'd a thought a hurricane hit the place. One empty can of cat food sat on the floor next to the refrigerator. I opened the refrigerator door, and the stench of rotten food made me gag and my eyes water. I turned to run out the front door and tripped over a bottle. When I got up, I looked up and saw her. Just sitting there in the corner of the room. Behind a turned-over keg, wild-eyed and shaking, with her mouth wide open. It was Cher. They just left her there like some empty bottle they were through with." Tears fell freely on to my arms. I sat just as still at the courthouse the day the jury convicted Suzette and LaRue of child abandonment and neglect.

I put both my hands over my eyes. "Cher stayed in the hospital for two weeks, dehydrated and in shock. If it hadn't been for that one can of cat . . ." I bent my head down and tried not to bawl like I had when I grabbed her up in her soiled clothing and ran out the front door of that blue shack. It was the last time I really cried in front of Cher. The doctor at the hospital told me this was no time for sissies. Cher needed rocks, not mud.

I never heard Miss Claudia leave the room, but I felt the soft touch of her bony hand on my back. My face was hot, and when I leaned up, I saw her standing before me with a glass and a lace handkerchief.

"Take a sip of Coca-Cola," she said, handing me the handkerchief at the same time. She sat in the wingback chair next to me. We were silent for quite some time. I figured she wanted to make sure I had gotten it all out of my system. Or maybe she was waiting for an ending. If only I had one to offer.

I blew my nose and cleared my throat. "They found LaRue and Suzette two days later. High on crack, in some fleabag in Las Vegas." I inhaled and blew the air out hard like I imagined a marathon runner would do headed towards the finish line. "Suzette had even been selling herself," the words trailing with the last puff of air. "She's in prison, not in a state home. I lied, okay?"

I looked at Miss Claudia, waiting for her to scream and kick me out of her house, to do something, anything. But she just sat there with her head tilted towards her shoulder.

"I'm sorry for lying to you. Look, I know how this must seem to you with me and my history . . ."

"Now, you've done nothing but try to take the girl and give her a decent raising. Does she know about all this?"

I jingled the cubes of ice in the blue-swirled glass and shook my head. "I know I ought to tell her. But she's a good girl. And with all the drugs and mess kids get into." I suddenly looked up at her as if I had another bright idea, "Do you want me to leave?"

Miss Claudia pulled herself up by the arm of the chair and gripped her cane. I learned long ago nothing made her madder than to have someone rush over and help her get out of a chair. Leaning on the cane, she turned her head and smiled. "Erma Lee, what do I have to do to convince you that you're family now? And that's what families do, they bear burdens. I love you and Cher."

I looked down at the Oriental rug and shook my head. The words *I love you* sounded different coming from her than they did when I tried to drill them into Cher.

She caressed the strands of hair pulled neatly back on my head.

"Can I offer advice? These are burdens we can't bear. Cannot control. Whenever I face times like these, I just put them at the Lord's feet."

I did not respond, but simply sat still and studied the swirls of navy and burgundy that jumped at me from the Oriental rug. I wanted to shrink into the swirls and become part of the carpet. Instead, I clasped her hand and closed my eyes tightly. *Would God hear my prayer?* I wasn't worthy like Miss Claudia. I was silent and let her lead.

We prayed for protection of Cher and for peace of mind. She even prayed for LaRue and Suzette, people

I was sure the good Lord had long given up on. When it was over, she hugged me tightly. "We have our crosses to bear, you and me."

I never fully explained to Gerald why I couldn't go to the steak house with him on Friday night. I told him Cher was on restriction and couldn't go to the skating rink. It embarrassed me that he brought dinner to us that evening. As he placed plastic bags on the counter, I knew the Lord was answering part of the prayer already. Gerald's presence seemed to lighten the tension that ran between Cher and me.

As typical of our fights, after two days me and Cher were speaking again. In that way she was like me. We were too no-nonsense for pouty bickering. She entered the kitchen Monday morning downright chipper. Even kissed me on the cheek before she went to the bus stop. All day, I felt guilty for trying to force her into accepting something Mother Nature had not intended, to hate a parent.

After determining how much it would cost to host a skating party for ten, I sat at the kitchen table to figure up how far my bank account could stretch for a skating party. Sixty dollars was the bare minimum for a party, and with the light bill due next week the numbers in my register just wouldn't cooperate. Reluctantly, I approached Miss Claudia with the idea of a loan. But I made her sign a piece of notebook paper stating I would pay her back by June 15. "You didn't take us to raise," I continued to remind her.

The truth shall set you free. It's one of the few

lessons I still remember from my days attending Sunday school and church with Aunt Stella. But telling the truth about Cher and Suzette to Miss Claudia gave me insomnia. As I laid there in my bed hearing the clumps of pine straw drift down on my tin roof, I was all tight inside. All I could think of in the first few nights after my confession was that spring day twelve years ago in Shreveport. I had dismissed it out of my mind when Suzette entered prison, and now LaRue had drug it all back up. *All this is his fault.* I kicked the sheets until they clumped together at the end of the bed. I sat up and sighed at the stillness of the room. Turning on the lamp, I picked up a pencil and notebook.

With a pillow as a bumpy desktop, I put little dots beside each point I wanted to tell Suzette someday. All the questions and details that led up to my discovery that spring day in Shreveport. All the holes I had not allowed myself to fill during the trial, vowing to never speak to her again.

I sat with the pencil dangling between my fingers like a cigarette. Thinking of issues to discuss in this imaginary world, I swung the wild strands of hair out of my face. The movement brought Gerald's perfect daughter to mind. Even I had to admit, with all her high and mighty ways, Marcie was a success. I saw it in the way Gerald grinned at her sassy one-liners, or at how he shook his head and chuckled at the cookout when she told him he was serving the salad all wrong. His daughter had become what he and Leslie expected and hoped for. Beside the pencil dot on the blue-lined paper, I wrote the last point I would address with Suzette: Why?

"This little thing ain't half bad. Sounds pretty good," Gerald said, examining the pink radio I had transferred from Cher's room to the counter of the kitchen. After asking Gerald over for dinner, I asked Cher if I could borrow her radio.

"The old me would've just pulled it right out without asking," I reminded her at the skating rink.

"You're trying," she said and got out of the car.

After a second pork chop, I decided I had to do it before my heart tore out of my chest. Gerald was still holding the biscuit on the edge of his plate when I ventured on shaky ground. "This is some of the best corn," he said, using the biscuit to guide the kernels onto his fork.

"Hey, I need to talk a minute," I said, clinching the paper napkin into a ball. I was glad the radio was softly playing to provide distraction. *The truth shall set you free,* I heard Aunt Stella's pastor scream from old files in my mind.

Gerald looked up, holding the serving bowl of fried corn. His green eyes looked bigger than usual. He probably thought that he really didn't know me. Maybe he thought I was going to announce I had put poison in his pork chop. "What's on your mind?" He calmly put the corn back on the table without taking a second helping.

The feeling of dread almost overtook me, and I wanted to run out the door. The long forgotten image of seeing Bozo, breathing heavy with a red nose, blocking my escape drifted into view. I glanced at my unlocked and unblocked door. The words came first in a whisper and grew in volume when I didn't see Gerald push the dinette chair away from my kitchen table and leave. Halfway through the story of my daughter, son-in-law, and the horrors they created for me to find that day in Shreveport, I wanted to stop and laugh. *It's a joke. It's not all as bad as it sounds,* I wanted to say.

At first the only sound was Travis Tritt's voice singing about a quarter and calling someone who cares. Gerald shook his head, almost in time to the music. He looked up at me and scrunched his eyes, calling attention to the deep wrinkles in his forehead.

"Dog," he whispered.

I began clearing the table as if I had just reported about a successful daughter who was like some Martha Stewart and lived in a three-bedroom brick home. A daughter like his own. When I got to the sink and began spraying water on the remnants of greasy fat, I felt his thick arms wrap around my shoulders. The width of his chest lay against my back, and his mustache tickled the edge of my ear. "You done good with Cher. You ought to be proud. You're a good woman, Erma Lee."

He felt inviting, and part of me wanted to lean my back against him and fall into his tight grip. But I continued to spray the water on the white dish until the spots of pork lard were washed away and the presence behind me had slipped away to the couch.

I told two people I had known only a few months the

secret I had been unable to tell old friends like Roxi, who I'd known for twenty years. The people I spent decades working alongside at the plant simply thought Suzette had moved to Las Vegas and worked at a blackjack table. The unstable lifestyle was my excuse for raising Cher. Roxi and the other folks in Cross City may have known of the punches I put up with from Bozo's direction, but they never saw the licks Suzette left on my heart.

Gerald almost ran into me when I turned to retrieve another pot. "Oh," I said, balancing myself by putting my hand on his shirt. The touch was forbidden, and I removed my hand. He was carrying the corn and salad dishes. I took them without looking into his eyes. Just when I had poured dishwashing soap on the dishes, he pulled me around to face him. His pull startled me, but I softened when he stroked his hand up against my face.

"There's some people on this earth don't seem worth the clay God used to make them. It just don't make sense when I hear stuff like that." He was looking over my shoulder at the radio.

"Look, I shouldn't have said nothing."

"That's just like you, ain't it? After all the crap you been through, you still worrying about somebody else."

I looked down at the bright white tennis shoes, washed especially for our date. The touch of his warm hand on the back of my neck drew me to his inner being.

"When you gonna let somebody care for you?"

All I could do was shrug. Just as I opened my mouth to say something funny, a trick I was learning from Miss Claudia, he leaned over and put his mouth on mine. Feeling the bushy hairs of his mustache on my lips, I leaned all the way into him. Before I knew it, my hand was on the back of his neck, pulling him down tighter into my grasp.

At first, I hoped the ringing of the phone was happening at the trailer next door. Thinking it could be Cher, I pulled myself into reality and broke free.

"Hello." My lips tingled from his kiss.

"Erma Lee." The voice was so faint I first thought it was LaRue calling to harass me. "I need some . . ." The phone on the other end hit a hard object. A chill ran from the base of my skull to the pit of my stomach.

"Miss Claudia? Miss Claudia, is that you?"

Fifteen

*T*he automatic sliding doors to the emergency room were not opening fast enough. I pounded my foot on the black carpet and held the blood-soaked dishrag on Miss Claudia's nose. Just when I was about to kick the glass door open like some kick-boxing champion, the glass slowly separated.

A black woman dressed in white with an ink pen dangling around her neck approached us. She opened the wooden doors of the treatment area and patted the black mattress of a vacant gurney. I thought the lady had ESP and knew we were in grave need the second we walked through the door, but then I remembered that the front of Gerald's shirt was darkened with Miss Claudia's blood. The strongest woman I knew hung in his arms with the limpness of a dead squirrel.

By the time I unlocked her kitchen door with my key, Miss Claudia was in a pool of blood. Lying in the living room near the table with the telephone. All I could think when I first saw her was that she had been stabbed. "Meanness is just taking over," she would say whenever Richard would report a new crime announced on his scanner. But when Gerald lifted her shoulders I saw the crimson flood coming from her nose. The fluid caked the front of her lavender house-coat like streaks of paint.

Oh, good, just a nosebleed, I thought. I got the dish towel thinking that I could squeeze her nostrils together and stop the bleeding. But like most problems, it was not that simple. She was unconscious, and nothing seemed to stop the steady flow.

"We'd better not wait for an ambulance," Gerald said. "I can get her there faster." He cradled her in his arms and gently lifted her off the floor. The silver cane sparkled next to the red pool.

As we pulled out of her driveway, I saw Richard's apartment lights over the garage. When I pictured her calling him numerous times before she gave up and dialed my number, anger flushed through my blood. Turmoil made me want to seek blame, and Richard was convenient. My insides rumbled like a creaky roller coaster. As her mashed down hair lay in my lap

175

and her face tilted to the side producing a steady flow of blood on my white shoes, I couldn't help but think this was it. *Aneurysm* raced through my mind until I wanted to scream out to prevent the doom my brain was creating.

Beneath the eerie glow of outside streetlights, I knew my life would change for the worse if I lost her. In my need to find a new life on my own, I realized I had become utterly dependent on her. I stroked her thick hair, hoping to calm her. "You the unluckiest person I know," Mama told me on several occasions throughout my life. She was right. Nothing good ever lasts long enough.

"I've ordered a blood transfusion," the young doctor with round wire glasses told us in the waiting room.

"For a nosebleed?" I wondered out loud. And then I pondered whether this young man even knew what he was doing. *He probably doesn't even need those glasses,* I thought. *He probably just picked out the Grandpa Jones pair at the drugstore to make him look like he's wise.*

Before I could question his medical schooling, like I even could, he was gone in a blur of green.

Gerald blew a massive amount of air out of his mouth. *Frustration,* I decided when he placed his thumbs on his pants pockets. A white supremacist shouted at us through the television, and we stood there looking at each other.

"Y'all need to fill out these forms," the black woman with the pen hanging around her neck said. When I took the clipboard from her, the woman softly patted my hand. *Why keep love in your heart when you can give it away for free,* I imagined Miss Claudia saying.

While I knew some personal details of Miss Claudia's life, the thick white forms made me realize how much I didn't know. Birth date, social security number, insurance, and medical allergies. I sighed out loud, vowing to learn the details and officially become the blood relation she made me feel I was. "I got to call Richard for some of this stuff."

"Tyler here," he answered on the tenth ring. His tone was all business. Music blared from his radio, and code numbers squealed out from his scanner. The background noise gave away any pretense that he was answering an office line.

"This is Erma Lee." I started to just lay it out, but then feared he might have some kind of nervous fit over the shock. Miss Claudia would never forgive me if I caused him to relapse.

"My fair Mrs. Jacobs. To what do I owe the pleasure?" He laughed and then went into a coughing fit.

"It's your Mama. Nothing serious. Well, we hope not." As I presented the facts as I knew them, he was silent. "Blueberry Hill" played softly in the background.

"Patricia usually handles all Mama's health matters."

"Yeah. Well remember her and Doctor Tom are down at that convention." I pictured Patricia at a luau that very minute, walking around poles with fire at the ends of them. "Now you've got to help me here. I need . . ."

"Hospitals and I don't get along. My nerves can't take the ruckus."

Neither could mine. "Man, nobody's asking you to worry yourself by coming down here." I saw Gerald turn around and look at me. "I'm sorry, I'm just real tired. Now let's start with her birth date. Do you know that?"

By the time Richard massaged his memory and provided the necessary information for the hospital forms, Gerald had already called Marcie and his pastor. "They got a prayer chain going right now," he said with tremendous confidence.

I knew most Miss Claudia wouldn't want everybody all in her business, but decided it might make him feel better and didn't say any more.

We sat there in the waiting-room chairs with connecting steel arms and watched the pimple-scarred supremacist rant and rave over the airwaves. "Thanks," I said when Gerald turned the television off. We were the only ones in the room, and the black lady sure did not object when the screams of insult were replaced by silence.

Who could I call? I didn't want to call Kasi because I figured she'd be all dramatic and make Cher believe Miss Claudia was fixing to die. So I just sat there. Without any prayer circle. My last prayer had been with Miss Claudia for Suzette and LaRue. A total waste of our time. God's too, for that matter. *Missoura*, I suddenly remembered and stood up. I'll call the lady who first taught Miss Claudia to pray. Only thing was, I couldn't remember her last name, and with no phone number I would have to call directory assistance.

I'm making me a notebook full of key information

about Miss Claudia when this is over. I sat back down with my arms folded. I was ashamed of my slouchiness in caring for my employer, my companion. The clock went through two spins of its hour hand while I mentally filed away information on Miss Claudia from A to Z.

Gerald turned the television back on for the late news, and the weatherman was predicting a scorching day. "Really, you can go on home now. Cher is spending the night at Kasi's. And I'm just going to stay here." Before Gerald could reply, his almond-shaped eyes widened. The doctor walked towards us with slouched shoulders.

Dear Lord, please don't let her be gone, I silently prayed without thinking.

"She's real weak. She's lost a tremendous amount of blood. It doesn't help that she's anemic. Are you her daughter?"

Yes, I wanted to cry out. But I shook my head no. "Housekee . . . Companion," I said. "And I'll stay with her."

"Rochelle will give you her room assignment." He half turned and looked at the black woman sitting at the reception desk.

"Doc, what you reckon got her in this fix," Gerald asked. "I mean, everybody gets nosebleeds."

"True. But nosebleeds usually aren't complicated by leukemia either," the young doctor said. He never saw my gaping mouth while he scribbled something inside his steel notepad. Although he could not tell on the outside, I was in need just like the other patients behind the light brown doors with the red signs that said *Do Not Enter*. My spirit was curled up on that tiled floor in the same position we had found Miss Claudia in.

The ache in my neck woke me before I heard the new shift nurse enter. I watched the heavyset nurse tightly adjust the tape that held the white swab under Miss Claudia's nose. *Good. The bleeding seems to have stopped.*

As soon as the nurse retreated to the light of the hallway, I rearranged the tape so it didn't pull Miss Claudia's skin and put the bed railing back up. She looked so pale. The one age spot on the right corner of her forehead look bigger than usual. I stroked her hair with the palm of my hand, thinking she would be upset to know how awful she looked.

At six o'clock, I called Patricia. I was pleased with myself that I could remember the name of that fancy hotel in Marco Island. "Richard told me he was calling you," I whispered into the phone next to Miss Claudia's hospital bed.

"Lord, Erma Lee. And you believed him?" Patricia sighed. "We'll catch the next flight out, and I'll try to be there by noontime."

"Try not to worry about her. We managed."

"You'll never know how relieved I am you were home. Can you just imagine Richard trying to handle all this?" I heard Patricia snort from the other end of the phone, all snug in her cozy bungalow.

Patricia's disgust with Richard made me feel honorable and helped take away some of the guilt for not having all Miss Claudia's medical information. "Uh, one more thing," I said, looking over my shoulder at Miss Claudia. Her chapped mouth was open, and her eyes shut. "The doctor said something about . . . well, I didn't know she was this sick . . . I mean real sick."

The silence on the phone line was frightening. Maybe Patricia did not know about the leukemia. I bit the edge of my lip and searched for something to say.

"Who told you? Mama doesn't want anyone knowing about it." The same shrill tone she used to discuss Richard was now directed at me.

"Well, the doctor said something about . . ."

"Erma Lee, I have all the confidence in the world in you. Now, I know you won't talk about this. We don't want Mama to become a case for pity. She flat-out won't have people feeling sorry for her."

I almost told Patricia that Gerald knew, but decided against it. This will be a good test for Gerald's honor, I thought. "I'll be right here when you come."

"Hey." Her voice was weak, and she ran her tongue over cracked lips.

"Hey, yourself." I rubbed a piece of ice over the thin lips. "You liked to scared me to death." *Death. Why did I have to bring up that word?*

She slapped the ice cube with the tip of her tongue and cleared her throat. "I just didn't know who else to call."

"I'm glad you did. I just got off the phone with Patricia, and she'll be here before lunchtime."

"Oh, Lord. I went and ruined their trip," she said and

turned her head to look out the window at the bright orange sun, which was rising over a mass of pine trees.

"Well, they gave you a transfusion. Put some new juice in you," I said with a chuckle that failed to make her laugh.

She was so still that at first I almost panicked and thought she wasn't breathing. Her sigh made me know she was still with me. "This is the beginning of the end. I just know it. Up to now everything was just like normal and now . . ."

I refused to play games with this smart woman. To make her out to be some little child who stays in the dark while adults speak in hushed whispers. "I know about it. About the leukemia, I mean. The doctor must've thought I already knew."

The IV monitor beeped, and she turned to face me. Her hazel eyes were wild and glassy. "Listen, you got enough to worry about. I don't want you studying about my problems too. Now I plain won't have it, hear?"

I cradled her bony hand in my palm and was careful not to touch the tape that secured the IV line in the blue vein. "You're my only family down here," I said, not telling her what I really wanted to say. That as far as I was concerned, she was my only family—period. "It's not a one-way street. My problems just can't be yours. We got to help each other or this relationship ain't worth squat. And I know better than that."

The second beep of the IV machine was shriller. Her hazel eyes misted in tears, and she patted my arm with her free hand. I wanted to reach down and hug her so hard that the poison would ooze out of her system. But I held myself back, thinking that she might burst into tears and embarrass us both. "Now let me go get the nurse and tell her this thingamajig just hollered at us."

She giggled and dabbed the corners of her eyes. When I entered the brightness of the ammonia-washed hallway, I thought of Gerald and his prayer chain. I turned the corner towards the nurse's station and thanked God with my eyes wide open. I thanked Him for the words and strength that I had found inside Miss Claudia's room.

"Y'all got plenty of money. She'll just have to go to one of those hospitals where they do special tests." I squeezed the empty coffee cup to the point of cracking and then released it. "My old plant manager took his wife all the way to Duke University when she got breast cancer. And now she's back teaching school." My eyes shifted from Patricia's dark-circled eyes to the blue-uniformed women serving food in the Southeast Alabama Medical Center. I wondered if I looked as homely behind the counter at Barton Elementary.

Patricia rubbed her temples with her two pinkie fingers. "We've been through it and through it with her. She's adamant about this now," Patricia said. Her voice sounded like any minute she would take off into song, like they do in those old artificial-colored movies Cher and me watched on rainy Saturdays.

"Has she talked to more than just one doctor?" I asked and opened my arms on the table. I fought the notion that I was overstepping my place. Patricia was acting only a touch mentally stronger than Richard.

My shoulders flinched when she slapped the glass tabletop. Her diamond rings hit the glass as loud as a bell chime. She closed her eyes and smiled that big toothy grin. "You know, honey, I realize you're trying to help. But sometimes it's just a little bit hard to come in on fourth quarter and start playing quarterback." There was only one quarterback in this game. And only one head cheerleader. Patricia had double duty. I smiled sweetly and nodded.

"Now, you know we just appreciate you to pieces," she said, patting my hand the same way she would've patted the heads of third graders in the lunchroom line. "We just have different roles." She looked at her watch. "Oh me, I know you're worn slam out. And I need to go check on Mama."

In the hallway, Patricia reached over and lightly kissed the top of my ear. I wondered if she was trying to do one of those haughty air kisses and missed. "Now, you go home, draw you a nice hot bath with lots of bubbles, and just *relax*."

But I did not relax as Patricia ordered in her fakey voice. I picked Cher up at the house and headed straight for the library. "I don't want Miss Claudia to die," Cher sheepishly said in the car.

She needs rocks, not mud, I reminded myself. "I don't neither. That's why we're gonna fight this thing. And we're gonna make Miss Claudia fight too."

Cher was amazing on the Internet. She whizzed around that thing like she was driving a Corvette through an obstacle course. Before I knew it, she was making that computer screen come up with doctors' names from Montgomery to Seattle, all specialists on leukemia. I watched her from a distant table and twirled the key chain on my index finger. The foreign environment with its cases of musky-smelling books and humming computers made me feel as though a spotlight was on me and any minute a college professor-type fellow would come out from behind a shelf and say, "Go away. You don't belong here."

"While Cher's on the computer, why don't we pull some books," Mrs. MacIntyre said behind me. I followed her blouse of yellow hummingbirds and couldn't help but feel proud that the librarian knew Cher's name. When I was going to school that was always a sign of a real smart girl, a good girl. All the same, for the sake of privacy I warned Cher not to tell the librarian Miss Claudia was the patient. "My great-grandmother's got leukemia," Cher told a frowning Mrs. MacIntyre.

The days that followed were a bonding experience for Cher and me. Every day after school, she would come home with a new printout from MedLine or some other Internet page describing the latest in leukemia research and treatment. Mostly the words seemed to run together in some mixed-up language. But since I always made good marks in science, I found it all interesting whether I knew what it meant or not.

Instead of battling over LaRue or Cher's self-appointed new last name, we spent our evenings reviewing papers and books with coded graphs and illustrations. Lymph nodes, immuno-suppressive therapy, T-cells, and blasts were road signs for our mission. Chronic myelogenous leukemia, according to a heavy book with a black cover, was not a fast killer. "Sometimes people live for five, even maybe ten years after they get it," Cher read. She leaned over the book with her hands stuffed inside the back pockets of her cut-off jeans. I knew by the way her wild brown eyes gazed up at me she was seeking reassurance. I held the fat book and ran my finger under the words that streamed together like Chinese. "How 'bout that," I said and handed the book back to her.

But it was the part in the book on blasts that worried me. The section I hoped Cher had overlooked. Later when Cher was asleep, I sat at the dinette table, and the low-hanging light cast shadows on the cell charts. My finger slowly crept along the pages and delivered me to a destination of worry. *Blasts, the point in leukemia when the white blood cells take over the bone marrow and prevent the marrow from making enough of the cells and platelets. The blasts overwhelm the system: the white cells needed to fight infection, the red cells that carry oxygen, and the platelets that help blood clot.*

My eyes locked on the words that predicted the blasts would take over Miss Claudia's organs and glands. I looked into the darkness beyond my kitchen window and saw the orange outline of Kasi's truck across the street. Under the hum of the lightbulb, I added blasts to my mental list of enemies, right under LaRue and Bozo.

• • •

"I just need my rest," Miss Claudia said the second day home from the hospital. I closed the bedroom door and stood still, listening to her breathe and feeling helpless. Her sinking spell, as she called the hospital episode, put my butt in gear. While most of the stuff Cher lugged home from the library was over my head, I did find something I could make sense out of—good groceries. Cher checked out a book on nutrition for leukemia patients, and soon I found myself in Winn-Dixie squabbling with the produce manager over the spinach. The acne-scarred man never understood why the nutrition book said spinach had to be a bright green, not a dull color.

Driving to Gerald's one Saturday afternoon, I stopped by a vegetable stand that an old man ran at the edge of his farm and bought a mess of squash and a watermelon. But my feasts were only successful in spoiling Richard. "I want you to get some more squash. That was the freshest mess of squash," Richard said, getting up from the table with his half-tucked napkin sliding down the front of his pants. I ignored his request and studied the dark yellow squash and chips of cooked onion, which had been creatively moved around on the plate Miss Claudia left outside her bedroom door. Nothing I did made her eat or even crack a remark. Her only communication with me was an occasional, "When you get a minute, could I have some more tea?" And when I knocked on her door with a crystal pitcher of sweet tea and a glass of ice, she'd faintly say, "Just leave it by the door. I'll get it directly."

• • •

"She just ain't acting right," I told Gerald.

At first I thought he was ignoring me when I saw him cast his spinning rod in the center of the murky pond. He had called me early that Saturday with an invitation to go to the weed-infested spot known to Wiregrass natives as "Kingfish Hole."

"Well, she just probably don't want you feeling sorry for her," Gerald said, reeling his shiny silver rod.

"I just don't understand why she won't take treatment. I keep putting papers that Cher finds on that computer under her door. You know, about new medicine and stuff," I said, looking down at the knee-high weeds around me.

"Dog," he yelled and quickly reeled in his limp line. "That was a big 'un." The light thud of the line weight hitting water made a ripple across the black surface. "She's lived a good life. She knows where she's going."

I put my hand on my jeans and held the grooved cane pole with my other hand. "Yeah. She's gonna die is where she's headed. I can't believe . . ."

He stopped reeling his line for a second and looked at me. His mouth was partly open, and the brim of his blue Ford cap cast a shadow over his eyes. Even his mouth was good-looking. The tickle of his mustache was still fresh in my mind. I looked quickly away at my bobbing red-and-white cork. Nibbling. That's all I ever get.

"No, she knows she's going to heaven," he said as matter-of-fact as if he had been giving me the time.

I glanced at him, but he was mumbling something undetectable and reeling his line back to shore. "Dadgum it," he said and stomped his foot.

His ways and tongue were foreign to me. *How could he be so confident in thinking he knew everything about Miss Claudia? Most likely he thought the same of his first wife. That she was safe and secure in a land of peace. Probably why he doesn't drown himself in drink.*

The second time he stomped his foot in protest, I let go of figuring him out and laughed.

"Hey, hey," he said, pointing at the spot where my cork had disappeared under the water's surface. The pole bent forward, and the weight at the end made me think that the pole would surely break in half. The slick pole pulsated in my hand, and I leaned towards the lake. My mind told me to give up and realize whatever had snatched onto my line would get away. Gerald stood behind me and gripped the pole. His hands were warm and rough on top of mine.

"No, let loose. I want to do it myself," I yelled. I grunted and moaned, pulling the heavy pole upward and towards the pond's bank. Before I knew it, the water was splashing around the edge of the lily pads. "No," I screamed when my wrists began to burn. I gritted my teeth and lifted the heavy pole over my shoulder.

Gerald held the big-eyed bass by the corners of its mouth. "I bet you he's a six-pounder."

Driving home in Gerald's truck with my prize secured in the orange cooler, I removed the rubber band and let my hair take off in a fury. Wind swept through the open windows and lifted the ends of my hair on a wild ride. "Well, ain't you something," Gerald said and brushed the corner of his mustache.

Each breath from the hard-hitting wind filled me with energy. There had been too many times in my life when I had wasted time thinking about opportunities that nibbled but never bit. I concentrated on all the good things that were happening in my life—my new life. And Miss Claudia was at the top of the list. She would not nibble and retreat. She would stay with me, I would catch her completely. I was determined more than ever to get her out of her box, the one she crafted behind the mahogany door on Elm Drive.

Sixteen

"*N*ow, this is her ulcer medicine," Patricia said, holding up the prescription bottle in Miss Claudia's living room like she was doing a Mary Kay sales pitch. "And these are her blood pills," she said. Patricia held the bottle at arm's length and read the label. She nodded and placed the bottle with the others on the silver platter. "Now Erma Lee, I only want you handling the medicine."

I nodded and sighed softly. The house on Elm Drive had been under Patricia's rule ever since Miss Claudia went into hibernation. Every time she called from school wanting to know an update, I felt like hanging up on her. But then I would remind myself that the strangeness in the home would pass and soon Miss Claudia would be back to her old self.

"Now, I don't want Richard touching these bottles," Patricia said with her hand cupped to her mouth. "Last time when Mama was having ulcer problems, he gave her a hormone pill." The red lips parted, and her eyes rolled up to the penciled eyebrows.

The rows of orange bottles reminded me of Miss Claudia's age and condition. *Blasts,* I thought and quickly pushed the negative thinking out of my mind, choosing instead to think of the prized catfish. Even at eighty, Miss Claudia was "so happening," as Cher described her best. Only I hated that silver tray lined with prescription bottles.

"She's just down in the dumps," Patricia would whisper and pull the bedroom door behind her. Usually I stood in the hallway, leaning slightly to try to catch a glimpse of Miss Claudia before the heavy door slammed shut. I only managed a peek of her burgundy wingback chair. So often I wanted to knock Patricia out of the way and walk right in. If I could, I'd tell Miss Claudia something cute I heard one of the kids say in the lunchroom line. She always liked their young outlooks on life and often would repeat their comments days afterward.

After two weeks, I began to worry that the stuff I shared with Miss Claudia about Cher's troubled start in life and the lies I told her about Suzette and her not being in prison had damaged our relationship. The tension was only made stronger by Patricia. She would

191

shake her puffed-out hair and stick her lips out like a pouting child. "Not today," she would say each time I asked if I could see Miss Claudia. "She's asked for privacy." My lip was slit from the steady clamping of my teeth.

I am only hired help, I would remind myself and then ball the dish towel, throwing it as hard as I could into the sink.

The creaks and pops of the trailer siding would echo while I laid still in bed trying to get inside Miss Claudia's mind. She had refused treatment for her leukemia, she was not eating hardly anything, and now she had gone against her very nature and become a hermit.

Her good-looking pastor with wavy black hair was not even invited in to see her. The poor man had no clue what was really running through Miss Claudia's blood. "Just simple anemia," Patricia told him when he asked about her mama's condition. One day after I had been staring at the pastor's shiny white teeth, I found myself calling out to Miss Claudia's God. "Show her some mercy," I said, as if a friend had been standing at her doorway. "You're the only one who can get behind that heavy door and pull her out of this."

Gerald was patient while I worked on strategies to reach Miss Claudia. And every time the latest plan failed, he would silently listen to my discouraging words on the other end of the phone. If Marcie was at his house fixing his supper or washing his clothes, she always answered the phone. I would promptly hang up before she could get the word *hello* out of her mouth. I could only worry about so many things at one time, and whether his prissy daughter really did or did not like me was one thing I couldn't take at that time.

Along with steak supper on Friday and Saturday nights, the Houston County horse show arena became another tradition for Gerald and me. As vice-president of the Rough Riders Horseman's Association, Gerald made sure the sand arena was tilled and all the bulbs in the stadium lights worked properly. Two Saturday nights a month, the arena was set up for pole-bending and barrel-racing competition. Cher would even skip skating and join us. I like how it felt having her seated in the truck between Gerald and me as we pulled into the arena's gravel driveway.

While me and Gerald sat above the arena in the stadium seats, cheering Donnie on during the barrel races, Cher walked alongside the horse trailers. She would talk to the owners and admire the horses tied to the side of the trailers. The trailers were directly opposite the stadium seats, and if she disappeared for more than thirty minutes, I'd stand up until I spotted her over the trailer tops. "You're as bad as an old mother hen," Gerald would tease me.

For acting so low-key the rest of the time, Donnie sure got worked into a frenzy during the pole-bending event. He'd stick his skinny butt up in the saddle and lean over his horse, guiding the animal around each pole. "Yip yip yip yip," he'd yell when circling the last one. I guessed that yelling explained why he had the logo airbrushed on the side of his trailer.

After every event, we would walk around the arena to the red horse trailer with a black Tasmanian devil painted on the side. The word *Donnie* was stenciled above the wild figure. Each Saturday evening Donnie would circle around us carrying a fresh horse blanket and getting ready for the next event. Cher took her usual place at the head of Paintbrush and was pulling his mane out from under the halter strap.

"You made good time out yonder," Gerald said, never noticing Cher feeding the horse a carrot stick she had hidden in her overall pocket. Donnie was busy putting the fresh blanket on Paintbrush's back when he saw Cher. "Are you stupid?" He snatched the carrot from Cher's hand and tossed it to the ground. "He'll colic if you feed him when he's hot," Donnie yelled. The horse raised his ears and lifted his brown head, still chewing the few bits of his forbidden treat.

Cher took two steps backwards and rubbed the sweetness of the carrot on her overalls. "Sorry. I just . . ."

My tongue was weary from being bitten at Miss Claudia's, and I was not about to bite it someplace I was not getting paid for. I moved closer to Cher.

"Ain't no need to get your panties in a wad," Gerald stepped forward and clamped his wide palm on Donnie's bony shoulder. "She's just learning about horses. Ain't you, Cher?"

I saw Gerald's fingers squeeze in around the skin that protected Donnie's shoulder blade. Donnie gasped and managed to spit out, "Sorry," before Gerald released the bone.

Gerald hadn't yet turned on his blinker to the Westgate Trailer Park entrance when he turned to look at me. "How about y'all come go to church with me in the morning?"

I could feel Cher's brown eyes fixated on me, wondering what my response would be. My foot nervously tapped on the floorboard. A man like Gerald, with his own prayer chain, probably thought all good women went to church. His first wife even went to Wednesday night prayer meetings too. I looked over at Cher.

"That sounds real nice." Cher wrinkled her brow and cut her eyes away. By my sweet tone Gerald must've thought I was the best peanut-brittle maker on Homecoming Sunday.

Nestled among a dozen oak trees and a patch of pines, Wiregrass Community Church looked inviting with its whitewashed block structure and small gold cross on the steeple. "The moss on those trees looks like earrings hanging down," Cher said when we climbed out of Gerald's truck. I had no time to notice such decorations. I was too busy pulling at my trusty white dress with big black flowers. All I needed was my slip hanging out the first time I met Gerald's church members.

"Foller, how in the world are you?" asked a little man with red whisks of hair on his freckled head.

"A. J. Ferguson," Gerald introduced the man while we stood on the green indoor-outdoor carpeted church steps. Three other men stood off to the side, puffing on their between-Sunday-school-and-church cigarettes.

A robust woman with loose brown curls stepped

195

from behind two white doors. Behind her I could hear the faint strains of piano music. She was at least sixty, and I thought it kinda funny how her long curls bounced and her dark eyes sparkled. Her head looked like somebody had cut out a picture of Shirley Temple and pasted it on a worn-out, lumpy body. "Oh, we got visitors," she said and handed me a bulletin. Gerald introduced her as Brownie, A.J.'s wife.

Before Gerald could introduce Cher, I seized the opportunity. "And this is my granddaughter, Cher Jacobs." I accented *Jacobs* the way a cheerleader would the word *touchdown* at a football game. The church house offered the perfect opportunity to remind Cher that she was truly a Jacobs by law and the last name LaRouche was filthy.

Later over a plate of Colonel Sander's original recipe I would learn Brownie's real name was Gladys. But ever since she was a kid, people called her Brownie on account of how bright her brown hair was. An identification marker that I imagined required a regular supply of Miss Clairol. Gerald knew all these details from his parents, charter members of the church, who now slept alongside Leslie in the cemetery behind the white-steeple church. I was grateful I couldn't eye the gray and white tombstones from the church parking lot and never strained my neck too far for fear of catching a glimpse of Gerald's first wife's resting place.

Lee Avery couldn't have been more than thirty. Certainly he was younger than any preacher I'd ever had contact with. Then again, other than the occasional funeral or wedding, that was not often. He stood in the church aisle next to Gerald's self-assigned fourth pew. The young man made me feel sorry for him by the way he nervously juggled his big black Bible from one hand to the other. Gerald introduced us, and I tried to smile real big at him, hoping to give him a little encouragement.

Lee had a pasty-colored face and a pointy nose that reminded me of a hawk's beak. He was nothing compared to that good-looking man of God who visited Miss Claudia. What remaining black hair Lee had on the top of his head spread out in thin pieces to form the shape of a black spider.

I sat there that Sunday morning speaking to the members of the congregation who wanted to meet Gerald's lady friend, as one old man called me, and I thought of Aunt Stella. She would've liked this church. But then again I guess Aunt Stella liked any church. Not even Mama was surprised when her older sister called that summer day and invited me to Vacation Bible School. Daddy had just left town for good, and if it hadn't been for the nursery that cared for my younger siblings, I could not have gone.

"All that church does is build up air castles," Mama said while I cleaned out her black lunch pail. "You gonna go there and get religion and then walk right out the door and get bit by the real world. You best learn to depend on yourself."

But as usual, I ignored Mama. Every morning that July week of Bible School, after Mama left for work, I'd get my brothers and sisters cleaned and dressed. "Y'all smell so nice and clean," Aunt Stella would say as I directed the fruits of my works into the white station wagon with the missing hubcap. During the drive to church, I liked to count how many times Aunt Stella would say things that were opposite to Mama's sour ways. How she would giggle at my youngest brother's questions in contrast to Mama's snappy responses. Or how on the ride home when my sister Lurleen would spill some of the Kool-Aid dispensed by the church ladies, Aunt Stella would casually reach back and hand me an ever ready napkin to dry up the red liquid. If Mama would've had a car that nice, she would've put a knot on Lurleen's head and one on mine too for letting the accident happen.

But Mama was not there in that hot, sticky car. The white station wagon was our oasis. While we sweated against the black plastic car seat and memorized Bible verses, Mama sweated over an industrial-strength Singer sewing machine. Years later when I went to work alongside Mama at the Haggar factory, I came to terms with why she was so jealous of Aunt Stella. Having a husband killed in Korea and no children were only minor inconveniences compared to raising seven children after a husband goes AWOL from his family duties.

The steps leading up the pulpit at Wiregrass Community Church were fancier than the steps in Aunt Stella's church. Her church steps were simple wooden ones. I know because I felt the stickiness of fresh varnish on them when I rested my elbows on them and joined the church.

All I knew that day was Brenda Singleton said her

mama told her before she left home that she wanted Brenda to join the church the last day of Vacation Bible School. My mama had only opened her black lunch pail that morning and asked, "Is this tuna or chicken salad?" before heading out the torn screen door.

Brenda had long slipped away from me and was in the embrace of the flat-nosed preacher. He kept dabbing his red forehead and nodding for Brenda's mother to play another stanza of "Just As I Am" on the piano while more kids migrated towards the steps. During the second repeat of the third verse I looked around in horror to find myself with my brothers and sisters and other children too young to make such decisions. The only other kid my age left in a pew was Bubba McAllister, the biggest and most hateful boy in school. The next thing I remember, I was face down on the sticky varnished steps leading up to the pulpit, joining Antioch Missionary Church.

"I'm just tickled pink," Aunt Stella said and nuzzled me into the softness of her bosom and underarm. "Your mama's next. Change is a-coming."

I'm just grateful that Aunt Stella thought gambling was a sin and never put any money on her prediction. Mama moaned and bellyached about going to my baptism two Sundays later. But after I had washed and dressed all the kids, she ran out of excuses. Little did she know her bickering only reinforced what Aunt Stella had told me about the devil having Mama by the tail. My brothers and sisters sat patiently in a line on the couch arms and cushions. I promised them all a candy bar if they acted nice. "I got no time to take part in your foolishness, girl," Mama yelled from the bathroom. I could hear the whips of the brush running through her coarse-cropped hair.

The horn from Aunt Stella's station wagon blared just as I was zipping up Mama's cotton shift. Like a herd of cows expecting feed from the automobile, the kids ran out the door and took their usual places inside the backseat compartment. I gave up my regular spot in the front for Mama and said a silent prayer for her best behavior.

"This is the day that the Lord has made. Let us rejoice and be glad in it," Aunt Stella announced before Mama could close the car door.

"I'll rejoice," Mama said, slamming the door, "whenever you get this thing moving and get some wind circulating. I'm 'bout to burn slam up."

The Pearl River was nothing new for me. Before Daddy left, while I could still be a kid, I went to the river all the time. I loved riding the tire swing and falling carelessly into the oil-colored water. It did feel weird walking into the same water that I used to play in, dressed in my only good clothes. When the cool water splashed against the hem of my cotton dress, I half expected to hear Mama revolt. "Don't take one more step and mess up that dress." But all I heard were the choir members humming "Shall We Gather at the River," while the big-faced preacher, who's name has been long lost, declared my membership into his church.

The dunk was fast and furious. It only hurt when he pinched my nose, but was over as quick as a shot of penicillin. Aunt Stella stood by the bank to greet me with her beach towel. A white one with brown letters spelling out the word *Coppertone*. While I hit my head to get water out of my ears, I couldn't hear all the amens, but I could see everyone mouth the word. Everyone but Mama. She looked away in the distance towards the tree-covered riverbank. After the pastor presented me with the little white Bible with my name spelled out in gold letters on the bottom, I was hopeful. I cradled the good book in both hands and lifted it in Mama's direction. She casually shooed me away as if I was a pestering housefly and returned to her steady gaze.

Two Sunday mornings later, when I returned to my Sunday school class to retrieve that white Bible, which I had mistakenly left behind, I realized how I ranked in the church family. Mrs. Penny Jackson, my Sunday school teacher, was talking to the preacher about children who needed second-hand clothes for the upcoming school year. My last name rang out like someone had shouted, "Freeze." Leaning against the classroom door frame, I could see the white spike pumps and the baby blue edges of Mrs. Jackson's crinoline skirt. Her voice sounded so twangy. "Yes, my goodness. That poor little Collins girl. Definitely. Might as well add the whole family for that matter."

"What's her first name again?" the pastor asked.

"Erma Lee. Every time I see her in that dingy dress, I feel so sorry for her I just don't know what to do. Poor little thing. Her mama's just a pure heathen to boot."

"We've been looking everywhere for you," Aunt Stella said after the church service. She found me in the parking lot sitting in her station wagon. My brothers and sisters leaned on the open window and overflowed behind her green skirt. "I got a stomachache." I unglued the sweat-matted hair from my forehead and leaned back against the sticky car seat. "I just didn't feel like going to church today."

I continued to claim a stomachache every Sunday morning until I had done what Mama thought was impossible. I wore my sweet Aunt Stella down. Silly as it may be, I still stood out on the front porch every Sunday morning at nine-fifteen, half expecting and half dreading to see that black spot from her missing hubcap rounding the corner of our rooted-out driveway.

The nudging of Gerald's elbow delivered my thoughts back to Wiregrass Community Church. "Yonder's Marcie," he said, pointing to his firstborn with the cleft of his chin. She was standing at the front of the church talking with the pianist, a thin woman with bright red hair twisted in a loose bun. Soon a pudgy girl with short wiry hair joined them at the piano bench. Marcie put her knee on the bench and placed her hand on her hip. She was leaning over, animated by the group topic. Her back was to us, so she missed Gerald's wave. But the pudgy girl saw him, and soon the others turned to face us.

"There's Marcie," Gerald kept repeating as if he was seeing Miss America in his place of worship. In an attempt to satisfy whatever it was that made him keep calling her, I finally lifted my hand and waved. The energy it took to lift my hand could have been saved. Marcie's mouth cracked a little, and her green eyes widened. Only the pudgy, wiry-headed girl waved and smiled. The type of uneasy smile that told me she expected somebody to jump out any minute and say she was on *Candid Camera*.

Marcie never did join us in Gerald's pew, choosing instead to sit in the front row with her husband, Chase. After the offering, she took to the stage for children's moments and invited all the little ones down to the front. Marcie held the mike and tossed her long blonde hair behind her shoulder so often that I almost got tickled. It was like she was in some sort of beauty pageant with her legs glued together and her left shoe pointing out towards the congregation. Her right white pump was properly placed behind it. When she began telling a story about trust, I sort of felt sorry for this young lady who was queen of this country church. Could I blame her for disliking me? Here I was the lady friend, sitting in the same pew her mother had, probably the night she was killed by the drunk driver.

Lee stood behind the pulpit, and his voice cracked with the frailty of an embarrassed altar boy. But any pity I had for the spider-haired man was soon lost. With each second he gained more momentum, and soon I watched as he confidently walked away from the podium. Finally he stopped long enough to sit on a yellow padded stool, as sure of himself as any night-club singer.

"Somebody once told me praying to my Savior is a

sign of weakness. Well, Mr. Gentleman, let me tell you right now, I am weak. I sin. Yes, ma'am, I do. Every day. I fail Jesus time and time again. But are you ready for this? Listen to me now. Jesus has never failed me."

"Amen," an older man yelled from the congregation. Before I could tap Cher on the leg to stop her from staring at the man, she had already turned back to face Lee.

"Jesus loved me before I loved myself. I told y'all before that I'm a nothing. Who would ever have thought Jesus would have called a something like me to preach his Word. I've done it all, lived it all, and lost it all. I've been so low that I stole money from my grandma's social security check to buy crack. But praise God, when I was sitting in jail after robbing a liquor store on a winter night, my grandma didn't give up on me. She came to visit me, and I'll never forget it. Her eyes near 'bout drowning in tears, she begged me to lean on Jesus."

"Preach it," Brownie yelled from the pew behind me.

"She said that she had prayed for me to reach rock bottom. She sure did. My own grandma prayed for me to be in jail. And then she told me why. Because when you're lower than a snake's belly and you're lying there looking at the mud, all of a sudden you can look up and realize that the Lord is your Everything. Surgery on sin's cataracts, she called it." Lee's chuckles made everyone else follow along.

Once the chuckles died to a few coughs, Lee suddenly fell, stomach first, on the stool's yellow padding. A few members gasped and leaned forward, probably thinking that he had a heart attack from all his excitement. Lying face down with wisps of his black hair dangling from his pale scalp, he held his microphone close to his mouth. "Jesus tells us in Matthew to take his yoke and to learn from him. For Jesus is gentle and humble in heart, and you will find rest for your souls. To rest. That's what Jesus wants to give us. He wants us to rest on Him, to lean on Him. And friends, Jesus will carry our burdens. He's the eternal stool we can all lean on. He's not saying you will be burden free. But Jesus does promise us a love and peace that passes our human understanding."

Cher was leaning forward, hands on her chin, with her elbows propped on the pew ahead of us.

"People, that's why I'm here today and not in the graveyard somewhere. I leaned on Jesus. I turned my soul to Him and asked Him to take over as leader of my life. Getting off that crack had nothing to do with religion. It had everything to do with me leaning on the everlasting Lord. Not religion, but a relationship. Not religion, but a servantship. Not religion, but a friendship."

"Amen," Gerald softly said. I doubt anyone else other than me heard him. But I did not flinch. The unattractive young man's words cut through my ears like a scalpel. Somewhere in a Louisiana prison my daughter sat at the level of a snake and needed to hear this message. I pictured her soul empty and drained.

"And don't sit there thinking who else needs to hear this message," Lee said, suddenly standing. A few sprigs of his hair still stood on end like he had undergone an electric shock. "We're all the same in God's sight. We all have to take the same step regardless of our circumstance."

"The church is not a place for anybody who thinks they're perfect. We're a hospital for hurting people. Do you know the One from Galilee who can heal the weary and bear your yoke? The Word tells us no one comes to the Father except by Jesus. All you have to do is call on Him. Ask Jesus to forgive you of your sins. Confess Him to be the great I Am who was crucified and rose on the third day so we may have eternal life in glory. Folks, the Jesus who died for us gives us a second chance. What truer friend could we have?"

Gerald's wide index finger, manicured with automotive oil, guided my eyes on the page of the battered hymnal through the stanzas of "Turn Your Eyes upon Jesus." The humble voices rang out against the steady strum of the piano. I was too tired to sing. Too tired of predicting, fixing, and controlling. *Hush, just listen,* I imagined Aunt Stella telling me. Gerald's low, deep voice echoed in my ear. "And the things of earth will look strangely dim in the eyes of His glory and grace."

"Mama wants a glass of orange juice," Patricia said the following Saturday morning. She entered the kitchen, the part of the house I claimed as my territory. She smelled of Miss Claudia's flowered perfume and carried a wooden tray with a plate of wheat toast. One piece was torn at the edge as though some tiny mouse had nibbled it.

I started to protest and demand that Patricia make

Miss Claudia eat. *Now we're at the point where she won't even eat toast.* I yanked the refrigerator door open so hard Richard's physician appointment cards slanted under the rainbow magnet. "All right. Let me get her some Florida sunshine," I said with an edge to my voice.

Patricia ignored me and studied the yellow legal pad she held out in front of her. "Oh, Lord. Doctor Tom slipped up and invited the Thompsons." The way she threw her teased hair back and fanned the pad in the air, I expected her to pass out any minute. I would step right over her plump waist and barge into Miss Claudia's room. "Lauren Thompson said she'd rather take a beating than attend Cotillion with Margaret Linville. And Margaret's daughter is coming out. So naturally I have to include her." Patricia's bright pink fingernail began scanning the guest list.

Did Lauren whatever-her-name-was even know what a beating felt like? I wondered as I poured the orange juice into the crystal glass. *And for that matter, did Patricia even know the black-and-blue souvenirs left by licks to the flesh and soul?* But Miss Claudia and me knew. All the more reason I should be the one seeing after her. While Patricia shook her head and scratched off names on her pad, I pushed the white swinging kitchen door open.

"Now, you know Mama's not up to visitors," Patricia said, not looking up from her list of Wiregrass's social best.

I wanted to lash out at Patricia. To tell her the secrets Miss Claudia shared with me. I watched Patricia's

207

broad khaki rump twist down the hallway with Miss Claudia's glass of breakfast, lunch, and supper. I hated Patricia that moment. Hated her for making me feel less than the person I knew Miss Claudia respected. Hated her being lucky enough to have a mother like Miss Claudia and not having the sense to appreciate her.

"Girl, you got to be either crazy or sick to miss Mel Gibson. You feeling all right?" Kasi asked and fluffed up her platinum hair in the reflection of my living-room mirror. The one with the red Coca-Cola logo on the bottom, won, most likely, by a member of Miss Trellis's family at a traveling carnival. Now the soft-drink-inspired furniture was part of the extra hundred-dollar rental collection I paid.

"No, really, y'all go on," I said, not even bothering with a reason why I didn't want to join Kasi, Laurel, and Cher at the dollar movie.

My mood struck faster than a migraine and caused me to want to curl up into a ball on my bed. *Come on, gal, you been through worse than this,* I reminded myself. The usual strength visited me for a second and then evaporated like smoke from a fired shotgun.

"I just reckon that leg's giving her a fit," Gerald said on the other end of the phone. I was sorry I even answered. Part of me hoped it was LaRue calling for Cher. I was in the mood to cuss and blame to damnation. LaRue would've been the perfect specimen. But I should've known better than to think he would call Cher. Their communication was always her financial responsibility.

"Don't worry about her. She's got a strong constitution." Gerald's tone sounded too fatherly, and I resisted hanging up.

A sigh is the only noise I could make. He made his feelings known about my worry about Miss Claudia the day at the lake. I heard the sounds of squealing brakes and fast-paced music. *More than likely he's watching TV and not even paying a bit of attention to what I'm trying to say about Miss Claudia.*

"Marcie just left. You should've seen this place when I come in from the shop. I bet you I could eat supper off the kitchen floor it's so clean."

I raised my free hand up in the air and rolled my eyes. "Well, I guess . . ."

"Her and Chase are going out to eat tonight. They got a new barbecue place. Old boy I used to go to school with opened it up. I was thinking maybe we could . . ."

"Uh . . . be right there," I yelled and paused a second. "Let me go. Somebody's knocking at my door."

"Uh, no, I better hang on to make sure nothing's the matter. You know with Cher's sorry daddy and everything. Go on and see who it is. I'll hold the line."

Instead of being mad at him for telling me what to do, I felt guilty for lying. I walked over and opened the door. "Hey," I said real loud. The chirps of crickets and a steady beat from a bullfrog filled the night air. Feeling stupid and nasty for pulling a trick on the only man who would help me if I needed him to, I dreaded to get back on the phone.

"Oh, it's Miss Trellis checking to make sure our electricity is on. She said hers is off. I'll call you back, okay?"

"Oh, okay. You going to church with me tomorrow?"

I ran my hand over my slick hair and rolled my eyes. "Well, I . . . Hey, I better go check my breaker box. You know, for any problems or anything."

I hung up the phone feeling stupid and more guilty for wanting to avoid him. The conversation exhausted me even further. I collapsed on the bed and wondered if the paralysis I was feeling inside was a sign of a stroke. *Who would care for me?* I then shut my eyes in horror, thinking of a mandatory return to Cross City. More than likely I would be put in Piney View Nursing Home. My only visitor, besides Cher, would be the occasional vision of Mama. *"If you'd listened to me and kept your tail at home, you wouldn't had no stroke,"* she would surely say.

My body was very still as I stared up at the brown spot on the corner of my bedroom ceiling—a leak, long ago repaired, but its victim permanently damaged. Maybe Mama was right. Maybe liberty and freedom were meant for the chosen few.

Freedom. That's where I was heading before LaRue stuck his head out from under his rock. Cher's phone conversations with him were never mentioned, but I knew they were there. Like that brown leak stain on my ceiling, Cher's calls to LaRue were things I wanted to ignore. She was walking away from me and everything I had tried to do for her. And now even Miss Claudia was becoming distant. "She ain't no different from the rest, honey child," I said up to my spotted ceiling. "All you got is ol' Erma Lee."

Gerald's pastor's voice floated through my mind. His tenor voice echoed words of freedom and support. Eyes closed, I lay on the bed and felt my stomach rise with each breath. I pictured the young preacher leaning on the yellow padded stool, his hair all spiky like Kasi's. Instead of giggling like I did the first time I saw the sight in person, tears began to roll down the sides of my face and drip in my ears. The inner strength that had gotten me through beatings, through Suzette's wasteland, and beyond the county lines of Cross City, Louisiana, was as far away as Timbuktu. "I got nobody," I screamed out into the empty trailer. My words bounced back from the kitchen.

Turn your eyes towards Jesus, look full in His wonderful face. And the things of life will go strangely dim in the light of His glory and grace. The words I heard at Gerald's church were as loud as they had been the day I was too stunned to sing them. Stunned because the inner strength that held me all those times before had collapsed, just like Lee had on the yellow padded stool. I wanted his stool. I wanted his peace. Gerald's peace. The peace Miss Claudia once had.

"Jesus, help me," I called out. "Please forgive me for resting on my own stool. I need you to take over here." The bountiful tears that fell on my bedspread were a backwash from a sewer system long filled with clogged waste. "Forgive me for my sins. Forgive me for always wanting to be the boss," I cried out. My arms stretched upward, not sure what to do next.

When I finally opened my eyes and wiped my salty,

211

wet cheeks, I expected something, anything. I tiptoed through my narrow hallway inspecting the paneled walls. An angel, a new body, a different view of my earthly belongings, I'm not sure what I expected, but I knew something was different.

The rabbit-eared TV, Cher's pink radio, the burnt-orange refrigerator door, they looked the same. But when I turned towards the Coca-Cola mirror and saw my bloodshot eyes and blotchy checks, I felt lighter. The reflection of my own eyes as they pierced through me was level with the red Coca-Cola signature on the mirror's corner. Examining the puffy brown eyes with streaks of red, I visualized resting on an indestructible steel stool. I pictured myself soaring over Courthouse Square in Wiregrass and around the Haggar factory in Cross City. Soaring on the everlasting stool, far above tribulation and trials.

The screech of the screened kitchen door reminded me that I needed to pick up a can of WD-40 at the grocery store. I held my hand against the white wood and eased the door closed. Suddenly, I felt like a trespasser coming into my usual place of sanctuary. *They really should lock the doors*. I made a mental note to get onto Richard.

Gunfire echoed from the big-screen TV, and Richard was sunk onto the sofa like some pitiful soul long shot out of his misery. The front page of the *Wall Street Journal* blanketed the top of his chest. His head was thrown backwards on the sofa, and his bare feet were propped on the coffee table. Richard's clipped snores were the only evidence that he was a living person.

Richard was supposedly Miss Claudia's attentive caregiver this evening. Patricia was a few miles away at her big home on the golf course honoring Wiregrass's next generation of Patricias and couldn't be bothered with caregiving. A Cotillion. A coming-out club, she'd called it. Now I was in such a club. A club with Miss Claudia. The floor creaked with each step, and I prayed that my new membership would pull her out of the haze that clouded her.

The big grandfather clock by Miss Claudia's bedroom door registered the time as nine-seventeen. I stood at the door with my hand on the gold knob and looked down upon the stand that Patricia had placed to hold plates of uneaten food. A container of Wendy's French fries sat on a rose-trimmed china plate. Dinner provided by Richard, I assumed. Funny, on the way over to Miss Claudia's house I was jubilant and felt like I was going to bring her back. Now, with the opportunity to report what happened at the trailer, I felt foolish. *She'll think I've lost my senses,* I thought. *What if she's sleeping?*

The coughs behind the heavy door gave me an excuse to enter. I was concerned when I heard the coughs, I would tell her. My arm pushed the door open, and at first I thought I was in the wrong home on Elm Drive. She sat with the usual red Bible on her lap, but the greasy hair slicked back from her forehead and the pale face were unknown.

"Erma Lee, what in the world?" She pulled at her powder blue silk gown and turned her face from me.

213

"I'm not feeling up to company. Now, I just need time and . . ."

"I asked the Lord to come into my heart," I said so fast I could barely keep my tongue inside my mouth.

The steady tick from the grandfather clock was the only sound for a few moments. Miss Claudia tucked her head down and smoothed out the thin pages of her Bible like she was dusting off a relic.

Because I feared she might ask me to leave, the words poured out of my mouth. I described the sermon, the emptiness, and now the fullness I felt inside me. She smiled and dabbed the edges of her sunken eyes. I didn't want her to feel sad about all this and, in fact, tried to act as though the last time I had entered her room was yesterday, not three weeks ago. She motioned for me to pull the wingback chair close to her bed. Her cold, bony fingers enclosed mine.

Miss Claudia handed her open Bible to me. The paint-chipped fingernail marked the spot I read. *Therefore, if anyone is in Christ, he is a new creation; the old has gone and the new has come.* I wanted to run down the stairs and toss Richard's newspaper up in the air like people do with confetti on New Year's Eve. Like a new year, I was celebrating a new life. Miss Claudia's red Bible told me so. The thin pages were lined and marked like a trusty road map. I saw how her road map brought her through the desert and wilderness. At a dead end with nothing but kudzu in front of me, I wanted to follow.

"Tell me the details again. You know, about the dogwood bloom and the resurrection and all that." I knew in my gut that she would either come out of her misty haze or ask me to leave.

Miss Claudia softly sighed and then formed her chapped lips into a, smile. Her words of hope eternal fell upon me with the force of driving rain.

"If you want me to, I'll go down front with you," Gerald said on the way to church. He'd been so happy when I called him with the news of my decision that he insisted on taking Cher and me to church.

I adjusted the air-conditioning vent towards the truck ceiling. Cher moaned and turned the frigid air back towards the passenger window. She hated sitting in the middle of Gerald and me, complaining that she never had enough room because of Gerald's mounted cellular phone under the dashboard.

"What you mean, go down to the front?" I thought of the sticky wooden steps that I had leaned on during Vacation Bible School. "I've already done that."

"Well, yeah. But you told me last night you just joined the church back then. You said you never really accepted the Lord before."

My newfound peace was evaporating as fast as the foggy spots on Gerald's windshield. I dreaded walking down the long aisle at the end of Lee's sermon. Suddenly, I felt naked just thinking of standing before the congregation. What would Brownie and the other members at Wiregrass Community Church think of me? The lady friend, one old man had called me during my first visit. The lady friend, coming to take the place of poor sweet Leslie, stolen away from them by a drunk.

And there would be Marcie to deal with. She'd probably run out of the church crying with the line of friends trailing behind her. Friends who had known Leslie and hated Gerald's new lady friend for snaking into his life. *"I bet she ain't even really saved,"* I imagined them saying in chorus, patting Marcie's heaving shoulders in the church parking lot.

"I'm freezing," Cher yelled. With one quick slap at the air-conditioning vent, the icy air stung my face.

At the close of worship that day, Miss Claudia's words echoed through my mind. *The Lord lives inside you now. You're never alone. He's your strength.*

While the plump girl with wiry brown hair sat at the piano and flipped through a faded green hymnal, Lee stood at the front of the church with his hands behind his back and licked his lips. "We offer this time as a chance for decision. A chance to accept the Lord Jesus Christ as your Savior and a chance to join this church by statement of faith in Christ." Soft piano notes began to drift over Lee's words. "Wiregrass Community Church sure ain't perfect, but praise God, we're trying. If you feel led, and only if you feel led by the Holy Spirit, won't you come."

"Just as I am without one plea . . ." Before the church members could finish the first line of the song, I slipped out of the pew alone. Part of me said to keep my tail in the pew. *Girl, you've been through all this before,* my mind kept repeating during Lee's invitation to come down front.

But Gerald was right. The first time I walked the

aisle in a church was because I thought it was the proper thing for a girl my age to do. After all, Becky walked that day during Vacation Bible School, and her mama was the church pianist. Whether I was baptized one time or two hundred, I was determined to make sure every letter of this contract was signed, sealed, and delivered.

My newfound church members were too important to risk dragging the late Leslie's husband down the aisle with me. Any woman who went to church for Wednesday night prayer meeting had to be a church member like Aunt Stella—the type who organized Bible School, kept up with the sick folks in the hospital, and helped cook fried chicken for dinners on the ground. Walking down the aisle, I tried to force myself not to think of Leslie. *This is a sacred moment,* I kept repeating in my mind. But when I made it to the front and grasped Lee's long fingers, I couldn't help but think I was probably standing in the same spot where Leslie's casket sat during her funeral.

Uneasiness was soon lost to the kind words from well-wishers who came by to greet me after Lee announced my decision of faith.

"Hey," Marcie said in a singing kind of voice. I caught myself opening my mouth, trying to match her excitement. She flipped her hair and lightly hugged me. "I'm just so happy for you," she whispered in my ear. The cinnamon scent of her chewing gum lingered long after she walked towards the group of women gathered around the piano.

After lunch, Cher reported she saw Donnie roll his

eyes when I stood at the front of the church with Lee. All that day, Cher's sighs and general bad attitude reflected an ugliness that I still was excusing as puberty. *Oh well, at least I had a whole bunch of people be nice to me. I just got to think about them.* I surprised myself with my enthusiasm.

"Mama told me about all the changes in your life," Patricia said behind the big wooden desk. Her teased brown hair never moved as she nodded and grinned. "And she told me how you came over to the house Saturday evening."

"Now, I know I shouldn't have, but . . ."

Patricia shook her finger. The finger-shaking told me to keep quiet and let her give me a tongue-lashing. *If it wasn't for her, I wouldn't have any money coming in,* I reminded myself. *Just smile and agree.*

"No, it was good you went and shared your little news with Mama. I'll be honest, I think it helped pull her out of that spell she was in."

I kinda giggled and felt foolish. "You mean it?"

"Honey, she's on cloud nine today," Patricia said and snorted with laughter.

Watching Patricia gain her composure and straighten the shoulder pad under her blouse, I realized that it was the unpredictability of this woman that made me nervous. Much like I'd get nervous whenever Bozo would lean against the open door on late Friday afternoons with a lone beer dangling from the ring of plastic circles.

"Oh, she's got all sorts of projects lined up. Doctor

Tom was just about to treat me to supper when she called, so I didn't have a chance for her to get into everything." Patricia wrinkled her nose and closed her eyes.

"Did she mention getting treatment?"

Patricia's chin dropped, and her ruby red lips puckered. "Now Erma Lee, I told you up at the hospital, Mama's made up her mind. She refuses to be throwing up all the time and having people make a fuss over her." She looked down and shuffled a stack of files. "She can live for years without getting to the bad stage."

"Yes, ma'am. But it's just . . ." the words were coming out before I knew what was happening. "Well, Cher and me have been looking on the Internet, and there's some good . . ."

"Honey, have you heard a word I've been saying?" She closed her eyes and offered another toothy smile.

I moved up to the edge of my chair, expecting to be asked to leave.

"Now, I called you in here to talk about something pleasant. I'm just running out of closet space," Patricia said. When she looked under her desk, I saw a hole in the mound of teased hair. "With you starting to attend church now, I knew you'd need some new clothes." She stood holding a big black garbage bag, its top tied in a yellow bow. "Since it seems like I'll never lose any weight, I thought I'd pass along some of my smaller sizes." Her nod let me know it was all right if I spoke.

"How nice," I said, trying to act excited. Thirty-five

years after Vacation Bible School, I was still on the needy list.

The lumpy bag barely fit under one arm. I used my knee to balance the bag and opened Patricia's office door.

"Oh, one more thing," Patricia said and pointed a silver envelope opener at me. "Let's just keep my generosity between us." She added a wink and a lick of her glossy lips. "I can't do for everybody like I'm doing for you."

Feeling the searing heat escape the gray trunk lining, I stood in the school parking lot looking down at my donation. The big black bag tied with its yellow plastic strip looked like a body bag in my trunk.

My fingertips burned against the top of the car trunk, and I slammed the lid down. The old white-and-black dress I took with me when I left Cross City was old and wounded, but I didn't have to strip self-respect to wear it.

Seventeen

A pearl white Lexus was parked in my usual spot in Miss Claudia's driveway. *One of the Sick Parade ladies from the church,* I decided and parked on the side of the street.

"Erma Lee," I heard Miss Claudia call out before I could close the kitchen door. "I'm here in the living room."

I smiled and pushed the white swinging door open. *At least she's out of that bedroom dungeon.* I was proud of myself for being the one who drug her out.

She sat on the edge of her chair. By the uneven poufiness of her hair, I could tell she must've done it herself. "You know my pastor, Dr. Winters, don't you, Erma Lee?"

The tall man I regularly watched depart Miss Claudia's home from the kitchen window stood up and buttoned the top button of his suit. His smile and dark eyes were full of appeal, and I felt my face grow red when he reached for my hand.

Just when he started to speak and most likely say that he had never met me, I blurted out, "Oh, I know who you are." I pulled the long ponytail around my neck hoping to hide the warmth I could feel. "I mean, I saw you from the kitchen. You know, when you left. So—"

He and Miss Claudia laughed, and I tried to chuckle, not sure if they were making fun of me. His gelled hair, dark eyes, and broad shoulders seemed at odds with my new pastor. The man that stood before me could be a TV preacher. I wondered if he had ever considered such work.

Dr. Winters pulled at the ends of his suit coat and listened to Miss Claudia go on about me and how I had become like one of her own. The hotness drifted up my neck to my checks. "And she just accepted the Lord too," Miss Claudia added.

"Well, fantastic," Dr. Winters said and offered the dimpled smile again.

I nodded my head and folded my arms over my white uniform top, trying to hide a stain of spaghetti sauce.

"Erma Lee, I called Dr. Winters over here because I have some exciting news. I have a purpose, and you're a part of it."

A beep that sounded like an oven alarm went off. Dr. Winters pulled a pager from his belt and mashed a button. "Excuse me, ladies. The office is calling. I'm afraid I must go."

"Oh, so soon? We have a phone if you need to check in with anybody," Miss Claudia said, pointing to the living-room table.

Dr. Winters clutched Miss Claudia's hand. "And I appreciate it, but we have some business going on back at the church. Now, I'll be looking forward to our announcement this Sunday."

At the door, the man of God raised one eyebrow and smiled at me. "And Emily, it was very nice to meet you. I do hope you'll join us one Sunday with Miss Claudia." He pulled his gold-and-blue-striped tie slightly out of his coat, and the material rose to attention.

"I hope so too," I said, never bothering to correct him about my name. *A man with his responsibilities had to be so busy*.

Sitting in Miss Claudia's wicker porch swing, I listened to her describe hours of prayer about the leukemia. Between clips from the automated sprinkler system, I learned her time in solitude was a deep depression over what she thought was surely a decline started by that anemia and the nosebleed. "Right after I accepted the Lord, Missoura told me that the best way to combat the devil is to get off somewhere by yourself and pray nonstop. Praying in the closet, she used to call it." Miss Claudia twirled the loose ends of the swing chain between two fingers. "I wanted to make sure I'm doing the right thing about not taking any treatments."

"Well, me and Cher have been working on that. We pulled lots of stuff off that computer at the library."

Miss Claudia put the palm of her hand up and closed her eyes. Like a schoolchild being directed by a traffic cop, I stopped talking.

"Sugar, I appreciate everything you and Cher tried to do. But in the end, the decision is mine. Now, I've lived a good long life. The Lord's been good to me. But I need to face this without being hooked up to all kind of tubes and urping all the time."

"But they got new medicine that won't make you throw up."

"I know all that. I read some of those papers you stuffed under my door," she said and patted my leg. "The doctor said it might be a couple of years before I get into the, you know, real bad stage."

"Acute," I said, finding the word I thought she was seeking.

She grinned at me. "You really did read all that mumbo-jumbo."

I looked down at my black rubber-soled shoes. She was not going to brush this aside like some little joke. Deep down I was mad at her for giving up, for not trying to fight the disease that was building in her bloodstream.

"I don't expect you to agree with me. But I don't want you having hard feelings towards me, either. I'm going to need your support. Erma Lee, I had a calling."

I looked up at her. Her hazel eyes were still weak, but her lips bore the perfect pink lipstick that was her calling card. "What sort of calling?" I asked.

The scent of Miss Claudia's favorite Estee Lauder perfume danced around the porch with the soft afternoon breeze. "When I was in my room I did a lot of Bible reading. No matter how many times I read something, I always pick up a different message." She chuckled out loud. "Well, after you came in and shared your good news with me Saturday night, I stayed up late reading the book of Deuteronomy. I read for the millionth time about the people of Israel wandering around for forty years looking for that promised land. And when I got to the part where the Lord told them, 'You have dwelt in this mountain long enough,' the words just jumped out at me."

She watched the clapping water rise from the ground and circle the rows of yellow butterfly bushes and pink azaleas. "I asked the Lord to help me move on with the plans He has for me. And to live with the strength to find His plan. Well, do you know, during the night I dreamed about a house. A bright yellow home with all kinds of women and little fellers in it. Kinda like a refuge. Women who been in a mess . . . you know, with men beating them," she whispered the last words like she did not want to embarrass herself or me.

She was silent, and the voices from the Houston County sheriff's office drifted from Richard's scanner.

His garage apartment window was open, and I couldn't help but wonder what mysterious explanation he would provide for Miss Claudia's vision. Then she looked at me with all the seriousness of a college professor. "I don't want you thinking I'm some kinda fanatic. But I'm telling you now, the Lord gave me that vision. He wants me to do this."

"I think it sounds real nice," I said. Coming from someone else, such a notion would have made me laugh.

"You and the good Lord pulled me out of that wilderness. See there, Erma Lee, God used you."

"Well, now I don't know about that," I said, shocked that God would want to use a messed-up something like me. Her vision was more believable than her compliment.

"That's why I want you there at church Sunday when Dr. Winters announces a plan to put all this in motion. And I'm going to kick off a fund-raising drive by writing the first check," she said, as self-assured as the best politician in Houston County. "But I'm going to need you in on this, Erma Lee."

Me? Was she out of her mind? I could barely pay the light bill every month.

"We know what it's like to have your flesh and spirit whipped. You can help keep everybody on track with what our women need."

I was silent and watched the stream of water circle around Miss Claudia's yard. My lack of education, training, and brightness slapped me like the water hitting the blooming bushes.

"I'm taking a step on faith here. I need you," Miss Claudia said and squeezed my hand. Her eyes widened, and she leaned towards me. By her side, the feeling that I couldn't do anything worthwhile evaporated. It just simply floated down the porch on Elm Drive and three hundred miles back to Cross City.

Driving away from the skating rink after making the first deposit for Cher's birthday party, I felt good. With the radio turned up, I tapped the top of my steering wheel and declared that I was living life at its fullest. I couldn't remember a time in my life when I had been free of major complications. LaRue was still a bad cold that Cher couldn't shake. But I decided that sooner or later he would grow tired and stop taking her phone calls. If only he knew she was telling her friends that her last name was LaRouche. Responsibility was the most effective pesticide with him. *Afraid he might have to financially support her, he'd walk away for sure,* I thought.

The next day, Miss Claudia pushed the point, and I attended Mother's Day services at her church. "My church service starts at nine-thirty. We'll have you over to your church in plenty of time." As usual Miss Claudia had it all worked out. Even though I was nervous about my baptism the same day, I gave in.

Gerald didn't seem to like her plans too good. "I just hope she gets you over to *our* church in time. I'd be glad to come get you to make sure you have enough time," he said.

"I appreciate it," I said, secretly loving the attention,

"but no sense in that. We'll manage."

By the time we went back to Miss Claudia's house for her offering check and the offering check she paid for Richard, we were late. The organ music vibrated the church foyer, and a bald man with wire-rimmed glasses kissed Miss Claudia on the cheek. "I just hate being late for church," she kept repeating.

The bald man swung open the wide, white doors leading in to the church sanctuary. Organ music swelled, and I saw Dr. Winters dressed in a black robe, sitting at the church altar in a big wooden chair. The church was twice as big as my new church home and had red carpeting with light brown pews.

I was hoping we could slip in a back pew. But Miss Claudia was determined to go down to the front. She was dressed to the nines in a pink linen suit and a white hat with a pink rose stuck on the side. By the way she had gone on about Richard getting up early to clip the rose out of her garden, you would've thought he had broken into a florist shop.

"Hello, everybody," she said in a stage whisper, waving her hand. Singing voices engulfed us as she slowly made her way down the aisle nodding and winking at different members of the congregation. *Would you just hurry up*, I wanted to yell. At that moment, I thought of Patricia's charitable contribution and the clothes in my car trunk. *Maybe I should've broken down and worn one of her hand-me-down designer suits.* The ol' standby black-and-white dress and Cher's sunflower outfit sewn by Miss Claudia decorated our backs.

I looked straight ahead and dared to make eye contact with the people standing on either side of me singing a hymn of thanksgiving. Their glares cut through the rayon dress. Probably thinking Cher and me were some pitiful lost souls Claudia Tyler found by the side of the road and brought to the church house to be redeemed. *"And the poor thing with no husband,"* I imagined them saying. Escaping strands of hair tickled the back of my neck. Soon heat crept up my neck to my cheeks. *I ought to have known better than to let Cher talk me into putting my hair in this bun.* When I'd almost decided she was going to just walk up the altar steps and sit with Dr. Winters, Miss Claudia eased into the second pew. Behind Dr. Winters, I saw Patricia in the choir. The poor thing looked bigger than usual dressed in the cream choir robe. She held the black hymnal in the palm of her hand, and her mouth was wide open.

I turned to place my white Bible and pocketbook down on the pew, and my eye caught Prune Face in the pew behind us, singing a hymn of praise with the same tired, scrunched-up look that she had whenever she visited Miss Claudia. Since I had taken on a new life and wanted to do right, I smiled and mouthed the word *hello*. She quickly glanced at me and then, just as fast, looked up towards the choir.

"Let us rejoice," Dr. Winters said. He raised his arms, and the black robe spread like wings. "Many segments in today's society are in need of our love and care. Today, as we celebrate mothers across this land, I think it fitting to announce plans for a new mission. Recently, I had the honor of meeting with Mrs. Claudia

Tyler and learned how God has spoken to her about a mission to reach hurting people. In the week ahead, I will call some of you and ask that you work on a committee to see how First Methodist can help women and children of domestic abuse.

"And this project, I believe, is a worthy cause. If I may tell this, Miss Claudia," the pastor looked directly at Miss Claudia, raised his eyebrows, and smiled. "Miss Claudia shared something when we met. A play of words that I hope symbolizes our covenant at First Methodist. After describing what the Lord laid on her heart, she looked me straight in the eye and asked, 'Why should we keep love in our hearts when we can give it away for free?'"

Chuckles swept throughout the church. I kept waiting for someone to yell "Amen." Finally the pastor began clapping, and others in the church followed. My hands stung from cheering the woman whose linen-covered elbow touched my arm. Miss Claudia looked down and slightly shook her head. When no one was looking, I slid my hand on top of hers. Feeling the sturdiness of the diamonds and emeralds in my palm, I thought of her previous life of hardship. A life no one in the room knew about, not even her own daughter.

To Gerald's surprise, we made it to Wiregrass Community Church in plenty of time. Lee took me by the hand and carefully guided me down the small steps that led into the church's baptismal pool. The small concrete enclosed body of water looked more like a bathtub than a pool. I stood on the steps, out of the congregation's view, while Lee introduced me and told of the decision I made by asking Jesus Christ into my life. He seemed not the least bit self-conscious standing waist deep in the water.

A small crack that ran from the drain helped me forget the prying eyes of people who would be inspecting me. My loose, long hair hung over my shoulders and down to the base of my elbows. Just when I thought I might turn and run, I remembered Lee's sermon from last week. The one about the woman in the Bible, worshiping Jesus by pouring perfume on his feet and wiping it with her hair. My eyes left the crack when Lee's arms extended towards me. I felt like some kind of beauty contestant as he helped me down the steps and into the water to face the crowd.

When Lee spoke of Jesus' resurrection and how I was making a public commitment, I looked straight ahead at the beige walls on the other side of the pool. I did shift my gaze slightly to the right to get a better idea of how the church looked from the higher viewpoint. My view reached over the choir members' bald spots and big hair and settled on the congregation. I saw my supporters in the third pew.

Gerald had his arms folded and was looking real serious. Miss Claudia draped her arm over Cher's shoulder, and whenever she turned her wrist, her diamond ring shimmered with a radiant light—much like the light I knew I would see if I got killed like Leslie by a drunken driver or, worse yet, a drunken ex-husband. I didn't want everybody to know I was looking at them, but I wanted more than anything to brand the details on my brain. Deep within my spirit, I knew the day would be a hallmark in my life, like the birth of my children and the birth of Cher. I stood very still, trying not to splash water as Lee spoke.

Lee held up his fingers and put them side by side. He told the congregation how baptism is only a symbol. He said the real difference was when I asked Jesus to forgive me of my sins and to come into my life. Seeing how I really didn't mean it the first go-round, I decided not to tell Lee about getting baptized during Vacation Bible School. I didn't want him to think I was putting on to try to get Gerald to marry me or something.

"Baptism is just a public declaration. The heart is where it really counts." Lee turned and smiled at me. Then, with those two long skinny fingers, he illustrated what I was about to do. He tilted his left finger down and still had the right finger upright. His bony fingers now looked like a cross. With Lee standing behind me, I went under the water. I visualized that cross, the one the Son of God died on to pay my debts to the Creator. The smell of Clorox on the white handkerchief Lee held over my nose and mouth was so strong, I feared I might gag and claw his hand for mercy. But the fear gave way to peace, and I felt Lee's hand lift the back of my head, pulling me out of the water.

There at Wiregrass Community Church I rose that Mother's Day with wet hair and the smell of bleach burning my nose. A thunder of "Amens" bounced off the cinder-block walls. I wiped my eyes and felt refreshed, like Jesus must've felt when He rose out of the grave after hanging in torment.

The stark white Sunday school room was my

dressing room that morning. With a towel wrapped around me, I sat on a beige metal chair. The chill of the icy surface caused a shiver to creep down my spine. Staring into the blackness of the chalkboard, I felt a drop of water run down my bare leg. The faint voices and muffled organ notes of "To God Be the Glory" drifted like background music in a dentist's office. On the third verse, I knew I'd soon have to walk down the aisle and take my place in Gerald's pew. But every time I tried to lean forward, I could not move. My brain wanted my butt to sit tight in the metal chair. To memorize the clean feeling that the most expensive bar of soap could not match.

Miss Claudia seemed just as comfortable at the Golden Corral as she had been Easter Sunday when Cher and me lunched with her at the country club. Since Doctor Tom and Patricia went to see his mother in the nursing home, Miss Claudia had no one left to celebrate Mother's Day with but Richard. And his usual case of Sunday morning sinus prevented him from leaving the house. So instead of the fancy crystal and soft piano music of the country club, Miss Claudia sipped her iced tea from a gold plastic cup and listened to Marcie carry on about a trip to Charleston.

"I'm going to a convention for the Sheriffs' Association," she said with a flip of hair. Ends of blonde hair barely missed the brim of Miss Claudia's hat. "I'm Houston County's senior dispatcher, that's how come I'm going. And I just don't have a thing to wear." Marcie leaned closely towards Miss Claudia as if they might share a secret language.

After ten minutes of jabber, Marcie looked down to cut her sirloin, and Miss Claudia winked at me. The knots inside my stomach prevented me from eating more than two bites of chicken. I was grateful for Marcie's trip. Her bragging kept conversation away from Mother's Day and the absence of the woman who brought her into the world.

When I directed the Lincoln back to its proper spot in her garage, Miss Claudia sat still long after Cher had gotten out of the car. "Erma Lee, just remember when everything is right with you spiritually, like right now, that's when the devil will come after you with a vengeance." I halfway nodded and pulled the key out of the ignition, never realizing the real devil was only six miles away.

Saturday was so hectic helping Miss Claudia and washing my own clothes that I didn't have a chance to sort through the mail stacked on the kitchen counter. Now I quickly opened a manila envelope with Bozo's first-grade scratchy penmanship. Inside was a sticky note advertising John Deere tractors. On the note he had scribbled brief remarks: *My lawyer's looking at papers. I'll sign them when he says to. Tell Cher to behave.* It wasn't a love letter, but for Bozo any words minus vulgarity were a major breakthrough.

"Yes," I yelled out loud and wondered if Cher could hear me over the radio playing in her bedroom. Digging deeper into the envelope, I pulled out two cards.

One was a birthday card with clowns. Opening it, I found a twenty-dollar bill and the words *Love, Pop* written on the bottom. So it would seem like Cher had more gifts, I put it aside and decided to give it to her at her skating-rink party.

The other card in the envelope didn't have a return address. The sunflower on the cover with the words *Happy Mother's Day* made me first think my son might have sent the card. But when I looked inside, the bright blue words jumped out at me with the force of a rattler in a 3-D movie.

I just stared at her name and pictured her dressed in prison clothes and writing this from inside an iron cell. I took Suzette's card outside and stood behind the trailer, reading the words as though the bright flowers on the front were something pornographic.

Dear Mama:

I've been thinking about you a lot lately. Don't know if you know this, but I got my GED. Fixing to start taking some college credits too.

I got a new counselor who said I should do this— that I should send you a card. I'm still trying to get my head all cleaned out. If you will, please tell Cher I've been thinking about her too.

Happy Mother's Day,
Suzette

I read her words three times and tried to analyze the handwriting to make sure the same girl who ran away from home to marry trash had actually written the kind sentences. Her former penmanship had evaporated as a late morning haze in my memory. Almost thirteen years had passed since we had spoken. The day she entered the Louisiana prison system was the day I buried her. The rehabilitated ghost had found me.

Inside the trailer I took the card and placed it under my mattress. With Cher talking to LaRue on the phone, now was not the time to get her more confused by telling her that her mother had awoken from the dead. I poked the card until the words were permanently hidden under the mattress. Only then did I feel assured that the happy sunflowers would not shine out and be discovered by anyone lifting the edge of the frayed mattress.

I hung up the phone three times before I finally dialed her number. Then I closed my eyes and prayed for strength. "Hello," her thick-accented voice said. Her voice was heavy on the hell part of the word, and I wondered if I sounded as backwoods on the phone.

"Hey, Mama. It's me." With my eyes still closed, I tapped my nails on the kitchen counter.

"You done decided to come back?"

"Well, no, I just . . ."

"Then you must be calling for money. Now I told you back yonder when you got your nail mashed up, I ain't got it. And with you up and quitting your job . . ."

"Mama, I didn't call for money." I sighed and rolled my eyes. *Why was I making myself miserable like this?* "So did you get my card?"

"What?"

"Your Mother's Day card? I sent it last week."

"Ain't come yet. You talked to Bozo?"

"No, but I got a note from him. He was pleasant

235

enough. He even sent Cher a birthday card. You know her birthday is next Saturday." Mama never could remember Cher's birthday. *Why bother? Since she never gave Cher a birthday gift while we were in Cross City, she sure won't give her one now.*

"Well, you done messed around and waited too long. Bozo's got him another woman. They tell me she's a big shot down at Wal-Marts. Makes good money. Drives a nice car. And he told me he's gonna sign them divorce papers. Before the ink is dried, he'll marry that gal. You mark my word."

"Really," I said with an excitement she never caught.

"Well sir, it's just too late for you. He's done put you down the road. I just never did understand, Erma Lee. The man makes a good living. Oh well, it's done too late is all."

"Yeah, I guess so. Well, I got a good job here working at a school. And . . ."

"Working at a school? You ain't qualified for that."

The old bitter feelings began clawing their way up my chest. I tried counting to ten like I did when Cher was nasty to me.

"Hello. Anybody there?"

"Yeah. Uh, well, I work in the cafeteria. Oh, and I help with a real nice older lady in the afternoons. She's been real good to me."

"Mmm-huh," she mumbled. "You best be careful. They act nice, and next thing you know you're out of a job for getting all in their business. You and the girl like it down there? Your cousin Lucille's telling every-body you ain't called her or nothing."

"Now, I went by to see Lucille when we first got here." I sighed and smiled, knowing there was no winning at this game. "We're doing good. Really. And I, umm . . . got baptized today."

"What? You done been ducked once. Down yonder at Stella's church." Another long sigh. "For crying out loud."

"I didn't understand then. I was just joining a church. But now I feel good about . . ."

"Well, I know this call's running up a big bill. Tell the girl I said hey. After Bozo signs them divorce papers, no telling when I'll see y'all."

"No telling," I said and hung up the phone. Looking out my kitchen window at Kasi scrubbing the wheels of her truck, I wondered if Patricia and Richard knew how blessed they were.

I leaned against the pantry door and tried to mentally shovel the hateful thoughts out of my mind. The image of me signing the divorce papers separating me from Cross City was my strongest shovel. And alongside Bozo's name on the divorce papers I added the name of the woman who was forced by nature to let me come into this world.

Eighteen

The first meeting of the First Methodist Rescue Home committee was held at Benson's, the chain department store that was once Miss Claudia's late husband's Emporium. Miss Claudia had planned a late lunch to give me time to finish up at the cafeteria. Opening the heavy glass door to the store, I might as well have been escorting the First Lady.

"Well, looka here," a woman with tight curly red hair sang out behind the Elizabeth Arden counter. As soon as the woman pulled off half-glasses decorated with little sparkles and hugged Miss Claudia, all sorts of people gathered. Miss Claudia glowed in front of her audience.

"How's your mama and them getting along?" she asked the black man who kissed her cheek.

"Gracious alive, you've lost so much weight I liked to not have recognized you," was another comment offered to a woman who tucked her chin and giggled.

Fearing being crushed against the glass makeup counter, I moved towards the rows of clothes hanging on metal racks. Casually I looked at the tag on a denim skirt. I quickly released the tag when I saw it marked as seventy-eight dollars. Another sign I was out of place in Miss Claudia's world. A world where even a meal was a big to-do.

The Confectionery was located on the top floor of the store, and by the time we arrived at the little restaurant, the group was already assembled. I stopped dead in my tracks when I saw Prune Face seated at the table, frowning and talking at the same time. The two other ladies were recognizable from the list of people who called on Miss Claudia. Funny, they all sort of looked alike to me with their bluish tint hair, cut and teased above their ears. Only Prune Face and Miss Claudia had unique hairstyles. Prune Face's ashen blonde color that dried her face out even more, and Miss Claudia's pretty soft black hair with light gray streaks.

"I beg apology for my tardiness," Miss Claudia said and adjusted her lilac scarf.

I stood behind her waiting for instructions like some little lap dog. I took a step backwards and almost knocked down a woman carrying a tray with glasses of iced tea.

"Easy," said the black woman, balancing the tray.

"Oh, I'm so sorry." I reached out to help her bring the tray to the table. I could feel the eyes of the First Methodist ladies on me like hawks seeking a fresh kill.

The black woman's silver glasses hung low on the end of her nose, and she rolled her eyes up at Miss Claudia. "Lord a mercy, you better get over here and give me a hug."

"I planned lunch here especially so I could see you, Mavis," Miss Claudia said with her arm around the thick-shouldered woman. "How you getting along?"

"Ornery as ever. How you?"

"About the same," Miss Claudia said.

The ladies at our table slightly grinned and reached over to remove glasses of iced tea from the tray.

"Mavis, I want you to meet Erma Lee. She's my new companion."

"Lord, you got a full-time job trying to keep her in line," Mavis said and playfully hit Miss Claudia's shoulder.

My eyes followed Mavis's broad white skirt into the kitchen. I fought the urge to follow her. Washing dishes and cooking were what I knew, not carrying on a conversation with women with too much time on their hands. After an endless supply of chitchat about grandchildren and sick people in the hospital, Miss Claudia outlined her plans for the home.

"This home ought to be a sanctuary, don't you know. A place where we can build women up," Miss Claudia said, raising her hands upward.

"Claudia, this sounds just precious," Prune Face said, pouring a packet of artificial sweetener into her iced tea. "But where on earth do you imagine this little place being?"

"Franklin Martin has a pile of land he can donate," said Mrs. Larson, the heaviest of the group. She nodded, and a lump of fat bunched under her chin.

"Oh, he'll do no such thing," Prune Face said. "That man won't even come to church regularly."

"Well, we might keep him in mind," Miss Claudia said and winked at Mrs. Larson.

"Y'all ready to order?" Mavis asked, clutching a small green pad. She used a pen to push the sliding eyeglasses back onto the bridge of her nose.

While the others ordered, I studied the menu, carefully looking for the least expensive item. Nothing was under seven dollars.

"Doll baby, what you want?" Mavis finally asked.

"Umm, just a tossed salad with Thousand Island dressing."

Mavis put her hand on her hip and looked down at me. "A tossed salad? You know you want more than that."

I glanced around the table and saw the high-class

eyes staring back. Their saggy sockets seared my neck. "No, really. I just . . ."

"That's how she keeps that schoolgirl figure, Mavis," Miss Claudia said.

Mavis departed, shaking her head and mumbling something I could not detect. I wanted to jump up and tell her that I was an impostor. *"Give me an apron and put me to work,"* I wanted to yell.

"Erma Lee can help us to know what younger women need from this home," Miss Claudia said, smiling at me.

"She's experienced some of this, I suppose," Prune Face said with a quick shake of her blonde hair. Prune Face was thumping another pink bag of fake sugar. I stared at the mechanical way her wrinkled index finger launched from behind her pink thumbnail.

"No, Elizabeth. She's just younger than you and has more sense," Miss Claudia said. Her chin pointed upward, and the hazel eyes cut sharply towards Prune Face. The laughter from the other ladies caused me to raise my head. Prune Face rolled her eyes and tore the empty sweetener bag in half.

The cookout was all Gerald's idea. An early birthday present for Cher, he told her. For me it was a double celebration. School had let out for summer the day before the get-together.

The smell of burning charcoal and chicken fat drifted over Gerald's backyard. Various members from Wiregrass Community Church congregated around makeshift tables designed by Gerald. Marcie and

241

Chase were away at her convention in Charleston, and Donnie was watching his girlfriend ride in a horse show up in Eufala. It was Cher's night. My only disappointment was that Miss Claudia was too tired to come.

"Man, you went all out," Lee said and pointed to the white table spreads.

"It ain't much," Gerald said, tucking his hands in the pockets of his jeans. "Just a sawhorse on either side and a piece of plywood. Erma Lee got the tablecloths from K-Marts and arranged them flowers."

"Well, you shouldn't have said nothing. It looks like Martha Stewart was here," said Lee's wife, Sonya. She laughed and folded her arms over her chest. Sonya covered her arms over her chest a lot. I decided she must be embarrassed about the pounds she carried. Whenever I was around her I always tried to tell her how pretty her skin was. And every time she would lean forward and say, "You think?" Every time I complimented Sonya, I felt taller, a little more like Miss Claudia.

A.J. and Brownie helped Gerald flip chicken breasts on the grill while me and Kasi ran in and out of the kitchen carrying necessary dinner items to the table.

"I won't know how to act in front of no preacher," Kasi said when I pointed Lee out in the crowd.

"He's the same as you and me. Please, he's even been in jail." I didn't want her to think my preacher was some holier-than-thou.

Kasi closed the refrigerator door with her foot. "Get out. What for?"

I repeated the story Lee told during his sermon. "Anytime, you know, you want to come to church, I'll be happy to have you ride with us." I shocked myself by sounding too much like a know-it-all. The last thing I wanted to do was to sound like one of the people who used to knock on my door in Cross City forcing religion on me. "I sure ain't no expert. But I tell you, I feel the best I have in . . . well, forever, I guess."

"I expect that man out there has a little bit to do with that good feeling," Kasi said, lighting a cigarette and then pointing the red tip towards Gerald.

I stood on the back porch and watched Gerald walk with Cher and Laurel to the corner fence. He opened the fence gate and put a halter on Donnie's horse. Cher put her tennis shoe in Gerald's palm, and he lifted her onto the chestnut-colored animal. He fastened two ropes on either side of the halter and then handed them up to Cher. Seated on the horse, she held her back straight and surveyed the crowd. When her eyes fell upon me, I gave her a thumbs-up and opened my mouth real wide, trying to imitate a surprised cartoon character.

Gerald lifted his right arm high and showed her how to pull the horse towards the left. The slowness in his arm movements told me he was gentle with his teaching. He pushed the brim of his ball cap and squatted on the ground as if he was sitting in an invisible chair. The way he chewed at the end of a blade of grass reminded me how earthy and attractive he was. I couldn't help but wonder how different my life might've turned out if I'd met him thirty years earlier.

After supper, Gerald put on the porch floodlights, and Brownie slowly walked down the back-porch steps carrying the chocolate birthday cake she made. "Okay, everybody. Looks like it's time for the birthday girl," Lee yelled and began leading the group in singing "Happy Birthday." Brownie bit the edge of her extended tongue. Her ringlet curls bounced each time she took a cautious step down the porch. I watched Cher's expression and grinned as wide as Patricia.

Cher looked down at the ground and then back up towards the crowd. Her full lips formed an angelic smile, and the way her brown eyes twinkled from the lighted candles made my eyes swim with emotion. My baby deserved all this and more.

My body slightly twitched when I felt Gerald wrap his arms around my shoulders. He stood behind me and propped his chin on the top of my head. At first I stiffened, wondering how this display of public affection would go over. But when no one gave us a second look, I exhaled the concern and let my shoulders fall under the weight of his tan arms. The heat from his body and the steady breath against my hair felt reassuring. My hand reached up and rested against his wide hand. I squeezed his skin hard and massaged a rough place where a blister once had been.

The crowd looked ghostly against the backdrop of the porch floodlights and flickering birthday candles. But their glowing faces only gave me peace. Absent only of Miss Claudia, the group assembled before me was my life now. They put a blanket of comfort on me and made me feel like I was as good as anybody. In their presence ugliness vanished as easy as the sun, which slowly sank behind Gerald's pasture. *Happy birthday to you. And many more.*

Cher and her five birthday guests crowded into the small camera booth and pulled the black curtain. I looked at the brown skates underneath the curtain and imagined the shrill giggles that were erupting within. The same giggles that were drowned out by the base-thumping speakers in each corner of the skating rink. I tried not to worry about how much money Cher was wasting on silliness and reminded myself this was a special day.

"If you want them to do any games, it's gonna cost extra," the little woman yelled to me. She looked like a fifteen-year-old boy with purple glasses and short black hair cut over her ears. A haircut Mama would consider stylish.

The music vibrated against the beige-carpeted walls. Blue lights made the skating rink floor look like a flat piece of ice. "All they want is one game," I yelled back. "How much is it to do the . . ."

"I'll pay for the game," Gerald yelled from behind me. He presented a twenty-dollar bill over my left shoulder. I snatched the money before the little woman could reach up and claim it.

"No, you're not neither," I said, cutting a glance over my shoulder. "Just go on with the game and put it on credit for me." The little woman wasted no time skating away and blowing her whistle. Credit was something I had learned to despise. Far too many women had worked next to me at the Haggar factory because of its bondage.

To top the night off, I was almost forced into a nervous breakdown by having kids as small as six years old skate around me like trained circus monkeys. Every time I almost tripped over one, I hated that I couldn't afford to rent the entire rink.

"I wish you'd let me help," Gerald said with his hands tucked inside his jeans pockets.

"You've done enough already." He had given Cher a birthday gift of ten skating passes, not to mention the cookout.

Over his shoulder I saw Miss Claudia and Patricia enter. "Miss Claudia's here. Go get Cher."

Gerald waved towards the corner of the skating rink where Cher and the girls had gathered for their credited game. Cher and Laurel were skating backwards and forming the letters to YMCA while the song vibrated the building. I smiled, thinking of how Cher's own mother used to dance to the song and form the same letters with her arms. Suzette was just about the same age at the time. I turned to focus on Miss Claudia before the image of Suzette's letter could appear in my mind.

"For goodness sake. And I thought the cafeteria was loud," Patricia said with fingers plugged in each ear. "Mama, if we stay long, you'll be running out of here in a fit."

"I'm not the one with my ears plugged up," Miss Claudia screamed.

Cher skated over to the bench we sat on. "Come over

here and give me some birthday sugar. Or are you too old for such as that now that you're fourteen?" Miss Claudia asked and hugged Cher.

The five birthday guests skated over to where Cher stood and watched as she opened Miss Claudia's gift. Some of the girls cut their eyes cautiously towards Patricia.

"Oh, I see lots of my former students. What pretty young ladies y'all turned out to be," Patricia said, looking each of the five up and down like she might purchase them.

"Oh, my gosh," Cher said, dropping the brown box and pulling out a short red sundress and navy short set.

"That's nice," one of the girls said. Another rattled off a name brand that sounded like Greek to me.

"Thank you, Miss Claudia." Cher leaned down to hug Miss Claudia's neck. One of her skates slipped on the carpet, and she stretched lower into her arms.

"I love you, you know that. And I want you to come see me in these new clothes now," Miss Claudia said.

Watching Cher tuck a loose strand of hair behind her ear and pat Miss Claudia's shoulder, I silently thanked God for not letting Cher turn out like her mother. Her mother, who was locked up in a Louisiana cell and was so fried out of her mind from drugs that she wouldn't have the sense to accept a free gift.

After two weeks of working for Miss Claudia on a full-time summer basis, I was worn out. Not by the work-load, but from trying to negotiate a medical break-through.

"Cher found out about a new trial they're doing up in Birmingham. They say one man was cured by this new stuff."

"Patricia was going to help me fill out these papers the city needs after her tennis lessons. And I declare, here it is a quarter after three." Miss Claudia stretched her arm and studied the gold wristwatch.

I gritted my teeth and polished the silver teapot as hard as I could. Miss Claudia had been ignoring my every mention of treatment. Her lack of interest was worse than being hardheaded—it was downright stupid. That was the part that made me the maddest. All she wanted to do was play developer for that foolish rescue home.

When I would find the medical papers Cher had pulled from the Internet still lying on the cherry dining-room table without so much as a finger smear, I hated that rescue home even more. I even tried leaving clinical trial papers in Richard's garage apartment right on top of his trusty police scanner. But the battle of wills was too intense for a nerve patient.

Within days, her dining room was converted into a makeshift office. Church elders, city councilmen, and people from United Way called on her at all hours. Anybody who would listen to her talk about that home was offered a seat under the crystal chandelier.

"Missoura, we need this place something awful. I just thank the good Lord you and Aaron opened up your home to me." Miss Claudia placed the fat black ink pen down on the dining-room table. "If it wasn't for you, I'm sure I'd be dead or in jail, either one."

Missoura sipped her iced tea and cautiously glanced at me. The type of glance somebody might give a little child who had walked in during adult conversation. She cleared her throat and knocked twice on the cherry table. "You 'spect I need to talk to the pastor and bishops about this?"

"I certainly think it'll help." Miss Claudia leaned forward and held her hand up. "Oh, and be sure to get them to attend the city council meeting next month. They're going to discuss setting aside some money to help with all this. It's real expensive, don't you know."

Missoura slightly turned her head and wrinkled her weathered brow. "How you feeling? You looking mighty pale."

I refilled Missoura's tea glass.

"Oh Lord, I'm fine. Haven't had any more problems since that mishap."

"Mishap," I mumbled. Ice and liquid clanked into Missoura's glass. "She was in bad shape. And won't even talk about getting treatment."

Miss Claudia's hazel eyes were locked on me. It seemed like an hour before she blinked. "Missoura, if you get your church involved, just be sure to tell them the rescue home will be a place where privacy is respected and people mind their own business."

"I'll have this bed ready for your nap in just a minute," I said in clipped tones. The starched white sheets popped off the mattress with a quick yank.

The tap of her cane against the hardwood floor was as faithful as a compass telling her location. Would she lift the cane and hit me across the back for disrespecting her in front of her trusted friend? Part of me wished she would and put me back in my role as simple housekeeper. I always thought the title *companion* sounded too personal anyway.

"I think we need to clear the air," she said.

"Ain't nothing to say." I pulled the pillowcase off with my back still to her. "I got out of line and apologize is all."

Her hand rested on my shoulder, and I closed my eyes, pushing down the tide of turmoil that swelled inside me.

"I want to at least look at you," she said.

Biting my lip, I turned around to face her.

"I understand why you said that to Missoura. You think I'm making a mistake by not taking treatments, don't you?"

"No, it's your business. Whatever." I suddenly realized I sounded like Cher and felt ashamed for skirting around my anger.

"I know better than that. But I can't make you talk. If that's how you want to do me," she said with a shrug and turned to walk away.

"Yes," I yelled before she had taken the third step from me. "I think it's a mistake. There, I do."

She stopped, and her cane caught the edge of her Oriental rug. The end of the rug curled up to reveal a dark pad. She turned her head and studied my reflection in the mirror on the chest of drawers.

"It just doesn't make sense. You got money to buy medicine. You could go to some of those trials I gave you papers on." I dropped the pillow on the bed and slapped both hands on the hips of my jeans. "You can get better. You just don't want to." I sat on the naked mattress and put my hands over my ears. I took the offensive towards stopping Mama's voice. The voice I expected to hear any minute telling me that I would be at the unemployment office by day's end.

"I want to live my life the way I want to live it," Miss Claudia whispered. She was sitting in front of me in the high-back burgundy chair. "Do you remember how constrained you used to feel when that man in Louisiana would knock you around?"

I lifted my head and looked into her eyes.

"Well, I sure do. Luther Ranker would tell me what I could wear. When to go to town. When to have supper fixed. When to go to bed. He'd control when I went to the bathroom if he could. And the day I learned he was lost at sea, I stood on the porch of that broken-down shack and promised myself I'd never be controlled like that again." She balled up a fist so tight, I thought she'd punch me out if I tried to change her. "And let me tell you one thing, Erma Lee. I won't spend what time I have being controlled by some snake oil that may or may not make me throw up, that may or may not put me flat on my back in that bed."

I looked down and slowly shook my head. "But those papers show . . ."

"They show lots of things. And for somebody younger, that's probably just the trick. But it's not for me. I got my purpose now."

"But see there, you could get cured and be around to

enjoy the rescue home and everything."

She closed her eyes and smiled. "Sugar, I appreciate your concern. Really I do. But I got enough battles to fight with this mess without having to fight you too."

At that point I wished she would have fired me. The grandfather clock outside her door struck three, and I wanted to run before the fairy tale ended.

"You're mad at me, aren't you?"

"No, don't be silly," I said.

"I know you. It's all over your face. But it's my life, don't you know."

The turmoil in my stomach tracked up my chest and throat with the rage of a tornado. *Don't cry,* I ordered and looked out of her bay window. The bright green oak leaves glistened in the afternoon sun.

"Come on over here." She patted the arm of her chair.

I knelt by her chair and let her rub my cheek with the back of her cold hand.

"I'm going to need your support and your prayers," she said. "But I'll be honest. Most of all, I need you. We'll make it through this. We're survivors, you and me."

But I was tired of fighting for survival. I placed the side of my face on her lap and turned my head away towards the bedroom window. Spanish moss swung carelessly on an ancient oak limb just outside the window. Had it not been for the stains left on her navy skirt, she would've thought I was napping instead of crying.

A fine mist of rain fell when I pulled up to the building

with faded letters, Westgate Trailer Park. I ran into the white cinder-block office and almost slipped when opening the door.

"Careful. All I need's a lawsuit," Miss Trellis moaned behind the wood-paneled counter.

While making out the rent check, I listened to her describe the bad case of sinus she was collecting with the change in weather.

"How's that wayward home coming together?"

"You mean the home for abused women," I said, wondering if she had Miss Claudia's home wiretapped.

"Yeah, whatever Claudia's a calling it." Her nubby hand rested on the roll of her chin.

"They're pulling the money together. Still looking for a location." I zipped my wallet up and turned to go.

"They tell me Claudia's gone plumb Negra crazy. Wants to get all them into it. She always was the beatenest thing to make over a Negra. Next thing you know they'll be taking over the place."

Waves of her nasal voice sent a chill through me.

"That's just like her to want to stir up trouble. Always something for that bunch."

The bitterness was contagious. Before I could help myself my hand had already slammed the counter. Miss Trellis jumped backwards, and the black vinyl chair that held her tilted to the side.

"All that woman's trying to do is help people. I've heard you run Miss Claudia into the ground until I'm sick and tired of it. Your problem is you're so eat up with jealousy you might split wide open. At least she ain't some broken-down hag like you. All the time watching that TV and talking trash about everybody in town."

The plastic blinds flew sideways when I swung the office door open. I didn't turn around when I heard her say, "And they say you got baptized. Huh, some Christian you turned out to be. I'm a mind to evict hypocrites."

The worst thing about being poor was having to compromise. I didn't sleep a bit that night wondering what I would do if there was an eviction notice on my door the next morning. I could never ask Miss Claudia to let me live with her. I prayed for options and direction. Upon hearing the recording that my cousin Lucille's phone number had been disconnected, I realized options were miracles meant for others.

The next morning I went behind my trailer, my home with Miss Trellis's name on the title, and picked a handful of wild daisies. The bottoms of my jeans legs were still wet from the dew when I walked into her office.

She was sitting at the counter sipping coffee while Katie Couric and Matt Lauer talked about their upcoming vacations. When I entered, her beady eyes drifted towards the door.

"Good morning," I said and held the flowers up in both hands. "I picked these for you."

She slurped the coffee loudly. "Ummm." She patted her flat gray hair and continued to look at the television.

"I hope you'll accept my apology." I wondered if this was what Lee meant last Sunday when he said Christians have to die to self. Every inch of my self wanted to throw the flowers at her greasy hair.

Matt Lauer said, "But first this is *Today* on NBC," and then the volume blared when a man named Crazy Ed screamed about low car prices.

Miss Trellis took her time in turning towards me. "Now what you want?"

I forced a smile and repeated the apology.

She moaned and closed her eyes. "I don't know. It sure does hurt a woman to get cussed the way you done me."

"Cuss?" *Don't fall for her trap and create another argument.* "Yes, ma'am. Like I said, I worked myself silly yesterday. And just . . ."

"Working yourself over that Negra house, I reckon." Another moan and a drawn-out slurp of coffee followed.

I looked down at the once white floor. A dead roach rested in the corner. "I best be going."

She coughed and played with the white sailor collar of her duster. "What you got there?"

The bright golden flowers seemed out of place in the brown-paneled office. "Here. These are for you." I handed over the flowers, tied together with a stray piece of ribbon left over from Cher's birthday party.

"Well, I do know. For me?" She widened her tiny eyes, making them appear normal-sized. Anyone who walked in would've guessed she had just won a sweepstakes. "Ain't none my tenants brung me flowers before."

I watched from my parked car while she sniffed the

255

flowers. My neighbors lined their vehicles up next to her office and waited to exit Westgate. I cranked my car and added the faded Monte Carlo to the lineup. Ready to face the bright world.

The car-wash business was Cher's idea, and soon she and Laurel had all the business they could handle. They started with Patricia's and Miss Claudia's cars, and before long vehicles were lined up on the cracked asphalt in front of our trailer.

"Miss Trellis is going to have a fit," I said and counted seven cars.

"I've already thought of that," Cher said. She smiled and pulled the green wad of cash from the back pocket of her cut-off jeans. "I told her we'll wash her minivan for free once a week."

I didn't say it, but I wished I was as bold as Cher. She pulled in good money with that business. Only thing was I had to make her split the revenue evenly with Laurel. At first Cher put in to pay Laurel a percentage of the business, arguing that it was her idea to start with.

Since Kasi worked the night shift at Graton Electronics, she was around to keep an eye on the girls. The summer routine became standard. Kasi would supervise the girls from sunup to one in the afternoon and then drop them off at the public swimming pool, five blocks from Miss Claudia's. At five I'd pick them up.

Fearing someone might actually witness her getting into my paint-starved car, Cher insisted that I pick them up at the softball field next to the swimming pool. "You're late the first time and I'm pulling right up to the front gate," I warned. But every day she and Laurel would appear around the corner of the metal porta-potties right at five, their hair slicked back and their tanned feet protected by plastic flip-flops.

One afternoon during late June, while Miss Claudia napped, I slipped away to make my credit record clean again. The twenty-five dollars I owed the skating rink for Cher's birthday game was one worry I'd be glad to have off my shoulders.

The red-and-white metal building looked so different during the daylight hours. Rust collected on the grooves around the glassed front doors, and the dirt parking lot was littered with crushed soda cans, ciga-rette butts, and a beer bottle or two.

Hoping to prevent future customers from ending up with a flat tire, I kicked a brown beer bottle towards the woods. A loud thud rang out from the rows of pine trees. But my eyes remained on the spot of sand my shoe had dug up. Shimmering against the sunshine was the edge of a photograph. A clump of brown sand and two crushed cigarette butts hid the rest of the picture.

Thinking some poor child had used his drink and candy money to sit inside that overpriced picture booth and then lost his purchase, I pulled the edge of the photo out of the sand. I fanned the strip of paper, and specks of sand soared in the air. I kept walking towards the glass door, shaking the photograph, and wondering if the boy-looking woman inside the rink would even bother to find the celluloid's proper owner.

My hand was on the glassed entrance door when I

looked down to inspect my find. Staring up at me in Technicolor was Cher and the face I had cursed thirteen years earlier. The four-strip of pictures showed different expressions, but there was no denying the smirk that connected to the darkest period of my life.

His hair was cut short, and if I hadn't known better I would have guessed he was somebody respectable, like a salesman or a banker. Not a convict who peddled drugs, pushed his own wife into prostitution, and abandoned his baby daughter in a crack house. The same baby daughter who looked up at me from the piece of faded film.

The muscles in my calves tightened, and I leaned against the rusty metal siding. *He's here,* I kept repeating to myself, staring into his face. My mouth opened, and soon a mist of spit covered LaRue's smile.

Nineteen

*T*he little woman with purple glasses had already thanked me for paying the twenty-five-dollar debt. Suddenly I realized that in the stillness of the empty skating rink I could not use noise as an excuse for my loss of words. The only noise I heard was a man advertising new microwaves on her portable radio. She stood still looking at me like she thought I might ask for change.

"Oh, yeah, thanks," I said and turned to go. When I reached the glass door, I pulled the picture out of my jeans pocket. I held the frayed edge up to the little woman. "Umm. Does this man come in here a lot?"

The little woman ran her hand through her short hair, and it showed no aftereffects from her jostling. "He came in here maybe once or twice. Kinda hard to keep tabs on everybody and be the deejay at the same time."

"Yeah, I bet," I said, thinking that I sounded like a detective. "Can you think of the last time he was here?"

She turned and began pulling compact discs out of a wooden drawer. "Maybe a week or so. Listen, we just can't police every little nitpicking thing. People expect us to be full-time baby-sitters."

"No, I'm not saying that. Just wondering is all. So thanks, hear?"

Before I got to the edge of the black foyer mat, I heard her. "Then I guess he's really not her brother."

I glared at this little woman who was wearing the same red T-shirt she had worn during Cher's party. "No, he's not. And I'll give you another twenty-five dollars if you call me the next time he walks in here."

The next week the photo of Cher and LaRue stayed in the forefront of my mind. Each night I would torture myself with the truth. It became a ritual. I'd lock my bedroom door, cradle the gray shoebox, and pull the faded photo from the left black shoe. And then looking into his energetic eyes, the ugliness of LaRue's world would pound me again with a fist full of hopelessness and fear.

Nothing seemed to pull me out of my misery.

Gerald's calls were met with an I'm-too-busy tone of voice, and Miss Claudia's rescue home was nothing more to me than a rich woman's fantasy.

Even when Miss Claudia held up the newspaper with the photo of her standing before the city council, I only said, "That's nice," and continued dusting the porcelain dogs in the living room.

"Well, my land, Erma Lee," she said, creasing the paper for clipping, "you could crack a smile for me."

I never told Gerald or Miss Claudia anything about my discovery at the skating rink. They could never understand all I had to lose, I convinced myself. Repairing automobiles and planning rescue homes were top items on their agendas. "Just stop worrying about it and pray," they would most likely tell me. And I did pray. But another part of me wanted to prepare a battle plan. Just like those blasts I had read about on the computer, the ones I worried would take over Miss Claudia's body, LaRue was a blast on my peace of mind.

"If I didn't know better, I'd think you had a man on the side," Gerald said with a chuckle.

I managed to hold the phone receiver and turn up Cher's radio louder so she would not hear my words. "Now, you know that's a lie," I said, stretching the phone cord to the fullest length. "Miss Claudia needs me to help stuff some fliers she's sending out. Something about a fund-raiser for the home."

"Umm." He sighed and then was silent. If he was trying to make me uncomfortable, it worked.

"Maybe tomorrow night?"

"I've done promised Marcie I'd go eat with her. You want to go?"

"No, no. I think you need to spend time with them on your own. It's fine. Really."

"Hey, maybe Cher and you can stop by tomorrow. Maybe I can talk Donnie into letting Cher ride."

I never made any promises before hanging up the phone. My mind and stomach were churning in anticipation of the butt-chewing I was fixing to give.

My life was beginning to close up again just like it had before I moved to Wiregrass. Secrets and half-truths. Gerald would never know that the little woman from the skating rink had called just before him. He did not know that I was about to see for myself the spell LaRue cast upon my Cher. The sharp labor-intensive pains knotted my insides into a ball, and my heart beat so fast I thought it might rip wide open. A birth of deep-seated bitterness was soon to be delivered.

Slamming car doors, giggles, and the occasional wave of music from the skating-rink doors were my only company while waiting for LaRue. Crouching in the piney woods next to the metal building, I felt my breathing became deep and burdensome. On bended knee, I watched the red brake lights of various trucks and cars as peaceful parents dropped off their children into the safety of the metal building. *Am I out of my mind to be doing this?* I wondered.

Then the horror of getting caught hiding next to the skating rink popped into my head. *A child molester,* any observer would think. Me, a grown woman, sitting in the woods leering at unsuspecting children as they entered the glass door sticking dollar bills into their pockets and carrying skates over their shoulders.

As easy as a movie runs across a drive-in screen, the words in Suzette's letter inched along the ridges of the skating-rink wall. My breathing slowed, and I pictured myself as a lioness I had seen on the Discovery channel, still and cautious. I had no choice but to take it slow. Cher would rebel for sure if I stormed out and chewed into LaRue for everything under the sun.

A cramp formed in my right calf. When I stood to shake my leg, they walked out. He had the same cocky strut I remembered when Suzette first brought him to the house. His shoulders were pulled tightly back, and his arms slightly bowed. And he was swinging his keys on his thumb like he had no care in the world. Prison had made him bigger. He was more muscled than the lanky young man I remembered. His tight black T-shirt and jeans made every muscle look rock-hard. The black work boots seemed strange on him. I had never known him to work a full-time job longer than eight months.

When Cher put her arm around his waist and he said something I couldn't understand, I wanted to jump out and scream. But I just froze as they walked closer to me. *What would he do if I made myself known?*

All he knew about me was what Suzette told him and what he witnessed during the fewer than five meals he shared at my table in Cross City. The part of my life he knew were the chapters I hated. The one-time Edith

Bunker clone who took it on the chin more than a few times. All LaRue knew about me was that I never had the courage to risk facing anything other than the misery, which was too convenient to depart.

He paused to light a cigarette and blew the smoke into the heavy night air. The red tip glowed as hot as the fiery hell I pictured him facing. They stopped by a white van with a paint-spotted ladder attached to the top. *Most likely living meal to meal by ripping off unsuspecting widows.* Promising to paint their home and then, after getting a down payment for supplies, fleeing to the next town. Empty promises that Cher would now face.

His van engine was turning over for the second time when I fled the piney woods, heading back towards my car parked on the other side at the 7-11 store. Briar bushes pulled hard to hold the legs of my jeans, but I fought back and managed not to lose much time. My feet did not stop until I found the black asphalt of the 7-11. With the exception of a little tow-headed boy hanging out of a car window holding a robot soldier, no one even noticed me.

I quickly cranked my car and, when I stomped down hard on the gas pedal, noticed the green sticker weeds that dotted my jeans. The squealing of my tires was an accident, but I knew as soon as I pulled onto the highway I would have to gas it to catch them. Soon the white van with the ladder and the dent on the driver's side was in my sight. I squinted my eyes for a license plate, not knowing what I would do with the number. But I felt obligated to gather the information all the same. Typical, LaRue placed a "Lost Tag" notice in the back of the van window. The black childlike letters placed on brown cardboard made him seem all the more trashy.

The window they sat next to at McDonald's had a film on the bottom portion. In the parking lot of a strip mall next door, I sat in my Monte Carlo and mentally scripted out their conversation. "I'm making good money now. I want you to come live with me. You belong with your real daddy. Wouldn't you rather live with me in my big nice home?" Lies LaRue shared that clouded Cher's mind just like the window film that blocked my view of them.

The white van pulled up to the skating rink thirty minutes before I usually picked up Cher and Laurel. I circled the 7-11 store parking lot to give him enough time to drop her off. When I pulled out onto the highway, LaRue was stopped at the edge of the skating rink waiting to get back on the highway. I slowed my car and let him pull out before me. The white van bounced when he directed it onto the road and then sped off. My rubber-soled work shoes slammed down on the gas pedal. I swerved in and around truckers to keep the swaying ladder in my view. At the next intersection I saw him in the turning lane and followed.

The Garland Motel was as dreary of a place as anyone could imagine. The long row of rooms connected to a main glass office. The buildings were painted a strawberry pink color and made me wish for a bottle of Pepto-Bismol. A couple of the doors were open, and I could see TV sets glowing in the darkness.

While I watched from my car, parked in front of the office, LaRue got out of his van and went inside his rented room. Room 107. I repeated the number three times.

With the car engine running, I thought of what it would take to make him leave. To get him completely out of Cher's life. If I had money, I would've confidently walked to the door and lightly tapped. Being too good to step inside, I would've been careful not to touch the dead-insect-spotted door and made him kneel before me while I propped my checkbook on his head and scratched out his price. A payment to ensure he would stay away from Cher for good. But before the red light could come on my dashboard telling me I had overheated my car, I retreated back to the skating rink. At each stoplight, the old bug of worthlessness settled deeper. I envisioned the fever transforming me more into the dingbat clone LaRue associated me with.

"Did you see Diana Jarvis trying to skate with Tad? And I'm like, *hello,* do you think he's even interested?" Laurel leaned over and climbed into the backseat.

"No way. She did not," Cher said, fastening her seat belt.

If you'd kept your butt where you belong, you'd seen it too, I wanted to yell. But I drove in silence listening to them discuss skating-rink gossip like two Junior Leaguers in training.

Why bother helping Cher? Why try to lead her in the right direction? She's going to turn out just like all the trashy genes running through her veins. Soon the words that I received from Suzette danced around my mind. A reminder of the cost I paid the last time I had given up on my offspring. And now the Louisiana prison system had the pieces of the person I let break apart.

"What did you do all night?" She opened the refrigerator door and took out a liter of Coke.

"Nothing much. Watched a little TV. Talked to Gerald. You know, stuff like that," I said, locking the front door and reminding myself to talk to Miss Trellis about a chain lock. LaRue had probably been in the same cell with a convicted kidnapper and learned many new tricks.

"I am *tired*," she said between sips of brown fizz. "We washed fifteen vehicles today. Fifteen."

I wanted to slap the orange plastic cup right out of her hands. *You think I don't know anything,* I wanted to scream into her face. I wanted to pin her down on the couch and scream into her ears. To make her know about the level of danger she was putting herself in. "Why don't you just get a shower and go on to bed," I politely said. And then I placed the cap back on the Coke bottle and returned it to the refrigerator shelf.

The running water and the whining pipes echoed in my bedroom. I could hear Cher's radio playing behind the bathroom door. I stood at my bedroom dresser and looked at the photo taken of us at Miss Claudia's home during Easter. She was only a young 'un, I thought, caressing the photo of us with Cher's arm around my waist. But then again, Suzette was only two years older when she brought LaRue into our lives.

Roxi was the one who told me Suzette was planning on marrying LaRue. It was right by the snack machine in the Haggar factory break room.

"My baby girl, Alberta, say she's up at that school flashing around a ring and everything. I said to myself, now I know Erma Lee don't know nothing about this here." Roxi lifted the metal flap and scooped up a package of cheese crackers. "Because that child needs to go on and graduate first, you know what I'm saying?"

After work I drove deep into the woods to find Bozo and his logging crew cutting down money, as he called his work. I spotted him in the yellow skidder. His face was scrunched up behind the glassed driver's box. He paused only to wipe sweat off his forehead with the base of his arm. The skidder clamped the freshly cut pine trees in its mechanical claw as tight as the hold I worried LaRue now had on Suzette.

His face was redder than usual, and when he reached me, he mumbled something that sounded like, "What?" Bozo had ordered me never to interrupt his work except in dire emergency. The loss of my daughter to a boy I heard had served time in juvenile detention for breaking and entering was worth the risk of interrupting him. Bozo bit his lip and shook his head when I told him the details Roxi shared. "That sorry . . . What you reckon we oughta do?" he asked and leaned lower inside my car window. At first I stuttered, not thinking I would be the one to come up with a solution.

I remember pulling away in my car, bouncing over

the rough grades in the makeshift road and thinking how far I had come. Little did I know it was the first and last time Bozo would actually agree with any plan I developed without throwing a dish or two at me.

After I searched her bedroom and found the tiny fake gold ring stuffed inside a pair of gym socks, the battle cry began. "We love each other," Suzette screamed.

"You don't know nothing about love," I yelled back. "He's nothing but trash. Just some old thing that looked a second time at you."

"And what you figuring on doing for a living? You gonna have life as good as you got it here, gal?" Bozo had stopped by the Brown Jug after our conference in the woods. His words were thick and slow to depart his mouth. He tried propping his thumb on the grease-soiled pants, but then slid his hand down to his thigh for a sturdier grasp.

Suzette was crying and pulling her hair like something gone wild. "I don't care. I don't care."

"You better care. You're only about to ruin your life is all," I shouted back and stomped my foot.

"He *loves* me. Get it? You're jealous," she said, wiping her eyes and nose with the back of her hand. "He told me you'd act this way." Suzette lunged forward and stuck her finger in my chest.

Her unusual anger caused me to take a step backwards. I felt the edge of the round dining-room table across my buttocks. I had expected her to curl up and beg forgiveness, handing over the cheap ring so I could give it to Goodwill. "He don't even know me."

She leaned into me and screamed like fire might

erupt from her tongue. "Mama, he knows you better than you know yourself. You're bitter and hate your life so bad you want me to be miserable too."

"I, uhh . . ." The edge of the table pressed harder against my backside.

"You're so jealous you're turning green. I'm getting out, and you're still here," she screamed and lifted her arms up in the air.

Each word hit me deep within my being. My daughter knew the truth that I would not allow myself to realize. Thinking I might collapse to the floor, I broke one of my house rules and sat on the edge of the table. *How could she ever say that about me? All I wanted was for her life not to turn out like mine.* My arms and mouth were open, but words and sign language were not forthcoming.

"I ain't gonna stand here and let you disrespect your mama like that," Bozo said, pulling the thick black belt off his pants. He swayed inches away from the new TV stand. Each pop against his belt strands caused me to flinch, unsure who would be the victim of his fury.

"Don't you touch me." Suzette kicked her foot and pointed at Bozo. "LaRue said he'll kill you if you lay a hand on me."

Bozo laughed and caught the edge of the TV with his hand. "I'd like to see that runt try."

"Just let me go free. I want to be free," she screamed and pulled her hair again.

"Get over here to me. I'll give you something to carry on about," Bozo said as he grabbed Suzette's arm. Each strike against her bare legs made her voice louder. "I *hate* you!" The gurgled words rang out between pops of the belt meeting naked skin.

Calmly sitting on the table, which was bought with dreams of peaceful family meals, I watched Suzette run in circles. The scene looked like slow motion. Bozo's left forearm muscles protruded from under his rolled-up sleeves. I remember thinking the sight looked like a clip from a movie I once had seen. A cowboy breaking the spirit of a wild mustang. Bozo's hand swung the black belt, delivering conformity with each strike. Strikes meant to make her finish school, to make her listen to her mama and daddy like a good girl, to make her forget LaRue LaRouche.

When he hit her kneecap with the silver belt buckle, it was finished. She fell to the floor sobbing. Brown hair tangled with sweat and saliva hung in her face. "Maybe now you'll get your lessons and stop running around telling everybody you're getting married," Bozo said. He tossed the belt on the sofa and headed towards the bathroom for relief.

"It's for your own good," I whispered. Her cries had long been exhausted, and only a shrill whimper was heard. "I did this because I love you." I often wonder if she ever heard my words. My words of truth and experience. Tough love they call it nowadays. Two days after Bozo sought to break her dreams of love, I awoke to find Suzette's bed empty and a note on her dresser telling us not to look for her. By then she and LaRue had already married.

The water in the shower stopped, and the music from Cher's radio grew louder. I looked at myself in the bedroom mirror and pictured the red welts that spotted Suzette's legs. The recollection of fiery streaks of skin made me look away.

Tough love and truth steered Suzette into destruction. I lifted my head up towards the brown-stained spot on the ceiling and pleaded to God for wisdom. Divine power was the only chance I had, my last chance at getting it right.

Gerald had never showed up at Miss Claudia's unannounced, so I was frightened when Richard yelled from downstairs, "Oh, Erma Lee. You have a gentleman caller." Richard's laughter rang up to the sunroom louder than any doorbell.

I almost broke the white blade off the ceiling fan. Climbing down the stepladder, all I could think was that Gerald was here to tell me that something horrible had happened to Cher. Something tragic that LaRue most likely had caused.

"What's the matter?" I asked before my foot hit the last stair step.

Richard's head was still bobbing from the outbreak of giggles. "You're all excited with the love bug."

"Just tell me where he is." His silliness wore on my last nerve.

Richard's point directed me to the side porch outside the kitchen door. When I found my unexpected guest, he was sitting on the porch swing slowly drifting back and forth. "Hey," he said, turning to look at me. His wavy hair was creased from where his cap had been. The same cap that now rested on his knee.

I stood still in front of him waiting for his news.

"This a bad time?"

"You liked to give me heart failure." I slapped the side of his shoulder and joined him in the swing. "I thought something was the matter with Cher."

"No. Uh-huh. A lady who works at the courthouse had a bad battery and called me. Since I had to come this way, I decided to pay you a call." He thumped the brim of his cap. "You don't reckon Miss Claudia will get mad?"

"She won't care. She's napping right now anyway," I said and dismissed his concern with a swipe of my hand.

"How's she getting along?"

"All this going on about that rescue home has just about worn her out. I don't like her color today. Looks a little gray."

"You never know. The nap might do her good."

I wanted to knock some sense into Gerald's head. *Don't you get it? She's got leukemia, not a cold.* I wanted to lecture him on white cells and how the evil blasts were the enemy. Instead, I wrinkled my brow and stared at him. A stare he never saw because he was busy molding the brim of his cap.

"Stopped by the feed store this morning," he said, plopping the reconfigured cap back on his head. "Old boy that runs the place, old Lee Roy Billings, he's done started a bowling league. Needs three more players. I was thinking of signing up. Reckon you want to put your name on the list?"

I thought of the Haggar factory bowling team and the

272

handful of times I had filled in when Roxi couldn't make her usual Wednesday night slot. It was fun, but Bozo never let me play on the team full-time. "You do this, and next thing I know you'll be running around town like something gone wild," he said after I mentioned the idea. But now that I had freedom, I worried about Cher's chance to run wild and spend more time with her new and improved father.

"I better not," I said. "Miss Claudia's really not doing that good. I never know when she might need me. You know, I wouldn't want to put y'all on the spot if I couldn't show up or something."

Two redbirds flew to the bird feeder next to Miss Claudia's rosebushes. "Look," I said and pointed towards the feeder. The crimson red feathers were a distraction, just like the quails were for Gerald the day he brought me to his secret meadow.

Gerald admired the birds and smiled. "Want to go to supper tonight?" he asked, not looking away from the flutter of red. "We still ain't tried that new barbecue place down on Highway 84."

"I've been wanting to try it," I mumbled. The creak from the swing was soothing, and I considered shutting my eyes, playing like I was asleep. "It's just that tonight I have to take Miss Claudia to prayer meeting." He wrinkled his brow and frowned. "They're voting whether to put the rescue home in the old house next to the church." I repeated what I had overheard Miss Claudia say during endless phone calls to church members.

"I understand," he said. The frown and the sigh that

273

followed certainly did not seem to show his understanding.

"This is the big night. You know she's worked real hard to get everybody to support this and everything."

When he got into his truck and rolled down the window, I stood at the edge of Miss Claudia's sidewalk. My hands were hidden inside my jeans pockets. Before I could offer dinner at my place, his truck phone rang, and soon he was discussing a special part he had ordered from the Chevrolet place. Between words into the mobile phone, he waved to me and lazily grinned.

When he drove away, I wanted to run after him and jump on the back of his tailgate. To hit on the back of his truck window and ask him to pull over and hold me tight. To let me feel his tight, secure grip. Instead, I quickly pulled my hands out of my pockets and waved before he had completely disappeared under the umbrella of oak limbs.

The bony blue-veined hands were manicured. The bright red fingernail polish matched the red Bible she had nestled in her lap. I could tell Miss Claudia was a little nervous by the way that she kept squinting at the cuckoo clock. Richard was sleeping upright on the sofa, his legs propped up on the blue-and-yellow-flowered ottoman.

"Jesus looked at them and said, with man this is impossible but not with God; all things are possible with God." Miss Claudia closed her eyes and repeated the verse. I joined in closing my eyes and soon felt

274

guilty that all I could see was LaRue and Cher in his white van. *Stop it right now,* I told myself. *This is a big day for Miss Claudia. She worked hard to get people to support this home. She doesn't need to hear your problems and get more burdened.*

The cuckoo sounded five times. She gasped and suddenly opened her eyes.

"We got plenty of time," I reminded her and leaned back in my chair.

"But I still got to do my face, don't you know." She grabbed the silver-tipped cane and began the journey to her bedroom vanity table. "I don't want the rescue home to miss any votes because I showed up at the meeting all pale-faced and ran them out the church door."

To keep from wearing the same dress to church, I went out on a limb and wore my short skirt and blouse that Miss Claudia made for my first date with Gerald. Sitting in her usual pew in the First Methodist sanctuary, I pulled the skirt down, trying to make it seem longer. Finally I pulled the hymnal from the rack in front of the pew and placed it over my legs, nodding my head and pretending to be familiar with the songs that I flipped through. I could hear Miss Claudia's voice behind me, greeting each church member as they entered. *Better than a seasoned county politician,* I thought.

"I don't believe we've had the pleasure."

I looked up and saw the good-looking pastor. He looked as polished as any movie star in a pair of linen khakis, a white shirt, and blue blazer. Thanks to a vacation in Hawaii, his skin was more tan than usual.

"Hey. Yeah. We met. I'm Erma Lee Jacobs." He put his index finger on his lips and pondered the name. "I work at . . . I mean, I'm Miss Claudia's companion," I said and flipped the ponytail over my neck.

"Oh, yes," he said and leaned back with his hands folded in front of him. "Now, I'm staying completely out of this vote whether we should purchase the property next door for the home. I hope Miss Claudia knows that."

Before I could say anything, Miss Claudia appeared and snaked her arm under his elbow. As they talked about dollars and plans designed by the committee of which I was an honorary member, I looked at the stained glass next to the pew. The mixture of gold and white showed Jesus in a robe. The color in his eyes shot out with golden rays from the setting Alabama sun. If it hadn't been for the jerking motion of the man below the stained glass, I would have meditated longer on the beauty of it all.

The man sitting in the pew below the glass was twitching his head and mumbling something crazy. What hair he had hung down the base of his neck, and every so often he would scratch his reddish orange beard. He was dressed in a dingy white shirt and stained blue jeans. *Hired help like myself,* I imagined. Most likely hired to cut the strip of grass in front of the church. By the way he had dirt stains on the shirt, he must've just turned off the mower. Not wanting him to feel like I was judging him, I scanned the rest of the church body.

My eyes fell smack dab on Prune Face. "Now, did you call all the people you were supposed to, Elizabeth?" Miss Claudia asked. Prune Face and her hunchbacked husband slid into the pew behind us.

"Oh, you better believe it," she replied in a snorting sound.

"Evening," I said and slid the hymnal a little lower to cover my knees. Prune Face looked down at me and took her seat.

"How you do," her husband said. Prune Face snapped her pointy head around and looked at him. *That piece of trash ought not to mix with us,* I imagined her eyes saying to him in some sort of code that only many years of marital agony enabled him to understand.

By the time we had sung the second hymn, I noticed the man under the stained glass twitching his head faster. My first thought was he must have slept wrong on his pillow and developed a kink in his neck. But when he stood up once and then quickly sat back down, I knew his problem was beyond poor sleep. Since the entire congregation was standing and singing, I doubt many saw him.

"Tonight we have a different type of Wednesday evening service," Dr. Winters said. His buffed nails rested on the sides of the white podium. "Tonight we will address three issues of church business. Two are routine budget matters. But the third is about helping those less fortunate. Something First Methodist has always sought to do." He cleared his voice, and that's when I heard the man under the stained-glass picture of

277

Jesus. I couldn't make out what he said, but it was loud enough for Miss Claudia to lean forward and look in his direction. The elderly couple ahead of us also glanced towards the commotion.

"Let us open our hearts to prayer now and seek divine guidance on how to address these matters." Dr. Winters closed his eyes and smiled. "Dear Father, we seek you on how to help those less fortunate in Houston County and the surrounding areas. We ask for your guidance . . ."

"I tell you how you can help."

A gasp erupted from the congregation. Eyes shot open and discovered the man with a twitch standing below Dr. Winters on the church floor.

"Oh, my stars," Prune Face said behind us.

"You can help by being Christians is all." The man's head suddenly jerked towards his right shoulder. His shirt seemed dirtier under the light beaming down upon the pulpit. "Y'all say you're Christians. I sat right out front tonight. Right out yonder by the front door. Not a one of you even spoke. You drive up in your fancy cars and fancy clothes. Not a one of you spoke." He scratched the bald crown of his head and mumbled beyond the understanding of human ears.

I looked up at Dr. Winters. His blue eyes were wide and his knuckles were white, clinching the sides of the podium. The elderly man with silver hair and a light blue sport coat in front of us slipped out of his pew and walked towards the twitching man.

"And y'all call yourselves Christians." The guest's voice cracked when he repeated the words. But he did not resist when the elderly man took his arm and led him through the side doors next to the organist. I heard the man's voice one last time. "I am a Christian." His declaration was muted behind the heavy brown door.

The ruffle of programs and a couple of coughs were the only sounds that echoed in the sanctuary. It seemed like hours watching Dr. Winters lick his lips and sip water from the crystal glass placed next to the podium. Even I looked down, feeling pity in knowing all too well how the visitor felt. From the corner of my eye, I saw Miss Claudia look down and slowly shake her head.

"The man has obvious mental challenges and needs our prayers," Dr. Winters finally said. He removed the pressed white handkerchief from his coat pocket. "That man, like many others, needs our help." Dr. Winters dabbed the glistening spots from his tanned forehead and, as smooth as shifting gears on a foreign luxury car, opened discussion on placing Miss Claudia's vision of a rescue home next door to the church.

"Well sir," a distinguished older man with a gray mustache said, "looks like to me we're setting ourselves up for trouble." The crowd mumbled, and I turned to see many heads agreeing with his comments. "Don't get me wrong now. I'm all for helping the little ladies. But putting that thing smack dab next to the church is just asking for trouble."

A woman about my age stood up. Her soft voice cracked when she spoke, and she gripped the pew ahead of her. "I hadn't planned on saying anything, but

I don't care if this home for battered women is across town or across the street, we've got to stand up and help."

"Darling, I'm all for helping." The older man stood back up. "We just got legal considerations. Now, I served as circuit judge for sixteen years. I know how jealous husbands can be. We just don't need this place next door at the old Jackson home. What if some nut case shows up and shoots the place up on a Sunday night? That thing could happen while we're all walking out to our cars after church."

Seven church members seemed to speak for the entire body that Wednesday evening. With the exception of the woman my age and one older lady who coughed so much I could barely hear her, all the comments were negative. All the talk of decreased property value and potential gunfire from irate husbands suddenly made Miss Claudia's vision of safety sound dirty. She never looked at her church family as the comments flew faster than the automatic bullets they feared. She simply adjusted her glasses and stared at the bowl of sunflowers sitting on a table near the spot where the surprise speaker had made his accusations.

"As a committee member, I started not to say anything," Prune Face said. She stood up from the pew and turned towards the crowd. Looking at her from behind, I discovered one of her secrets. Underneath the curls of ash blonde was a beige pad, visible at the base of her so-called hairline. *A falsey on a falsey.*

"But after meeting upon meeting with city council members, United Way, and other churches, I cannot in good faith put this home near our beautiful church." Prune Face sat back down and was straightening her skirt when she saw me. With her looking right at me, I rolled my eyes and slowly turned my head towards the front of the church.

"And I don't mean any harm at all by saying this," the older man said with his hand placed over his heart. "But tonight with that poor man." He paused and closed his eyes. "Well, let me just say if this home opens next door we'll see many more like him. All sorts coming around here. Half of them probably drug addicts and the like."

If I had more education, I would've stood and said something about the old man's comments. *And he calls himself a judge.* When I turned to read Miss Claudia's reaction to the judge's comment, she had disappeared.

"Ladies and gentlemen, as you all know, this was my proposal for our church." Miss Claudia stood in front of the church, both hands on top of her cane. Her sweet half-smile told me that she was giving in and walking away from her vision. She had been a member of this church for fifty-two years, she had told me on the drive to the service. She was a part of this world, and there were unspoken rules to follow.

"I still believe this home is what God wants. Whether it's done here or elsewhere makes no difference. Because the One who calls me is faithful, and He will do it."

"Amen," the woman who stood up and defended the home said.

"What troubles me more is some of the talk I've

heard tonight in the Lord's house." Miss Claudia glanced at Dr. Winters and sighed. "I declare, how far have we gone when we're not moved by what we've seen by that man who spoke to us? When all we do is argue and carry on? It is the call for us to be the light for Jesus. And quite honestly, it hurts me to say all I see are dull bulbs." She bit her lip and cleared her throat. I looked down at my bare legs, longing to go put my arm around her. Dr. Winters approached her, but folded his arms when she raised an eyebrow at him.

"And Judge Harland, I beg your pardon. But you're out of line with some of your remarks. The women needing this home are not the bottom of society's barrel like you said. They're decent, smart women who've been punched down to the bottom."

"Amen," I yelled out. The echo of my voice against the high walls made me flinch. I quickly cut my eyes to see if anybody was staring at me.

After Miss Claudia took her seat, a floor vote was taken. If Miss Claudia was successful that evening, it was in making sure the defeat of her home would not be unanimous. The church would not support a safe haven for battered women within ten blocks of First Methodist. But the church noted its moral support for a home placed elsewhere in Wiregrass.

We left through the side door, the same one that the undesirable had earlier exited. We walked through the hallway with white Sunday school doors on either side. Photos of new members and children's hand-painted prints on construction paper decorated the entrances. I trailed behind Miss Claudia, not knowing how to handle her disappointment. Our shoe heels and her cane tapped, out of sync, on the beige tile floor.

While Miss Claudia put on her nightgown, I called Kasi to make sure Cher was within her sight. "You old mother hen. Her and Laurel are laying here on the floor watching a scary video," she said. I hung up wondering if Cher had complained to Kasi about me calling and checking on her like it was her first overnight trip.

I poured the steaming water into a china tea cup. The white Sleepy Time tea bag floated to the top.

"Thank you, sugar." She sat in her bed and looked grayer than usual against the mahogany headboard. "You're going to spoil me yet."

"A little spoiling will do you good," I said and placed another pillow against her neck. "I hate how everything turned out. You know, with the home and all."

Her hazel eyes looked tired and weary. "This is where faith comes into play. Now we just sink in our heels and pray, knowing God will do it." She sat the white china cup down on the tray and stared at her armoire.

"I've been a member of that church ever since I married Wade Tyler." She rubbed the tea-bag label between her red fingernails. "Oh, even back in those days it was snooty. Only thing was, I prepared myself for it."

"After Wade married me, he sent me off to Miss Porter's. Some high-brow finishing school in Atlanta." She laughed. "That poor old thing earned every penny with this backwoods girl from Apalachicola, Florida. I learned how to eat, how to walk, and especially how to talk." Miss Claudia pressed her back firmly against the pillows, clasped her hands, and pursed her lips together until she looked so prissy that I burst out laughing.

"She taught me to drawl the letter 'I' out so I didn't hit it so hard and sound crackery. I declare, I was just too precious for words." Miss Claudia closed her eyes and stuck out her tongue.

I leaned into the wingback chair. I liked laughing with her. For me it was the same type of feeling I imagined LaRue and Suzette got from cocaine.

"But Miss Porter didn't have to teach me about clothes. I was the craziest thing over clothes you ever did see. And after living with Nettie in the quarters, I knew how to make those flashy dresses like she used to wear." Miss Claudia slapped her bed. "Can you imagine if all those high-society women at Miss Porter's would've known I learned my taste from a colored harlot."

She wiped the tears of laughter from the corner of her eyes. "But no, I was so excited when I got back to Wiregrass and those ladies in the church accepted me. All their sweet little luncheons and circle meetings. It wasn't until Wade died that I really stopped playing church and got into a love relationship with God. That poor soul tonight was the final straw. His words hit me square in the eye."

"I know. I even wanted to get up and say something to that old judge."

"No, not Judge Harland. He's always been a little touched. I'm talking about the man who looked so pitiful." Miss Claudia gazed across the bedroom at the closet door.

"I declare, it was just like the Lord spoke to my heart the very minute that man opened his mouth. That man could've been me, before Miss Porter's school." She was quiet and looked into the cup of tea sitting on the tray. "You know, Erma Lee, I'm ashamed of myself. I should've told that church. Told them that I was one of the women they feared having near their precious church house."

"At least you had the guts to get up there to start with."

She rested the back of her head against the tall headboard. "All these years, I'm still hiding behind smoke and mirrors."

During my drives home from Miss Claudia's I began circling around the Garland Motel. Each time I maneuvered my car by the glass motel office, the air would get caught up in my chest and I would have to remind myself to breathe. I'd sit in my humid car hearing the steady rap of crickets and the occasional roar of a semi truck and think of ways to destroy him. A bomb planted inside his white van. A sniper planted under the faded green slide by the weeds and high grass. The spot at the motel where a swimming pool must once have been.

As I watched the usual motel clerk with short brown hair and square glasses stare at *Wheel of Fortune* on her office TV, I reminded myself that revenge belonged to the Lord. I thought of the Bible readings

Miss Claudia and me did on Paul and how he had a thorn placed in his life that the Lord would not take away. Miss Claudia said we do not know what Paul's thorn was. Who knows, maybe Paul had a LaRue in his own life. "Lord, please take him away from here," I prayed for the thorn that sat inside room 107.

If one thing Bozo's drunken fury taught me, it was that life had to go on whether I was smiling or not. Frowns always drew too much attention. To prevent Gerald from thinking anything out of the ordinary was going on in my life, I invited him to supper.

Earlier that day Miss Claudia met with the city planner about using city funds for the rescue home, and Richard offered to go with her. "No need bringing your credentials up to the poor man. Everybody knows you have your law degree. Just let me do the talking," Miss Claudia instructed. Looking into the mirror of a small compact case, she drew her red lipstick, and Richard lifted sofa cushions searching for his car keys.

After they left, I went home to do some last-minute cleaning for Gerald's arrival. Cher's little pink radio blasted country music while I dusted, swept, and mopped. Whether I wanted to or not, I was going to force myself to be in a good mood. The floor slightly bounced like a trampoline as I danced around the sofa, sorting through the clothes and linens I had cleaned earlier in Miss Claudia's washer.

LeAnn Rimes's voice trailed down the narrow hallway. I fumbled over the words trying to sing along and carry Cher's fresh-smelling bed linens at the same time. Chicken-fried steak, sweet potatoes, and black-eyed peas. I selected the menu for Gerald's dinner and stretched the pale yellow sheet over the corners of Cher's mattress. I was still thinking of a dessert choice when I lifted the bottom edge of the mattress with my knee and tried to force the shrunken sheet over the corner. Down by my bare foot on the box springs, I saw what looked like a long, skinny spitball. The wrapped ends and the black burnt markings convinced me the object was not a classroom nuisance. My weight fell to the bed, and I held the joint of marijuana in the palm of my hand as if offering a guest a piece of candy. In the second it had taken me to drop the mattress, the thorn in my life had grown to become a poisonous tree.

Canceling the meal with Gerald was the last thing on my mind. I jumped into my car and sped down the asphalt driveway. Blood boiled in my ears, and I dared Miss Trellis to step out of her white block office and get onto me for speeding in her trailer park.

Cher never saw me pull into the main parking lot of the city swimming pool. The section Cher had forbidden me to enter. The squeals and splashes of the young kids who lined up behind the high diving board drifted into my car. My eyes searched through the windshield for the green bathing suit she had purchased with car-wash earnings.

She was standing with Laurel and three other girls behind the chain-link fence in the back corner of the pool. *Probably talking about how her no-count daddy can get them all a supply of pot*. I pounded the black asphalt parking lot with my lace-up work shoes.

Laurel was the first to spot me. Her mouth dropped, and she tapped Cher on the arm. When Cher looked at me and rolled her eyes, I wanted to run up to the fence, stick my fingers through the metal gaps, and yank a handful of her brown hair. She put her hand on her hip and said something to the girls. Waiting for her to walk through the side gate, I folded my arms and tapped my finger.

She moaned like I was an inconvenience to her sun-filled day. "What are you doing here? You're supposed to park by the baseball field."

"Get your stuff and get in the car."

"Uh, I still got another hour . . ." Cher lifted her hands up in the air.

"I said now."

She looked over her shoulder at Laurel and the others standing behind her. Casually she walked over to the gate, and Laurel handed her the plastic shopping bag containing a sunflower sundress and towel. She draped the towel over her shoulders and placed the black sunglasses, another car-wash revenue, on her face.

"What's up with you?" she asked in a whiny tone.

With her lagging behind me, I stomped towards the car. "Just get in the car."

She never made it past the hood. "I don't feel comfortable with this, you know. You come down here and embarrass me. And won't even tell me what this is about."

The car door squeaked when I opened it. I stood behind the door glaring at her. "Get your butt in this

288

car, young lady. And I mean *now*."

"No. Not until you tell me what your problem is." She tilted her head back towards the baking sun.

I slammed the car door and bolted towards her so fast, she took a step backwards. "Let me just show you what my problem is." I pulled the joint out of my jeans pocket and held it in front of her peeling nose. Before she could reach up and take the offering, I closed my hand and hid it back in my pocket.

She stared at me with her mouth open. "I just . . . we just found it."

"You just found it, huh? Try another one on me."

"Laurel's boyfriend . . ."

"Can't you even take responsibility? I told you. But, no ma'am, you wouldn't listen to dumb ol' me." I raised my hands in the air and turned my back to her. "I told you he was trouble. And now he's got you all strung out on drugs, just like your sorry mama."

Cher opened her arms like a defensive tackle ready to launch. Her mouth was gaping open. "How did you . . ."

"Don't stand there acting like you pulled one over on me neither." I turned to face her, so mad her image made me feel heat behind my eyes. "You don't think I've seen you with him. Those nights riding around town smoking God knows what in that white van."

"This has nothing to do with my daddy. Laurel's boyfriend gave it . . . And why do you care if I see my daddy?"

"Because he's trouble, girl." I put my hands on my hips and leaned down towards her face. "He ain't nothing but a cokehead and never will be nothing more."

"You're not telling anything, you know. He already told me about all that. He's changed now."

"Huh. He'll change the day his toes turn up and the undertaker puts him in the ground."

She grimaced at me and squeezed her hands into two fists. "Oh, you make me so mad," she screamed and stomped her foot. "He said you'd do this. He said you'd come between us. Just like you're doing."

My scrunched up eyes reflected back at me in her fancy sunglasses. "I saw what he did to your mama. The man's poison, Cher."

She leaned towards me and screamed, "You're nothing but a sorry liar."

The cracking sound from my hand meeting her face echoed down the parking lot and towards her friends. For an instant there was no splashing water or laughter from the pool area. Just an uneasy stillness that made me hope the situation was a nightmare and that I'd soon awake to hit the snooze button.

Her prized sunglasses, first scouted out in *Seventeen* magazine, landed on the pavement. She looked up at me, and the red indentation on her cheek outlined the spot where my long fingers had settled.

Before I could open my mouth, she ran in between parked cars and towards the dense trees behind the swimming pool. Her white plastic bag rattled in the wind, and with each stride plastic flip-flops slapped at her feet.

"Get back here," I yelled over the splash and squeals

of innocent kids. Normal kids enjoying their carefree summer day. Once she had disappeared beyond the shrubs and trees, I picked up the designer sunglasses and noticed a crack on the front of one lens.

Twenty

*A*fter searching the woods behind the pool, I walked over to Laurel and the girls Cher had been talking with.

"You seen Cher?" I asked Laurel.

Laurel bit her paint-chipped fingernail, shook her head, and looked at the other girls. They stared back at me with the same blank look Cher had given me after I slapped her. "Laurel, stay here. I'll be back in a minute," I said and walked to my car.

I drove around the side road of the swimming pool, looking deep within the pine trees and oaks that filled the woods. The area was as long as a city block. A convenience store sat at the end of the street. I asked a young woman pumping gas if she had seen a fourteen-year-old in a green bathing suit. "I sure haven't," she said with her hand planted on the car trunk as if there was not a worry in the world.

If LaRue had not been in town, I wouldn't have gripped the steering wheel as tightly as I did. His high-cheek-boned face was the first thing that popped into my mind. I just hoped Cher had not thought of him too.

"You mean that good-looking feller that drove the

van with the ladder on top?" the Garland Motel clerk said. "He's done checked out."

"Do you remember what time?"

"Baby, I reckon it was about two hours ago," she said, adjusting the big square glasses on her nose. "Why? He ain't in no trouble I hope."

"I hope not either," I said and heard the silver bell at the top of the office door ring when I left.

Riding around the streets of Wiregrass, searching for my biggest asset, I felt trapped. Roped in my own frustration and torment, I drove down Elm Drive and passed Miss Claudia's big brick home twice before convincing myself to stop.

Walking up the side porch to the kitchen, I could see Miss Claudia through the tall windows. She was at the stove heating up the pot of field peas I had cooked for lunch. Richard sat at the table reading the newspaper. They looked content and safe. Just when I turned to leave, Miss Claudia saw me on her porch and held up her hand.

"Erma Lee, what in the world," Miss Claudia said at the screened kitchen door.

"Cher and me got in a fight. I thought she might be here." Not wanting her to see my hands tremble, I tucked them in the back pockets of my jeans.

Miss Claudia wiped her hands on a dish towel with little red cherries. "I'll be watching for her," Miss Claudia said and patted my arm. "It's difficult at her age, don't you know."

I halfway smiled and turned to go.

"Let me hear as soon as you find her," Miss Claudia said. Even though it was hours before dusk, she turned the porch light on when I turned to go.

At five I returned to the swimming pool to pick up Laurel and hopefully Cher. "She hasn't come back?" Laurel shook her head no to that question and every one I asked about Cher on the drive back to the trailer. Had Cher said anything out of the ordinary? Did she mention anything today about her real daddy? Was there a place she knew of where Cher might be? Laurel would simply stare straight ahead and sniff her nose.

"You remember how it was when we was girls," Kasi said, standing at her trailer door. Laurel slipped under Kasi's arm and disappeared. "I bet before you get supper fixed, she's at your door acting like nothing's the matter."

Kasi took a drag of her cigarette and blew smoke over my head. I postponed telling her about the joint I found under Cher's bed and how Laurel's name was tossed into the conspiracy. For all I knew, maybe it was Laurel's marijuana cigarette. Maybe LaRue had nothing to do with it at all. Maybe Cher was right and he had changed.

"That boy ain't nothing but the worst kind of trash," I remembered Mama saying the first time she met LaRue. It was the part of her I was glad I inherited, the commonsense part. And the common sense I had always respected would not play a game of make-believe on Kasi's wrought-iron trailer steps.

Before the toilet had flushed the joint down to the septic tank, Gerald was knocking at my door. He was expecting chicken-fried steak, and all he would find would be my brain dipped in a batter of worry and fried in a grease of regret.

I dished him the highlights of Cher running through the woods and never mentioned LaRue. "A misunderstanding," I explained to Gerald. He would think trouble was my middle name if I told him all the details. And besides, the motel clerk said LaRue had already checked out. Probably already in Montgomery, riding the streets searching for drugs or a fresh widow he could con into a paint job. At least that's what I walked around the trailer silently praying.

"You checked down at the skating rink?" Gerald asked with his brow wrinkled.

I stood in the kitchen with my arms folded, shaking my head no. As much as I wanted to look at him, my eyes froze on the torn piece of gold linoleum around the edge of the pantry. The strip had long been ripped away from its base and flapped carelessly towards the pantry door.

"Let's ride up there. Maybe she decided to mess around with some of her friends." Gerald fingered the metal clump of keys on his belt loop.

The jingle from the keys sounded like the first note of a telephone ring, and I looked up at him. "Uh, no, you go on. I better stay here. You know, in case she calls," I said and glanced over at the phone.

My arms were still folded against my chest when he engulfed me in a hug. I could smell exhaust fumes on his plaid shirt. I wanted to release my arms and wrap them around the thick back and lovingly squeeze him.

I wanted to tell him that I was glad he was here and that I needed him more than ever. But I stood still and held my breath under the weight of his gentle touch. Just when I thought my lungs might explode from the lack of oxygen, he let go.

"I'll be back directly," he said, jingling his keys once more before closing the trailer door.

The sun descended beyond the tops of the pine trees. I watched from my kitchen window and prayed for a sign that Cher was safe. The silence of the room weighed heavy on my heart.

My faithful bed, which had been my altar a few weeks back, became my resting place once again. I knelt down and placed my elbows on the frayed white blanket. "Lord, you know this situation. You know where Cher is at this very minute. Please bring her back to me. I just can't stand this," I cried out in a loud voice. I opened my eyes and looked up at the brown stain on my ceiling. I pictured my words reaching the top of the thin ceiling and bouncing back down on me.

The slamming car doors outside made me trip over my feet. I practiced what I would say to Cher, nothing heavy but enough to let her know she created a stir: *Girl, do you know how worried sick I've been? I'd just die if something happened to you.*

But peeking from my bedroom miniblinds, I saw only Miss Claudia and Richard slowly making their way towards my door against an orange light from the setting sun.

"I didn't want to tie up the phone line in case she called," Miss Claudia said as I helped pull her up the last step to my trailer. "I beg apologies for just showing up, but I've been worried to death."

"Just all to pieces," Richard said in a loud whisper. A line I'm sure he had memorized from the numerous times it had been delivered about his own mental state.

Updating them on Gerald's search, I was too upset to be uncomfortable about them seeing my humble home for the first time. My home that would fit inside the space of Miss Claudia's formal living room.

"What about that other little girl she's friends with?" Miss Claudia asked. She tucked the coffee-stained pillow between her back and the couch.

"You mean Laurel? I've asked her. She just sat there like an idiot staring out the car window."

"If Gerald comes up empty-handed, we should call the authorities," Richard said. The authoritative tone was a hint of the lawyer Miss Claudia said he once was.

I twirled the ends of my ponytail and felt my eyes grow wider. The very idea of having the law involved would make it a real emergency. It was not that way at all. *Cher will call from McDonald's,* I kept telling myself. *Probably when she goes to buy something to eat and realizes all her car-wash money is still in the red coffee can on her bedroom dresser.*

"Well, let's not call the road patrol just yet," Miss Claudia said, staring at my frozen expression. "I imagine Gerald'll find her down at that roller rink."

I twirled my hair into a knot and fought off the evil images that flashed through my mind. *She's not in a muddy ditch dead somewhere, she's just skating in cir-*

cles—thinking things through. I closed my eyes and repeated the assuring words.

When Gerald opened the door, I saw the darkness of the night and heard the crickets chirping outside. He looked down at the grease-spotted cap he held in his hand. "They ain't seen her."

I wasn't sure if the ringing in my ears was from the blood rush that his words produced or from the crickets outside the tin walls. "Call the law," I mumbled.

When I opened the door, the old man next door was standing at his kitchen window with the blinds yanked wide open. The sight of two patrol cars at Westgate created a minicrisis. Kasi was standing on her steps with the door wide open. A peaceful glow radiated from her TV.

I was thankful the officers had not pulled up with their sirens blowing and blue lights spinning. If Miss Trellis was in the office watching one of her home-shopping channels, she would've surely seen the officers drive in her trailer park and would appear at my doorstep any minute.

Idle chitchat and clips of static from the officers' walkie-talkies drifted around my living room. The photo they had requested stuck to the plastic protective cover, and I noticed my hand shaking when I tried to pry the celluloid away from my wallet.

"Y'all do a fine job. Just fine," Richard said. "I have one of those new trunk police scanners so I know everything that's taking . . ."

The door knock made Richard shut up and the rest of

297

us flinch. Gerald moved to open the door, and I pulled hard, freeing Cher's face from the plastic photo cover. Just as I was handing Cher's photo to the black officer, Kasi entered with her hands on Laurel's shoulder.

Laurel looked down at the floor, and Kasi glanced nervously around the room. "Hey," she whispered. "Laurel knows maybe what happened. She got all scared when the cops came." Kasi smacked her chewing gum and played with the tag inside Laurel's orange T-shirt.

The static grew louder, and the officer adjusted a knob on the walkie-talkie attached to his hip.

"Well, go on," Kasi said with a slight push of her hand.

"Umm. Well, you know Cher wants to see her daddy and all," Laurel said. Her hands and words flew in circles. "And since you didn't want her to and everything, she planned to anyway."

I held my breath, dreading what her next words would be. I felt the heartbeat of fear make a path up my neck.

"Tell them what she said this morning," Kasi said, pushing Laurel's shoulder again.

"Well, okay. Okay," Laurel said, closing her eyes as if now she wanted to remember all the details. "She was gonna meet her daddy again today. You know, leave the pool and see him and stuff. Then come back in time for you to pick us up. Okay." Laurel cut her blue eyes up at me and quickly looked back at the floor.

"Meet him where? I looked everywhere," I said,

fighting the urge to knock a knot on her blonde head.

"Down at the store," Laurel whispered.

I thought of the convenience store that sat on the edge of the woods behind the pool. My version of events played out in my mind like a horror movie. In the time I spent walking around those woods calling for Cher like she was a lost dog, she made it to the store and rode off in a white van with a lost tag.

"Who's the father?" the deputy asked.

"LaRue LaRouche. I got custody of her."

"Man," the other officer said. His exhaustive tone said it all. A lost cause. A waste of his time to hunt down a man who fathered the girl.

"He's been in prison." My voice was beginning to shake with fright. "For drugs and child abandonment. He's just, dangerous. Plain dangerous," I said loudly.

"Oh, God," Kasi said. She hit Laurel on the back of the head. "How come you didn't say nothing before now?"

Laurel rubbed her head and sank her shoulders lower. "Cher made me swear not to."

The flurry of details swarmed around me. Where was the last address for LaRue? How did Cher get in contact with him? Where was the last known phone number for LaRue? I provided as much information as I could to the officers. My mind was in a million places, thinking where Cher might be and what trouble she was already in with that no-good driving her.

"I should've forced her to stop calling him," I said, handing the latest phone bill to the officer.

"You can't worry about that now," Miss Claudia said. "Just dismiss it from your mind."

While I jockeyed questions from the two officers in the living room, Miss Claudia, Richard, and Gerald congregated at my dinette table. I could hear their muffled whispers and the creaking chairs when they leaned forward in conference. Miss Claudia asked Gerald if he knew LaRue had been in town. Gerald reminded her how private I was. I wanted to get up from the sofa and storm the twenty steps to the dinette table and tell them I didn't appreciate being talked about in my own home. But I remained on my rented sofa and offered "I don't know" to more questions from the officers.

The plastic clock on top of the TV read eight thirty-nine when the officers left. They assured us an All Points Bulletin would be released from Wiregrass to Shreveport. Soon Miss Claudia, Richard, and Gerald would leave too, and the emptiness of the trailer would wrap around me and try to suffocate me with despair. Looking into Miss Claudia's sunken hazel eyes, I cussed myself for being selfish.

I lightly touched Miss Claudia's cream silk blouse. "You ought to go get some rest."

"You don't mind me," she said and tapped her cane on the floor. "Gerald has a good idea."

"I hate it. But I know how the cops are. Even if they send that notice out, other towns will sit on it less somebody's there to push them." He pushed up the brim of his cap. "You reckon we need to head on to Shreveport?"

I thought of the time LaRue and Suzette left Cher

300

behind in the drug house. They ran to Las Vegas. "He may not be there, though," I said. The very words felt like they were coming from somebody else.

"If you ask me, it's as good a place to start as any. He'll have to change out that van or get caught sure enough. I imagine he's got a set of old boys in Shreveport who'll help him out."

"Gerald's right. Time is the advantage right now. He's easier to catch before he slips off again," Richard said.

I tried to stand upright and not let the situation overtake me, but my shoulders slumped at the very thought of not seeing Cher until she matured and realized what a mess she made. "I know, but I just can't run off to Shreveport."

"You can and you will," Miss Claudia said. "I'll give you an advance to cover the gas and motel."

"If we go ahead and leave, we could make it by dawn," Gerald said.

I studied him carefully. "We? Oh, no. I won't have you taking off . . ."

"Hey," he said with a point of his finger. "I don't want to hear another word about it. I'm going. Period."

Before Richard and Miss Claudia left, at her request we gathered in a circle to pray. Miss Claudia led the prayer and asked for my comfort and Cher's safe return.

I felt paralyzed by the whole situation and distant from God. Like the pictures in my mind of Cher mangled and torn on the side of a road, I kept pushing away the question of why God would let LaRue take Cher, fearing that if I allowed myself to ask such a question I would surely never see her again. To distract my mind, I lifted my head and looked at the three people gathered around me. Miss Claudia held her head upright, and her red lips moved with words of mercy and deliverance. Gerald and Richard obediently had their heads tucked down.

Miss Claudia made out a check, squeezed me tight, and stood at my door waiting for Richard to make it down the steps first. "Let me hear from you, now." She closed her eyes and smiled. "I'll be wrestling for you and Cher in prayer."

The prayer chain did not end with Miss Claudia. While we were driving down the highway, Gerald got on his truck phone and sought prayers from Pastor Lee, A.J., and Brownie—and, of course, Marcie. I didn't mind any of the rest of my church members knowing about the situation, but I figured Marcie would just gloat over it. *"Now Daddy, should you be this involved?"* I imagined her asking on the other end of the phone.

And I could tell by the way he said "yeah" and then cut his eyes over at me that that was exactly the type of questions he was getting.

If it hadn't been for Marcie's job at the sheriff's department, I admit I would've been in a worse fix. Her computer matched LaRue's phone number with an address. If it hadn't been for that piece of help, I would've demanded that Gerald not call her.

I looked out the truck window and watched the neon roadside lights flash by me. *"I liked to got fired using the computer system for that address,"* I imagined Marcie saying the next time I saw her. *The humble shall inherit the earth,* I reminded myself and quickly wrote down LaRue's address on the back of a crumpled gas receipt.

Since we left so late, I tried to sleep on the way to Jackson. As my head bobbed with each worn-out spot on the interstate, I thought of Cher and how I had slapped her. Other than a few spankings when she was little, it was the first time I hit her. I retraced the steps that brought me to the end road I faced. If only I could go back and keep my cool. If only LaRue would have just left us alone. *This was all his fault.* The anger that fueled me was greater than my natural need for sleep.

In Jackson, we stopped at Shoney's and traded seats. I hadn't been under the steering wheel more than ten minutes when Gerald's whistling snores began. He filled the passenger seat with his arms folded and cap's brim pulled low over his forehead.

Behind the wheel, I fantasized about making a speech at LaRue's hearing for kidnapping Cher. Even if she went voluntarily, I decided I could get him on kidnapping because she was in my custody. That young lawyer of Miss Claudia's could figure out a way to make it happen. "Legal loophole" I've heard it called on the news.

During my testimony, a history of his destruction of my family would be offered. I would borrow one of Miss Claudia's hats so I would look sophisticated. Sorta like Alexis used to wear on *Dynasty*. While tractor trailers and cars passed by me, I chose my words carefully. After my comments, I would stop in front of LaRue and stare so long he would look down at the floor. Compelled by my testimony, the jury would sentence him to either life in prison or the death penalty. Since I had not made my mind up on whether any person other than LaRue should get killed through the justice system, I left the option open.

A chill ran over me, and I cut the air conditioning down. My strength was beaten back down when the thought of how I wanted to stand up and defend Miss Claudia's rescue home during the church service crossed my mind. *Who do you think you are?* the darkness asked. *You couldn't even stand up in a church, much less a court of law.* And suddenly the pride of securing LaRue's torment was sucked into the air-conditioning vent and landed flat on the asphalt where it was promptly pounded by Gerald's tires.

When we arrived in Shreveport, the downtown casino lights were just beginning to fade against the rising sun. I steered Gerald's truck while he offered directions. Little Haven Apartments were located in the Red River section of town. Judging by the torn window screens scattered across the patchy-grassed lawn, the apartment complex was just LaRue's style. Nervous energy, which had been building in my chest, faded when I failed to spot his white van in the concrete parking lot.

"Hadn't seen him in two weeks," the man behind the counter said. His words fought with the roar from the window-unit fan. If his hair had been longer, he could've passed as Santa Claus, maybe even fatter. "He left here with checks bouncing ever which a way. He burned you too, eh?"

"He owes me," I said.

"He had one of those girlie-show girls piled in there with him. She told me she was staying down at the Decadence Inn but got kicked out." He paused to chew the end of his pen. "She's not bad-looking neither."

"You remember her name?" Gerald asked.

"Starts with a M, maybe. Anyway she works down at the Pink Palace. Smack next to that place I told you about. Decadence Inn."

I used the pay phone next to the apartment building to call the Shreveport police station. Two different people told me that they didn't know anything about an APB for LaRue. I provided his name and a description of the van. "Please, please, send it out to your people," I begged the second sergeant I spoke to.

"What's he wanted for?"

"Umm, kidnapping."

"You the mama?"

"Grandmama. Yes. I got custody of her."

"Oh, yeah. Okay. We'll get the notice out for you."

The phone line went dead. I lifted my foot and finished crushing a piece of broken Budweiser bottle on the sidewalk. "These people just don't get it," I told Gerald and slammed the phone down.

After spending the day driving around and around the Red River district, I decided that I must now know every fleabag motel clerk by name. The feeling of defeat settled deeper when we passed the Pink Palace. It was all lit up with white and yellow marquee lights. The image of Cher dancing around on tables for drunk men forced me to close my eyes and grit my teeth. The stinging that comes from lack of sleep rested behind my sockets.

The motel room had two double beds, and if the bed had been made of feathers, I don't think I would have slept any better. While Gerald called home to check on Donnie, I brushed my teeth. Any nervousness I felt about sleeping in a motel room with Gerald was washed away from the hours riding in the close compound of his truck. Before he could get out of the bathroom, I was sleeping, fully dressed, on the multicolored bedspread.

I awoke the next morning with a beige blanket placed over me. Gerald opened the door with two paper cups of coffee and a bag of doughnuts. I jumped up thinking of the wasted time I was spending lying in bed. Time given to LaRue's advantage, so he could run off with Cher forever.

"Settle down. It's only six-thirty," Gerald said and placed the green-and-white paper bag on the table.

Recalling the old saying that if you tell your husband your dreams before breakfast they come true, I ate my doughnut in silence, while Gerald held the map of Shreveport and outlined our search. Even though he was not my husband, he was the closest thing to a boyfriend I ever had, and I was not going to risk it by letting him know all the nightmares I had about Cher's whereabouts.

The Pink Palace lived up to its name. It was a stucco building painted a pink so bright it hurt my eyes when I saw it at the corner red light.

"This place looks rough," Gerald said outside the building. "Maybe you need to stay in the truck."

I looked at the top of the tinted-black glass door and saw two dead mosquito hawks hanging from a spider web. Secrets had gotten me to the point where I was. Now I had to lay it on the line for Gerald as well. "I've been in worse, I can assure you," I said.

Indeed, the darkness of the open room and the smell of stale cigarette smoke was similar to the places I had pulled Bozo out of during our thirty-plus years of marital bliss. Only difference was, this place had a small stage surrounded by mirrors. A crystal ball, like the one at the skating rink, hung from the ceiling. My eyes were adjusting from sunlight to blackness when I saw the outline of a skinny man carrying a brown box.

"We closed," the man said and placed the case on the bar. He looked about sixty, and his forehead was made high thanks to a sharp widow's peak at his hairline. His black hair was slicked back with some type of greasy substance.

Gerald moved forward, and I followed behind him. "Hey. How you doing?"

The man pulled out a pocketknife and slit open the case. He looked up with his brow wrinkled and his mouth partly open. "All right. But we're still closed."

I folded my arms and wondered if Gerald was tough enough to handle the situation I had put him in. While anybody could look at him and know his massive size would intimidate a skinny man like the thing that stood before me, Gerald lacked the harsh tongue that I imagined the skinny man had picked up from hard living.

"We ain't here for that." Gerald pulled the photo I found in the dirt at the skating rink from his shirt pocket. Gerald laid the faded photo on the bar. "You know this feller? Some of his people's needing him."

The man continued opening the case of Wild Turkey and squinted his eyes down at the photograph. "Man, do you know how many people walk through them doors?" The man grinned and shook his head.

"One of the dancers here lived with him," I said behind Gerald's shoulder. Gerald half turned and looked at me.

The man sighed, dropped his knife on the bar, and picked up the photograph.

"He's got short hair now," I said. The man wrinkled his brow again.

"Oh, yeah," the man grunted in a way that made me think he wanted to laugh. "Sweet Magnolia. We put her down the road. She's always picking up one stray or another here. Just got in the way of business." The man pulled bottles of brown liquid from the case.

"You know where we can find her?" Gerald asked.

The man stopped and put his pocketknife back in his jeans pocket. "I ain't her daddy."

I stepped forward. "We don't want trouble with her. I just need to find LaRue. You know the man in the picture. It's about my grand . . ."

"Lady, I ain't getting in the middle of whatever mess you got."

Gerald put his thumbs on the waist of his jeans. "We just need to see if that dancer knows where this other feller is. Now if she quit, it looks to me like you'd have some address on her for tax stuff."

"That's it. Now go on and get out of here." The man waved his arms at us like he was shooing cattle.

When I turned to go, a loud thud and cussing rang behind me. The skinny man's head was mashed down on the bar, and his arms were twisted behind him. Gerald straddled the man from behind and jerked the man's arms. "You reckon you can remember that address now?" Gerald said through gritted teeth.

We left the darkness of the Pink Palace with the address of Magnolia's sister, written on a white cocktail napkin. As my eyes adjusted to the light, I wrinkled my brow and glanced at Gerald. I worried he'd erupt again if I looked at him too long.

We rode in his truck three blocks before he said a word. "Don't forget to buckle up," he said and smiled at me. I put the seat belt on and felt his hand on my leg. "Be looking for that street on your right," he said and gently patted my leg.

Leaving the dancer's sister's home, I felt as low as any human could. The young girl stood in the paint-chipped doorway holding a baby dressed in diapers. A torn brown recliner sat on the front porch. Its yellow stuffing dangled at the edge of the rip. The girl couldn't have been a day older than twenty-one and bit her lip when we asked about her sister.

"Is she dead?" she asked and blew up at the wisps of black bangs that fell in her eyes. She had never seen LaRue before, but by the way she described her sister, she was definitely his type. She told us how her sister had been strung out on heroin for the past two years. How she always had boyfriends who furnished fresh supplies.

Thinking I might not be able to stand, I put my hand on the flakes of white paint peeling from her door frame. "Do you know where she's at?" I asked. A stream of drool dropped from the baby's bottom lip.

"Only place I know to tell you is that old motel next to Pink Palace. I heard they been selling out near the old fairgrounds too. She probably hates my guts. But you know, I got kids in the house and everything. I can't be having that kind of stuff going on."

Gerald cranked the truck and, before he pulled away, I turned to get one last look at the house. Not really a house, but a shack that looked like spots of snow had stuck to the brown wood. "I'm so sorry to drag you into this," I said, never looking at Gerald and not really hearing his words of encouragement. No matter what he said, I felt I had dirtied his soul by introducing him to a way of living so foreign to his own. *Maybe lies weren't so bad after all.* We continued to romp through the Red River section of Shreveport, searching for a beat-up white van.

By the third day we had logged more miles and driven through more seedy motel parking lots than I care to count. The scenes of Shreveport were beginning to look the same. Although Gerald never said anything, I could tell by the way he would sigh and rub the corners of his mustache that he thought we were wasting our time. We saw every white van in Shreveport but, of course, each one was newer and had a proper tag. The one I searched for was driven by a loser and someone who most likely was halfway to Las Vegas by now.

"You know, Erma Lee, she is fourteen," Gerald said after we drove away from McDonald's.

At first I ignored his comment and continued to unpack our lunch. But by the time I scattered his French fries on the opposite end of his Big Mac, I was about to pop. "What does that mean?"

He took a sip of Coke, and I could tell if he could come up with another topic he would have. "It's going to be hard for the police to pin him with kidnapping when she left on her own free will."

I tore open the packet of ketchup and poured it on my hamburger, tossing the empty packet to the truck floor out of spite. "She most certainly did not leave on her own. He told her a pile of lies to get her." I slammed the lid of the Big Mac shut and tossed the box back into the bag.

"All I'm saying . . ."

"I know exactly what you're saying. Look, if you don't want to be here, then just drop me off at the motel."

He sighed again and rubbed the corner of his mustache. "You know I ain't doing that. I just don't want you to get all disappointed if they don't lock him up."

"You're as bad as that old police sergeant. Didn't you

hear that girl's sister say how strung out she is on dope? If the police pulled him over right now, I guarantee you they could get him on a drug charge alone." I looked out the window. The trash that littered the sidewalk was easier to look at than Gerald. "And nobody asked you to come here. You decided and might as well say told me . . ."

The sudden swerve of the truck slung me against the window. I heard a hard thump when my head hit the glass. Gerald's truck suddenly was on the other side of the highway.

"I saw him." Gerald leaned over the steering wheel.

"What? You sure?" I asked, rubbing the back of my head.

"He passed right by us. He's got that ladder on top, right?" Gerald floored the gas pedal.

After constant disappointment, I was surprised when the nervous energy returned. When I saw the faded brown cardboard with the words *Lost Tag* on the back of the white van ahead of us, I liked to have jumped right out of the truck.

"Don't get too close," I said, remembering a TV movie where the mother blows up a car to keep from having her children taken away.

Evening was settling in when the white van pulled into a small motel connected to a flea market. An old rusty farm tractor surrounded by three black oil barrels marked the boundary between the motel and the flea market. A cloud of dust rolled over the van, and like a ghost LaRue appeared from the driver's door. He was dressed in a sleeveless T-shirt and the same tight black jeans he had on the night I saw him with Cher. A girl with stringy red hair dressed in cut-offs and a yellow bikini top got out of the passenger side.

We sat in the truck surrounded by silence, waiting and watching near the motel office. *Lord, please give me Cher,* I silently prayed. Without a care in the world or a sign of things to come, LaRue strutted inside the opened motel door.

"That him?" Gerald asked.

I nodded my head and looked down at my long nails. The vision of the same nails slicing LaRue's face took over where reasoning left off.

Gerald picked up the mobile phone and dialed 911. A man naked from the waist up walked out of the room next to LaRue's. A silver belt buckle dangled below his big stomach. He walked around in circles, scratching his head and yelling. The man was a minor distraction to the pain and rage that was building inside me. Rage not only at LaRue, but also at myself for not confronting him when I had the chance in Wiregrass. Rage that I let my lack of self-worth stop me from doing what was right for Cher.

"Let me see, this place is off Highway 71 just outside of town. Yes, ma'am." Gerald was looking towards the motel office when I opened the truck door.

"She's run off," I heard the fat man yell and scratch tuffs of hair on his head. The rolls of stomach fat shook when he stopped and looked inside LaRue's open motel door. When the man turned to face me, I saw a scratch mark with fresh blood on the side of his face.

His gray eyes looked wider and more glassy with each step.

"Erma Lee," Gerald yelled behind me. But I keep walking over rocks and sand, hearing more clearly the guitar jam that played inside LaRue's room. "Erma Lee," Gerald's voice grew closer. I could hear his boots pounding towards me. The old tractor surrounded by tall weeds and barrels was ahead on my right. "Erma Lee," Gerald yelled once more and I walked faster towards the ground-shaking music and the man with the drooping belly.

"Grandma." I stopped, thinking at first I had imagined the soft voice. I turned and saw Gerald running towards me and then looked in the direction of the rusty tractor. In between the high weeds and the tractor, Cher was crouched down behind one of the black barrels. Her lip was swollen, and the faster I ran, the redder the cake of blood looked on the corner of her mouth.

When I reached the tractor, I saw the fat man running wild-eyed towards Cher. The man yelled with his arms outstretched. Cher screamed and used one hand to push backwards into the dense weeds. Her other hand was holding together the torn strap of her sundress.

I tried to run faster, but it seemed like slow motion, watching the fat man's outstretched arms move closer towards Cher. "No, no, no," Cher kept screaming and crawling backwards. When the fat man reached down for Cher's neck, I gritted my teeth and jumped forward, landing next to the barrel. I looked up to find Gerald's hand pulling the man upright by his wiry hair.

I was struggling to catch my breath when I heard Gerald hitting the man in the face, the crush of fist meeting bone.

Cher was shaking uncontrollably. I could barely keep my arms around her. All I could think to do was rub my hands over her bare arms and tell her everything would be all right. Each syllable got caught in my throat. I knew if she could understand my words, she would know I was lying. The rattle of her teeth only stopped when I pulled her head into my chest and held her jaw shut. The twitching jawbone jarred the palm of my hand.

Thinking the shakes must be a need for warmth, I lifted her. Her head twitched against my shoulder. Running towards the truck, I passed the fat man pinned down on the hood of the rusty tractor. Gerald's bloody fist mechanically pounded the man's face. "Gerald," I screamed and continued carrying Cher towards the truck.

I placed her in the passenger seat and saw the ripped bra straps. Her hand was glued to the torn strap of her sundress. She rolled towards the passenger door and whimpered a sound I'd expect from a wounded dog. "I'm here now, baby," I repeated over and over.

When I cranked the truck and turned the heater on, I saw LaRue standing outside his room, holding the inner portion of his arm. My eyes locked on his, and if he hadn't moved so fast, I would've run him down. He jumped into the white van and spun dust around the tractor where Gerald was still pounding the fat man's face.

Anger took over where my common sense left off. I jerked the steering wheel and the truck spun around. Soon we were on the highway gaining on LaRue. The paint-spotted ladder on top of his van bounced with every dip in the road. The truck speedometer read ninety-five. Sweat formed from the heat and rage and ran down my neck.

When he turned onto a county road, his right back tire came off the road and the ladder on his roof turned sideways. We flew past a road sign ordering forty-five miles per hour. I was so close to him, I could see the wavy hair on the back of his head and the evil in his eyes each time he glanced at me in his rearview mirror. All the words I had planned to say in court would be said here, on judgment day. I slammed my foot on the gas pedal even harder.

I heard the sirens before I saw them. Two patrol cars were coming towards us in the opposite direction. Suddenly I saw the red in LaRue's only working brake light. My feet pounded the brake pedal. And the scream of Gerald's tires locking onto asphalt made me clinch my teeth and extend my arm to protect Cher from flying through the windshield. All I saw was a flash of the green pasture across the road when the truck spun to the left and crossed into the opposite lane. When we finally came to a stop, I was looking in the direction from which we had come.

The sirens grew louder, and when I looked into the rearview mirror, LaRue's white van was airborne, flying towards the side of a convenience store. Gerald's truck vibrated when the red fireball erupted behind us. Cher screamed, and I pulled her head down towards the seat. The weight of my body landed on top of her. "I love you. I love you," I screamed into her ear.

Twenty-one

*T*he only time I cried was when I looked down at Cher in the hospital room. Deep asleep, thanks to the liquid dripping into her arm, she looked angelic against the white sheets and white hospital gown. Her brown hair was tucked behind her ears, and her swollen red lip glistened from the antibiotic cream.

I sniffed and wiped away the tears with my palms. In the silence of the room, it was my chance to mourn her loss of innocence. The doctor said she had not been raped, but the fat man's attempts and the blows she took from the struggle could not match the blows I imagined her heart had received. I had failed to protect her from the wickedness of this world. Wickedness that ran through her very blood.

The tears fell on my T-shirt and temporarily released frustration and bitterness. The battle with the one thing stronger than whiskey in tearing my family apart was over. With Gerald at the police station giving his statement, it was my only chance to cry in private. I refused to let Gerald and Cher see me shed one tear.

At first, the sheriff's deputies wanted to charge Gerald with aggravated assault. The fat man's cheekbones were shattered into a bloody pulp. They even took Gerald in for questioning. My heart fell to my feet when I got back to the seedy motel that day and saw Gerald sitting in the back of the patrol car. But Cher's statement helped get him off.

The fat man had a full grocery store for LaRue: a stash of heroin and three grams of cocaine. A dealer who regularly bartered for his trades, the fat man offered LaRue his next hit for the small price of Cher's innocence. I curled my fist and hit the blue plastic cushion of the hospital chair.

As it turned out, vengeance really was the Lord's. When LaRue's van went airborne, it crashed into a propane gas tank at the convenience store. The fireball created from cans of paint in the van and the gas proved to be LaRue's final sentence. The officer said the woman normally posted at the cash register was lucky enough to have been stocking milk on the opposite side of the building. The poor old thing escaped with third-degree burns. Another victim to add to LaRue's resume.

His charred body hid the needle tracks, but heroin secured its mark on LaRue's insides. The autopsy showed he was tore up on all kinda dope when he crashed. I often wondered if he meant to plow into that white propane tank. To somehow escape the responsibility he would finally face or to do away with the turmoil that I imagined brewed in his soul.

Forgive others as Christ has also forgiven you. The words played in my mind like a tape recorder on maximum volume. And try as I might to release LaRue for final judgment, I knew he would be a hindrance until I could forgive him. *But that day would have to come tomorrow,* I decided as I tried to shake the image of his blonde hair afire.

I positioned my back against the hallway pay phone so I could watch Cher sleep. "No matter what, the Lord still loves you and Cher. There's a whole lot of meanness in this world. But God still remains." Miss Claudia's words sounded weak on the phone.

A pity party is what I wanted, not comfort. I wanted to scream and ask why I was being punished with all this turmoil. Why did everything bad happen to us? I rolled my eyes and yanked the phone receiver away from my ear. Her words of spiritual strength were not welcomed. I would've hung up if it'd come from anybody else. I wanted to lick my wounds. Question God. Shake my fist. But deep inside my spirit, I was fearful as much as determined not to go backwards. It could always get worse.

The motel Bible rested on my lap so long before I finally opened it that the book had become a heater on my skin. I read the first chapter of 2 Corinthians every ten minutes until I had the passage just about memorized. *For just as the sufferings of Christ flow over into our lives, so also through Christ our comfort overflows.* The fancy-typed words were a shot, protecting me against the pity virus that hovered over me. And sitting in the vinyl chair in Cher's hospital room, I closed my eyes, put my hands on the sheet, and forced thanks to the Lord for bringing Cher back to me, wounded yet alive.

Gerald said little after the incident. When he came into

the hospital room, he only looked at Cher for a minute or two and would disappear to the lobby. Checking out of the hospital, I had to let Gerald put the bill on his credit card. "Now I promise you seventy dollars the first of the month until I get you paid back." I was humiliated to ask for help, but after the admissions clerk informed me my HMO did not insure us out of state, I had no choice.

"I liked to killed that man with my bare hands," Gerald said. He touched the elevator button and massaged his index finger.

"He deserved every bit what you gave him."

"But I done it for all the wrong reasons." Gerald moved to let an orderly pushing a wheelchair past us.

He never said any more about the matter, but as I watched how he gently lifted Cher from the wheelchair into the truck, I knew what he meant. I figured Gerald beat the fat drug dealer for what he represented just as much as for what he did to Cher. He beat the demons out of that man. The same demons that caused the drunk in Wiregrass to get behind the wheel of his truck and kill Gerald's wife.

Gerald pushed up the brim of his cap and cut his eyes towards me from the driver's seat. Right then, his eyes and lazy smile gave me a warmth that could only be matched by Miss Claudia. He had cared enough to drop the customers who were scheduled to have their automobiles worked on, to put the miles on his truck, and to risk being arrested. All that trouble to vindicate me and to save Cher.

Cher's head rested on my shoulder, and she stared

straight ahead, never saying a word. On the interstate, I could see through the corner of my eye the backdrop of Shreveport in the side mirror. But I never looked back. Looking back at the city that produced heartache for me and my baby would be like Lot's wife looking back on Sodom and Gomorrah. And I had come too far to be turned into a pillar of salt.

The first week back in Wiregrass, church members took turns bringing supper to us—something I had no idea people did unless someone in your family died. But then again, I guess they figured that a part of Cher did die in Shreveport.

In the daytime hours, Cher went with me to Miss Claudia's and would lie in front of the TV. At night she would go straight back to her room and turn her radio on. Even Laurel's presence at the door would not get her to come out.

The evening Lee and Sonya brought a pot of chicken and dumplings to us, I was at a loss. All week Cher had not spoken a word. Even the most basic questions were answered with a shake or nod of her head. Her behavior reminded me of the struggles I had gone through with Miss Claudia. *You have nothing to be scared of anymore,* I wanted to yell into Cher's face and shake her shoulders. But the vision of her permanently handicapped like Richard prevented any tough measures.

"Erma Lee, have you thought about a counselor?" Lee asked. He watched Sonya set the cardboard box of casseroles on my dinette table.

Head shrinkers, Mama called them. I knew all about them from Suzette's stint in prison. "If she won't talk to me, what makes you think she'll talk to somebody she doesn't even know?" I spoke in a stage whisper and pushed my hand towards the floor, trying to make Lee speak in a softer tone. Cher was only steps away, locked behind thin bedroom walls.

Lee put two fingers up to the thin lips. A few black strands of hair stood like electricity was running through him. "Sometimes we hold back with the ones we're closest to," he whispered.

"And to be real honest with you, that hospital bill and the trip up there set me back." I had vowed to never again speak the word *Shreveport.* "Don't you think you could just talk with her? You know, maybe pray with her or something?"

Lee propped his hand on the kitchen counter. "You got it. But you know, prayer is a two-way street. What good is it if all she does is block my words out of her mind? I think prayer with counseling is the best thing here."

"What about Andra Kintowsky, down at the community center?" Sonya said. She looked at Lee and folded her arms.

"That's a good place to start. Andra is the best I know of. Why don't I call you with her number? They tell me there's even a plan for hardship cases." Lee nervously looked away when he said the word *hardship.*

Cher waited in the stark white lobby, staring at the loud television mounted on a corner wall. I met with Andra first. I knew I must have messed her name up by the way she responded.

"It's just like Sandra, only drop off the S. Don't worry about it, hon," she said and squinted up her round nose.

Andra said the word *hon* a lot. She was petite and stylish with a layered blonde hairdo. She told me she grew up in northern Ohio and moved to Wiregrass after her husband graduated medical school. She informed me that he was the medical director at the local rehabilitation hospital and they had a five-year-old son. "So now, hon. What about you?"

What could I say to match her wonderful home life? I'm sure twenty minutes later, after I offered highlights, she was ready to sign me up as the patient. Even so, I left nothing uncovered. Her blue eyes only widened when I told her how I found Cher in the crack house after LaRue and Suzette ran off to Las Vegas. "And I've never told Cher that. I always thought it'd be too painful for her, you know. And now with everything that happened, well, I reckon she saw enough for herself."

Andra tapped a pencil eraser on the wide desk calendar. "But you're still going to tell her, right?"

I looked down at her shiny black shoes with big square heels. Shoes like the ones Cher looked at in her fashion magazines.

"Hon, closure is going to be critical for Cher." Andra leaned forward and chopped her hand in the air. "Absolutely critical."

After Andra met with Cher for only ten minutes, she

brought her back to the lobby. For that little bit of time, I was glad I only had to pay five dollars. "You qualify for our sliding fee scale," the young receptionist said and smiled real big. *A giveaway program for the pitiful,* I thought.

A daytime story roared so loud on the television, I had to lean forward to hear Andra. "Cher and I agreed to meet weekly for a little while," Andra said, smiling, with her hands on Cher's shoulders. "See you next week, hon." Andra winked and turned back down the sterile hallway.

Walking to the car in the searing June heat, I pulled a pair of sunglasses from my pocketbook. They were not identical, but as close as I could find at K-Mart to the ones that broke the day I slapped her. To keep her from getting nervous, I handed them to her and looked away at the Hispanic man cutting the row of shrubs in front of a sign that read Houston County Mental Health Center.

"Thanks," Cher whispered.

"What'd you think of her?"

"I liked her shoes."

I clapped my hands and threw my head backwards. "I knew you'd say that the minute I saw them things." When we slid into the scorching car seats and rolled the windows down, a chill drifted down my spine. I thanked God for His mercy. That day marked the first time Cher had said two words to me since her return home.

Two days before July fourth, the divorce papers were

signed with much less fanfare than I expected. No fireworks or celebration cookout. Just the young lawyer and the dining-room table at Miss Claudia's house. Her lawyer brought them to me when he dropped off some other papers for Miss Claudia's signature.

Bozo agreed to pay fifty dollars a week in child support. I had arranged for half of each month's payment to go into the college account I opened for Cher down at the bank. The papers I signed said Bozo could visit Cher one weekend a month and two weeks during summers. But with his new love interest, I doubted Cher would be hearing from him anytime soon. I never did call and tell Bozo about LaRue. *He would just blame it all on me anyway,* I told myself as I finished polishing Miss Claudia's baby grand piano.

"Cher, you 'bout ready for our lesson," Miss Claudia yelled to Cher. "Your grandmama's got the piano all nice and shiny for us."

Cher turned off Miss Claudia's television and stumbled into the formal living room.

"And remember where middle C is now," Miss Claudia said, placing Cher's thumb on the correct key.

The piano lessons began after Cher started her marathon TV watching. "I just see that screen sucking her brain out," Miss Claudia said to me. Soon piano lessons became a way for Cher to turn off the TV and for Miss Claudia to turn off worry over the rescue home.

While Gerald and me were away looking for Cher, the city council manager promised Miss Claudia a portion of the city budget would include funds for the home. She was still lobbying local churches. Every morning she would sit in her dining room, with papers scattered all over the table, talking to local pastors and community leaders.

Miss Claudia's pastor, Dr. Winters, visited once after the church voted to turn down full sponsorship of the home.

"Miss Claudia, I wish there was more I could do." Dr. Winters shook his head and picked a piece of lint from his olive slacks.

She pulled her glasses off and slowly twirled them around with her fingers. "Oh, but Dr. Winters, I think there is more."

"What? Yes, indeed. Anything at all for you, Miss Claudia."

"You can get down on your knees and pray for the church. Too many of them are playing church rather than worshiping the Lord."

When Dr. Winters's beeper went off, Miss Claudia never let up. "I want to quote you something from Timothy," she said and picked up her ever handy red Bible. "For God did not give you a spirit of timidity, but a spirit of love, power, and self-discipline." She raised her arm in a militant fashion. "Power."

When she raised her voice and repeated the word, Dr. Winters dropped his pager and disappeared under the table trying to find it.

"Notice how I put the emphasis on *power*. Do you think we showed power when that poor man came to our church looking for somebody to be nice to him?"

"You're right, of course, but others are very comfortable with our worship service. This revival kind of thinking . . . well, it's just old-fashioned," Dr. Winters said on his hands and knees under the table.

"Revival? I'm talking about a Christian attitude, don't you know," Miss Claudia said. She lifted the lace tablecloth and looked down at him.

I noticed his pager by the china cabinet and scooped it up. "Here it is."

"Awh," Dr. Winters yelled when he crawled from under the table and bumped his head on the section piece.

The pastor fumbled to place the pager back on his belt loop. "And I pray that you'll have boldness to preach the truth and not be so bashful," Miss Claudia continued.

"Thank you, Emily," he whispered. Dr. Winters waved to Miss Claudia, and before I could run ahead to open the door for him, he was backing the Lexus out of the driveway.

I bit my lip. But when I walked into the dining room and saw Miss Claudia chuckling, I tilted my head back and liked to died laughing.

"Bless his heart. The man's got the backbone of a jellyfish," Miss Claudia said, wiping tears from her eyes. "And don't you know, if I didn't have a cent to my name, he would've never stepped foot in my place." She flung her hands to the side. "I'll pray for them. But I tell you one thing," she pointed directly at me, "the Lord spoke to me that night at church. God may be everywhere, but not everywhere is God."

I had no idea that Miss Claudia would really take me

up on my offer and go to my nondenominational church. But when I came to get her, there she was on the steps of her white-columned porch, dressed in a red suit, matching hat, and white gloves.

"Look who I got with me," I said to Gerald. Miss Claudia giggled behind me.

Gerald stood and let us enter the pew. His smile was not very broad. By the way he cast his eyes to the side, I sensed he was not happy with Miss Claudia's appearance. But if he wasn't, Marcie certainly was.

"So good to see you again," Marcie said, hugging Miss Claudia's neck.

"Let's see . . . I recall the last time we were together, you had a big trip someplace," Miss Claudia said.

Marcie slung her hair over her shoulder and stuck her chin up. "Yes, ma'am. Charleston. Oh, it's just so pretty down there. I had a grand time." She hammered down on the word *grand*. "And how are you, Erma Lee?"

When Marcie walked away, Miss Claudia held the church bulletin to the side of her mouth and pinched my arm. "I mean to tell you, she's just a regular rounder."

That afternoon Gerald called to check on Cher and me.

The echoes of Cher's radio played in the background. "She seems to be doing good. She likes that counselor, Andra. Just like Sandra but drop off the S."

"And what about you?"

"Busy helping Miss Claudia get ready for that big city council meeting. They're finalizing the budget for the house and everything."

"Hmm. Well you reckon you want to slip off and get some barbecue this evening?"

The thought of leaving Cher alone still terrified me. "Well, I sorta promised Miss Claudia I'd help send out some letters about that meeting. And Cher's got a video she wants to watch on Miss Claudia's VCR."

"Well, you know, I got a VCR over here too."

"Oh, I know. What about tomorrow night?"

"Got a horse meeting up at the clubhouse. You wanna come?"

I closed my eyes and imagined what he would say if I asked if Cher could come along too. He probably thought like Kasi. That I was mothering Cher too much. "Well, why don't you call me tomorrow at Miss Claudia's."

Cher walked into the kitchen, and I moved to let her get to the refrigerator. I watched her pour Coke into a glass and stroked her hair. I really didn't hear Gerald's tone of voice change. I just remember the sudden dial tone.

"Yeah. I'll see you, hear?" he said and hung up.

"She's opening up more," Andra said in the lobby of the mental-health clinic. Audience screams from *The Price Is Right* echoed throughout the lobby.

I wanted to ask if Cher blamed me in any way. "So she's getting better?"

"Hon, the kid's been through a lot. It's not a Band-Aid fix." Andra reached over and patted my shoulder. "She wanted things to be one way very badly, and reality forced her to see they were not."

"You talking about LaRue and Suzette?"

Andra tucked strands of blonde-streaked hair behind her ears. "I really think she needs to hear the entire story. How you and your ex-husband came to adopt her. Quite frankly, there's only so much I can do to help her. We need all the pieces to build the puzzle."

Cher was smiling when I saw her walking down the long clinic hallway. She was carrying a clump of bright-colored material in her arms.

"Look," Cher said and held up two shirts. "Andra gave these to me. Do you know how much I'd have to pay for these?"

"Not a bit of telling," I said, thinking of my own charitable clothing donated from Patricia. The designer labels were probably molded from the car-trunk humidity by now.

"See ya, kiddo," Andra said with a wink.

During the car ride back to Miss Claudia's, I wanted to give Cher the missing pieces Andra talked about. In my mind, I carefully selected the words so it would sound like I was talking about somebody else. But my limited vocabulary could not change the picture of her real mama and daddy dumping her on the floor like the empty beer cans I found gathered around her thirteen years ago.

Three times I took my eyes off the road to look at her. She was still smiling and examining the two shirts Andra gave her. And each time I looked over at her, I convinced myself she could not handle the truth. *She's just not ready,* I repeated to myself and grew frustrated at Andra for putting me on the spot. I could tell Cher was not ready by the fragile look in her brown eyes. Never once did I look into the rearview mirror and look at my own eyes.

That evening I made a leap that I felt Andra would be pleased with. I lifted my mattress, pulled out the letter Suzette sent, and drafted a reply on a piece of Cher's notebook paper.

The words flowed out of me as if I was writing a newspaper article on the last days of LaRue's life. I purposely left out words like *your husband* or *Cher's father* and kept it strictly business. *He is dead now,* I wrote at the bottom of the letter. *I hope we can all live in peace.*

Ending the letter was the hardest part. I didn't know whether or not to sign off with the words *Love, Mama*. The day she entered the prison gates, I tried hard to let Suzette die in my mind. This would be my first communication with her since that day. And most likely my last. I finally signed the letter *Mom*. Mom always sounded cold and detached. Something Yankees the likes of Andra labeled the women who bore them.

The next day I watched from Richard's garage apartment while the postman collected my letter from Miss Claudia's mailbox. I tried to picture the stops the letter would make along the way and the surprised expression upon Suzette's face when she opened the envelope.

After so many years, would Suzette's surprised expression look the same? The same bitten lip, wide eyes rolled slightly upwards. Dumping cigarette butts out of the gold-colored ashtray, I felt sorry for her and the added turmoil my letter would probably cause. *Maybe I shouldn't have sent it,* I thought. The sudden crackle of Richard's scanner jabbering about codes that only the police and Richard could decipher made me jump.

I never entered Richard's apartment unless he was away. This morning he was at the eye doctor getting a new prescription for his glasses. "Just hit the middle in his room," Miss Claudia told me about Richard's garage apartment. "He's got so many papers all over the place to where he's the only one who can make heads or tails of it. It's part of his research, don't you know."

The tip of my black work shoe was just about to press the vacuum-cleaner start button when I heard the whiny voice shoot out from the scanner. I looked at the black box with the red light on channel 23 and studied the silver antenna. Marcie was not speaking the same codes I heard earlier. Codes of speeding violations and emergency assistance. Her high-pitched voice was so vivid I could picture her facial expressions with each transmitted word.

"I hate that things aren't working out between you and her. But like you always told me . . ."

"What's that?"

Hearing Gerald's voice, I turned the volume up.

"Well, I'm just going to say this," Marcie continued. "You've always said when you lie down with dogs you get up with fleas. And ever since you almost got arrested in Shreveport," she whispered the word *arrested,* "I've had a bad feeling about you hanging around her."

Gerald's sigh sounded like something scratching against the phone receiver. His truck phone was clear enough for me to hear a Garth Brooks song playing in the background.

"I'm sorry. I should just keep my mouth shut," Marcie said.

"I heard that," I said and put my hand on my hip.

"It don't matter. She's so busy worrying over that old lady all the time, I already decided to leave her alone."

I leaned on the edge of Richard's leather couch and a stack of old *U.S. News and World Report* magazines, piled on top of the armrest, tumbled to the floor.

"I think it's best," Marcie said. "You raised two kids. You don't need another one to take on with that grand-daughter. And anyway, Annie, that woman I told you about in the judge's office, she keeps asking about you. Her divorce is final now. Kids all grown. She's real classy and just as cute as she can be."

When I scrambled to turn the volume down, my shoe slid on a slick copy of *U.S. News and World Report*. I twisted the knob in the wrong direction, and Marcie's voice blared across the room, "I'm fixing you a casse-role for supper tonight." My heart was racing when I finally managed to make the voices go away. Leaning against Richard's leather couch, I looked down at the scattered magazines. Red letters against a white background shined from one of the covers: *Divorce in the Millennium.*

Twenty-two

"Oh, I just know that good report is a sign," Miss Claudia said in the passenger seat of her car. She clutched her fists and raised her arms in victory. Her monthly visit to the oncologist showed that her white blood cells were holding their own.

"I declare, I feel stronger already." She gripped my arm, and I guided her up the brick steps. A white wooden sign with the words *Cut Ups* dangled above us. "Now, while I'm getting my hair done, don't forget to run by Benson's and pick up that dress they're holding. I plan on wearing it tonight when I give my talk."

The talk was her final pitch to the city council. Miss Claudia stood before the group in a bright blue dress with a multicolored scarf tied loosely at her neck. Her freshly painted fingernails rested on the podium. She cleared her voice and nodded to each of the nine council members.

"I'm tickled to stand before y'all this evening and present a request for funding of a project that has pulled all of Wiregrass together." She looked up from her notes and smiled.

She leaned against the podium and tilted her head dramatically to the left. "We got a petition here showing more than eleven hundred folks in Wiregrass want their tax dollars to make a difference." Miss

Claudia slightly turned and nodded at Missoura and the pastor. The big man with gold glasses and a shiny brown head eased up and handed the cardboard box of petitions to the city manager.

"The people are saying that a rescue home for battered women is needed in Wiregrass. I believe I'm not out of turn when I say we've all been blessed. We all have a safe home, I pray. And now it's time for us to stand up and help those who are living in pure you-know-what. To help these women and little children find the same security that we are blessed with.

"Now through churches, the United Way, and private donations, sixty percent of the cost to start the home is covered. I ask that you do the right thing and stand by your preliminary budget to fund the remaining forty percent."

Several board members nodded and smiled at Miss Claudia like I'd expect they'd do for a six-year-old singing a solo for the first time. A woman, her brown hair in a tight permanent wave, sat at the end of the council chamber sipping her coffee and flipping through white papers. The silver-haired man next to her leaned back in his swivel chair so far I thought he'd tip over. The creaking of his steady rock echoed during Miss Claudia's remarks.

When she finished, Miss Claudia sat next to me and listened as the next speaker, a young bearded man with a protruding belly, placed his thumbs in his blue-jean pockets and complained about the lack of funding for the baseball program. Following him, several other people voiced concerns that Wiregrass, once the Little

League capital of Alabama, was falling behind with a washed-out field and shabby uniforms.

Before I knew what was going on, the council member with the tight permanent moved to increase funding of the baseball program by seventy percent. "Second," said the man tilting backwards in the swivel chair.

The city manager raked his hand over a few remaining blonde hairs on his shiny head. He looked at Miss Claudia from his table next to the council members and shrugged his shoulders. She craned her neck and bit the bottom part of her lip.

"What's up?" Cher whispered to me.

Not meaning to copy the city manager, all I knew to do was shrug my shoulders and look at Miss Claudia. Her eyes widened, and she inched forward on the black padded chair. Squirming in the seat was a last-ditch lobbying effort.

"Bless it," Patricia said the next morning. She patted Miss Claudia's arm with one hand and scooped the remaining cheese grits out of the saucer with the other.

Richard chewed his bacon and nodded at each attack Miss Claudia offered the city council. "That city manager sat right there in his office and promised Richard and me it was a done deal."

I poured Patricia another cup of coffee, and Miss Claudia shook her finger faster.

"And what about that? Tying up good taxpayers' dollars on some baseball mess." Miss Claudia leaned over her china coffee cup. "When I could drive around this county and find forty women by sundown who look like they got hit with a baseball bat."

"Mama, parents go plumb nuts over sports. I know. I see it at school all the time." Patricia dabbed her glossy red lips with the white napkin.

"Well, I'm ashamed to live in a place where the needy take second place to new Little League uniforms." Miss Claudia shut her eyes and tightly folded her arms.

"Oh, now, Mama, you mean no such a thing," Patricia said, handing me the empty grit bowl.

Miss Claudia never opened her eyes. "I most certainly do."

"Now, Mama. This town's been good to us," Patricia said. I was sure, by the way she lifted her voice, she would break out into song any minute.

"I guarantee you, Daddy would've gone down there . . ." Richard began before Patricia rolled her eyes towards him.

"Remember now, most the people on that city council and their parents before them were good customers at the store," Patricia said. "They helped secure a mighty nice lifestyle for us."

I was putting the pitcher of milk back into the refrigerator, when Miss Claudia looked up at me. Her sunken, hazel eyes locked on me, and she shook her head.

With me in the room, I could only imagine how hard the situation was for her. I figured she looked at me and thought of the world she survived and looked at Patricia and thought of the world she had carved out for herself. I tensed and waited to hear once again the words of evil acts. To hear the words that would remove her children from the life of privilege in Wiregrass and transport them to the black-and-blue times she faced at the hands of Luther Ranker.

"I'm just plain sorry is all," Miss Claudia finally said and looked down at the untouched plate of bacon and grits. "I let them down."

"Bless it," Patricia said once more and placed her hands on top of Miss Claudia's bony fingers. "Now, Mama, you fought a good fight. Nobody expected you to do this but you. I know how much that little home meant to you. But there's other stuff you can work on."

As Patricia offered a list of projects sponsored by the Cotillion Society, Miss Claudia once again looked up at me. Before her eyes could latch on me, I turned and faced the sink full of grease-spattered pots.

With the piano strands of "Victory in Jesus" echoing in my ear, I led Miss Claudia and Cher out of Sunday morning services. If it hadn't been that church was the only place Cher seemed remotely interested in going to, I would have stayed home. Sitting in the back pew and hearing Marcie impart her words of wisdom during children's moments was nauseating. I had to open my white Bible to the passage about Jesus drawing the line in the sand and telling the crowd who wanted to stone the prostitute that he who was without sin should cast the first stone. I read Jesus' statement six times before Marcie disappeared and Lee began his sermon.

Only once when leaving church did I glance back and see Gerald talking to a new church member. Standing next to his regular pew, Gerald smiled and shook hands with the red-headed lady. *A fresh catch,* I told myself. When Brownie saw me and waved her black Bible, I stopped in the aisle and spoke to her.

"I'll just wait for you in the car," Miss Claudia whispered. Cher followed closely behind her.

I had gotten used to Cher wanting to run off and not speak to anybody. But this was a first for Miss Claudia.

When I liked to knock old Mrs. Greer down, I turned around, begged forgiveness, and walked towards the light of the open church doors.

Lee was still talking to Miss Claudia when I stepped outside the door.

"It's not over yet. We just need to keep praying and that home will make it here yet," he said, holding Miss Claudia's hands.

She looked down at the green outdoor carpet and her shiny beige pumps. "We'll see."

Walking to the big Lincoln parked under one of the oak tree limbs, I tried to think of an encouraging word or something funny to say. But the cloud of disappointment hung as low as the moss from the trees.

Pictures of castles and islands with white block homes replaced the letters, petitions, and file folders that had populated Miss Claudia's dining-room table.

"And look here, Mama," Patricia said, pointing to the castle. "Some places we'll see date back to the 1500s." She lightly tapped Miss Claudia's shoulder.

"And this one here's where y'all are staying, right?" I asked, trying to show enough interest for myself and Miss Claudia.

"Yes, on the last portion of our trip," Patricia said and then hid the brochures to the side of her hips. "Now, I just hate to run off and leave you all upset, Mama."

"Nonsense," Miss Claudia said. "Your twenty-five-year anniversary only comes once."

"Well, that's what Doctor Tom said. But I just can't imagine a whole month on a cruise." She fanned her face with the brochures. "Mercy."

The day before her journey, Patricia reviewed the steps to take in case of an emergency. Miss Claudia was still standing by the window when she left. She had a spot where Patricia had tattooed a red lipstick print on her cheek. She was holding the heavy gold curtain apart and watching Patricia drive away in the silver Mercedes. "I've been studying about Patricia. Maybe we need to follow her lead. Just get away for a spell." She turned and smiled at me.

"Well, sure. I mean you talking about going to Panama City or up to the mountains?" Listing all the places I had experienced through the vacation stories of others.

"*Southern Living* ran a big article on St. George Island last month. Down in Florida, near where I'm from," she said, gazing out the window. "Back then, there wasn't even a bridge to the place. Now they got all sorts of fine homes there."

"I bet this will get Cher excited," I said, letting her

know I refused to leave Cher behind.

"It's time," she whispered. Miss Claudia continued to stare at the light that seeped through the window sheers. "I just believe it'll do us all a world of good."

Gerald called the day I packed my clothes into our makeshift suitcases, a dozen paper grocery bags. I said nothing of the month-long stay Miss Claudia planned in Florida. *Buddy, why don't you just go on and try that woman Marcie wants you to sample?*

Before Gerald could finish telling me about the new alternator he was installing, I snapped a quick, "Well, let me go, hear?"

Hanging up the receiver, I convinced myself he was better with the woman I heard Marcie describe as classy. A woman with the elegance of Miss Claudia, Patricia, or Andra. A woman Marcie could talk to about clothes and the latest hairdos. *It's for his own good,* I thought, and tried to follow Miss Claudia's rule about topics I could not control. "Just dismiss it from your mind," she'd always say whenever I brought up a useless worry.

"Hon, here's my home number in case you need me," Andra said the day before we left. Her frosty white fingernails slid the thick paper across her desk.

"Now, you don't think me taking Cher down there this long will mess nothing up?"

"Honestly?" She leaned forward and propped her chin on the manicured fingernails. "It's up to you and Cher now."

Afraid that Miss Trellis would hold my envelopes

over a hot steamer and get all into my business, I gave Kasi responsibility for my mail. Not that I had anything earth-shattering coming from the postal service, but there would be the first installment of Bozo's child support and a few coupon fliers I might use when we got back.

After Kasi closed her trailer door, I felt a penetration of guilt for not telling Gerald we were going away. To me a month away from home might as well have been a year. And even if he was through with me, if he happened to call or stop by, his good-natured spirit would cause him to worry about our welfare. I tapped on Kasi's vinyl door.

"If you see Gerald, just tell him I'll see him in a month." The very words made me feel strange, like I was in one of those old late-Saturday-night movies Cher and me watched on TV. A plot suited for a rich woman running off on a European holiday.

"Awright. I'll sure do it," Kasi said and blew cigarette smoke into my hair.

When we passed the green sign with the orange sketch of Florida welcoming us to the Sunshine State, Miss Claudia became restless. She pulled at her pants and twisted in the seat every few miles.

"Thirty more miles to Apalachicola, Mama," Richard said. He filed a mileage report each time we passed a sign noting the number of miles to Miss Claudia's former home.

By the time we entered the city limits of Miss Claudia's old hometown, I was lost in the view. "This is just beautiful," I said, looking down past the gray water and onto the marble courthouse and the square blue inn with white latticework. An old Victorian mansion and two-story brick buildings formed Apalachicola's main street.

Miss Claudia sat in the passenger seat gripping the blue material at the knees of her slacks. The sun shining through the passenger window made the drops of sweat on her lip glisten like early morning dew.

"In all my years, I've never been here," Richard said from the backseat.

Cher leaned against the front armrest. "Does it look different to you, Miss Claudia?"

"Mmm-hmm," Miss Claudia replied, never looking at the little fishing village outside her window.

I gripped the steering wheel and cut my eyes towards her. But as soon as we passed over the bridge and the town was behind us, Miss Claudia released the grasp on her pant legs. Rows of navy wrinkles were all that remained.

Cher leaned on the back of the seat while Miss Claudia's Lincoln coasted down the long bridge to St. George Island. Pine trees and sawgrass dotted the edges of the bay side.

"Forgotten Florida," Richard called the island.

After we picked up our house key from the real-estate office, Miss Claudia asked me to stop at the corner of the main road. Her eyes grew wider when she ordered a bushel of oysters from a man with a red umbrella in the back of his truck. A white sign spray-painted with the words *Fresh Seafood* propped against the back truck tire.

"Those things are nasty," Cher said and stuck a finger in her mouth.

"Sugar, you haven't lived until you've tasted an oyster from Apalachicola Bay," Miss Claudia said. "We're going to be regular big shots shucking oysters tonight."

I laughed harder than the situation warranted, relieved that the salt air we had driven hours to find was working its magic.

The island had one main road that stretched from one end of water to the other. Other than three real-estate offices, a convenience store, two restaurants, and a brightly painted pink building that sold ice cream and rented videotapes, St. George Island was made up of homes. We drove to the end, next to the gated state park. Two sand dunes covered with tall brown grass greeted us as the Lincoln pulled into the gravel driveway. The beige stucco building, held high off the ground by four large stilts, was pushed far away from the other homes. Rows of sugar-colored sand dunes were our closest neighbors.

Cher jumped out of the car and headed towards the beach. "Don't you get your clothes all wet," I yelled behind her.

We unlocked the door to discover four bedrooms and a large screened porch facing the beach. The home looked like something out of one of Miss Claudia's magazines. Three big white columns separated the kitchen and living room. "Cher'll be happy," I said and pointed to the VCR and library shelf packed with videos.

I placed Miss Claudia's luggage in the big bedroom that faced the emerald water. She sat on a white chest at the end of the bed and clasped her hands.

"This place looks brand-new." I pulled back the floral drapes and opened the French doors leading to the screened porch. The tinkle of wind chimes echoed, and a soft breeze made the sheer curtains sway in all different directions.

"Good gracious alive." Miss Claudia took a deep breath of the salty air. "I don't know what kept me so long."

Twenty-three

"The man next door's from Albany, Georgia," Richard announced before lunch. "He has a fine boat parked down at the marina. Mentioned us taking a fishing expedition."

Miss Claudia winked at me and placed the bowl of boiled shrimp on the table. "Did you wash your hands?"

While Richard was sanitizing himself, a thud from outside vibrated the floor. The sound of Cher racing up the steps became her calling card. A red-and-white-striped beach towel was wrapped around her, and her hair was slicked back with salt water.

"I'm going to lay out and get *darrrrk*," she said, twirling around in circles.

"Watch out or you'll knock something over," I said and brushed the crystal sand from her cheek. Seeing her acting childish was a welcome change to the shell-shocked young woman I first dropped off at Andra's office.

By the end of the first week, I settled into a spoiled, carefree lifestyle. A way of life I imagined people on the *Lifestyles of the Rich and Famous* lived. But it took another week to lose the nervous edge that I ought to be busy with some household chore. With such a compact house there was little cleaning. Just the daily washing and cooking. Plenty of time was left to sit on the beach watching Cher ride the waves on the yellow-and-black boogie board that she secretly talked Miss Claudia into buying. After the afternoon dishes were washed, I would walk down the white sand beach and check on the progress of the fishermen, who kept their rods nestled inside PVC pipes, hidden deep within the sand.

Miss Claudia originally suggested that we continue our daily Bible study. It was my idea to meet on the front porch just before sunrise.

Miss Claudia stared at the white sand scattered on the porch floor. "Erma Lee, why do you reckon God put a stop to the rescue home?"

I sipped a cup of coffee and ran my fingers through loose hair. Orange rays were rising over the dunes on the side of the house. "When we first got back from picking up Cher, you know, over there."

346

Miss Claudia nodded, offering a detour around saying the word *Shreveport*.

"Lee's sermon the first Sunday back was on *circumstance*. He said when you go through bad stuff and don't have answers, you got to focus on Christ. That's just how he said it, Christ—not circumstance. We can either let the circumstances control us, or we can ask the Lord to carry it for us."

Miss Claudia rocked in the wicker chair, and the roar from the waves grew stronger. "But I know the Lord wanted me to move forward with that house. I just know it."

"Then you did your part. And I know I'm not telling you stuff you don't already know," I said and playfully pointed my finger at her. "But we all got a free will. Even those city council people."

"Free will. Yes, indeed." She looked through the porch screen. Her lonesome eyes trailed a sea gull flying inches above the waves.

"Now I want to tell you something. Are you listening?"

She glanced at me and half smiled.

"All right. We study this here Bible to know how to live like Christ. And if there's anybody on this earth who does it, it's the woman sitting in front of me," I said, tucking a strand of hair behind my ear. "You make your mark on so many people, I couldn't count them if I had to. I see how you leave people feeling better. How you let them know you love them." My voice cracked, and I quickly looked down at the rocker's peeling white flakes. "I know cause that's how you done me. And well . . . I love you for it."

The creaking floor caused me to look up. The edge of her baby blue duster was next to my rocking chair. Before she walked inside the house, she squeezed my shoulder. I sipped coffee and witnessed the first rays of sunlight easing over the island and into the water. The squeeze of her hand made me feel light. Light enough to step off the porch and join the group of pelicans flying over the beach in a V-shaped pattern.

During the days that followed my pep talk, conversations with Miss Claudia were superficial. She was cheery enough, laughing at Richard's corny jokes, making over how Cher's arms were being defined from all her swimming, telling me how good the fish was, but never anything deeper. Even the morning Bible studies seemed rehearsed and stilted.

"Erma Lee, I need you to pack me a sandwich and a handful of potato chips," Richard said while I scrubbed the breakfast dishes.

"What you got going on?" I asked and turned sideways. Richard was putting Cher's suntan lotion on his arms and hands.

"What in the world?" Miss Claudia propped her hand on the kitchen bar.

"Matt, you know, our neighbor, is taking me trout fishing. He said this place has the biggest . . ."

"Well, you can't do that," Miss Claudia snapped.

I turned around with soap bubbles still on my hands.

"Now, Mama, we're just going fishing. I took all my medicine this morning."

"Have you even been out on a boat in the past twenty-five years? You have no earthly idea how you might carry on."

"And neither do you." His right arm stretched out frozen. The white and orange bottle of lotion tilted in his hand.

"I reckon I know enough. I'm the one who saw you hooked up to those tubes when you fell out in a spasm that day in court," Miss Claudia yelled. "Liked to give me and your daddy a heart attack seeing you that way."

"It's just a boat. A boat," Richard said. A drop of white suntan lotion fell to the floor.

"You're special, you know that. You can't do like other men. That boat will be loud and bumpy. Your nerves will just go all to pieces."

Richard stormed into his room and came out with a white cap with the word *Florida* stitched in orange thread across the front. "Never mind the sandwich, Erma Lee. I'll stop by the store on the way out."

"Richard, I'm warning you. It's trouble. I feel it." Miss Claudia held the door and yelled down the stairs. When Richard's shoes no longer stomped the wooden stairs, she closed the door.

She stood planted at the door until the awkward silence forced me to speak. "I know you're probably thinking about what happened to your first husband."

"What?" Her pained expression made me wonder if she questioned whether the man who just ignored her really was a nerve patient after all.

"You know, with Luther Ranker getting lost at sea and everything."

She wrinkled her brow and shooed her hands.

"That was a long time ago," I said. "This man's boat is probably top dollar. Well, there's not even a cloud today."

"After Richard came to live with us, I stayed worried to death he'd have another nerve attack. His daddy even hired a man to put soundproof insulation in the walls of the apartment." She eased down on the sofa. "We liked to lost him the first time. Oh, Erma Lee, I just can't bear to lose another child." Her hand trembled when she shaded her eyes.

I knelt beside the sofa. "He'll be fine. You won't lose him over no fishing trip. It might even do him good."

A steady chime drifted from the porch. The high-pitched toll was too closely akin to a wail of mourning. I blocked the noise from my mind and chose instead to focus on the feeling that my knee was falling asleep.

Miss Claudia's weak eyes fixated on the black TV screen. "My poor Beth. She was just the tiniest thing you ever did see. So vulnerable to the meanness."

Her white blouse felt slick when I rubbed her shoulder. "Now, that was a long time ago. Your first baby's at rest."

"Oh no, no, no." Her eyes widened, and her mouth gaped open. She moaned in a way I had never heard before, neither a sound of pain or pleasure. A stream of drool trickled from the corner of her mouth. Thinking she was having a stroke, my first inclination was to call an ambulance. Keeping the wild-eyed stare, she got up from the sofa and drifted to the door. "I can't stand this mess," she slowly said, her eyes closed and her hand on the gold doorknob. "I just can't stand it. Run me up to the cemetery."

Unsure of Miss Claudia's mental state, I let Cher stay behind on the beach. Miss Claudia was quiet when we reached the top of the big bridge guarding Apalachicola Bay. She leaned against the car window and stared at the two-block city.

"Over yonder is where Luther kept his boat," she said and pointed to the spot where a restaurant now stood.

As if the years had rolled back upon our arrival, she called each building by its name known seven decades ago. When we came to the spot where the local bank stood, she tapped the passenger window with her red fingernail. "Old Man Maxwell's store. Good riddance."

She never said to pull into the cemetery, but when I saw her point towards the small graveyard across from the gray stone church, I turned on the blinker. Spanish moss from the oak tree branches dangled above the black wrought-iron gates through which we passed.

Slick green leaves from a magnolia tree hung over the area Miss Claudia was drawn to. The edges of the headstones hinted at the white they once were. Age and weather had turned them a sooty black. A simple concrete cross marked the spot where her father was buried. "You know, I still thank God every day for my daddy. If it hadn't been for that good, sweet man, I might've never had enough trust to find Wade Tyler."

A few steps farther, she stopped and looked up with

her eyes closed. I adjusted my sunglasses, trying to watch for any signs of buckling legs.

"Erma Lee, I got something to say. And I want you to hold your tongue until I'm through."

She pointed the end of her cane towards the tiny headstone. Ranker was the only recognizable word on the black-streaked stone.

"We put my little Beth here, next to Daddy. I always imagined the good Lord sending Daddy for her the night she passed. Luther wasn't supposed to come home early that night. He said he wanted to take the mullet nets and fish until sunup. But shortly after midnight, I heard him groaning on the front steps, straining to pull the wet rubber boots off his feet.

"Beth was just two then. The poor little thing had been running a fever all day. The doctor was over in Gulf County. I made do the best I could. The wet rag worked for a little while, but by the time Luther got in, she was pulling her blonde curls and screaming at the top of her lungs.

" 'You better shut that young 'un up,' Luther yelled from the bed. His tongue was never thick from whiskey, just from meanness. I bounced her on my hip and pushed her face into my nightgown, hoping to drown out the screaming. But she'd only gasp for air, throw her head back, and scream louder.

"All I could hear were screams. Luther's screams. My baby's screams. And before I could gather my senses, I was screaming too. Screaming that I hated Luther and saying all the foul things I had tried to bottle in my throat in days gone by. I still can see the crooked purple vein in his temple, big and bulging, when he stood over the rocker and screamed into my face.

"That was the one time I thought he'd really kill me. You know it was the strangest thing, I'd prepared myself for death. Even welcomed it. But when the time came, I didn't give in like I thought. With every ounce of strength I slammed my knee between his legs. He fell on the floor, rolling back and forth, eyes wide open.

"Beth looked like something gone wild. My baby's hair was hanging in her face and inside her mouth. She just kept screaming while I ran with her into our bedroom. I grabbed Luther's wallet and slipped on a pair of shoes, still listening to him in the other room moaning.

"The old front screen door hung by one hinge. I remember thinking how easy it was to kick open and wondered why I'd never tried it before.

"We made it to the first porch step when I felt the stinging fire of his work boot against my neck." Miss Claudia's hand trembled when she rubbed her neck just as if the bruise was still fresh.

"When he hit me with his boot, I turned just a touch. And when I did I saw the flash of his fist coming at my eye, knocking me sideways down the steps. I landed on the bottom step, and he jumped on top of me. It only hurt for a few punches, and then my face felt numb. I kept trying to arch my back, hoping Beth would crawl out from under me. All I could feel was a lump underneath my spine. Like a sack of flour or something. 'My baby! My baby!' I kept trying to scream, but nothing came out of my mouth but blood."

Miss Claudia took two steps backwards, and I helped her to a marble bench. Brittle, dead magnolia leaves and moss covered the seat. Her glasses had slipped to the end of her nose, and a line of sweat trickled down her temple.

"*Accident,* they called it. The doctor only found a tiny spot of blood on the side of Beth's head. I always hoped she died the minute she hit that porch step. The poor old doctor tried to comfort me by saying she probably would've died from the fever anyway.

" 'I hope you know you killed her,' Luther said the day after we buried her. 'You squashed her like a roach,' he'd say over and over until I would feel my teeth chattering from nothing but pure rage.

"I spent the next month thinking of a way to end it. I had an idea to stow away on one of the fishing boats. When they were deep in the Gulf, busy working, I'd sneak out from under the tarp and ease myself into the water. But Luther pushed me before I could ease into anything.

"The night he slapped me in the kitchen for not frying the mullet crispy enough, I got up from the table, barely making a sound. He continued to eat his swamp cabbage and grits and complained about prices paid for grouper. A slap was nothing but a love tap for Luther. I liked to not even flinch when he struck me. Just like I didn't flinch when I saw the knife lying on the counter.

"I can still see the flakes of silver-and-blue fish

354

scales left on the blade. That's all I remember, those shiny fish scales. Pretty, like diamonds or something. And the next thing I know, I'm standing behind Luther's chair looking at the knife sticking out of the side of his neck and listening to him gurgle for air. He tried to turn around, but slipped sideways and hit the floor. Silly the things you remember. The loud thud from the fall reminded me of Old Man Maxwell's store and how he used to throw sacks of feed on the wooden floor.

"Every light in the house was on when I went running to Missoura and Aaron's place. They told me later I was beating on the door and screaming that somebody had killed me. If it had been anybody else I'd run to, I'm satisfied I'd be in the nervous hospital, don't you know.

"Aaron's forehead glowed with sweat when he looked down at the hateful man who furnished his paycheck. I know most he was studying what might happen to him if any of this hit the streets.

"I helped Aaron wrap Luther in a sheet, trying to make myself believe that the body we rolled was a rag doll. A doll, nothing more or less, with some of the stuffing missing from its neck. I helped load the crimson-soaked sheet into Aaron's wagon. An hour after the saloon closed, the town was quiet. Aaron headed west with the wagon. When he found the fresh-tilled soil roped off with white cord, he put Luther away for good."

Miss Claudia gripped my arm, and I pulled her from the bench. She was stooped over. The tip of her cane shook when she lifted the end and pointed to the brick two-story building with the words *Rexall* painted on the side.

"Aaron had heard some men say concrete was to be poured for the old bank building the next day. So there, Luther Ranker was sealed away for good. After he buried him, Aaron took Luther's boat over to St. George Island and burned it. Before dawn, Missoura and I took their little rattletrap boat and picked him up. We took turns fighting the waves with the oars. Funny, I remember gritting my teeth and pulling that heavy brown paddle, all the while thinking if I'd known I was this strong, maybe things would've turned out different.

"We timed our move to Wiregrass. I went first as the pitiful young widow looking for work to pay bills because her husband was lost at sea. Missoura and Aaron came six months later.

"I'll never love a man more than Wade Tyler for seeing that they had work. My second husband never knew all what went on here. It's just not fitting to talk about such things. Whenever I thought about that night, I just changed it all in my mind to a part Vivian Leigh or Bette Davis might play in a picture show."

A bird chirped off in the distance, and we moved slowly down the brick path to the car. Passing rows of headstones, I felt my head swimming with the words that had been poured into it. I leaned to the left, steadied myself, and put my hand on her pointy elbow. Even if I would've had words to offer, I doubt my mouth would've produced them.

Once I cranked the car, I sat still, gazing at the magnolia tree that guarded the headstones of her secrets.

"I've bottled up that mess until, at times, I thought I'd take a running fit," Miss Claudia said and patted her upper lip with a lace handkerchief.

I wanted to tell her it was going to be all right, but my lips bonded together. Instead, I shifted the air-conditioning vents on her and pressed my foot on the accelerator. The deepened roar of the car engine was the only sound I controlled as the car struggled to the top of the tall bridge leaving Apalachicola.

"Nobody's been truer friends than Missoura and Aaron," she said and shook her head. "No, siree. When I married Wade Tyler, I felt so guilty for my good fortune. But Missoura led me to the answer. We knelt by my fireplace, and I asked Jesus to forgive me and to take over my life." She turned to look at me with her eyebrows raised. "Now, not to say I didn't struggle. I declare, sometimes it's easier to pray and ask the Lord to forgive you than it is to accept it yourself."

When the car was on the highest point on the bridge, Miss Claudia sighed and looked out the window. The second-story windows of the Rexall building were framed in the rearview mirror. A monument too tall for a man as sorry as Luther Ranker.

A steady drizzle fell on the beach. Cher watched a video, and Richard talked about his adventures at sea. Grease spattered and hissed each time I turned his catch of red fish in the skillet.

Richard leaned on the kitchen bar, and in between my nods and fake laughs at his fishing tales I cut my eyes towards Miss Claudia's bedroom. The white door had been closed since we got back from the cemetery in Apalachicola. I was scared to death that I had done the wrong thing by giving her an extra nerve pill the night before. Since then, every time I checked on Miss Claudia, she'd just lick her lips and mumble something about needing rest.

After the supper dishes were cleared, I eased the bedroom door open. The tinkling sound from the wind chimes was the only sign that movement existed in the darkened room. Light from the opened door spread across her bed.

"You doing okay?" I asked.

She slowly pulled the floral print bedspread off her. When she leaned up, her matted hair looked like someone had stomped on her head. And I wondered if Luther Ranker had ever styled her hair in a similar rat's nest with his work boot. An injustice buried under a building that now gave out medicine to free people from pain.

She coughed and squinted her eyes. "Where am I?"

I froze and felt my heart skip a beat. "Now, you know where we are. We're down here at St. George Island having a big time." I walked over to the nightstand and turned on the shell-shaped lamp.

She squinted her eyes tighter and reached for her glasses.

"I been dreaming," she said and raked her red fingernails through the black-and-gray waves of hair. "Just awful things. Just not even fit to talk about."

"Then we just won't talk about them." I sat on the

edge of the bed, and my hand rested where her feet poked up under the sheet.

"I ought not of burdened you with all that talk at the cemetery."

"Now, you don't worry about that."

She licked her chapped lips, and I went into the adjoining bathroom. When I handed her the Chapstick tube, she tried to laugh. "You gonna spoil me yet."

"That's my job, remember." I reached over to pick up the empty water glass from the nightstand, and she grabbed my arm.

"I hope you don't think less of me. You know, for what I did. I just felt trapped. And then . . ."

"And then, we forget about it." I rubbed the dry, scaling skin on her arm. "Now, this morning I went ahead and studied the Bible without you. Even though you was in here playing Miss Sleeping Beauty."

She smiled and ran her fingers through mine.

I grabbed the red leather Bible from her nightstand. "When I read this I knew I'd heard you say it before. It's in Isaiah," I said, flipping the thin pages and hoping I could find the chapter without her assistance. *"Forget the former things; do not dwell on the past. See, I am doing a new thing. Now it springs up; do you not perceive it? I am making a way in the desert and streams in the wasteland."*

Her bony fingers squeezed my hand. When I looked up, her smile was so sweet and innocent that it looked like it belonged on a little young 'un instead of a confessed killer.

"I saw that and thought about the first time you read

it to me. Our way was made out of the desert. You got nothing to worry about anymore. When you and me asked the Lord to forgive us, we got it without any extra work."

Days later, after supper, Miss Claudia went with Richard to see the fishing boat he and his new friend had been using to supply many of our meals. During the time alone with Cher, I discovered just how hard it was to practice what I preached.

The thin pad of my flip-flops made squeaky noises each time I lifted my foot off the thick sand. The sound made me shrink and bite my lip like I used to whenever somebody would run their fingernails down a chalkboard. To distract myself from the sound, I looked up and waved to Cher.

She was riding the boogie board on her knees. Rolling waves pushed her towards the white sand shore. Purplish clouds hung low behind her, and the sun waited in the chute for its departure. By the time I reached her, Cher had propped the board against the beach chair.

"You missed me wiping out," she said, running the back of her hand across her nose. Two strips of white, dead skin peeled upwards on the tip.

"Lord, I don't see how you stay on that thing."

"Richard tried it," she said and laughed.

I held my hand on my stomach and howled. "And Miss Claudia thought he'd have problems fishing? She'd have a natural-born fit if she knew he was out there on that thing."

We walked towards the state park, between white dunes and the departing tide. I looked down at insect-sized white crabs racing from one hole in the sand to the other. *If life could only be so easy—to know exactly which hole to run to.*

Cher was still talking about a surfboard she had seen at the beach store when I jumped in all or nothing. "You don't say much about it. You doing okay and everything?"

Cher was still smiling. Her thoughts most likely still with the surfboard she desired. She nodded her head and looked down at the sand.

We stopped long enough for me to slip off my flip-flops, then we continued walking along the edge of the shore. The cool waves tickled my toes, and Cher laughed when I moaned. *She's doing fine,* I thought and kicked the clear saltwater towards the sky. I felt relieved that her counselor would be satisfied with the way I had cared for her. I could just picture me sharing the good reports with Andra. When I shared the report, Andra would most likely be standing in the white-walled clinic hallway, smiling and widening her blue eyes.

Cher didn't look up from digging her big toe in the sand. "How come you let my mama marry him?"

I stopped and turned towards Cher. The sun was hanging low behind her. I wanted to ignore the question and tell her to turn around and watch the start of the sunset. My heart began to race. Cher's toe disappeared deeper in the soft sand.

I noticed she did not refer to LaRue as her father. She

omitted his name the same way I had all those times before. *Him* or *that man* were words used as scabs to cover up the wounds LaRue had left on our lives.

"Tell you the truth, I don't know," I said and sat down on a cascading bank of sand. I studied Cher and the sinking sun behind her. "She just up and ran off with him. Suzette was legal age to marry. Her home life wasn't great. I know that. But believe me, I begged your mama not to marry him," I said and then worried how that sounded. "But you know what? If those two never would've married, there'd be no you. And whether you know it or not, you are the best thing in my life. Always have been. You got the world by the tail, girl."

She glanced at me sideways and then continued burying her foot in the damp sand. "How come my mama let you and Pop adopt me then?"

The question had been asked by Cher a hundred times before. The first time I stuttered and coughed a lot. Soon the answer became scripted in a format I'm sure Cher could recite. A half-truth of prison sentences and sickness to drugs. I could see Andra's raised eyebrows and hear her instructions that the rest of the healing was left up to me.

I breathed deeply and tasted the mist of sea salt on my tongue. "Cher, I want to be honest with you, I really do. But this thing flat won't be easy. For me or you. Come over here and sit with me, please." I was afraid she'd think I was babying her too much. "I just want you to help cut some of this wind off me."

Cher pulled her feet out of the sand and never stiffened or shrugged when I placed my arm around her damp shoulders. The warmth of her sun-soaked skin helped steady the rhythm of my heart.

I started from the day I couldn't get anyone to answer the phone at the little rental house in Shreveport. And never once did either of us cry when I told the story of finding the best thing in my life discarded next to crushed beer cans and a charred sofa. I just held her tightly around the shoulders and watched the tip of the orange sun slowly dip under the sea. Staring at the pink and blue strokes across the gray sky, I picked my words carefully. Words of lost dreams and hopeful tomorrows.

Later that evening, each time I looked at Cher, she shied her eyes away from me. When I joined Miss Claudia, Richard, and Cher to watch television in the living room, she got off the floor and went to her bedroom. I heard the laughter from the situation comedy on TV, but never saw the humor. *Congratulations, Erma Lee, you blew it again.* I stared at the white bookshelves. Part of me wanted to call Andra and chew her out for dictating that I should tell Cher the whole truth. Andra was probably some quack who couldn't get a real job in the hospital and ended up at the community health center helping charity cases like Cher.

I tossed and turned in the bed, chastising myself for listening to Andra. *What kind of counselor do you call yourself?* I wanted to yell. I pictured Andra with her perfect hair, sleeping in a safe, warm bed with her doctor-husband. Cher was better off with my version of just part of the story than the whole nasty mess. I punched my pillow and slung my hair back.

The door squeaked, and I squinted my eyes. All I could make out was an outline of a body. Her arm latched around my waist. The smell of Cher's strawberry-scented shampoo kept me steady.

"You couldn't sleep neither?" I asked.

"Remember when I was little and you used to snuggle with me?" She moved closer against my back. "You said I'd say 'snuffles,' and you'd know what I wanted."

My chest shook when I giggled, and I turned my head to glimpse her in the corner of my eye. The moonlight streaming in from the window blinds made the side of Cher's face look blue. "Yeah, you and your snuffle." My chest shook again, and I hoped she couldn't tell I was fighting off a cry.

"This new book I'm reading, the one about the girl who rides in horse shows and makes money for her family," she said and squeezed my stomach harder. "There's this woman in the book they say is like an iron fist inside a velvet glove."

"Umm, she sounds mean."

"She's not. She's just tough," Cher said and locked her foot around mine. "Like us."

Twenty-four

*W*hen our four-week beach holiday was over and we arrived at our rusting trailer, a note from Gerald was sticking between the rubber lining of the door. The block letters were written on the back of a NAPA envelope. Judging by the dirt and smear of ink on the envelope, it had been there a while. *Just trying to catch up with ya. Hope you are good.*

Cher ran to retrieve the mail from Kasi's, and I fought my way through the thick, hot trailer air. Having told Cher about Suzette's letter during my confessional, I lifted my mattress and pulled out the note.

When Cher entered carrying bills and junk mail, I started talking before she could put the stack on the kitchen counter.

"I put your mama's letter in there on your bed. Just take it in and talk with Andra about it." I felt uneasy trying to play counselor and me with no education.

The following week, Cher announced she was writing Suzette and wanted me to help her. I sat at the dinette table staring at the paper full of Cher's articulate lines about her episode in Shreveport. I bit on the end of the pen, trying to look as if I was capturing my thoughts, but only a blank slab appeared. My other letter to Suzette was strictly business. LaRue was dead. The words were colder than a morgue most likely would use to announce the death of her former husband.

"Just write how you feel," Cher finally instructed and poured herself a Coke.

Advice coming from Andra, no doubt, and for a lot less money. I drug the pen across the page. I tried to make every letter straight and perfect: *We had a real nice time down in Florida. Cher is so tan. But you know me and how I can't take the sun. I hope you're good. Mama.*

I looked at the note and read my part again. I was lying. Suzette had been locked away for thirteen years. She didn't know me. The real me. Just like I didn't know her. The words on the note sounded cold and calculated, something I'd expect my own mother to write. I quickly picked up the pen and added the word *Love* to the closing.

"I believe Mama's out of those little blue tablets," Richard said. "I'm going to the drugstore to get a refill."

"She's needing some more toothpaste too," I said and smiled at Richard. Not that he could handle anything urgent probably, but I was pleased to see him taking more interest in caring for his mother.

Standing at the sink washing the lunch dishes, I could hear Miss Claudia's soft voice echoing from the dining room. "Oh, the island's so grown up you'd hardly recognize the place, Missoura."

Upon our return to Wiregrass, Missoura was Miss Claudia's only visitor. With the rescue home no longer a consideration, there seemed little reason for others to visit. If they only knew she had leukemia, I'm sure the

Sick Parade from First Methodist would've still been calling. Rinsing off the china plates, I decided I didn't blame Miss Claudia for not telling her fellow church members. Pity was the worst dose of medicine anybody had to endure.

Beyond the hushed whispers and occasional laughter, I was sure Miss Claudia told Missoura that I now was a member of their secret sorority. I could tell by the way Missoura would smile at me and nod her tiny head while I stood holding the crystal pitcher, waiting for her to get the last sips of iced tea before refilling her glass. I felt valued knowing I was trusted enough to protect the secrets buried under a drugstore.

Wiregrass's downtown cafe was filled to capacity. The eatery with the mobile marquee in front of its doors claiming south Alabama's largest buffet bar became a regular stop after Miss Claudia's oncologist appointments.

Inside the square-shaped building clanging forks and a local country music station competed for air space. Miss Claudia used her plastic tea glass to brush away my question about her doctor visit.

"Well, he had to say something, now."

"Just some nonsense about me starting blood transfusions."

"Well, you're going to do it, aren't you?"

"I told him, I'd study on it. He promises there's nothing to it. Just needs to recharge my cells is all. How about you going to the dessert bar and getting us some of that banana pudding?"

I grabbed her bowl and marched up to the food bar. She never wanted to discuss her health with me, and it never stopped me from being mad at her for a few minutes. If I was her caregiver, her companion, or whatever it was she called me, I thought there were a few things I needed to know.

When I licked the dab of yellow pudding that missed the bowl and landed on my finger, I saw Gerald through the glass top of the food bar. Through the thick glass his head looked wider than usual. A man on the other side of the food bar prevented me from seeing who Gerald was with.

I walked around the rows of baked potatoes and salad supplies, smiling and thinking how surprised he'd be to see me. When I got to the end of the bar, I saw a woman with curly black hair and lots of makeup sitting across from Gerald. She was talking and batting her eyes at the same time. Three strands of gold necklaces and matching gold hoop earrings with little angels decorated her. *Classy*. The word I remembered Marcie using on the police scanner to describe the type of woman she wanted Gerald to have.

"Excuse me," a man with a potato loaded with clumps of sour cream said behind me.

"Sorry," I mumbled and moved over a bit. When I turned back to face the loving couple, the woman had her painted faced scrunched up and her red lips puckered. Watching her pinch Gerald's cheeks made me want to throw up right there beside the container of melted cheddar cheese.

"The pudding's especially good today. Won't you try

368

some?" Miss Claudia asked. Whip cream nestled in the corner of her mouth.

I forgot to tell Miss Claudia to wipe her mouth off. My energy was spent convincing myself that Gerald was better off with the decorated woman. A woman his daughter would accept. A woman Marcie could shop and play little dress-up games with. A woman Marcie would require her brother to like. *They would all be a happy little family and live happily ever after*. I watched Gerald pay at the cash register for his romantic luncheon. After he placed a toothpick in the corner of his mouth, Gerald let the woman put her hand around his waist.

Soon the white napkin I balled up and tossed into my salad plate soaked up the excess honey-mustard dressing.

"That little girl from United Way sent me the sweetest letter," Miss Claudia said.

She was reclining on the sofa recovering from her weekly blood transfusion when I handed her the envelope. While I sorted the mail and threw out junk pieces, she read parts of the letter aloud.

"We fought a good fight," she said, holding the letter up in front of her face. "She says they'll continue to seek funding for the rescue home. Umm."

Miss Claudia put the letter down and shook her head. "I declare, I reckon I'll have to wait until I see the Lord Almighty to find out why that home never came to pass."

I poured her another glass of iced tea. "Like you tell

me, you're just gonna have to dismiss it from your mind. Besides, the way I figure it, if we had all the answers, then what would we need God for."

She opened her mouth and tilted her head to the side. "Well, anyway, I probably never would've thrown a fit and run off to my old stomping ground if the house would've come through."

"See there. And that trip done you good," I said, hoping the scab from old hurts in Apalachicola really had fallen away.

"Yoo-hoo," Patricia said the minute she entered the kitchen door. We heard her voice before she appeared.

"I'm back from holiday," Patricia said in a fake English accent. Her voice drifted towards us as she walked through the kitchen.

A big straw hat wrapped in a floral scarf balanced on her teased hair. All in one swoop, she put the photo album on the coffee table and placed a kiss on Miss Claudia's cheek. She kissed three fingers and waved in my direction.

When Patricia opened page one of her photo diary, I slipped out the kitchen door. I knew she wouldn't inquire about how we managed without her until her snapshot tour of the Mediterranean was completed.

Cher's weekly visits with Andra were cut to every two weeks. Cher sat in the lobby with the blaring television and worked on the journal Andra wanted her to keep. Walking down the hallway to Andra's office, I vowed that I would not look for the book and read it. I'd had my fill of telling and hearing secrets. Besides, after actually seeing Gerald with another woman, I wasn't sure I could've taken the hurt I figured rested in the pages of Cher's journal.

No matter how many times I walked the long, stale hallway to Andra's office, my hands would grow clammy. The steel desk and the report I received on Cher's progress and my ability to parent always put me in mind of going into a principal's office.

I hadn't closed the office door when Andra put her arms around me and patted my back.

"Hon, I'm proud of you for coming clean with the kid." Andra showed me her perfect white teeth the same way I imagined she smiled at her little boy when he brought home a drawing with a gold star.

And a gold star couldn't have made me any happier. Andra said Cher was coming to a breakthrough. My eyes widened, and I sat on the edge of the brown seat while Andra explained Cher's progress.

Andra pointed out that Cher was discovering she could love her parents for giving her life, but they would probably never be the people she wanted them to be. Most people would've thought by Andra's toothy grin she'd found the cure for cancer. I could only think that, after all this time and money, Cher had finally discovered the very knowledge I tried to impart to her from the start.

"Now, I want to see her once a month. When school begins I'll reevaluate the situation." Andra sorted through a stack of blue folders.

"We'll see you next month," I said and opened the door.

"Oh, hon."

I turned to find Andra looking at me with her index finger held up and her blue eyes bugged. "I almost forgot," she said. "Cher told me she admires you. The way you've always stood by her. Just thought you'd want to know you're a hero."

"That's me, ol' Wonder Woman," I said and tried to chuckle.

Andra's toothy grin disappeared down into the sea of files on her desk.

Outside in the white walled hallway I folded my arms and held my breath, wanting to hold hostage the warmth that tingled down my spine. I repeated Andra's nasal-sounding words in my mind, trying to capture them the way I did Miss Claudia's Bible verses. Just like with the Good Book, I knew the words would be pulled out when days looked black and the distance too far.

Twenty-five

The first installment of Bozo's child support went to Gerald. I still owed him for Cher's hospital bill. Anytime the thought crossed my mind that Gerald had been good to me, the image of the woman at the cafe floated across my mind and I'd go right back to claiming he was like all the rest.

I was pulling the tinfoil off the Jiffy Pop popcorn when the phone rang. "Girls, y'all hush up," I said to Laurel and Cher. The pair had stretched out in front of the TV on the pallet I created out of blankets.

"How come you didn't let me know you was back?" Gerald asked.

"Oh, hey. Well, I been busy. You know taking care of old women and stuff like that," I said, hoping he'd connect his conversation with Marcie. The conversation when he said I was too busy for him to fool with.

"Yeah," he said.

I rolled my eyes at his lack of recall. I moved behind the kitchen pantry, hoping Cher couldn't hear me. The screaming from the scary movie on TV made his words hard to catch.

"I got your check in the mail. Now, no need to be in an all-fire hurry to pay me."

The sooner I'm done with you the better. "Well I wanted to go ahead and get it to you. It'll just have to be month to month."

"Listen, I ain't dunning you." His sigh was long on the other end of the phone. "Um, how's Cher getting along?"

"Doing real good. Listen, uh, she's got a friend over here. I was just fixing them popcorn so . . ."

"Okay, yeah. I'll let you go then. But, now, I won't see you at church tomorrow."

I breathed a sigh of relief. Fearing I'd have to see Gerald all shoulder to shoulder in church with his new Hot Mama, I had planned to skip. "Oh?"

"Marcie and Chase are moving to Montgomery. Lots happened since you been gone. Chase done got promoted to shift manager at the Firestone plant up there."

Too bad Marcie didn't get to spend more time shop-

ping with your new Sweet Thing. "Well, this popcorn's a-burning."

I peeled the tinfoil off the bag of popcorn and felt the steam sting my face. *It's for the best,* I kept reminding myself. He needs the woman with gold necklaces and fancy perfumes, not the caretaker of the young and old.

While Cher showered the next morning, I put my regular weekend call in to Miss Claudia. "You 'bout ready to go to church with us?" I asked and took a sip of coffee.

"No, y'all go on without me." Her words were muffled, and her voice deeper than normal.

I sat up on the edge of the slick vinyl dinette chair. "What's the matter?"

"Not a thing. I just got a little temperature is all. Tell your sweet little pastor I played hooky." She tried to laugh, but the sound turned into a cough fit.

"I want Richard to make you some hot tea. Have him put plenty of honey in it for that cough."

"Yes, Dr. Erma Lee."

"You know that's right," I said.

My attempt to be light-hearted grew into a heavy burden. By Monday, when I took Miss Claudia in for her blood transfusion, the cough was more frequent and the fever lingered.

"I don't like the sound of her lungs," her oncologist said in the waiting room. "I want a chest X-ray."

Waiting in the doctor's office lobby, I watched the small purple-striped fish swim in the aquarium without a care in the world. *We're having chicken-fried steak for dinner,* I kept telling myself. Miss Claudia loved it better than anything else I cooked. If I could just get back there and tell her my menu plans, she'd pull out of this. But the pictures I'd seen on Cher's Internet of leukemia cells congregating in the bloodstream kept flashing through my mind.

"For precautions, I'm admitting her," the oncologist said and rubbed his chin. "We'll get her on IV antibiotics and knock out this pneumonia."

When I finally saw Miss Claudia, she was already next door at the hospital, perched up on a gurney. My rubber-soled work shoes squeaked louder the faster I walked on the tiled floor. Each step made her face look grayer. The lipstick, which was bright red hours before, was worn to a faded smudge.

"Sweetheart, do you know where you are?" a big-butted nurse with orangey-red hair shaved over the ears kept asking Miss Claudia. Her words grew louder each step I made.

"You're in a hospital, sweetheart," the nurse yelled. Her words were robotic, and each vowel very exact.

By the time I reached the end of the gurney, I was jogging. The nurse leaned over Miss Claudia. Her patronizing questions made me want to land my black shoe square in the crack of her wide tail. "She ain't deaf, sweetheart," I said.

The nurse curled her upper lip, slung the steel pad on the gurney hook, and walked to the registration desk.

Beads of sweat decorated Miss Claudia's upper lip, and her hair was matted. Her fingers kept a steady crease at the edges of the white sheet. The appearance was every bit the elderly patient the nurse assumed she was.

But the Miss Claudia I know is nothing but typical, I kept assuring myself. "Don't you worry about a thing. The doctor's putting you in the hospital for precautions. You just rest now."

The days Miss Claudia spent in the hospital were an emotional roller coaster. Each time I pressed the number eight on the elevator panel, I held my breath. The box lifted me upward, and I prepared myself for another turn in her condition. One day Miss Claudia's fever was down and the doctors seemed pleased, and by afternoon the fever would spike again.

When I got off the elevator with a tuna sandwich for Patricia, I spotted her at the end of the hall talking with the tall, young, pointy-eared doctor.

I quietly placed the bag down on the vinyl bench in front of the big windows. At times like these, I wanted to be invisible. *As much as I worship the air Miss Claudia breathes, she is still Patricia's blood mother,* I reminded myself.

"I want some answers. You do know my husband is Doctor Tom Murray, the oral surgeon. So you're not dealing with your typical laypeople here."

The young doctor put his hands in the white pockets of his lab coat. "Yes, ma'am," he said and sighed. "And we're doing all we can. Her white blood cell count is through the roof. And while I'm waiting for the tests . . ."

Patricia closed her eyes and showed the doctor the

big white teeth. "I'm so sick and tired of you and your tests. Now just tell me what you think."

"Like I was saying. The normal cells are depleted in her bone marrow. The leukemia cells are just taking over. It's part of the phase known as the . . ."

"Blasts," I said, staring at the doctor's silver necklace.

The doctor and Patricia turned to look at me. I could feel my neck getting hot.

The young man looked back at Patricia. "It's called the blast phase because the leukemia cells are taking over."

Patricia shook her head and complained about his lack of experience and how she would transport Miss Claudia to the University of Alabama for better care.

Her clipped words echoed down the hall. I stared out the window at the peaceful pond below. The people reminded me of toy dolls, running and walking around the asphalt trail. Thanks to the departure of an afternoon thunderstorm, they were carelessly enjoying a break from the August humidity. I wanted to beat on the window and make them stop. To make Patricia shut up. To make them all understand that the enemy I kept praying would lose its way was taking over. The blasts first scouted on Cher's Internet had made their way over the fortress and into the promised land.

I stood outside Miss Claudia's door, watching Richard. He was at the end of the hall, sitting with his legs crossed on the padded bench, the exact spot where Patricia told him to wait. Patricia decided that if

Richard was in the room when the news was given, Miss Claudia would be so concerned about Richard's nerves, she'd miss the details.

So while the oncologist told Miss Claudia about the enemy's advancement, Richard and me held positions in the hallway. I leaned against the brown door and pictured the scenes I heard inside the room. The doctor's words were technical and without emotion. He described the journey the blast cells were taking, depositing their tumor bombs along Miss Claudia's bones.

"I see," Miss Claudia said in a voice deepened with congestion.

"Mama, they can put those high-powered antibiotics in you and make you better. Then we can worry about this other mess," Patricia said.

The silence in the room made me bite my thumbnail. I fought off the angry thoughts. *If she would've only tried treatment.*

"No," I barely heard Miss Claudia say. "I understand."

"Now, Mama. Use your noggin. Just a few more days and you might get rid of this pneumonia."

"And I might not. But one thing's for sure. I won't stay here being poked and prodded all the time," Miss Claudia said. "I expect it's time for me to go on home."

The beady eyes were on me tighter than a radar gun. Miss Trellis was standing at the cluster of trailer-park mailboxes, staring at me with her hands on the wide yellow housedress. When I put the last grocery bag filled with our clothes into the car, I finally lifted my hand and waved. Miss Trellis shook her head and wobbled back into the white block office.

"Where in tarnation are you running off to now?" she asked when I stopped to pay my rent.

"We're just taking a little vacation." I refused to let her know that we were staying at Miss Claudia's. Refused to let her get into the final details of Miss Claudia's business.

"Now, don't you go blaming me if somebody comes in here and breaks in your place. They libel to with the lights off."

The small TV on top of her counter was tuned to a shopping show. The announcer kept repeating there were only fifty more Scarlet O'Hara dolls left for sale. I handed her my check and smiled.

"I'm sure it'll be just fine." I visualized her negative comments bouncing off the shield of armor I mentally put on before entering her kingdom.

"The last time you ran out for an entire month." She leaned over the brown-paneled counter and pointed her fat finger at me. "Next time you best leave a light on. I'm telling you I don't want no trouble with break-ins."

I continued to smile and put my wallet back into my pocketbook.

"And by the way, I ain't talked to you since that old house of Claudia's got flushed down the toilet. They's lots of us glad that place never got off the ground. The only people I heard tell of who wanted it were the nig . . ."

She stopped speaking when I walked behind the

counter. Boxes stamped with QVC and Family Shopping Network logos were stacked around the wooden stool she sat on. Her mouth gaped open, and I wondered if she expected me to slap her the way my flesh wanted to.

I placed my hands on the sides of her shoulders and forced a big grin. "I love you, you know that?"

Before I walked out the door, I smiled as big as my mouth would stretch. Her own mouth pulled to the side like she had suffered a stroke from my forced kindness. Love might be free, I thought, but sometimes there was a price for delivering it.

Twenty-six

*C*her and Patricia settled into the upstairs bedrooms and, since Miss Claudia was in a hospital bed, I stayed in her bedroom. It was only fitting. A good companion ought to stay with her assignment.

"Now, remember we're not blood kin. Just don't get in the way," I warned Cher. She nodded and pulled underwear out of the grocery bag.

Patricia was more help than I thought she would be. She helped cook and even made up her own bed. Richard only appeared for his meals. Each morning whenever I filled his plate with scrambled eggs and asked if he wanted to look in on his mother, he'd say, "I'll see her in a minute."

To some degree, I understood Richard's reluctance.

Frailty did not become Miss Claudia. The chalk white face and the flat hair propped against pillows would make anyone think she was wearing a costume. Her hazel eyes, once sparkling with plans and compliments, rested in her skull like two marbles dulled from too many games in the sand.

"Inside that dresser drawer yonder," Miss Claudia mumbled and barely lifted her hand in the direction of the armoire, "you'll find what you need when this is over."

I ignored her and continued to tuck the sides of the blanket into the hospital bed. I hated that bed. The cold steel siding was an eyesore in her fancy bedroom.

"You hear me now?"

All I could do was nod.

Hospice sent over a sweet young nurse that was Miss Claudia's kind of people. "We want her as comfortable as possible. This should all be done on her terms," the nurse with the light brown skin told me. She also said it was our job to ensure Miss Claudia's stay at home was not complicated. There were no prying plugs and wires. And I told the nurse that a catheter wasn't needed.

The enemy may have taken her appearance, but even blasts of leukemia couldn't squash her spirit. It became a running joke whenever Patricia and I would lift her to use the bedpan. Miss Claudia would moan and gasp, "Maybe you girls will get me potty-trained yet."

Patricia and Cher were at the grocery store when I heard Miss Claudia ring the bronze bell Patricia had placed by the hospital bed. Richard never looked up from the plate of roast beef.

"I just can't hold it any longer," she whispered. The frown on her face always indicated a need for the bedpan. I tried to lift under the armpits; at least there was some flesh there. But each time she'd gasp when my fingers slipped over her bony shoulder.

Richard ate faster when he saw me standing in the kitchen doorway. "Can you help me lift your mama? Her kidneys need to act."

"I just . . . Can't we wait until Patricia gets back?" he asked, scooping kernels of corn onto his spoon.

Before I could think, I snatched the plate, and kernels of corn fell to the floor. "Now I've about had it with you. She's your mama, and God knows she's waited on you more times than she should've. The least you can do is pick her up so she can pee."

After I showed Richard how to lift Miss Claudia, he not only picked her up that day but every time Miss Claudia needed him. Whenever I tried to lift the sides of the sheets to change them, Miss Claudia would say, "Just let Richard."

Keeping track of the medicine was another task Richard learned. I administered the shots for pain into the IV tube that the hospice nurse secured in Miss Claudia's vein. But Richard worked with the nurse on the dose and time allowed between injections. He even color-coordinated the dosing schedules on three-by-five cards.

"Umm," Miss Claudia would moan when the pain hit

her. I learned how to prime the needle and inject the painkiller into her system in less than a minute. After the medicine had time to take effect and her face muscles softened, the first words out of her mouth were always the same. "You'd make a fine nurse."

When I walked into the kitchen, Patricia was holding an empty vial of painkiller.

"Erma Lee, it was too soon for Mama's shot," she said.

I felt my eyes widen and looked at the empty vial she was holding between her fingers. "What? Well, she said she was needing it, and Richard said . . ."

"Oh, me." Patricia threw her hands up in the air. "You're relying on him to remind you when Mama needs a shot?"

Patricia never saw Richard behind the porch screen door.

"Well, he can't even keep straight how many Tylenol he takes, let alone lethal medication. Erma Lee, really. Do you know what this could do to Mama?" Air spewed from her mouth, and her eyes rolled upward. "I'll just have to call the doctor and . . ."

Richard walked in and snatched the empty vial. "We've given this every four hours for the past three days now." He pulled a yellow index card from his shirt pocket. "Last shot was at eight oh-seven this morning," he read and looked at his watch. "It's twelve thirty-four. Past time for the shot."

Patricia wrinkled her brow and watched him walk down the hall to Miss Claudia's bedroom.

The day Missoura visited, Miss Claudia's breath was

shallow, and it was hard for her to talk. When I brought a straw for Miss Claudia's diluted iced tea, Missoura leaned over the hospital bed railing and held her hand. I lifted Miss Claudia's back slightly, and Missoura tipped the straw towards her mouth.

"Drink yourself some tea now," Missoura said. "You always say it's the house wine at your place."

Missoura took the damp washcloth from the bed rail and blotted Miss Claudia's chapped lips.

"I'm teaching Cher piano," Miss Claudia mumbled between gasps.

"Well, I be."

"Like you taught me. Remember?"

"Seem like about a hundred years ago." Missoura caressed the side of Miss Claudia's face.

The steady tick from the grandfather clock filled the room. Missoura kept stroking her cheek and smiling at the woman she'd help mold. Tears surrounded the coal-colored dots of her eyes, but she never looked away.

"We need a fresh washcloth." I snatched the cloth from the bed rail and ran down the steps to the washroom. In the dampness of the basement, I leaned against the washing machine, muzzled my mouth with the cloth that had brushed Miss Claudia's lips, and allowed myself to cry.

The smell of bacon drifted throughout the first-floor rooms. I put a third plate on the kitchen table, only to pick it up again. For a second, I forgot Cher had spent the night with Laurel.

"Mama said she wants to try a bite of bacon." Richard's words mingled with laughter.

"What?" I laughed too and opened my mouth, believing a miracle had taken place.

"She sure did. I asked her how she was feeling this morning, and that's what she said." Richard clapped his hands and sat down at the table.

"Well, I better get that gal a slice of bacon," I said and finished filling Richard's plate with grits. "Patricia's getting dressed. She said for you to go on and eat."

Placing the bacon on a plate, I walked by the staircase and heard Patricia slam the bathroom cabinet. *Plugging in those rollers, getting ready to make that hair big.* The grandfather clock chimed eight when I walked into Miss Claudia's dark bedroom.

She was sleeping with her head turned to the side, her mouth slightly open. I placed the plate of bacon next to her red Bible.

"I hear somebody's hungry for some bacon." The heavy burgundy drapes were hard to pull back, and my eyes squinted when sunshine filled the room.

Miss Claudia's face looked more pasty in the rays of light. "I said I made you some . . ." I touched her hand. "Miss Claudia?" My hand lightly shook the pink chiffon–covered shoulder.

A cough upstairs from Patricia and the tapping of Richard's fork against his plate. Those were the only sounds I heard. The sounds of ordinary activity. I stood as still as possible by the bed rail, balancing her hand in my palm. The selfish side of me kept looking at her chest, ordering it to rise up with life.

Now, you know she's better off, I kept repeating to myself. *You knew this would happen.* But my mind couldn't stop my shoulders from shaking or the sob that grew within my chest. I leaned down and kissed her forehead. The wrinkled skin was still warm. My tears landed and then rolled down the side of her face. *Why hadn't I kissed her before now?*

I covered my mouth and tried to muffle the sounds of loss. My loss. Not Richard's or Patricia's, but mine and mine alone. She was my mother too, but in a different sense. The mother that, as a girl, I had long given up ever knowing. And even while standing there in the stillness of the room with tears flowing, I somehow had the good sense to take in the room like a snapshot, knowing that my life would never be the same.

When I turned my head away from the hospital bed, I saw the armoire. The list was tucked inside the top drawer just as she promised. *Call hospice and Blakely's Funeral Home. Have them dress me in my lavender suit. Have Erma Lee, Cher, and Missoura sit with the family.*

With the note in hand, I rang the bronze bell as hard as I could. Richard was the first person at the doorway. He clutched both sides of the door frame, and his mouth slowly dropped. Hugging him tightly, I whispered, "She was proud of you for taking care of her." Then I made my way towards the living-room phone.

Patricia skipped two stairs at a time, barefoot and wild-eyed. A brown age mark decorated her plain face, and a drip of water fell from wet hair. She paused to look at me and bit her bottom lip.

After I hung up the phone, I realized my last task for Miss Claudia was over. I stood at the doorway of her room feeling the confusion of the moment and looking for a way to make myself useful. A glass half full of watered-down tea needed to be put in the dishwasher. The bell needed to be returned to its proper spot. Patricia and Richard hovered over her, locked in each other's grasp. Richard's cries only sounded louder because Patricia's face was buried in his chest. Their sobs grew softer with each step I made to the light of day. I walked to the side porch and sat in the wicker swing overlooking Miss Claudia's flower garden. The swing creaked when I turned my head away from the dots of pink and yellow and towards the empty black asphalt of Elm Drive.

The side porch was the same place I retreated to after Miss Claudia's funeral. While Patricia sat in the living room squalling and being fanned by three of her friends from the Cotillion Society, I sat on the swing dressed in my old faithful black-and-white dress, fanning away the stifling heat with the funeral program.

Cher was quiet and sat next to me with her legs crossed. During the service she softly cried and scooted close to me. Her body nestled against the soft spot under my arm. The only time I felt like bawling my eyes out was when the choir sang "How Great Thou Art." The image of Miss Claudia smiling and playing that one-two-three tempo flooded my mind.

But I just bit my tongue and squeezed Cher's shoulder tighter.

Patricia made Miss Claudia go back one last time to the church that let her down. "We can't hurt everybody's feelings," Patricia said when Richard voiced opposition to having the services at First Methodist.

"Gerald was at the funeral," Cher said.

"You saw him?"

"He was in the back. Sat next to Brownie. I saw them when we walked in."

Lee, his wife Sonya, and Brownie all spoke to me at the cemetery. But I never saw Gerald.

The screen door opened, and the chatter of the guests drifted to the porch. Richard closed the door and loosened his tie. I tried to picture him dressed in the same uniform twenty years ago, a hotshot lawyer. Try as I might, the image never materialized.

"All that chatter is wearing on my nerves." Richard held up Miss Claudia's red Bible. "Mama wanted you to have this."

I clutched the Bible with the torn corner and smiled. "Are you sure Patricia's okay with me having this?"

He looked inside the kitchen window and fanned his hands. "She's too busy with her sinking spells to pay any attention."

"You know I'll cherish it."

Richard slowly made his way down the concrete steps and walked towards the garage apartment. His suit pants hung loose in the seat, and the navy material gathered at the belt loops. "Mama loved you, Erma Lee. And so do we."

• • •

All my energy was drained from changing out of my good dress. I wanted to rest and dream about Miss Claudia. To pretend in sleep that she was still needing a ride to the beauty shop and offering me a dose of encouraging words along the way. There would be plenty of time to move on. But today I wanted to be selfish and mourn my loss.

I had just laid down when Cher knocked at my bedroom door. "We've got company," she said.

I pictured Brownie at the door with a pot of chicken and rice for our supper. "Tell them I'm taking a nap."

"You need this," she persisted and opened the bedroom door. "Now, come on and get up."

I sighed, got up, and slipped on my flip-flops. "Girl, I swear . . ."

Cher opened the front door, and Gerald stood on the steps holding a dozen red roses. "I knew you'd be feeling all low today, so I had the lady down at the flower shop fix these up."

I took a step backwards and grabbed my chest. In all of my forty-eight years, I had never seen so many flowers in such a big vase. Once, after I had threatened to leave Bozo, he sent me six roses.

The wide vase required Cher to use both hands when she placed the flowers on the counter. Red petals filled the kitchen.

"I know I should have said something at the cemetery." Gerald tucked his thumb inside his belt loop and looked across the street. "I just ain't good at such as that."

Every fiber of my being wanted to leap and wrap my arms around him. Words from the phone conversation with Marcie about other women seemed tiny and remote. "Gerald, you shouldn't have done that now," I said.

"Y'all got time to run out to the house? It won't take but a minute," he said and pointed at Cher.

Riding up the bumpy driveway to Gerald's home, I was prepared to see the woman that was with him at the restaurant now standing on the front porch. He probably told her that he felt sorry for us and had to do something to clear his conscience.

But when we pulled up to the faded white house, there was no sign of anybody. Just two horses and a scattered group of cows grazing in the field next to the home.

"Now, gal, you better shut them eyes," Gerald said.

"All right already. They're shut," Cher said, both hands covering her eyes.

The excitement was contagious. I looked around trying to figure out what Cher's surprise was. Gerald got out of the truck and walked to the side of the house.

"What's he doing?" Cher asked.

"I have no idea," I said and chuckled.

Gerald approached the front of the truck leading a black horse with a white blaze down the front of its head.

My gasp made Cher lean forward, her eyes still closed. "Grandma, I'm about to wet my pants."

We got out of the truck, and I led Cher by the arm.

A game-show host couldn't have been more enthused. "Open them eyes," Gerald yelled.

Cher opened her eyes and bent forward, and her mouth fell open.

"An old boy owed me money for putting a new engine in his truck. He couldn't come up with the money so we bartered on this mare. You reckon you'd care for her if I was to give her to you?"

Cher's hand trembled when she covered her mouth. She put her arms around Gerald, and he smiled that crooked way he had.

I winked at him and fought the urge to go up and squeeze him myself.

"Now, I'll board her for you, but you're gonna have to clean the stall and feed her."

"Gerald, I'll do anything, I swear," Cher said and pushed hair from her eyes.

Gerald led the way to the place he called his sanity. Cher rode behind us, seated on the horse in one of Donnie's saddles.

"Cher, now your Grandma's the only one who's seen this place," Gerald said when we reached the open field. He put his arm on my shoulder, and my eyes closed at the touch. I didn't have to be Andra or some fancy psychologist to know I needed the feel of his wide hand that day. The united feeling of warmth and being wanted were discovered in the grease-spotted cuticles of his thick fingers. If our relationship never grew beyond that touch, I knew I could count him as a close friend.

We stood at the edge of the brook and watched Cher

ride in circles around the meadow. "Remember to keep your toes pointed up and your hiney down," Gerald cupped his hands and yelled. I studied the way he squatted down on the ground and put a blade of grass in the corner of his mouth. Miss Claudia was right about him. He was the salt of the earth.

While Cher guided the horse through the brook, Gerald addressed it head-on. "I know things been rough on you. But . . . well I don't know. You mad at me?"

I looked down and pulled my big toe up against the plastic flip-flop. "No, don't be silly."

He scratched the gray stubble on his chin and looked back at Cher.

"You and that woman still dating?"

He cocked his head towards me and smiled. "You know about that?"

"I saw y'all."

"I only went out with her a couple of times. Marcie kept after me until I did. I don't know, she's nice enough. Just too high cotton for my tastes." Gerald walked to the edge of the brook and instructed Cher to tighten her reins.

While Cher and Gerald worked the reins, I looked around the lush green meadow and listened to creek water splash the rocks. The light breeze and its steady currents helped me understand why this place gave Gerald peace of mind during his hard times.

The blanket of trees and their limbs that bent down to almost touch the grass hugged me that afternoon. I didn't need a nap to dream about Miss Claudia. I sat on the stump of an ancient oak and wondered if she was standing in a similar place in heaven. I pictured her running wide open through an even greener meadow and throwing that silver cane farther than any javelin gold medalist. The cane would sail across the clear blue distance, and she would lift her head high, shouting eternal *Hallelujahs*.

Twenty-seven

E verything has a season. Lots of change came with the passing of that summer. Because of Cher's new horse, me and Gerald saw each other three afternoons a week and most Saturdays. We'd take turns buying Cokes from the drink machine at his shop and watch Cher practice in the meadow he no longer needed to keep private.

Cher started the ninth grade by joining the high-school band. I always said it was on account of Miss Claudia taking up time with her on the piano. The car-wash money she earned even paid for the clarinet.

Soon Cher started playing in the small Sunday morning orchestra at church. Although some of the older church members still complain to Lee that it's sacrilegious to have drums in the church house, I like the addition. Each Sunday, when the service ends and the congregation joins hands to sing "The Family of God," I stand tall on my tiptoes. Watching Cher's cheeks sink in as blasts of praise rise from the black instrument makes me feel even taller.

Suzette continued to keep writing us letters. A couple of times I have written her back without Cher's joint signature. I got to hand it to Suzette. She's trying. She's done so good with her schoolwork that her letters got me to thinking. And the day Cher began high school, I forced myself to go down to the vocational center and sign up for night classes. The retired math teacher who leads the class, Mrs. Hutchinson, calls the program General Equivalency Diploma classes. Patricia said she can get me a raise at the cafeteria the minute I get that certificate. But who's to say, maybe I'll make a nurse yet.

Cher wants us to see Suzette during Thanksgiving. I won't say I'm not scared of being disappointed that Suzette really hasn't changed as much as I hoped. Or that the sight of Suzette behind the glassed prison visiting room won't rattle me. But either way, I now have the real strength to handle it.

And I'm satisfied that two months ago Miss Claudia did a somersault in heaven when the doors to the Claudia Tyler Rescue Home opened at the old Piggly Wiggly. Richard laid the law down to Patricia. He demanded that the money earned from selling Miss Claudia's home be used to buy and refurbish the abandoned grocery store. I think the only reason Patricia held out from making a final decision for two days was because she didn't come up with the idea herself. After the sale, Richard moved out of the garage apartment and used part of his inheritance to buy a small brick house six blocks from Elm Drive.

The day the United Way lady asked me about volunteering, I waited a week before calling her back. Not because I didn't want to. I just never felt like I had my own life together, let alone was able to help somebody else. But I knew Miss Claudia would've been put out with me for giving in to those fears. So two evenings a week, when I help out at the shelter, I drive by Miss Claudia's old home. A young couple with a small blond-haired girl live there now. Sometimes I see them after supper, sitting on the porch swing. Driving slowly by the brick home with white columns, I shake my head and remember how intimidated I was of the fancy place that turned out to be the best school I ever entered.

Missoura was hunched over when she met me at the door. "I 'bout decided I'm too old for this volunteering business," she said with a hand propped on her hip. "I've done signed one girl in and washed a load of towels."

"Y'all been busy."

"Sheriff's office called, and they bringing one more from the emergency room this evening. Bless her heart. They say she got a little baby and a four-year-old." Missoura looked down and opened the tinted glass door. "Lord have mercy. I'll see you day after tomorrow."

I folded the towels in the lobby. The early newscast played on the corner TV, next to the portrait of Miss Claudia.

The first time I saw the painting was the day the

shelter opened. I joined Wiregrass's finest at the ribbon-cutting ceremony. Most the people I had met before at Miss Claudia's home didn't remember me. I had on the pink linen suit that Patricia gave me when we cleaned out Miss Claudia's closets. *This is not a handout,* I told myself the morning I put the suit on. Fastening the jacket's pearl buttons, I decided it was a gift, a part of Miss Claudia. The safety pins that secured the skirt scratched against my waist. But I didn't pay it any mind. I loved wearing the suit that day and slyly tilted my head down to the shoulder, where her signature summer-dew scent lingered.

Almost bumping into the reporter interviewing Prune Face, I overheard her official comments. "The minute I learned about this place I jumped right in," she said with clasped hands. "As Christians we must help the needy." Fearing I might gouge my elbow into her skinny chest, I moved towards the painting.

I got tickled thinking what Miss Claudia would say of her portrait. The artist showed an elegant Miss Claudia wearing a white and navy hat, her head slightly turned. I could just picture her looking up at the painting and saying, "Good gracious alive. Why did they go ugly up the place with this old thing?"

The shrill security buzzer made me jump. I released the switch and allowed a female deputy, a young woman carrying a baby, and a little brown-haired boy into the lobby.

"Evening." I tried to look upbeat and smile real big, just like the United Way lady taught us during volunteer training.

The twenty-something was wide-eyed and kept her hand on the head of the young boy. Her auburn hair was parted in the middle and layered down the sides. Black wiry stitches decorated the side of her cheek. One eye was green, and the other lined with red blood vessels and a purple bruise.

"You want to come over here and play while we sign Mama in?" I asked the little boy. He was dressed in a black wrestling shirt and looked up at his mother. She motioned with her chin, and he followed me to the plastic container filled with toys.

The deputy left before I finished explaining the policy to the new resident. My eyes drifted to the baby dressed in disposable diapers. "We left the house so fast, I didn't have time." She rolled her good eye towards the half-naked baby.

"I know. Don't worry about nothing," I said and waved my hand in the air. "We got clothes for y'all and everything."

Thuds from toys landing on the floor echoed while I completed the necessary paperwork. The girl balanced the baby in one arm and tried to scribble her signature. Each time she tried, the hand twitched wildly and only chicken scratch appeared. She sighed and put the pen to her forehead.

"Here. Let's try this." I placed my hand on hers and steadied the pen. With each stroke, her hand vibrated under my palm.

I led them down the dormitory hallway and handed over fresh towels and clothes. She opened her mouth, but nothing came out. I smiled and lightly rubbed her elbow. "Y'all sleep tight. Everything's fine now."

Turning off the lobby TV, I pick up toys scattered about the room. While I glance up at the painting of Miss Claudia, I clutch a miniature tractor-trailer and gaze into her eyes.

Nights like these, when the shelter grows still and the residents are tucked in bed, I stare at the painting and carry on a mental conversation with Miss Claudia. I update her on lives changed at the rescue home, Cher's horse riding and band practice, the new people in my night classes, and something funny Gerald might've said. But mostly I tell her how I long to hear her words of wisdom and to sit for a spell at the kitchen table on Elm Drive. And as crazy as it sounds, during those times I feel like she's gone away just for a little while.

Placing the tractor-trailer into the toy box, I watch the hazel eyes follow me. Those eyes, even on canvas, look right through my heart. The same heart that feels parched from the empty place she left in my life. And just then, from the brightest corner of my mind, I hear her drawl, *Why keep love in your heart when you can give it away for free?*